The

SWEET

BY

and

BY

Jeanne Mackin

The

SWEET

BY

and

BY

ST. MARTIN'S PRESS
NEW YORK

www.stmartins.com

Design by Kathryn Parise

LIBRARY OF CONGRESS CATALOGING-IN-PUBLICATION DATA
Mackin, Jeanne.
    The sweet by and by / Jeanne Mackin.—1st ed.
        p. cm.
    ISBN 0-312-26997-8
    1. Women journalists—Fiction.   2. Loss (Psychology)—Fiction.
3. New York (State)—Fiction.   4. Spiritualism—Fiction.   I. Title.

PS3563.A3169 S94 2001
813'.54—dc21

                                                                00-045988

First Edition: March 2001

10   9   8   7   6   5   4   3   2   1

ACKNOWLEDGMENTS

The American Antiquarian Society in Worcester, Massachusetts, and its knowledgeable staff provided a grant and support that helped in completion of this novel; I am in their debt.

Thanks also to the members of the Mostly Sundays Writing Group who provided valuable insights and useful critiques: Bonnie Auslander, Jane Crawford, Emily Johnson, Janis Kelly, Nicola Morris, and Linda Myers. Victoria Pryor was both agent and friend.

And, as always, special thanks to my husband, Steve Poleskie.

Then the kingdom of heaven will be comparable to ten bridesmaids, who, taking their lamps, went out to meet the bridegroom. Five of them were foolish and five were wise. The foolish ones took lamps but took no oil along with them, but the wise ones took along oil in the flasks with their lamps. And as the bridegroom delayed his coming they all grew drowsy and fell asleep.   —MATTHEW 25

. . . while it is undoubtedly true that evil spirits are attracted to an evil circle, in actual practice it is a very rare thing for anyone to be incommoded thereby. When such spirits come the proper procedure is not to replace them, but rather to reason gently with them and so endeavor to make them realise their own condition and what they should do for improvement. This has occurred many times within the author's personal experience and with the happiest results.

—SIR ARTHUR CONAN DOYLE

What is faith but a kind of betting on speculation, after all?
—SAMUEL BUTLER

The

SWEET

BY

and

BY

$\mathcal{S}$o you don't believe in ghosts?" Jude asked one evening, when the flames from the hearth cast dark, dancing shadows into the room. This was during our private Golden Age of Civilization, as he called it, before the accident, before the quarrel, before the separation: B.D. Before death.

"And you do?" I whispered back, nestling closer to him, my bare back pressed into his bare chest.

"Sometimes I wish I did. I would come back to you. But dead is dead, isn't it? 'We must needs die, and are as water spilt on the ground, which cannot be gathered up again.' "

"Listen," I said. "It's raining. Do you hear it on the roof? Spring rain. Another winter is over."

~

But sometimes, when we leave that gray season, we bring fragments of it back with us, into denatured nature, into the finite. Maggie Fox was one of those who, in seeking sanctuary, gave birth to a being that is neither angel nor devil, good nor bad, who is perhaps all things, and perhaps nothing. Maggie was one of those who makes truth even harder to define.

As was Jude, the beloved . . .

CHAPTER ONE

Eleusis, New York~1998

$\mathcal{B}$e open-minded," my editor Tom Riley said in his best editorial voice when I spoke to him last month about the article on
Maggie and her kin. "Consider, at least for a moment, all possi-
bilities. One can hope."

"Too many hope," I told him. "Usually for the wrong things.
Hope is sister to faith, and faith is a guest of honor who leaves
too soon or never arrives, but only keeps you waiting and looking
like a fool."

"You sound like a jilted Victorian virgin," Tom said. "It
doesn't suit you. At least it didn't use to. I'm not certain you
should take this assignment."

He cleared his throat loudly so that the phone against my ear
rasped and scratched. In my mind's eye I saw him in his Forty-

second Street office, sitting behind his battered oak desk, half hidden by books and manuscripts and back issues of *Savant,* pencil in hand, tap, tap tapping on his coffee mug. There is a sphinx on his desk, a tawdry brass thing that Jude gave him years ago as a souvenir of some private joke never explained to me.

"We'll put aside for the moment the question of faith," he said. "It's a difficult one, certainly not suitable for a long-distance phone call. But your mourning is taking too long, Helen. Perhaps writing a piece about Maggie Fox will be cathartic."

"Perhaps," I said, but did not believe.

His remark describing me as a jilted Victorian wounded. Jude hadn't jilted me, unless death counts as a no-show. His loyalty, in fact, had been my life raft, my dawn after the darkness. It had been complete.

The pencil tapped again. "Write about endings, Helen. But only if there is a beginning after the end. And I'll come visit in a couple of weeks, to see how things are going. I'm still not certain this is the right topic for you, now."

"Later, thanks."

Maggie Fox, the founder of the American Spiritualist movement, was a nineteenth-century farm girl who, with supple knee and toe joints and a taste for the theatrical, made the dead rise from their cold and lonely graves and speak again to the mournful living. Now is Maggie's season, when the earth sleeps under winter's lingering white shroud and life holds its breath, waiting for either miracle or disaster. March, not January, is the two-faced month that leads back to winter or lunges into spring. March makes fools of us all and March knows nothing of loyalty.

Maggie herself has been dead for a hundred years, and Splitfoot, the first of many spirits who conversed with her—well, the devil never dies. We will not let him.

As I go over notes from my last conversation with Tom and reflect on Maggie's life, a full moon casts shadows on the stubborn blanket of snow still covering the north meadow outside my window. The wind moans and whistles through the oaks and pines, as I imagine it did on that night of March 31, 1848, the night Maggie Fox began speaking with her spirits. I sit in my vast bed shivering, waiting to hear the knocking that means Maggie is here. I'll give this dead Spiritualist a chance, if for no other reason than to add spice to the article Tom wants me to write.

Okay, I'm ready. Speak to me, Margaret Fox, if you can. Tap at the window, on the wall, on the ceiling, anywhere you prefer. Make yourself known, be heard. Here, now, in this place. Focus all your straying atoms, if any still cohere to the personality and body once known as Maggie Fox, and answer my call. If you speak to anyone, it should be me. Who else has paid you so much attention lately?

Nothing? Silence? Only the wind in the snow-heavy pines? Where are you? Are you?

Wait. Did I hear something? Was that a tapping?

No. Of course not. The dead do not speak with the living. The dead do not speak at all. They have disappeared into nothingness, returned to the silent stardust from whence we came.

It could make a good beginning, though: journalist in bed with covers up to her chin, a howling wind, cold spots on the stairway, the fragrance of invisible lilacs in the air, a tapping from the wall, ghostly lights in an otherwise dark room, as Maggie Fox announces herself.

No, this is foolishness. If Tom and the magazine's editorial board wanted that kind of cheap sensationalism, they would have hired someone from the tabloids. I don't write for periodicals that collage the faces of politicians onto alien bodies or into the arms of starlets. I am a serious woman, a hardworking woman who has earned a reputation for accurate and unbiased reporting. I write for no-nonsense publications, and *Savant* wants someone who will stare the cult of Margaret Fox in the face and not flinch, not cower under the covers and start waffling paragraphs with maybes and *perhaps*.

Customarily I am not a hagiographer of spurious mystics. Numbers are my domain—sudden-infant-death syndrome rates in public housing projects, the number of fatalities from car accidents, the probability of a new and deadly mutant rain-forest virus popping up in Chapel Hill. Risk assessment. Odds. The chances are . . . Numbers are my refuge from chaos, not mystics and mediums.

However, I asked for this bizarre assignment from *Savant* because of the unusually large check that awaits me, a dollar a word for a definitive biographical essay, in ten thousand words, of one of the greatest frauds in the history of religion, an area replete with trickery: Maggie Fox, the upstate New York girl who used parlor tricks to make the credulous think they were speaking with their beloved dead ones—for a fee, of course. Maggie and I have that much in common. We are working girls with bills to pay.

My name is Helen E. West. I live in one of those little academic towns that dot the valleys and waterways of upstate New York. It is not far from where Maggie Fox first spoke with the spirits. Most towns here are named after Greek places and Greek heroes (or, like me, Greek disasters), and are filled with aged Greek Revival townhouses and mansions long since converted to interesting apartment houses with modern sculpture in the entrance, or disheveled fraternities with abandoned bathtubs in the front yard.

My own house is not one of those thin-walled apartments that carry the accumulated smells of graduate-student curry and garlic, marijuana and Marlboros, but a rambling, drafty, turreted, many-chimneyed farmhouse situated at the top of an old Indian trail–turned–road, named Piety Hill. My house, enlarged, updated, and otherwise improved—or ruined, depending on your views of historical preservation—suffers a plethora of Italianate overhangs, a Greek Revival porch, several Victorian sunrooms, and turrets tacked onto the original Federal facade. The house came cheap, with reason. More-recent owners lacked the means to repair roofs, replace windows, and, in general, to maintain that fine and required separation between indoors and outdoors.

The house came with ten acres of old farmland now given over to new forest growth and meadow, and seven rooms littered with four generations' worth of dusty yellowing books, threadbare Oriental carpets, mismatched china and linens, radios, gramophones, and other jetsam and flotsam left behind by the Barwell family. They have, according to the local historical society, now died out. There is no address to which I can send the trunks of clothing, the family photo albums, the schoolbooks and report cards from 1921 stored in the attic. I feel like an interloper, living among the dusty accumulations of others. I like this sensation. In such a house, loneliness is complete. There is no way to pretend that you are not solitary; there are no illusions here.

The one item in this house that is distinctly mine, aside from clothes and papers and the many overdue library books, is a Gothic Revival bookcase filled with volumes of Victoriana about the occult, inherited from my great-grandmother Clara. She believed in ghosts ("spirits" she called them, if they were friendly, and "wraiths" if not) and in communication between living and dead. She was the rule, not the exception. Ninety-seven percent of Victorian women did believe in life beyond the grave, in heaven and hell and those shadowy mists betwixt the two from which the dead sometimes appeared to the living. Maggie had much to do with this.

Of course, I can't blame Maggie personally. She simply filled a slot that is always present, it seems. She was part of the perpetual jest in the want-ads of the cosmos: *New culture being formed. Needed: carpenters, politicians, doctors, cranks.* The morning edition today carried a large story about a woman who is running for president. She claims to speak with spirits, one of whom is Lincoln, who endorses her candidacy. A group of survivalists in Idaho insist the end of the world is coming and they are in direct contact with God and his angels.

How much of this delirium is simply about loneliness? We and the world contrive to separate ourselves, one from the other in countless ways, and sometimes the solitude becomes over-whelming. A legion of devoted guardian angels and other friendly spirits seems a pleasant thing to anticipate. Even cataclysm adds spice to the day, and I suspect that this great longing for the com-pany of the dead is simply the chin-up obverse of the fear of death. If Jude were here, I'd ask him what he thought of guardian angels. We never discussed them.

Over my desk hangs a painting by my great-grandfather. A woman, her long dark hair streaming over white shoulders, sleeps on a sofa. There are dark circles under her eyes; her mouth is pale. An angel with multicolored wings and my great-grandfather's dark eyes hovers over her.

When Clara died of consumption, my great-grandfather washed and laid out the body himself, chasing away the female relatives and neighbors who normally performed this chore. He sat by her day and night until, exhausted, he fell asleep and they stole the body for burial. He didn't speak much after that. But he did keep a diary which was passed on to me when my mother died, along with the bookcase filled with Victorian books on the occult. The diary is filled with notes about weather and comments about ar-ticles read in *The Abolitionist*. But there is this comment, written a year after Clara's death:

> . . . bought a ticket on the public carriage to Rochester,
> thence to meet with Margaret and Katie Fox in a circle.
> Will Clara speak from beyond the grave?

Jude, my lover, who first introduced me to the world of mys-tics and religious anomalies, read every faded word of the diary, but found no other reference to his favorite medium, Margaret Fox.

Great-grandfather never remarried. I never married at all, nor did I have children—two activities no longer as closely related as they were in Maggie Fox's and Great-grandfather's time. Some current statistical studies claim I'm more liable to be attacked by a terrorist than get married. Single, middle-aged women abound whereas their male counterparts are as rare as the white Siberian tiger—and equally as skittish.

The nearest I came to "married" was my long-standing and intimate relationship with Jude Reid, a professor of classical studies. The relationship ended with his sudden and premature death three years ago. The average American male today can expect to live seventy-six years. Jude died at forty-five.

His wife, Madelyn, has already remarried, to a professor of macroeconomics. "I'm no good alone," she said in one of her infrequent phone calls. "I can't mourn forever. He would have wanted me to get on with my life."

I sleep alone now that Jude is gone. I have no desire to replace him. Some women deserve to be loved, some women just are, whether they deserve it or not, and some women, women like me, should be content with being wallflowers at this particular party.

I will be honest. It wasn't the money that made me accept the assignment to write about Margaret Fox: writing about Maggie keeps me connected to Jude. She was his obsession, his find, one of his gifts to me. Jude was a gift-giver. He brought me flowers, chocolates, ideas, names of people he thought would interest me, stories, scraps of history. In the hospital, during my recuperation after the accident, he came twice a day with an anecdote from Herodotus, usually one of the sexier parts. My favorite was the story of how Cleopatra swam under a bridge and tied pickled herring onto Antony's fishing pole to flatter him, since he caught nothing with his own skills.

I miss Jude, his stories, his little gifts, the feel of his eyes on me. I live in perpetual winter.

Some days I know that if Maggie were here I would let her convince me. I would be as easily gulled as one of the hundreds of widows or virgins who came to her, pleading to speak with the beloved husband, fiancé, brother, father, killed at Harpers Ferry or in the Glen Salt Mine or the influenza ward of Mercy Hospital. I would let Maggie draw the heavy velvet curtains, extinguish the lamps, pull the chairs into a circle, and command Jude to speak from beyond the grave. I would ask silly questions, like where did you leave the corkscrew and do you still love me now that you're dead or is it all over between us? Can you ever forgive me?

CHAPTER TWO

Hydesville, New York~1848

The women of the town were all gathered there under the tent, singing and praying, and sometimes one of them would fall to her knees and weep and wail and yell for Jesus to come to her. Then, the minister would stand before her, and put his hand on her forehead, and pray over her. The woman would grow calm again and the others would move closer to her, for protection, the way sheep do in the field when they sniff a strange dog. The devil was always just outside those close circles, waiting, hoping, looking for an opportunity. Jesus seemed more distant.

It was early spring, late winter, really, and it was cold and wet and the smell of damp wool was heavy in the air. Maggie Fox stood straight-backed next to her mama, trying to look pious, though her thoughts were not on salvation. She had not eaten all day. "Fasting is good for the soul. It will knock temptation out of you," Mama Fox had said. But twelve-year-old Maggie thought that going without breakfast and lunch put temptation into her, because now all she could think about was pork chops and applesauce. It was Wednesday. Pork chops day.

They had been at the tent meeting for ten hours already, praying and talking and singing and, when necessary, going for "little walks" when nature called. Maggie's throat was scratchy from the hymns and her head ached with hunger.

"Mama, can we go home soon?" she whispered, tugging on her mother's black wool sleeve. Half the assembly had already departed, worn out by prayer and the search for salvation.

Her mother pulled her arm away and buried her nose in her hymn book without bothering to answer. She prided herself on her stamina. Mrs. Fox did not leave a meeting till it was over.

Bored, Maggie looked at her little sister, Katie, who was asleep on the ground, curled up on the trampled brown winter field, thumb stuck in mouth and an angelic smile playing across her face. Her face looked whiter than normal, framed as it was by the dull brown bonnet. Her open hands looked like a picture of a starfish that Maggie had seen in her natural history primer.

Maggie nudged Katie with her foot. "Wake up!" she hissed under her breath. Katie squirmed away from the invading foot and stuck her thumb deeper in her mouth. "Wake up, Katie!" But Katie would not. And since she was only eight and not yet grown, she was allowed to sleep, while Maggie stood, stiff, hungry, and exhausted, praying for the prayers to end.

At dusk, they did. The tent was too big to heat and light, so nighttime brought salvation, but not the kind the congregation had hoped for; it was merely a respite, for Maggie and the other children and the husbands and brothers and sons back home, longing for their dinners, impatient for the womenfolk to finish their conversations with God and come home and wait on them.

" 'By-and-by, by-and-by. We shall meet in the sweet by-and-by!' " Mrs. Fox sang. Without losing a beat she leaned over and dragged Katie to her feet by her armpits. "Home, Katie. Wake up. We're going home . . . 'We shall meet in the sweet by-and-by!' "

Maggie, for the first time, wanted to dance and sing. It was over! But she had no energy. And she knew that come next week, it would be the same thing, and the week after that, and after that and after that. The happiest she could feel was a mild relief that soon, after the three-mile walk back was over, she could at least sit, and sip her tea and milk, and try and get warm again.

"Did you learn anything today, Maggie?" her mother asked when they were outside the dripping tent and had their faces turned to home. A very light rain, with large persistent snowflakes mixed in, was falling and making halos around the lanterns now dotting the pasture. The other wives were still mostly gathered at the tent opening, talking with each other and competing for the preacher's attention. But Mrs. Fox was new to this town, and still an outsider. People nodded and called "God bless you!" to her, but they did not smile; they did not stop her for small talk and gossip.

"I learned that we all have a guardian angel," Maggie said after a pause.

"You already knew that. Didn't you learn anything else? Or weren't you paying attention? Katie, stop sucking your thumb, or I'll put pepper on it."

"I learned that Jesus helps us when we are in need."

Mrs. Fox sighed. "You stupid girl. You already knew that, too. Maggie, if you don't stop your daydreaming you'll end up idle and even more filled with sin than you already are."

"Yes, Mama."

"Think about your own death, Maggie, it will come for you soon, and always sooner than you expect. Do you want to go to heaven or hell?"

"Heaven," she said, because she knew that was the correct answer. Deep inside her own thoughts she wondered, Where do all the dead people go? And can they come back, if they want, if they've been good?

The three of them, Maggie and Katie and their mother, walked slowly, even though a blazing hearth and hot food was at the end of the walk. They all thought, and did not speak, the same anxiety. Mr. Fox was at the end of the walk, too. Had he had a good or bad day? Much depended on that simple question.

Back home, it was soon obvious he'd had a bad day. There was a bottle, already empty, by his creaking rocking chair, and he still had his muddy boots on, not his house slippers.

"'Bout time!" was all he said when they walked in. "Get my dinner, woman. And you . . ." He reached for Maggie, who, already alert to danger, stepped quickly beyond his reach. "I told you to muck the horse stall this morning, girl. What about it!"

"I had to go to school," Maggie said, wishing she could suck her thumb, as Katie did, and knowing she'd get slapped if she did.

"School. Waste of time. When I was a child, children knew to obey. If that stall isn't clean tomorrow, you'll be sorry, understand?"

Maggie nodded, and went into the kitchen to help her mother. With precocious insight, she realized why her mother was so content to spend ten hours standing in the damp and cold of a tent, singing hymns, instead of staying at home.

Nighttime. Wind rustled the snow-heavy pines and howled through the plastered cracks of the log cabin like something alive and dangerous. Seasons have souls, and winter has the soul of a wolf. It devours.

Strong, cold gusts forced a sprinkling of snowflakes through the window cracks and onto a bed mounded with patched coverlets. Katie and Maggie huddled under the quilts, trying to warm and amuse each other through the long, frozen night.

"The wind is a wolf, but snow is dragon's breath. It starts out hot, then turns to ice," whispered Maggie.

"I didn't know there were dragons hereabouts. Never seen any," little Katie whispered back.

"Things don't have to be seen to be real, do they? Maybe they just don't want you to see them."

"Maybe." Katie, convinced, pressed closer to her sister. Both girls stared out the ice etched windowpane into the dark night outside, where the barren, snow-covered fields reflected moonlight and then stretched into a frightening emptiness. All color had fled the world. Even the plaid shirt on the scarecrow had faded to gray.

"See the scarecrow? It's waving at us. He's cold as a witch's teat. He wants to come in," Maggie whispered.

Katie snorted. "Scarecrows can't want nothing, silly. They're just spit and cloth and hunks of coal." Then, in an even softer whisper: "Why's he so mean?"

Maggie instantly knew she meant Pa, not the scarecrow.

"He just is. Jesus hasn't saved him."

Next week, meeting day came and went and Mrs. Fox stayed home. Mr. Fox had been drinking steadily and ranting that he deserved better, he deserved a wife who didn't gallivant all over the countryside thinking only about herself. The three women, Mrs. Fox, Maggie, and Katie, tiptoed around the cabin, avoiding the rocking chair where Mr. Fox snored and occasionally called out in his sleep. They made sure there was a full bottle by his side.

Then, on Monday, temptation seized Maggie just as her mother had always warned. That day, in the schoolyard, Mary Beth Brennan had boasted how her father had taken her downriver to see P. T. Barnum unload his tigers and clowns and two-headed alligator in Rochester.

Maggie went home and did all her chores and when they were done she chopped the wood, too, which was Mr. Fox's chore.

"Good girl," her father said. He had sobered up the day before and seemed a touch repentant for his bad temper. He pulled her pigtail and gave her a little smile when he saw the neat pile of wood she'd laid up next to the front door.

"Papa, the circus is here. Can I go?" She tried to look sweet and winsome, though she knew at such moments she was more liable to look cunning, and God does not like cunning, he likes innocence.

John Fox, who at the moment was God's representative, stopped smiling, and slapped her. "It costs a quarter each to get into that ungodly show!" he roared. "Do you think my pockets are filled with dollars? Are you trying to shame me?"

His anger was quick to rise but slow to melt. Once started, it built on little things like a flame licking at wisps of paper. The next morning, when she was slow about getting up and feeding the chickens, he pulled her from bed and threw her out in the snow in her shift. She trudged back and forth to the barn like that, barefoot and half naked, shivering, snow falling on her hair and shoulders. Her mother watched from the window, her mouth working in silent, continuous, and always unanswered prayer.

He was still on his high horse storming and ranting and looking at everyone sideways. Worse, he was inebriated again. *"Drunk!"* Maggie had yelled once, and her mother had slapped her for it.

"Respect your father!" Mrs. Fox said, though it was clear that all the things Maggie was thinking, she was thinking, too.

Maggie and Katie fled to bed to escape him.

But escape was not that easy, in a small cabin on snowbound nights when the darkness gnawed at the edges of anything hopeful and kind. Mr. Fox, his shirt hanging out of his pants, his jacket collar twisted, burst into the room. Maggie wasn't surprised. *Threes,* her mother said. *Bad things come in threes.*

"Good-for-nothings," he shouted. "Lazy Jezebels!"

16

Katie started to whimper. Maggie sat up and tried to stare him down. She couldn't.

"Out of bed." He grabbed her arm and pulled. "I've got something new to show you. You'll start to earn your keep around here." His words were slurred, his hand hot and clammy. Down the stairs, two at a time, Maggie twisting and half falling as he tugged her to keep up with his longer strides. Into the warm, cabbage-smelling kitchen, with its deal table and wobbly chairs.

On the table were two rat traps and in the traps, rats, squealing and red-eyed. Maggie smelled something hot and evil and looked for it. A pail of bubbling tar on the stove.

"Time to learn how to tar vermin," Mr. Fox said. "Watch." Carefully, considering how his hands trembled, his long, dirt-encrusted fingers released the wire spring of a trap nearest to him and grabbed the rat's tail before it could escape. Carrying it gingerly, he moved closer to the stove and dripped tar over the rat with a rusted spoon. The animal squealed and twisted, trying to bite, to escape. Maggie's heart shrank in her chest.

"Up to the neck. Not the head. Don't want it to die too soon. First, it has to run back to its hole. Then, we can kill the whole nest, 'cause the tar stain will show us where the hole is." He put the animal on the floor where it left a trail of tar as it scurried for the root cellar.

"Now, you do it." He pointed at the second trap. "And don't whine. Next year you'll be at the mill and you'll remember this as the good times. That cotton dust takes away any spare breath you're tempted to save for complaints."

"No. I won't!" Maggie shrieked, running to the other side of the table.

" 'Won't'? You'll do as I say."

"No, no, I won't!"

He pushed the table close to the wall, trapping her, then lunged across it and grabbed her by the black braid that hung down her back.

17

"Then stay the night with 'em," he yelled, dragging her to the cellar door. He opened it, and threw her down. She fell six steps then caught her balance but before she could run back up, to the light and warmth of the kitchen, he had slammed the door and bolted it. It was a thick, heavy door with new, tight hinges. Maggie knew she could never force it open by herself and her mother wouldn't help, for fear of Pa. There was no escape.

She had never been locked in the cellar before, not in this cellar, in Hydesville, in the haunted house. She hated him for this, with a hatred she knew would not go away in three days or four, when his darkness had passed and he asked her, as he sometimes did, to come and sit on his knee and give him a kiss. She would not. Not ever again. She wanted revenge. But how?

First, she must fight the night and the cellar, defend herself. She stumbled through the dark, feeling her way with her fingertips, looking for a shovel, a crowbar, anything that would be strong enough, long enough. Nothing. Except for bags of feed and a bucket of apples gone soft, the cellar was empty. Not empty. Rats.

She cowered against a wall, her teeth chattering. Furry bodies squirmed against her, red eyes glowed devil-like in the darkness.

If she closed her eyes, even in the dark they sensed her vulnerability and sharp teeth would test the skin on her bare feet. She soon learned not to drop off, to sit upright and widen her eyes so they couldn't close.

Maggie, huddled in a corner, fighting unseen enemies, flashed memories across the darkness of the cellar like a magic lantern show: the day last year when Papa brought them to this ugly town and awful cabin, the first day at the new schoolhouse, where boys plied each other with snowballs and the girls danced ring-around-the-rosy, tripping in their heavy coats and boots. "They live in the haunted house!" the Hydesville children had chanted. "Hey, Maggie, have you seen the ghost yet? Does it go 'whoo, whoo' in the night?" "Hush, children," the schoolmistress had hissed, but it was too late. Maggie had heard, and Maggie would not forget. Katie's teeth had chattered in fear.

"That cabin harbors a vexed spirit," whispered Orville Brown as he plucked pickles from the barrel and wrapped them in greased paper. His shopkeeper's apron was smeared red from the deer he was dressing in the side yard, and the color and smell of blood added luridness to the story he whispered to the two young girls. "A peddler. Murdered in the root cellar. That's what I heard. Everyone knows. That's why the place rents so cheap. Haunted." He laughed at the look on Katie's and Maggie's faces and stomped over to the flour bin to measure some for Mrs. Hughes.

The information simmered in the children's minds, coming to a sweet and dangerous boil like maple sap.

Another recent memory—a week after, gathered in front of the schoolhouse, Maggie and Katie accompanying their new classmates on a day trip to nearby Arcadia, to witness the new long-distance talking machine that had just been installed there. The telegraph machine operator was a tall man with a white beard and a touch of malignancy in his watery blue eyes. Black garters held up his white sleeves over his large hands and wrists. He pushed on a little lever and tapping noises filled the telegraph office. "I'm sending a message to my sister in Albany. See those poles and wires outside? I send a message by code and it goes along those wires to Albany, and her message comes back faster than a horse can carry it, faster even than the spread of old women's gossip."

The schoolchildren's mouths dropped open in awe and disbelief, except for Maggie, whose dark, knowing eyes narrowed in speculation.

"Can you talk to God and the angels?" Maggie had asked. "Can you send a message to my brother who's buried in the churchyard?"

"Maybe, little lady, just maybe I can." The telegraph operator winked at Maggie; she stared back, unsmiling.

Now, in the cellar and remembering, Maggie for the first time in her twelve years spent a night without any sleep at all and her mind opened like a book—not like a book waiting to be read, but like a book waiting to be written. In her new wakefulness and in her terror, she realized that the universe was waiting for her to tell it a story.

She mumbled to herself through the night, inventing a story of escape, of dragons slain, of a princess rescued. But what had she to do with princesses? Fantasy is useless if it hasn't borrowed some of its garments from reality. She wove another tale with the threads of the gossip she'd heard, a story of murder, of a body buried in that same cellar where she cringed. By telling it out loud, she took the teeth out of it, she declawed it, till murder and death and corpses were just empty, harmless words:

". . . and then, when the peddler wasn't looking, the greedy killer picked up the fire poker and crashed it into his head. Blood poured out of the wound, down the peddler's face . . ."

Maggie paused, thinking, and from overhead, through the gaping floorboards, she could hear her mother alternately sobbing and declaiming from the Bible in her thin, high voice. "Maggie, are you there? Listen, Maggie. Repent your wickedness. 'Then the kingdom of heaven will be comparable to ten bridesmaids, who, taking their lamps, went out to meet the bridegroom . . .' "

"He died with his eyes wide open in surprise," Maggie whispered back to the darkness, fascinated by death, by the new awareness that all people die and so would she, one day. She wrapped her skirt tighter over her feet as a rat brushed by. "The killer dragged the body into the cellar, where the hole was already dug. . . ."

" 'Five of them were foolish and five were wise,' " her mother's voice sighed. "Are you listening, Maggie? Let the Bible comfort you. He's asleep. Nothing more will happen tonight, but you know I can't let you out . . . 'The foolish ones took lamps but no oil along with them, but the wise ones took along oil in the flasks with their lamps. And as the bridegroom delayed his coming they all grew drowsy and fell asleep.' Save us, Jerusalem!" And then, in a whisper: "Now, sleep, Maggie. The night'll pass faster."

Forever after, when Maggie heard a woman weep, when she heard the Bible quoted, her own memory would add the squeak and rustle of rats.

She was allowed back up the stairs in the morning. Her mother bandaged the bites, and never said a word. A man was king in his house. Children were to submit and show respect, and keep quiet. Maggie didn't like to keep quiet. She had things to say, questions to ask.

"Mama, why do they put coins on dead people's eyes? Do they have to pay Jesus?"

CHAPTER THREE

Maggie had prematurely learned gratitude and fear and hate, and the knowledge was sharp as rat's teeth.

The next night, in bed again with Katie, watching the flapping scarecrow in the snowdrifted cornfield, she thought how wonderful it was to be in bed with sheets and blankets, high up from the floor, from the mice and rats, but under the wonder was resentment that she had learned what it is to cringe in a cellar all night.

"Hey! You're taking all the blankets," Katie giggled. She had her own bed, but the sisters liked to sleep together, especially in the winter. Two were stronger than one in this perpetual pitched battle between Papa and children.

In the winter, the bed they shared was pushed into the larger room where their parents slept, so that only one stove had to be loaded with wood for the night. "Only one room need be kept warm, this ain't that there Versailles in Par-ee," Pa said, pointing to last week's newspaper at the top of the kindling bin, and its headlines of riots in France. "I ain't no Louis Philippe with a crown and gold plates."

"Are we gonna do it?" Katie whispered, holding her white, starfish hand over her mouth to stifle another giggle. "The new game?"

" 'Course," she whispered back. "When Pa starts to snore . . . then we'll commence. You got the string from the shed?"

It was March 31, 1848, the evening of April Fool's Day.

Maggie, in bed now, waiting, heard the first soft *pffts* and *hummphs* of her father's deep sleep. The moment had arrived.

In that Hydesville cabin, in the dark winter night, a sound was heard, something between a thud and a tap.

Mr. and Mrs. Fox, tossing and snoring in their nightcaps, were light sleepers, as country dwellers must be, in case of fire, in case of foaling, in case the baby wakes or the hired hand doesn't. They immediately woke and sat up, stiff with alertness. They had heard the stories, too, about the haunting of their house. Mrs. Fox already believed in spirits. Whenever a thimble went missing or the stew wouldn't boil, she would ask the room in general: "Is there a bogey present?" No one ever answered before. That was about to change.

The thud sounded again, four, five times.

Mr. Fox, cursing, lit the oil lamp on the bedside table and pulled on a coat. Long shadows flickered against the bare walls. He went down the stairs to the door. It creaked open. Then shut. He came back upstairs.

"No one there," he said, scratching at his beard.

Four more knocks—*thud, thud, thud, thud*—in a broken rhythm that had nothing to do with the wind, or tree branches close to the house, or the loose front gate. Those were all familiar,

23

even comforting sounds. This sound was new and unknown, and therefore dangerous.

Mr. Fox scuttled from window to window, his nightshirt flapping at his knees, his long gray beard bouncing up and down on his chest. *Thud, thud* at the door, the wall, the window, the door again. Surprise and annoyance turned to fear. Where was the noise coming from?

Mrs. Fox covered her mouth with her fists but that didn't stop the chattering of her teeth nor the nervous trembling of her loose jowls. Her gray hair slipped out of her mobcap.

Katie and Maggie held their hands before their faces to hide their giggling, but as soon as Pa grimaced to shush them, their hands shot back under the covers, and the thuds started louder than before.

"What the devil . . ." cursed Mr. Fox, shaking a clenched fist at the ceiling. But the answer wasn't there. It was behind him, in the lumpy bed his daughters shared.

"Look, Papa." Katie snapped her finger, a skill only recently learned and one of which she was proud. The mysterious knock echoed the snap. Maggie, not to be outdone, snapped her finger four times. An answering knock sounded four times.

"Who's that? Who's there?" her mother asked, trembling.

A name. She needed a name. Maggie thought of her favorite name for the devil.

"It's Mr. Splitfoot," she said. "Listen." She snapped her finger three times. "Mr. Splitfoot, do as I do." Three taps obediently sounded.

"Saints preserve us," cried Mrs. Fox, clasping her hands together and trembling with excitement. "It's spirits." She fell to her knees. " 'And at midnight there was a cry made, "Behold, the bridegroom cometh. Go ye to meet him," ' " Mrs. Fox cried in ecstasy, swaying back and forth and weeping. " 'The bridegroom cometh!' "

Mr. Fox, less credulous, scratched at his bristling beard and stared at Maggie. She stared back. For the first time, he was the first to drop his eyes. Almost cringing, he took a step away from his daughter, from the hard glint in her stare.

"Ma, she says it's a devil. Get the hell off your knees," he told his wife. "I think it's a trick."

"I swear," Maggie said, opening her eyes as wide as possible. "It's not. It's Mr. Splitfoot." She looked at her father, stared at him again, and he would not meet her eyes. He had seen the hatred in them and knew he deserved it.

Maggie had found her voice, her power. She had made Papa drop his eyes and quake before her and the unknown; she had had revenge. She felt taller, stronger, fearless. There would be no retreating from this moment. She had chosen a path into her own future . . . or had it chosen her? Was there a second of doubt when she wondered who or what had been the instrument of this voice beyond the grave?

Carefully, so that Papa wouldn't see, she hid the apple and the string under the messy bed linen. The trick had worked. Now she was tired and wanted to sleep.

She would get no sleep that night.

Mrs. Fox, believing that the dead had spoken through her two daughters, could not contain her joy. Salvation was at hand. The barrier had been breached like the walls of Jericho. She fell to her knees, prayed, jumped up for joy, and fell to her knees all over again.

"Get up! Get up!" she called to her daughters. "A miracle has happened, and we must tell others! We must share the good news!"

"Ma, don't take on so," Mr. Fox said, putting his hand on Mrs. Fox's shoulder. "Just hold here, let me think." Maggie and Katie, still in bed, raised their eyes and made faces like those of angels on cards, though any fool could see Maggie's smile was a grin. "Girls, tell your ma it's a joke."

"Oh, Pa!" Katie said.

25

"It's not," Maggie insisted. "Something just come over me, just like that, and 'fore I knew it, I could tell some other . . . presence . . . was here. Jesus saves!" she added, for good measure.

"Mr. Fox, don't be one who sees and cannot believe," his wife reprimanded. "There has been a miracle here tonight. And I will tell others of the good news."

Hatless in her haste, dressed in a nightgown with an old wool coat pulled over her shoulders, she ran to the neighbors and invited them to come see, come hear, the miracle wrought by her daughters, her Maggie and Katie. Spirits had spoken!

Word spread from house to house down the single dirt street of Hydesville. Neighbor woke and listened, dumbfounded and hopeful, and went to knock on neighbor's door, and before dawn half the town had gathered in the cabin, including the most important people in town: the sheriff, the mill owner, several ministers, and one of the ministers' visitors, a Mr. Capron of Albany, who published a paper that circulated throughout western and southern New York State.

Thirty-five souls crowded, open-mouthed with yawns as well as awe, into Mrs. Fox's cramped little parlor, five people each on settees built for three, children kneeling on bare floor, servants and hired hands overflowing the hall.

Maggie and Katie, still in their sleeping gowns and caps but with blankets over their shoulders against the late-night chill, sat on straight-backed chairs in the middle of the parlor. They trembled with fear and exhaustion. Apples and strings could not be hidden and dropped secretly from their position on these chairs, in the middle of the parlor, with all the gas lamps blazing. What would they do? Admit the joke?

Katie was crying in fear which her mother mistook as shyness.

"Don't say anything," Maggie whispered to Katie; she templed her hands in front of her face as if she were praying, to hide her words from the gawking crowds of neighbors and townsfolk. "Remember when Joey got birched for cracking his knuckles in prayer meeting?"

Katie, wide-eyed, nodded.

"You could do it, too, remember? And so could I. Crack your knuckles when I do."

Mrs. Fox was busy pouring cider for the men and tea for the ladies and passing plates of butter cookies. This was the first time any of the people of Hydesville had paid her a visit. It wouldn't be the last. Years before, when she had first married Mr. Fox, she had dreamed of calling cards and afternoon visits with piano recitals and recitations of uplifting poetry. She had yearned for lace curtains and carpets on the floor, and a husband that other men deferred to. But children came soon and frequently, and there were recessions and stock failures, and gin became cheaper and cheaper as Mr. Fox, a man easily discouraged, gave up. She had once packed her trunk and bundled up the firstborn children, David and Leah, and left Mr. Fox. Nursing, her work was politely called. When people were making a mess being born or dying, Mrs. Fox was called to empty the slop buckets and boil the linens. It was a Mr. Thorpe, who died too slowly of a stinking, bloody flux, that sent Mrs. Fox back to Mr. Fox. Better cleaning up after your own than strangers.

Nine months after her return to Mr. Fox, Maggie had been born, and three years after had come Katie. Leah had grown proud as only really poor people sometimes do, and left, as had David, who had a farm and family of his own. Mrs. Fox, who had never ordered a set of calling cards, never hung anything other than muslin at her windows, was ready to believe, if belief could save her from the dismal failure of her life.

"Are you ready?" Mrs. Fox jubilantly asked the crowd. "Are you ready for this? Listen. Maggie, is there a spirit here in this room?"

27

Maggie hesitated a moment, then, wrapping her hands in the folds of the blanket, cracked her knuckles as loudly as she could. The sound was almost muffled by the stirring, heavy-breathing gathering, but enough people heard the sound that they gasped with awe.

"I heard it! I heard it!" shrieked Mrs. Troytan, the doctor's wife. "The spirits have come through!"

"Ask it a question," Maggie suggested. Katie had stopped crying and was watching her big sister with awe.

Mrs. Troytan scratched her chin and thought. "All right. How old was my little Bobby when he died?"

Maggie knew all Mrs. Troytan's children, for they shared the same schoolhouse. And everyone knew that Bobby had died last year, of a brain fever, when he was just three years old. She cracked her knuckles three times.

"Oh, Jesus," cried Mrs. Troytan. "Bobby, can you hear me? Are you here?" She turned in frantic circles, looking.

"Arnold! Can you hear me?" shrieked Mrs. White, widowed last year when Arnold had been crushed in a mill accident.

Beth! Baby! Jason! Enid! Louis! Grandmother! Father! The room echoed with the called names of the many dead. How was there room in heaven for so many dead? Maggie thought, listening and watching. The air in the parlor was feverish. People were praying and crying and hugging each other and staring quietly into the distance, fearful and hopeful at the same time. I should stop this now, Maggie thought. This will make God mad at me.

But when Miss Brayster begged to know if her fiancé was present, Maggie couldn't resist. She liked Miss Brayster, the school music teacher, liked the sad, fairytale-ish quality of her unhappy spinsterhood. "Oh, yes, he's here," she said. "Ask him a question."

"James! Do you . . . Do you still love me?"

Maggie cracked her knuckles twice. "Twice means yes," she said.

Miss Brayster wept openly, dabbing at her eyes with a dingy lace handkerchief that had once been part of her trousseau.

Hands reached for Maggie and Katie, clutching, pleading.

"Not all at once!" Mrs. Fox said, trying to take some control. "One at a time. They're tired, the little angels, can't you see? You'll exhaust them."

"Yes," Maggie agreed. "One at a time. And we'll use a special system. One knock means *A,* two knocks mean *B,* three knocks, *C.* You count as the spirits knock. Mrs. Cary, you start. You'll be wanting to know about Alfred."

Luckily, the people of Hydesville were very credulous and not overly imaginative. The questions they asked Splitfoot were easily answered with bits of information the girls had gathered in general-store and Sunday school gossip. How many children do I have and what are their ages? How long has little John been dead? Maggie, cracking her knuckles, answered so many questions correctly that a practical joke was about to turn into a new creed.

The game soon turned cruel, however. Spirits often have an axe to grind, so Katie and Maggie harvested all the gossip they had heard to create Splitfoot's tale of mayhem, and added to it the embellishments Maggie had embroidered aloud during her night in the cellar.

MRS. FOX: Are you a human being making this noise?
Silence.
MRS. FOX: Are you a spirit?
Two raps, for "yes."
MRS. FOX: Are you an injured spirit?
Two raps.

Maggie knuckled out the story in questions and answers, of a man who had been murdered in that Hydesville cabin, by an unknown person who had occupied it some years before; that he was a peddler murdered for his money. To the question of how old he was, there were thirty-one distinct raps. She also ascertained that he was a married man and had left a wife and four children. She studied her father's face all the while she cracked out these messages. He had a wife. He had four children. He could be wished dead.

The townspeople, unaware of the locked eyes of Mr. Fox and Maggie, grew hushed. Murder! Murder in Hydesville! And the dead can speak!

Maggie sat back and judged the effect. All eyes were on her. For the first time in her life, she felt safe. Nothing bad could happen, with so many people watching. Could it?

Two weeks later, Leah Fish, née Fox, sat at her breakfast table drinking chickory coffee and reading the Rochester morning paper. "Hush, Lizzie!' she said to the eleven-year-old girl sitting on the chair opposite. The child had been singing to her doll, but unfortunately Lizzie's voice was unable to replicate even the easiest scale or follow the simplest tune. This knowledge was painful to a mother who prided herself on a love of music.

"Sorry, Mama," Lizzie sighed.

Leah returned to her perusal of the paper, looking for possible ads for organists and piano players wanted for weddings, funerals, and public lectures. Instead, she found a notice that made her stand so quickly her chair fell over. Lizzie scrambled out of the way. " 'Hydesville Rappings'!" Leah read aloud. " 'Fox sisters speak with spirits'!"

And they hadn't contacted her. An event this large in her own family, and she had to read about it in the newspapers! Fuming, she grabbed Lizzie's hand, bundled her daughter and herself in heavy coats and tattered hats, and was out the door, heading for the canal ticket office.

~

Leah and Lizzie arrived in Hydesville covered with barge dust and a light frosting of snow, just as the family was sitting down to boiled cabbage and beef. Leah's brown eyes narrowed with disgust at the smell.

"Look who the cat dragged in," said Father Fox, chewing the cheap, gristly beef with gusto.

"Greetings, Father," said Leah, pushing her nose high into the air and brushing carefully past him to hug her mother. Over her mother's shoulder, she eyed her two little sisters, who stared back.

"How did you do it?" Leah asked, narrowing her eyes.

"Why, Leah! It's a miracle! The spirits speak with them!" Mrs. Fox protested. Mr. Fox chewed a mouthful of soggy cabbage and kept quiet.

"Maggie, come with me, dear," Leah said, taking Maggie by the arm so that she had no choice. "Now, show me what you did," she said, after the kitchen door was closed.

"I did nothing. The spirits spoke," Maggie insisted, trembling.

Leah slapped her hard enough to hurt, but not hard enough to be heard. "Try again," she suggested.

"Apples," Maggie said, refusing to cry. "And then we cracked our knuckles."

"And they believed it?"

Maggie nodded her head.

"Incredible. Yet . . ."

Rochester in 1848 was a boomtown riding the serpentine success trail of the new, hand-dug Erie Canal. It was a city of lumber mills and machine shops, garment manufactories and shoemaking plants. It was everything that Hydesville, democratic in its poverty, was not. For the well-off, for those flour, lumber, and sweatshop barons of Rochester's first industrial incarnation, it had a music hall and a library, a park with flowers in the summer and a brass band. For the poor, there were tenements and soup kitchens and hopelessness.

31

Leah lived in a shabby neighborhood where the crooked, wood-frame houses were gray with coal soot that no one had the energy to wash away. Milk was delivered already sour because the working class, with their fourteen-hour workdays, didn't have the energy to complain. The cowering street dogs were lean for lack of edible garbage. Leah's rooms were small and shoddily furnished; she longed for a stylish oak hall stand with a mirror and carved wreaths of grapes, and a hall in which to put it. She longed for a grand piano to replace the little square one she used for music lessons.

In need of cash, Leah quickly made the connection between her little sisters' prank and a new source of revenue. Young Johnnie McCabe, the son of Leah's coal man, had died recently in a Rochester grain warehouse accident—suffocated by grain, when he hadn't in years had enough of it to fill his belly—and hadn't the grief-stricken mother said she would give six months of her pay to hear his sweet voice again? Her friend, Rosa Hill, had just buried her firstborn, and longed to hear his prattle one more time.

Leah, child of the first years of Mrs. Fox's marriage—years of the drunken father, the desperate mother traveling from one religious revival to another, seeking salvation, seeking relief—remembered that the hat was passed at those revivals. Moreover, Leah subscribed to the improving lectures sponsored by the American Lyceum Association given at the Corinthian Hall. She knew how many heads, at a quarter a head, could be packed into that large hall, if the spectacle were interesting enough.

A photo of Leah from 1848 shows her in a dress of cheap, shiny material—it looks black, but was probably a brilliant blue to counteract the dimness of gas lamplight. Her hands are gloved, like a lady's, but what she hasn't yet learned is that while ladies wore gloves "even to wipe their arse," as Mr. Fox commented, gloves were always removed for a portrait. Leah will learn. For now, she smiles serenely, gloved hands in her lap, and looks at some invisible object over the photographer's shoulder. She looks pleased, as if she just had a good idea. Maggie and Katie, in their photos, always look a little guility, as if they are about to be found out.

When Leah returns to Rochester from Hydesville, she has little Katie in tow. Maggie refuses to go with her.

CHAPTER FOUR

*J*ude standing at the sink, looking even more masculine somehow in an apron, splashing water over the pasta plates, singing
loudly and off key . . .

> " 'Days and moments quickly flying
> Blend the living with the dead;
> Soon will you and I be lying
> Each within our narrow bed.' "

"Morbid," I had complained at the time.

"One of Maggie's. Don't you like it? How about this? 'By-
and-by. By-and-by. We shall meet in the sweet by-and-by!' "

I remember that now, and how he put his wet hand tenderly
on my breast, leaving behind a handprint on my sweater. I still

have the sweater, but the print dried long ago, of course—though I'm tempted to get out of bed and check. Maybe there's a little stain left behind, an indication that I was loved, that he touched me.

At four in the morning I sit up in bed, turn on the light, and grab my notebook. It's snowing again.

Jude, after he acquired his "upstairs privileges," as he called them, moved our bed by the window so we could see the meadow and all the way to that shadowy, mysterious line where the dark forest begins.

"*Lisière,* the French call it," he told me. "A shadow where two realities meet. My mistress has a sacred grove in her backyard." That was one of the things I loved about him: he could use dated words like "mistress" and not sound silly. Jude had been raised within the narrow confines of a strict religious sect—boys and girls in separate schoolrooms, the elders' word as law, no movies, no dances, no beer. Much of what he knew of the outside world, he had learned from old novels read by flashlight under the bedsheets. As a child, he had knelt, starved, obeyed, and kept silent. But when he was set free, at the age of eighteen, he never returned to the commune or the sect. His contact with his family was limited to yearly Christmas cards, sent spitefully since his mother and father did not celebrate Christmas.

"But I still hear them sometimes in my head," he admitted once. "I hear all the *no*'s and *don't*s and sometimes I even miss the little locked box of their lives."

The last time he saw my fields, they were like they are this night, knee-deep in snow except for sad brown patches where hungry deer have scraped the ground. Nothing moves in this frozen stillness, this more-likely hell than the overheated, noisy underworld dreamed by the Christians. Mary Shelley was right to sentence the unredeemable Dr. Frankenstein to the Arctic. Coldness is closer to death than heat.

It will be dawn soon. Perhaps I'll sleep then. "You are a

watcher," Jude told me once, "biologically destined by atavistic genes to keep the night fire burning, to stare back at the eyes staring out of the darkness, while all the other members of the tribe sleep." Like Maggie in the cellar, I sit up, wide-eyed, sleepless.

I crave sleep the way starving people crave food, with a desperate need that begins in the dark cave of our survival instinct, sweet sleep, with its seaweed dreams pulling me under warm waves of what was, its seashell echoes of memories, of touches, of Jude. Sleep is a brief reunion with my beloved . . . each within our narrow bed.

Jude's playfulness was often tinged with the morbid. I think he was, to use a word, mortally afraid of death, which of course makes his premature death, and my guilt, that much more terrible. In earlier times people like Jude found comfort in the mystical elements of their religion. But this is a harder century; we have Freud and the microscope and the self-help shelf in the bookstore. We examine, analyze, and explain. Mysticism has been outmoded. We are alone.

Just before dawn, I hear a branch tapping against the house, tapping a Morse code I can't decipher. This is the kind of noise Maggie would have heard, and noticed, and found a way to use.

And then, I sleep, just for an hour or two, before another day begins.

"Look," says my friend Alicia, bumping me with her hip since her arms are full of books. "Don't take this the wrong way. But you've become awfully . . . well, somber—you know? It's almost three years since Jude died. Can't you wear anything but black? I can't remember the last time I saw you actually wearing a color."

"Two years, eleven months, and one week. I like black. Doesn't have to be cleaned as often. Besides, black is all the colors merged into one. You just can't discern them."

My friendship with Alicia had survived the months that followed Jude's death because she viewed my mourning with the unflinching eyes of a scientist. "You're at stage one," she said. "Denial. Now you're at stage two: anger. Stage three, bargaining with death. Stage four: guilt."

Alicia is a mystery buff, when she's not doing free counseling on the side. Today, we're in Eleusis' best bookstore, stocking up on the latest paperbacks. Blizzards come up quickly in this part of the world and last for days. We've learned to keep a larder of canned foods and a basket of novels to get us through the worst storms.

She wears a long row of gold hoops in her multipierced ear and has dyed a pink streak on one side of her blonde head. When she gives scientific papers, which she does often since she is one of the leading physicists in the country, she removes the row of hoops and the streaks and dresses in gray flannel. Today she wears a hot pink jogging suit as she contemplates a row of gaudy paperbacks.

"Time to move on to the next stage, Helen. Acceptance. Time to live again," she says.

"I eat, I sleep, I work, I play. I paint my toenails and still crave chocolate. I'm going to start a diet tomorrow and take calligraphy lessons. Isn't that living?" I pull out a Ruth Rendell title. "Try this one. Nice plotting."

"You know what I mean."

I do, and it's more than my growing tendency to reclusiveness. There's a hollowness at the center of my life so great, it echoes if I drop any hope into it. Jude is dead, and I still hear that voice on the phone saying, *So sorry, Ms. West. He's not one of the survivors.*

Sorry. As if death is no more than a clumsy theatergoer who steps on your toes trying to get into his seat.

I like Maggie's grim reaper better. He, at least, was a prankster. Jude told me once about the prankster gods: Baron Samedi and

Loki, Zeus and Kali, Coyote and Cuchulain. Good stand-up material, he called them. Might as well wisecrack and duckwalk through eternity.

I met Jude when I was researching an article about historical family demographics; I needed figures on divorce in classical Italy and he had, the year before, presented an excellent paper to the Modern Language Association on just that topic. As a classical humanist he had a reputation for being sympathetic to the feminist agenda, a billing that made me wary from the start.

The chairperson of the journalism school, where I teach an occasional class just to keep my library privileges current, arranged our meeting by seating me next to him at one of her dinner parties. That is the fate of the single woman: strained dinner parties and trying to guess in advance whom you will be seated next to, what absent wife or girlfriend or same-sex partner you are standing in for. Most academics and professionals hate, or pretend to hate, such affairs. "Socializing," they call it, with a tone that suggests that sitting at table and eating a communal meal with mere acquaintances is akin to a visit to the dentist—good for you in the long run, but dreaded at the time.

I enjoyed dinner parties, though, in those days. I liked the well-prepared foods, the dressing up in something other than chinos and workboots, the arch conversations and usually harmless gossip.

The night I met Jude was a particularly strained dinner party. The theater historian kept chuckling to himself over how bad the Shaw festival had been last summer, the unpublished novelist was belligerent from rejection, and the somber feminist had just been appointed head of the notoriously underfunded Women's Studies Program. I laughed too much, and at all the wrong times.

The man next to me, Jude Reid, was blue-eyed and blond, with the long nose and high cheekbones that bespeak a Germanic ancestry. Later, when I knew him better—so much better that there were as many of his books in my house as my own—I would pick up one of his most dog-eared classics, Butler's translation of the Golden Ass, that ancient tale of magical transformations and dangerous love, and read a passage that described Jude to perfection:

> ". . . tall but nicely proportioned, slender without being thin, complexion rosy but not too red, yellow hair simply arranged, tawny eyes but watchful and with flashing glance just like an eagle's, face handsome in all its features, and a graceful and unaffected gait."

That was Jude. He was aging quickly by the time I met him; there was gray mixed in with blond, and a maze of wrinkles around the eyes. Those signs of mortality only added to his beauty, the way sadness helps to flavor joy.

His wife and teenage children were in England, visiting her family there. They had just separated. He told me that a little unhappily and a little shyly, anticipating in advance my reaction: Here was one more scholar who had done graduate work abroad, fallen in love with London and mistaken it for a woman, whom he had married and brought home as a kind of ultimate souvenir. That kind of thing. It happens often enough in Eleusis.

"I'm sorry," I said. I remembered what the house feels like when parents have decided to call it quits. I could understand why she went back to England while the details were worked out.

"So am I," he said. "I miss the kids."

He raised an eyebrow when he first heard my name. "Helen. It suits you. 'The face . . .' "

" ' . . . that launched a thousand ships.' I wish Marlowe had never written the damn play."

"Must have been hell in grade school," he agreed.

He was charming, as liberal humanists often are. Occupational hazard, I suppose, perhaps something in the curriculum. He mollified the feminist, flattered the unpublished novelist, drew out the eccentric theater critic, and addressed frequent little asides to me so that I did not feel neglected. Jane Austen would have found him exquisite, all that perfection—the perfect nose, perfect hairline, perfect suit, perfect manners; one could assume his lawn was free of weeds and there were no dustballs in the corner of his study. He made me feel inadequate, and even a little hostile.

"Your daughter plays violin and your son is president of his class, right?" I whispered to him over chocolate mousse pie.

He blushed perfectly. "Piano. Vice president," he whispered back.

Over coffee, in the music room where we had gathered, he sat next to me on the hideous horsehair Victorian settee, the kind that Mr. Borden had been napping on when Lizzie did him in. Victorian decor, that year, was required in academic upper-class homes, as a kind of stagecoach stop between the Scandinavian Modern which preceded and the neo-Gothic which followed.

"You are interested in Roman history, I understand?" he asked, lowering his formal dinner-party voice a notch, to a more personal level.

"No. Only their divorce rates," I said. "Sorry. Didn't mean to be so blunt."

"I admire the way you journalists get to the point," he said.

"No you don't. You find journalists crass and coarse."

He laughed.

"But not without perception, obviously," he said, lowering his voice even more. He leaned closer. His mouth curled at the corners when he smiled, making little dimples.

When the party broke up, Jude and I walked to our cars together. It was a spring night, warm and humid, and the countryside, even in the dark, seemed jumpy with new life. Frogs croaked gently from a nearby pond. An owl called from an old oak tree whose leaves, outlined in moonlight, were just the size of squirrel ears. It had rained during dinner and now warm mist created special effects around us, and the black ribbon of the road shone hazily.

A rock in the road moved. I watched. It moved again.

"A turtle," Jude said. I peered into the darkness, watching the turtle's sweet, clumsy slowness and the shine of moonlight on its shell. My father had given me a pet turtle for my seventh birthday.

"The Senecas had a village here where we're standing, before the Europeans came," I said. "They believed that the world moved on the back of a giant turtle and that it was bad luck to harm any turtle. The world would totter and go off course."

As I finished speaking, a car whizzed by, barely missing the animal. The headlights of another approaching car were already visible.

"Can't have the world totter," Jude declared. In five strides he reached the road and the turtle before the other car and deposited the turtle on the other side.

"Safe," Jude called as the car whizzed between us. He looked boyish in the moonlight, and it occurred to me that charm wasn't always bad.

And though the turtle was safe, the world did totter. I looked at him, at his perfect nose, and his perfect grin as he looked back from across the road, and even the quality of the pale, hard moonlight seemed to change, to grow brighter.

He called for lunch the next day. I agreed, if he would limit his remarks to ancient Rome. He did. But never have I heard a man speak so erotically of a dead culture. He discussed ancient Roman sexual practices in convincing detail and by the end of that lunch I knew, or thought I knew, exactly what our relationship would be: short, secret, and conducted entirely in bed. I was wrong. Jude was like one of those eighteenth-century etchings where two profiles are hidden in the shapes of vases or urns—sometimes you see the vase, sometimes the profile; on a good day, when your wits are sharp and your heart open, you can see both.

On our third "date," before we became lovers, he took me to religious services at a Catholic monastery. "This is the only place in the northeast part of the state where they still perform the mass in Latin," he said. "Living history." I sat stiffly next to him in the hard pew, overwhelmed and intimidated by the music, the incense, the robes of the priests, the formality of the language and gestures.

I was already familiar with this: a childhood Sunday morning had come back to haunt me. My childhood parish had a particularly fierce priest who lectured too frequently about hellfire and damnation. His was an Old Testament God, vengeful and ready to strike for the slightest misdeed. It's changed since Vatican II. But having left, I never went back, not till that Sunday with Jude.

Jude knew when to kneel, when to stand. He knew the responses. I wondered, a little uneasily, if he, raised in a strict cult from which he had fled as a young man, was now a convert to Catholicism. Perhaps belief becomes an addiction.

Afterward he explained a little self-consciously that he was interested, in a noncommittal way, in the sociology of religion, in the way God is named, defined, and celebrated. And then he said, "Dead is dead. There is no god, no afterlife. It is only the credulity of the faithful that interests me."

"It is the credulity of Maggie's followers that interests me," I say to Alicia, who is at the cash register paying for the Ruth Rendell.

"Right. You don't believe any of it?" She raises one eyebrow knowingly.

"Not a word. Or I should say, not a rap. That's what they called it when the spirits knocked out a message. Rapping."

"Rapping? Like a rap group? No, I suppose not. But think of the fun we could have with that bit of cultural overlap."

"Don't take this the wrong way," she says later, as we're driving home. "But you've looked better, if you know what I mean. Try some makeup. Are you sleeping?"

"Not much," I admit. "I never sleep really well when I'm involved in a long writing project. Deadlines. Stress. Weird dreams."

"And Jude's death is still on your mind. When you go into this no-sleep mode, you get paler than usual and the scars are more noticeable," she says, trying to sound motherly.

Instinctively my hands go to my face, where my fingertips quickly find the little ridges that radiate out from my left eye. *She's lucky she didn't lose her eye,* the doctor had said. *Lucky she didn't die.* He used the word *lucky* over and over, as if hitting a deer and going through a car windshield was a form of a lottery.

Perhaps it is.

CHAPTER FIVE

$\mathcal{N}$ever overlook the entertainment value of religion, especially new and exotic ones," Jude once said.

That was before we were lovers, when we were still behaving, still pretending this was a passing lust that could be ignored, still trying to put off the inevitable. We chose various forms of amusements and entertainments. Dinners at ethnic restaurants—out of town, of course, for discretion. Madelyn had returned from London and Jude had not yet found his own place, so the separation was more emotional than legal, and Eleusis is a very small town. So, we went to the movies and held hands in the dark. We played long games of Monopoly at my house, in front of the fireplace. We lived outside of society. Jude was willing to try anything, everything. There was a vulnerability to him, an emptiness that certain people seem to carry around with them, the way medieval lepers carried bells and staffs to announce their approach. We were both vessels yearning to be filled, although that role is traditionally assigned to the female. My emptiness was the less exotic form of loneliness, easily filled by the presence of the beloved.

Jude's emptiness was not as simple. It was the void that religious people feel when they have lost faith, the black hole of doubt, the vacuum of dogma no longer believed.

"I understand why the desert mystics spoke of the church as a woman, a mistress," he said once. "Losing faith is as physical, as painful, as losing the woman you most long to hold in your arms. I am an anchorite seeking his desert cell," he said. "Be the horizon that fills my eyes. Be God."

"Can't we just be friends?" I asked nervously.

"Maggie Fox played the role of priestess. I thought it was a role women enjoyed. Watch," he said. It was one month after the dinner party. We were having lunch in the musty, wood-paneled faculty rathskeller, still comparing notes on divorce in classical Rome.

With his hands held high in the air, with no physical movement, or so it seemed, he jerked the table at one end, then the other. Then, enjoying himself immensely, Jude grew bolder and used his knees to "float" the table an inch off the floor. Water sloshed out of our glasses onto the tablecloth.

"Spirit, are you present?" he whispered. The table dipped as if in assent then fell squarely back to solid ground.

"Easily enough done. Yet people fell for it." He seemed disappointed at how easy it was to create illusion.

"Wasn't that about the time that P. T. Barnum pointed out that 'There's a sucker born every minute'? Today those people would be seeing Elvis in supermarkets and watching for UFOs in their backyards," I said, mopping the spilled water with my napkin.

"We've all got to believe in something." He reached over and took my hand, massaging the third finger, the finger where other people wear a wedding band.

"The Greeks began the custom of wearing a band on this finger," he said. "They believed there was a vein that went from here"—he touched my finger just below the knuckle—"to the heart. How come you never married?"

"Too busy. That's the abridged version, of course."

Fearful that I would end up like my mother—married too young, too soon, starting with too much to do and finishing with long days of empty hours, and all the while waiting for him to come home, and then, after, for him to come back. There's no divorce for Catholics, only a kind of limbo of being neither married nor single. I escaped that first round of proposals, when the senior prom, the fumbling in the backseat, turned to white gowns and wedding showers—and the second round, when college exams and Mary Jane parties led to brief ceremonies in the park.

After graduation I moved to New York and threw myself into my work, wedging myself into small alternative weeklies and then the *Times*; then better-paying magazines—lengthy and sometimes dangerous assignments covering floods in India and malarial outbreaks in Kenya to establish my reputation as a front-line journalist. By my mid-thirties I was the lonely odd woman at dinner parties, the woman that wives did not trust. Seventy-six percent of married men have extramarital affairs. I contributed to those statistics, in those days when I thought that loneliness was the worst demon a woman could face. My accomplice was a fellow journalist, a competitor for top assignments, which added zest to the affair. We were lovers for three years before the miserly once-a-week allowance of sex and companionship became a worse demon than loneliness. His wife became pregnant and I sublet my New York apartment and fled to the wilds of upstate. Never again, I vowed.

"Good resolutions are useless attempts to interfere with scientific laws," said Oscar Wilde. "Who would give a law to lovers? Love is unto itself a higher law"—Boethius, one of Jude's favorite philosophers.

"Margaret Fox and her circle believed in marriage with spirits, in heaven," Jude said, still holding my hand. "Heavenly matrimony. Don't you think that's an oxymoron? The pagans had believed that marriage existed in the afterlife but, in the afterlife as in this life, it worked in men's favor: they could take as many wives and concubines as they wanted, while the women were required to be faithful to their one spouse."

"Now you're going to say your wife doesn't understand you," I said, using my free hand to stab a forkful of his pecan pie. The ceiling vibrated with the thumping electronic music of the student-cafeteria jukebox located somewhere on the floor over our heads. Intimate conversation was impossible, or at least risky, but we didn't have time to meet off campus because he had to teach a class in half an hour.

"As a matter of fact, she understands me very well," he said, pushing his piece of pie to the middle of the table, closer to me. "So does her lover, who was once a good friend. Ha. You're surprised. You thought only husbands got up to hanky-panky. Isn't that a bit antiquated of you?"

The music overhead changed from heavy metal to a softer acoustic guitar ballad. The student waiter poured us more coffee. Jude and I drank the coffee and considered each other over the rims of the cups.

He courted me in traditional manner, sending roses and chocolates and phoning three times a week. He took me to lunch every time I had to be on campus, and for long walks along the lake.

He called once at midnight to say there was a shower of shooting stars.

"I think in a previous lifetime you would have been a safari guide," I told him. "I feel like I'm being stalked. I've become the prey."

"Is it an unpleasant feeling? Being wanted? Being the prize?"

"No. Quite the opposite."

47

"Isn't this about the time Jane Eyre flees the wicked Mr. Rochester?"

"I'm not Jane Eyre. And honor is more complicated than the Victorians gave it credit for being."

Desire began to sabotage my senses. Colors began to seem brighter, fragrant smells stronger, when Jude was in the room. Colors faded to gray when he left; roses lost their scent. Electricity passed between us. He could finish my sentences for me and not get a word wrong or out of order from the way I thought them. The years I had lived before him lost their focus. I came to feel that there was much time to make up. I wanted him so badly I couldn't work.

We became lovers on a rainy early-summer night two months after our meeting. It seemed inevitable, as if all the choices had been made for us.

We were to have gone to the movies, one of those postcard-pretty Merchant-Ivory productions that leaves you hungry for chamber music and pink gin cocktails. But rain began to fall in heavy sheets and ripples of muddy water frothed down Piety Hill; going out seemed unwise. Without a word he closed the front door and took my hands in his. I will not forget the way he looked at me. Not as if I were merely pretty, or desirable, but as if I were the only woman, the single member of my sex. I was Eve.

He built a fire in the fireplace. I opened a bottle of Bordeaux and made a plate of toast, pâté, and Greek olives. When I returned to the parlor (I still can't call it a living room; the house, born before "living rooms," deserves some respect) it was silent, except for the crackling of the fire and the tapping of rain on the roof.

"No music?"

"No music," he said. His eyes were dilated from the darkness. He sat forward on the sofa, wringing his hands and staring into the fireplace. I put the plate on the coffee table, among the back issues of *Savant,* piles of dusty library books, and yellow notepads, and paused in front of him, giving myself one last chance for escape. He is still tangled up in a marriage, I reminded myself. A separation is not a divorce. But I did not escape. Instead, I took him by the hand and led him up the stairs to my bedroom.

When I call back that particular memory now, it seems to me that there were three people in that mussed and joyful bed. Jude. Me. And a future that died when he died. Time stands still now. It has frozen into a winter that will not end and there are monsters moving through the icy darkness. All the colors have faded, the roses are dead on the branch.

Tonight, when I wake at three in the morning, shoved out of my own dreams like a guest who has overstayed her welcome, the atmosphere in the bedroom seems different, as if things have been moved, reoriented to a different center. But nothing has been moved, it is my perception that is off.

Usually I prop up the pillows, pull the blankets closer and huddle in the still darkness, not brooding or weeping or making lists as other insomniacs do, but content to simply wait in a half-conscious state, either for dawn or that familiar restlessness that compels me to be up and working, even in the darkness of night.

But tonight, when I awake, I am fully alert, alarmed even. My face is hot with an adrenaline flush.

There is a knocking somewhere in the house. It is irregular, like Morse code, and soft.

Old houses are filled with noises. Any day when the temperature varies by as little as twenty degrees between morning and evening, this house groans and creaks and stretches and shivers like the entire percussion section of a medium-size orchestra.

This noise, though, sounds like heavy raindrops on the roof. But it is not raining. It can't—it is still cold winter, the season of silent snow.

Tap. Tap. It continues. Maggie?

49

Don't be stupid. And predictable. That's what happens to writers. Begin an article about arthritis in Iceland, and all of a sudden all the men at your next editorial meeting are named Olaf. Accept an assignment about swimming mortalities in Japan and the supermarket opens a new section of fresh sushi. Connection. Coincidence. Write about a spiritualist, and your house starts to knock at you.

Keep your head, Helen. An animal has taken up residence in one of the walls. That's what it is. An animal, knocking, banging, trying to find its way out, or perhaps burrow deeper in. Poor thing. To be trapped in such a narrow space, seeking warmth and finding instead a prison, a living grave.

My pity lasts only a moment. Fire is the greatest danger in these old houses. And most of the fires are caused by animals who have chewed or otherwise damaged wires in their marauding and burrowing. At three in the morning, I am scurrying up and down stairs, checking to be sure the fire extinguishers are in their assigned places. I must remember, tomorrow, to check the batteries in the smoke alarm.

The *pensione* where Jude stayed in Rome did not have a smoke alarm. After the fire the Japanese partnership that owned the building was penalized, I heard.

Sometime just before dawn the knocking, scraping noise stops and I fall asleep again. I dream of monsters moving through a cold, dark night, and of fire. When I awake the house is very quiet. Quiet as the grave, my grandmother would have said.

Perhaps the animal in the wall has died.

No, there it is again. Knocking. I definitely heard a knocking sound. It has started again.

It continues as I pull on another sweater and pair of socks and make my way downstairs to the kitchen and teakettle. It continues as I stir a cup of Earl Grey and toast a slice of bread, that loud *tap-tap-tap* that does not sound like a branch rubbing the house, or wood shrinking and creaking or any other noise I know. It stops only when I go back upstairs and sit down at my desk, to work.

Great. A haunting deadline. But I can't laugh.

In midmorning, as I'm going over some notes on Maggie and trying to figure out why the spellcheck on my laptop isn't functioning, Alicia sends an e-mail:

—What happened to the antimatter that was created during the Big Bang? We've misplaced eighty percent of the known universe, just can't find it. A single proton lives for billions of billions of years. Why can't we? There's a psychic festival at the Holiday Inn. Don't you think we need to go? Just for research purposes? It will be good for a laugh. Come out, wherever you are.

Alicia, I think, staring at the screen, show me a proton that goes bump in the night and I'll pay attention. Meanwhile, you're spending too much time in the subatomic-particle accelerator. A psychic fair? The mediums will just be manicurists and babysitters in funny clothes. But if I go out, on the way back home I can stop at the hardware store.

Okay, I send back to her.

The lobby of our local Holiday Inn is broken into the semblance of a medieval village with plastic tarps and blankets creating a weird effect of tents and shanties. Candles burn, and there is a smell of incense in the air. In each of twenty little alcoves sits a person, most of them female, with homemade posters balanced on easels next to their booths, advertising arcane skills for speaking with the dead or foreseeing the future. There are several artists who paint portraits of their clients' earlier lives and, sensing an opportunity, several people from the town's smaller, less conformist churches are also on hand to dispense literature and encourage attendance. *There will be a tent revival at the Green Street carwash on March 29.*

51

Don't you want to be part of it? asks a yellow sheet thrust into my hand by a youth standing under a potted palm.

"There will probably be a blizzard that day," I tell him.

"Jesus will keep us warm," says the youth.

The embarrassed manager of the hotel grins excessively. Alicia is rocking back and forth on her heels with pleasure. I am unhappy. It reminds me of the awful Halloween houses of my childhood, with peeled grapes passed around as eyes and sheet-wrapped balloons posing as ghosts. The fraudulent leaves a bad taste in my mouth; I appreciate the empirical, the knowable, the provable. This was, to use a country phrase, hogwash.

"Well, shall we have our portraits done up from the eighteenth century? We were both probably witches," Alicia says with enthusiasm. "Or perhaps stick with the more conventional, and go to that woman there, with the crystal ball."

"Madam Psyche and her crystal ball," I say without enthusiasm. "Then we won't have anything to carry home."

Alicia goes first, sitting down in the folding metal chair with a flamboyant swish of her patchwork skirt and warning the fortune-teller she wants only good news.

"I tell what I see," the woman replies sourly. Her sallow skin and a thick layer of green shadow on her eyelids gives her a reptilian appearance. Her fingertips are nicotine-yellow. "Twenty dollars, please."

The reading takes fifteen minutes, during which time Alicia is informed that a great sin of her youth has been forgiven her, a colleague is planning to sabotage her project, her mother loved her more than she ever said, and she will take a trip to exotic places. I roll my eyes in disgust, but Alicia stands and gives me a little push into the chair. I sit and hand over twenty dollars.

The fortune-teller looks into her crystal ball, and then into my eyes. "In three weeks, you will have a great celebration of life," she says.

Not likely. That's the anniversary of Jude's death, the day of his memorial ceremony.

She looks again into my eyes, frowning. "You have had a brush with death," she says.

"Yes," I say, angry and covering my eye with my hand. "A car accident."

Then the predictable patter: the trip to a new place, the unhappy episode (unspecified) that would soon be forgotten, the money I would earn next year.

"You will hear soon from an old flame you thought you would never hear from again," the fortune-teller says.

I'm tempted to ask for my money back, but did I really expect to hear anything sensible? "Is that it? Am I done?" I ask, rising.

"One other thing. You will meet a stranger. A man." Alicia, still standing behind me, clears her throat. This time, the fortune-teller rolls her eyes and has the grace to look a little uncomfortable. "I know. Silly, huh?" she says. "But you will. I see it. Soon."

"Tall, dark, and handsome?" Alicia asks.

"No. Tall, skinny, redheaded, not very good-looking."

"She prefers good-looking."

"I say what I see. Beauty is in the eye of the beholder."

"Now that's original," mutters Alicia.

On the way home I ask Alicia, who is driving, to stop at the hardware store on Main Street so I can buy rat poison and a sledgehammer.

"Work going that badly?" she asks, pulling over into a parking space in front of Tony's Hardware. The street has been plowed and dirty drifts of snow three feet high run like a miniature mountain range edging the sidewalk.

"I think I have an animal trapped in one of the walls. If it dies there, I'll have to open the wall and retrieve it, or live with the smell of rot and decay for the next twelve months or so."

"You country house-owners have all the luck," says Alicia, helping me push the car door into the mountain range of snow so I can get out. "I'll give you some new Sheetrock for your birthday. And when I find out which colleague is sabotaging which project, can I borrow the sledgehammer?"

"You didn't take any of that seriously, did you?"

She hesitates, then shakes her head.

Back at my house, Alicia doesn't come in for coffee. She's got a project going back at the lab and doesn't quite trust the graduate student she left in charge. Alicia, as far as I can tell, spends her days in a synchrotron, charting subatomic events that happen only when someone says they've happened. *If God closes his eyes, do we cease to exist?* Jude asked once, voicing an ancient fear. Perhaps we are only God's bad dream and we exist because his eyes are closed.

"You're worried about sabotage, just because some manicurist with a scarf wrapped around her head says she saw it in a piece of glass. Alicia, this isn't like you." I stand in my driveway, shivering, fumbling for the keys in my purse. Even with fur-lined gloves, my hands are numb with cold; great bursts of frost leave our mouths as we speak and hang in the air like cartoon bubbles for dialogue.

I can't remember a winter ever being as harsh as this one. But then, this is what I say every year at this time.

"It's not just because of her. We have this visiting physicist from France who's walking a little too closely behind me, peering over my shoulder at my notes, that kind of thing. He's making me nervous." Alicia pulls a face and I laugh. But I see she is anxious.

In the house, stillness reigns. Whatever was knocking before has stopped. I stand in the cold silence, clutching the sledgehammer and rat poison, challenging the silence. Nothing. The hammer and poison go into the broom closet and I make a cup of tea.

The hotel fire that killed Jude has made me queasy about fires, and I haven't built a fire in the hearth since his death. Now, I pause in front of that cold, ashen hearth, blanket wrapped around my shoulders, considering. Jude would have hated that fair, that reduction of philosophies of immortality to the lowest common denominator, to child's play. I feel disloyal for having gone.

God, it's cold. I miss the blazing fires that Jude used to build here. Yet I am drawn to this spot, to the memories, vivid as living people, who crowd around me.

Here, on many a snowy winter night, stood Jude, a drink in each hand, watching as I spread a blanket on the floor in front of the crackling flames. Once we fell asleep here and Madelyn, for revenge, called at five in the morning to wake us. "Rise and shine," she said. "Rise and shine, little adulterers." That was after her lover had left her and she was jealous of our happiness.

" 'Adulterer,' " Jude said, rising up on elbow. "From the Latin, 'to falsify, to alter.' Are we falsifiers, counterfeiters of passion?"

"We are not," I said. "Hang up the phone. I love you."

"Ah," he sighed, putting the phone down. "Love. The final justification. Then come alter me, my love."

Do houses absorb those moments? Does the house remember Jude?

CHAPTER SIX

Rochester, New York–1849

$\mathcal{L}$eah's first husband wasn't just an adulterer, he was a bigamist. While still married to a younger, trusting Leah, he absconded with the funds of their meager bank account, went west even before Horace Greeley made it fashionable, and took a second wife.

The world changes quickly and completely for certain women. Leah was one of them. One day she was a young mother with a husband to pay the landlord and green grocer; the next day she was abandoned and in charge of a wailing infant. Pride kept her away from Ma and Pa Fox as long as she could stand the hunger and the landlord's threats, but soon Leah resorted to the survival skills an abandoned woman of her era needed: platitudes of Christian charity, coquetry when safe, tears on rare occasion. She gave piano lessons in the afternoon, earning probably five cents a day, and wheedled credit from various sellers; when absolutely necessary, she begged a secret loan from her mother.

No wonder Leah, alone with a dangerously light purse and smarting pride, was so pleased to find that her younger sisters were capable of drawing a crowd, at a quarter a head. Talking with the dead looked like a profitable venture. Willful, sulky Maggie was going to be a problem, but Leah, older, stronger, more cunning, could handle her.

Leah had the play; she had the characters. She needed a better setting, more stylish props. She needed to relocate to a more respectable neighborhood. First problem: How to get out of the lease for her rooms, which had another year to run. She must have thought of the solution while still on the barge, as Katie and Leah's daughter, Lizzie, practiced table-turning and other pranks. As soon as she was back in her Rochester rooms, Leah put her plan into motion:

Leah sits by the window overlooking the dark, marshy square of grass she calls a garden where Katie and Lizzie, wrapped in woolens, have been sent to "take the air." Leah bends over her embroidery hoop and her dark hair, combed into smooth wings on either side of her face, sweeps forward as she dances her needle in and out of the cloth.

All at once there was, as Leah described it later in her family biography,

> . . . a dreadful sound, as if a pail of bonnyclabber had been poured from the ceiling and fallen upon the floor near the window. The sound was horrible enough, but in addition, came the jarring of the windows and of the whole house, as if a heavy piece of artillery had been discharged.

Snow heavy with melting ice makes such a noise, such a vibration, when it avalanches off a roof. But Leah preferred the ghostly and gothic explanations that would enhance the rapping performances of her younger sister and daughter. Her autobiography is filled with accounts of noises that sound like the pouring or dripping of blood, the marching of parades of spirits, the wailings and weepings and groans of the restless dead. Beds rise and spin, invisible feet trudge up and down stairs, the spirits even applaud each other . . . according to Leah. Maggie could have been an actress or a social reformer; Leah could have been a novelist to rival Le Fanu and the other Victorians who told tales of midnight deeds.

> I came to the conclusion that it (the apartment) was haunted, and decided to move out of it as soon as I could and find another house that suited me. . . . I was particular to tell the agent that I wanted a house in which no crime had been committed. For I believed that the house I was then living in, like the one at Hydesville, was haunted; and I presumed that in this case as in the other it must have had its origin in hidden crime.

Leah had found her lease-breaking clause: She claimed the rooms were haunted, and what respectable family could live in a haunted house? Considering the racket Leah made to prove this claim, the landlord was probably happy to be rid of them.

Second problem: Finding the funds for her better digs. She borrowed, probably, a little from friends and family and much from a professional money-lender, accepting a high interest rate and using her old parlor piano as security. Soon, she hoped, she would be able to afford a new one.

So, Leah, Katie, and Leah's daughter packed up their valises and boxes and moved into a freshly painted, freestanding little house in Mechanics Square, where proper little girls wore clean, white stockings and embroidered smocks, not burlap aprons, where the coalman and tomato-seller tipped their caps and said

"Thank you, ma'am" after each purchase and delivery. The house itself, with its chastely shuttered windows and front porch big enough for a potted evergreen and bench, had four different staircases connecting its two floors, as well as a balcony outside the upstairs parlor. Such a surplus of amenities would come in handy for various stage entrances and exits, both earthly and not.

Next Leah arranged the reunion of Katie and Maggie, who was still in Hydesville. Katie did not have the talent, the appeal of her older sister, and foolish Lizzie was prone to giggle at the most important moment of a performance. Maggie was needed. Leah wrote to her mother, explaining that Katie wept herself to sleep every night in longing for her sister (a lie) and that she, herself, felt only half alive, deprived of her beloved sister's companionship. (Another lie. She didn't like Maggie.)

Mrs. Fox, thoroughly perplexed at the strange twist her life had taken, was only too happy to leave Hydesville, where things had gotten out of hand. The Hydesville Rappings had continued, with Maggie presiding over them, and the little run-down cabin had become a major tourist attraction, more popular for the moment than Niagara Falls. Through Maggie, the ghosts rapped nightly, to a wide-eyed, trembling crowd.

What with all the attention, and the gifts, the flowers and embroidered handkerchiefs and leather-bound Bibles, Maggie felt like a princess. She no longer bothered to answer her father when he addressed her, but only put her nose higher in the air and turned her head in the other direction. Her revenge focused on the cellar, her prison, and in the course of one particularly interesting evening she cracked out a lengthy message from the murdered peddler saying he was buried in the cellar. Next day, most of Hydesville turned out to dig for his body. Maggie watched in glee as an enthusiastic army of farmers turned the hated cellar into a pit-marked, mud-filled ruin.

They found a few bones but not an intact skeleton, and had to give up digging when the cellar began to fill with water.

But the bones were deemed incriminating enough. There was mob talk of finding the former owner of the house and putting him on trial for murder. They would call on the dead man's spirit as the main witness, using Maggie as a medium. (Later, when Maggie carried these conversations with the dead well beyond the town line of Hydesville and into New York, Boston, and Philadelphia, there would be bizarre trials of the dead accusing the living, through mediums.)

Dead men. Trials. Ghosts. Her own Maggie acting uppity as a city-bred stranger. Mrs. Fox, watching all this activity from a bewildered distance, developed migraines. Could Maggie and Katie be deceiving them? Did her girls really speak with spirits? At some point Mrs. Fox simply stopped thinking, and accepted. Isn't that what faith requires?

She also accepted Leah's invitation and left home once more, towing along a reluctant Maggie, who had enjoyed being the solo star attraction in Hydesville.

Maggie, standing on the doorstep in Rochester, valise in hand, her old wide-brimmed hat caught by the wind and twisting as though it wants to fly away, glares at Leah who has just opened the door. "Come in, dear sister," says Leah. "My home is yours." Maggie catches the smell of tea and fresh-baked muffins, sees the darkly-painted green hall with the new fancy carved hall stand and thick carpet. She hesitates, knowing that this is more than a simple entrance, Leah is offering more than an invitation to tea. Her nostrils twitch in suspicion. Maggie hesitates, and the wind, as if to mark the moment, finally takes her hat in its grip and carries it down the street. "Let it go, Maggie dear. I'll get you a new one," Leah says with honeyed voice. But Maggie isn't fooled. She knows this is a trap.

Hydesville is behind her. Leah is in front. She must choose.

Maggie haughtily steps over the threshold. "Just for a few days, sister," she says.

Leah's new house, with its balcony and four staircases, suited her purposes perfectly and she quickly became an accomplished stage manager, somehow making it appear that the three little girls, Lizzie, Katie, and Maggie, were present, when in fact one or two of them were tiptoeing up and down stairs, pulling strings, dropping objects, making noises.

Every visitor to those rooms—and there were many—was treated to a spectral spectacle: tilting tables, books flying off shelves of their own accord, invisible feet marching up and down the stairs, rappings and knockings which Katie and Maggie proclaimed were messages from restless spirits . . . all done, as the saying goes, with mirrors, and with strings and levers—and supple toe and knee joints.

Entire murder scenes were enacted, with sounds of throttling, stabbing, scuffling, and groaning filling the parlor and terrifying the visitors. In the dark inner parlor where stiff brown velvet curtains excluded all daylight, the guests sat stiff with fear, holding hands, eyes tightly shut (as Leah required), as Maggie and Katie screamed and wailed and banged bricks together, then fled to the balcony to shake chains, or hopped up the stairs, making sobbing noises.

Maggie sometimes subverted the performances by moaning when they had decided she would drop something, by being in the corner instead of on the balcony. She was not without humor. For one afternoon caller, she made a spirit called Flatfoot pound out a distinctive Highland fling and Leah, forced to play along with this unplanned jest, sang the music for Flatfoot.

Leah's house, now crowded with little marble-topped tables, doily-covered chairs, little girls, astounded mother (Mrs. Fox stayed on) and many spirits, became one of the most popular spots in Rochester, falling somewhere in respectability between Mrs.

Farley's decorous tearoom and Rosy O'Leary's back room, which was rented by the hour to heavily-veiled women accompanied by "uncles" who sat too close, kissed too often, to be blood relatives. The knockings, as they were called, were entertainment with a higher purpose, to achieve greater understanding of The Beyond, the Other Side, so who could object?

And Maggie—what was she thinking at this time? How did she like living with older sister Leah, performing as Leah commanded?

Rochester was better than Hydesville. Rochester at least had gaslights on the streets and a sweet shop where she could go for a phosphate. Leah let her stay up late at night, and sleep late in the morning. Leah did not make her tar rats and did not throw her into the cellar when she was sassy, there was no cow to milk or chickens to feed, and there seemed no reason to work on her ragged, bloody *A-B-C* sampler, since she now had a Higher Calling than simple needlework.

All those things were improvements. But Leah was bossy and mean. She smacked Maggie when Maggie didn't do as she was told, and quickly. Resentment piled on resentment. Maggie was a deep one, as her mother too often complained. For the time being, she did as she was told. But she once again dreamed of revenge.

Inspired by improved surroundings, Leah began to change and focus the manifestations, from pranks by anonymous spirits to "visitations" from beloved dead ones.

Using the "spirit telegraph"—one knock for *A*, two knocks for *B*, et cetera—Leah "received" a message from her grandfather one early autumn night when several visitors had gathered in the little cottage and joined hands around the table.

My Dear Children:

The time will come when you will understand and appreciate this great dispensation. You must permit your good friends to meet with you and hold communion with their friends in heaven.

I am your grandfather,
Jacob Smith.

That "authorization" from a dear departed was vital. Leah and her little sisters were exploring unknown lands and not everyone agreed they had the right to trespass into that other world. There was talk, even threats made against them: *Let the dead rest in peace.* Eggs were thrown at the house; unsigned hate letters were pushed through the mail slot.

But if friends wanted to come and speak with the dead, who was she, Leah, to stand in the way of the spirits? If those same friends chose to leave a little offering in a plain envelope on the hall stand, how could she stop them? Leah upped the stakes. She let it be known that her little dead brother had come to her.

. . . and so long as I remained quiet and permitted the little angel to do as it wished to, without disturbing the conditions requisite to enable it to come so near me, there was no shrinking or withdrawal on the part of the Spirit, who had thus far reentered this mundane sphere to prove to us, beyond a doubt, that he still lived, and loved us. We could not doubt it.

Since her dear little spirit brother had come, could not other spirit children come through to those who missed them so desperately? Might they not comfort grieving mothers and sisters?

This new entertainment would have been staged at night, of course. We are so much more foolish and gullible in the evening than at noon. In the darkness, all the ancient fears rise up and dance around us, tickling the backs of our necks. At Leah's, there would be darkness in the close little parlor, with perhaps the hall lamp lighted but none in the room. They would sit at a table, their hands joined, their eyes tightly closed or covered with a scarf. Katie would moan or sing to cover the sound of Maggie's footsteps as she creeps beside the bereft mother and gently removes the client's hand from Leah's and puts her own little hand in the waiting palm.

Try this sometime: Sit quietly in a very dark and quiet room with your eyes closed, as a friend, with the lightest touch imaginable, puts his hand over yours. Even when you expect it, even when you know whose hand it is, the sensation is uncanny. We are all fools in the dark.

"Your son is here, Mrs. VanClyfe. Don't move. Any movement will frighten the little spirit away. No, don't take the cloth from your eyes. Remember that when Orpheus tried to see Eurydice, he lost her forever. The spirits don't like to be seen. They like to be felt. Let Albert comfort you. Let him take your hand." Leah's voice, I imagine, was particularly beautiful. And convincing.

Lines started to form outside Leah's front door.

But Maggie was already getting weary of her game. Perhaps Maggie, young as she was, already had regrets.

"Oh, no. You started this, little miss. You'll finish it," Leah hissed the first time that Maggie claimed to be too unwell to receive the "visitors" who came to the new Rochester house. "You'll do as I say, and you'll do it now!" Leah gave a hefty pull, and weeping Maggie was out of bed and on her feet.

"Powder." Leah grabbed the puff off the dressing table, then hesitated. "No. Red eyes and nose look real convincing. You'll go downstairs just like that. Now, march, young lady, and don't forget what I told you. The boy's name was Everett, he was six years old when he died, he was afraid of the dark. His mama wants to talk to him real bad. Say only good things. He's happy.

He plays all day with the angels. He knows he will be with her again."

Everett, Johanes, Marthe, Annie—other children who died so young they hadn't even been named anything but "Baby"— rapped on table and wall and prattled (Katie, standing behind a curtain, imitated a convincing toddler's voice of either sex) in Leah's parlor, to the consternation of skeptical fathers and the great joy of grieving mothers who still heard, even without Maggie's help, the sobs and wails of their dead children, mothers whose arms ached for the sweet weight of that dead infant, whose senses were quick and active with longing.

Not all the afternoon visitors were grief-stricken. Some came just for the entertainment, to be amused by invisible, dancing ghosts who pulled hair and tweaked feathers in hats, poured salt into the teapot, and made terrifying noises: moans echoed down the chimney; bodies were dragged across bare floors in the over-head rooms; shrieks issued from the pantry.

The visitors, blushing and blanching all at once, trembled and hid their eyes from what was already invisible, and then, having had a perfectly charming afternoon, always left a little something behind on the silver-plated salver on the hall table. New curtains appeared on the windows; meat was served at dinner. The Fox sisters wore new dresses and hats trimmed with silk flowers.

Think of Maggie at fourteen, a dreamer of both dreams and night-mares, larger than her own landscape, capable of seeing what others never even suspected. Think of the angry, cruel father, the rat-filled cellar back in Hydesville, the hopeful mother who still believed in redemption and better ways, the religious community, the faith and the sentiments. ("But surely as our Savior rose, / On Easter morn from Joseph's cave, / Shall all those mounds at last unclose, / And Christian people leave the grave," they sang in Church every Sunday.)

Beneath those exterior catalysts, curled like a lizard under a

65

cool rock, is Maggie's inner life. Perhaps she came early to that point, that emptiness that cries to be filled, so into it we drop the first things at hand: truth, fear, hopes of a summer afternoon, winter's desolation, anything to fill the yawning abyss. Her rappings might have partially filled that emptiness.

What could she not have been, had she turned away from fraud and lies? A great actress, certainly, someone to rival Bernhardt and Duse. A novelist, had she let her imaginings work themselves into words on the page instead of tales told into a dark night. A philosopher, perhaps, an earlier Dorothea Dix, a woman who understood grief and could make it turn tail and run. Such a woman could have had a future. Women like Maggie have only a past.

Maggie's clients came looking for footsteps into the unknown, for shadows, for remnants of love and the beloved, and she tricked them. She deceived them.

There is an end, and death is it. Life leaves behind odds and ends, but they are nothing more than dirty dishes at the end of the banquet, rumpled clothing at the end of the day.

CHAPTER SEVEN

$\mathcal{J}$ude left his robe hanging on the bathroom door. It is still there. I wash it every so often to get rid of the accumulating dust, and hang it back up. When my bedroom light is on and the bathroom door is open, the robe casts a reflection on the floor, making it look as though he is standing there in the bathroom, brushing his teeth, perhaps, or making faces at himself in the mirror. He did a great Cagney imitation.

It's a winter twilight now, and the shadow is there. I get up from my desk to close the door. The house is quiet. Perhaps it will stay quiet. I stare out the window, willing my eyelids to grow heavy. The field is empty and white except for little black scars where a deer has walked from forest to field and back to forest, leaving the sadness that occurs when a place, formerly filled with life, suddenly is vacated. For days after Jude's departure, his pillow stayed flattened where his head had rested, and carried the scent of his bay-rum aftershave.

I wake just a few hours after dozing off. The knocking has begun, coming from the room down the hall.

It starts as a staccato tap, quick and light, almost playful. I sit up and listen, more curious than anything else.

After a few moments the noise grows heavier, more insistent, with fewer pauses between the now dull thuds. Then it becomes so loud, so heavy, the walls seem to vibrate with it. I feel a moving sensation, as if I am vibrating, too.

I listen with all my being, as if this is a lesson that must be memorized. And then I rebel, jump from bed and turn on the radio, twisting the knob to the local college rock-and-roll station to drown out the other noise that now inhabits this house. Instead of heavy metal, the soft and sweet "Do You Wanna Dance?" sung by the Mamas and the Papas, insinuates into the room. Jude's favorite song.

Write, Helen. Fight back. I get out my laptop.

Dead is dead. The dead do not speak. That was the simple, unalterable truth that Maggie's clients could not face.

But Maggie's followers weren't alone, neither geographically nor historically. Today, the fastest-growing religions (the human race has had one hundred thousand religions at last count) are the charismatic ones, with their signs and miracles, their messages from the dead. Sixty-nine percent of people believe in miracles. Forty-seven percent of parents who have lost children believe their dead child's spirit has visited them. My chiropractor has seen guardian angels and spoken with her dead mother, she says.

We do not accept death.

Jude used to quote to me from Propertius' elegies. " 'Extraordinary attachments survive even beyond the fatal shore,' " he would declaim, working his eyebrows Groucho Marx style and standing in his "aggressive orator" stance, feet in ballet's fourth position, left hand on hip with elbow jabbing into the air, right hand waving over his head.

This last part will have to be deleted. I can't work it into the Maggie article. I turn the laptop off, and let the memories have their way with me.

"Of course, the Romans saw death for what it was," Jude had said, sitting next to me on the sofa. "A destroyer of routine and habit, an inconvenience, a break in the perpetuity of matter. For them, judgments were minimal and death itself could be bargained with. Their ghosts, for instance, were made of flesh and blood, had more to do with zombies than wispy white sheets. A ghost could be loved, held, kissed. At the end of Propertius' elegies, the dead Cynthia comes again to his bed."

"Sex with a ghost doesn't sound all that appealing—clammy at best." I poured more brandy into his glass, in encouragement. I liked his performances. We had a blazing fire in the hearth. Outside, it was snowing, but we did not need summer to be happy together.

"Then you've never read Berta Reese of best-seller-list fame. In *Death Is a Door* she highly recommends it, as part of the mourning process."

We talked about death as an abstraction, as lovers do. We wrote about it, thought about it, analyzed it, but as gamblers do—fearlessly, even coldheartedly, figuring odds. Very few of us are prescient enough, or honest enough, to admit that tragedy is an equal-opportunity event.

And then, suddenly, death became real.

One year after I had met Jude, I ran out of milk for our coffee and decided to make a late-night run to the convenience store. It had snowed heavily. The road was icy. The deer, crazed with starvation, stepped in front of my car as purposefully as if it wished to commit suicide. Einstein could explain this, but I cannot, because as soon as I saw the deer, and the deer saw the car, time stopped. I had oceans of time, enough time to remember the books I had planned to write and hadn't, the birthdays of friends and relatives I had forgotten, the boy in seventh grade who kissed me outside the school gym. I had enough time to think, No, not me! I don't want to die.

But though time seemed to stand still, the car kept moving, to the inevitable conclusion of flesh meeting glass and metal. The deer died. I did not; almost, though, I'm told. My right cheek needed eight stitches around the eye, which I almost lost, and there was damage to the spine, a head injury.

When I came out of the hospital two weeks later, my life became a round of physical therapists and cosmetic surgeons. Jude drove me back and forth between his classes, from surgical centers to rehab practices, from home to doctors' offices. He fed me, spoonful by spoonful, and held my head when the painkillers wouldn't let me keep the food down. He tucked me in at night and brought my morning tea and pills. I was not a good invalid. I didn't lay prettily in bed, smiling and accepting and grateful to, be alive. One day I refused to stay in bed at all and tried to manipulate my stubborn legs into the bathroom, only to end on the floor in an immobile, soiled heap. I stayed that way for three hours, waiting for Jude to come back from his classes.

"Isn't this romantic?" I quipped as he tried to lower me into the bathtub and my right knee still refused to bend because of a muscle spasm. "Isn't this just what every man dreams of? Taking care of a woman who can't even wash herself?"

"I think I can deal with the stiff leg and the messes," Jude said, lifting me under the armpits and pulling. "I did help raise children. But if the self-pity gets worse, I'm going to have a hard time, Helen."

Eventually, the knee bent. Eventually, the doctors and surgeons and therapists moved me past crisis to recovery. But it was a long haul for me, and for Jude. And the scar on my face, around my eye, was permanent.

"Gives new meaning to the line 'face that launched a thousand ships,' doesn't it?" I said bitterly to Jude one day. "Something like this could have prevented the whole Trojan War. Paris would have run in the other direction."

Jude and I were standing side by side in front of my tall mirror. He put his arms around me and hugged.

The scar looks like a thin, incomplete spiderweb made of slightly raised flesh. It is not hideous, not extreme, but it is the first thing people see when they see me. I have become a scar. For a while I parted my hair on the left so that it would fall forward over the right eye. But that tactic merely delayed, rather than prevented, the moment when stranger or friend could not help but let his eyes go from mine, to that scar.

Now there are few mirrors in my house. There is still one over the bathroom sink, where Jude shaved in the morning, and one in the guest room, since I rarely go in there.

"Do you fear death?" I asked Jude, several months after the accident. I kept reliving the moment when I had thought, "No, not me!"—worrying that I had cheated somehow, that a death was still due.

"I am afraid of the IRS. Death deserves its own verb, don't you think? Some new verb that would also describe how I felt when I went to the hospital and saw you unconscious with wires and tubes and needles all over."

"I knew you were there. I felt you; I think I heard you talking. You sang to me. 'Do You Wanna Dance?'"

"Well, you know me. Always too much to say, and out of tune when I sing. I talked to you nonstop. I yelled at you, once. When your blood pressure went so low the nurse started giving me sympathy looks. I yelled, and you came back. Do you remember that?"

"No. Nothing."

"Could you invent it? There's money to be had from that out-of-body stuff, you know."

Jude could not talk about death for long. It always had to

become a joke or a lecture. There could be no silence, no calm, when death was in his imagination. The few psychiatrists I know are still trying to come to terms with their own unhappy childhoods; doctors often have a morbid fear of illness. We choose the professions that promise to help not others, but ourselves, and Jude's academic profession provided clues to his deepest fear: his best-received paper had been on rites and rituals to stall or thwart the physical persona of Death in ancient Rome.

Was it fear of death that drove Maggie? Perhaps she meant eventually to believe, meant to move past the fraud, the practical joke, and become one of the faithful. I know agnostic and atheist Catholics who go to mass each Sunday, preparing for a time when they will actually believe the dogma, when they will be graced with faith. I tried it myself. After Jude's death I went to the monastery where he had brought me for mass. I tried to believe that he was out there somewhere, watching over me, being happy and peaceful. I couldn't. Once I was a smooth-faced child who caught snowflakes on her tongue and made snow angels. But now I'm not, and winter is long and cold and hostile, and Jude is gone.

It has snowed for three days, nonstop. Snowplows rumble up and down Piety Hill, clearing it for schoolbuses. For the first time I wish snow made noise as it fell. Perhaps it would cover the sound of the knocking in the wall. It comes now at three in the morning, like the first time, but also at noon, and again at six. The cyclical pattern indicates an animal, doesn't it? I wish the knocking would stop; it's setting my nerves on edge. If it is an animal, though, how can I blame it for trying to escape the cold winter outside these walls? *If it's an animal . . . ?* Listen to me. What else could it be?

The phone rings, interrupting this unwelcome train of thought. Alicia. Lunch.

Before driving into town, I lug out the sledgehammer purchased last week at Tony's Hardware and carry it into the room

I think the noise is coming from, the bedroom next to mine, from the wall facing the hall. It is a room I rarely use, having little need for more than one bedroom, a kitchen, and some work space. The air is heavy with dust and mildew and the smell of disuse. At some time it must have been a child's room—the faded, peeling wallpaper is decorated with ascending hot-air balloons which, in their time, were probably very gaily colored. Now they are gray and sad.

The wooden bedframe still in the room is smaller than usual. A child's bed. There is no mattress, for which I am grateful. It would have been home to dozens of mice. I tidied up the room when I first moved into the house, and two boxes of yellowed, crumbling schoolbooks are still propped against the south wall. Maggie would have known those primers, *Mrs. McGuffey's Readers,* with their crude drawings of cows and little girls in bonnets and fathers who all look like Old Testament patriarchs, probably like Mr. Fox himself. Maggie's red schoolhouse in Hydesville would have been only fifty or so miles from here. It's not impossible that she might have handled some of those books. I'll have to look through them someday, check the doodling in the margins and the signatures inside the cover.

But why did the noise, the animal . . . whatever . . . choose this room? It is pleasant enough. Two large windows let in plenty of light. There is nothing eerie here, aside from those cobwebbed boxes of dogeared readers which remind me of too many childhoods ended, too many children now just bones in the earth.

I hoist the sledgehammer over my shoulder and take a desperate swing at the wall, determined to make a hole large enough for the animal to escape. The wall caves in with a storm of plaster dust and crackling wood, and leaves a jagged hole some two feet in diameter. The noise reminds me of that smashing of metal and flesh before I was knocked unconscious in the car accident.

When my heart slows to normal, I stick my head in the hole in the wall, careful to avoid the pointed ends of the broken wood

73

studs that stick out of the plaster like a compound fracture. I maneuver my hand in next to my right ear, and turn on the flashlight.

Plaster motes whirl in the flashlight beam. A smell of mold. Darkness except where the light flashes. But no trace of an animal. Not even mouse droppings on the floor; though, judging from the noises I've been hearing, a raccoon, or at least a large squirrel, has been rummaging around this wall.

I was wrong. Or maybe I just guessed the wrong room. There are two other unused bedrooms. I heard wrong.

And now there's a very large hole in the wall.

A little weak in the knees, I start to laugh.

"So, what did the fortune-teller decree for you? Good or bad? I can't remember," Alicia says, a little too brightly, digging her fork into a ham-and-brie quiche. She looks tired. There are dark circles under her brilliant green eyes and her lower lip trembles a bit, as it always does when she is feeling stressed. She has dressed hurriedly. Her eyeshadow is smudged and she wears no jewelry, not even the familiar row of hoops in her left ear.

"Mostly good, except he won't be handsome, only tall. Why?" I chew a forkful of warm chicken-and-walnut salad and wait for her answer.

"Well, remember, she told me someone I work with would sabotage a big project I was working on?"

"Yes. And?"

"The department has canceled my work leave for next year. Jim Phillips talked them into giving the time to him. I'll teach his Intro to Physics course while he's off in France playing with quarks."

She eyes her quiche steadily, refusing to look me in the eye. Jim, chair of the physics department, has been promising her this leave for three years. She needs it to finish, and publish, her own research on quarks before someone else publishes first. Impossible now. No wonder she has lost her appetite.

"It gets worse. I'll have to leave, of course. I can't stay, if they won't support my work. But where will I go? This is the best physics department in the country." She is quietly sobbing now. Her shoulders heave. Fearless Alicia is weeping into her quiche. Diners at the next table give side glances to Alicia, noting her tears, then look at me, noting the scar, and then look politely away.

"This is a temporary setback. You'll get your leave next semester and then publish before Jim even gets his results tabulated."

"Maybe." She doesn't look convinced.

Over chocolate-mousse torte her mood lightens and her resilient optimism returns. Alicia, as she often points out, gets on with life a little less grudgingly than I.

"So what do you think?" she asks. Her lips pucker as she works a piece of chocolate in her mouth to get the fullest flavor. "Did the fortune-teller really see the future, or just read my mind?"

"She may have been slightly telepathic. Maybe some people have a sense of what other people are thinking, but I don't buy into this 'reading the future' theory. Your subconscious already suspected Jim of some treachery, and she picked up on that . . . if anything unusual at all happened. I stick with the 'lucky guess' theory."

"And what were you thinking of when she read your fortune? Have you met Tall, Dark, and Not-Handsome yet?"

"Not unless he's an extraordinarily large mouse running around my walls."

"Helen, you need to get out more. It's been three years."

"Not quite three years. There's a few more weeks till the anniversary."

"Isn't this what the Victorians did? Celebrated anniversaries of deaths? It's morbid, Helen."

"They were called 'heavenly birthdays.' And it was a way to maintain a previous relationship, when no new relationships were forthcoming. Few women had the chance to marry a second time or even a first, if he died before the wedding. A dead spouse or fiancé was better than none at all."

"Are you talking about the Victorians, or yourself?"

"Both."

CHAPTER EIGHT

$\mathscr{N}$ext morning, the day I had scheduled to begin the yearly garden cleanup—the raking of leaves not raked in the fall, the pushing back into the marshy soil the escaped roots of mum and liatrus—on this morning, the first day of spring according to a calendar as blind as justice, I wake to six inches of new snow covering the fields and roads.

It takes an eternity for warm water to finally trickle out of the shower, and while I wait I stand naked in front of the bathroom mirror, shivering and considering. I step closer, as if that woman in the mirror can comfort me as Jude used to, with his hands and mouth and belly. I touch myself as he touched me, stroking the breasts he kissed, the eyebrows he traced with his finger as if drawing them, the scar that trails my eye like a comet's tail. But my own touch, as unfamiliar as a stranger's, does not console. I step into the shower and let the now-hot water drive needles into my back.

The house is so cold that my breath frosts as I dress. The furnace doesn't thaw even the smallest corner of this fierce cold, but only rumbles helplessly like a dying animal, spewing out currents of hot air that turn cold as they leave the ducts. There's ice inside the windows. I pray the pipes don't freeze. I should buy more insulation and give the pipes another wrap. I should get out of here for a while. Maggie is becoming a kind of secretive boarder who never shows up at meals or to help with chores, but is nonetheless always there, always a presence. Everything I do— making fresh coffee, reading last Sunday's *New York Times,* watering the houseplants—makes me stop and wonder: Did Maggie take cream in her coffee? Did she enviously ponder the advertisements for the new cage crinolines in her newspapers? Did she fill her parlor with overgrown, grasping ferns and darken the room to a perpetual twilight with mocha-colored wallpaper?

I'll drive into town, buy pipe insulation, go shopping with Alicia and pick up a pile of books and papers the university library has unearthed about religious revivalism in nineteenth-century upstate New York.

In my car, driving considerably under the speed limit thanks to the icy road and my remnant distrust of roads, cars, and winter, I pass a black station wagon that has spun into the ditch and been abandoned. The tracks in the road curl and twist like skaters' patterns. Slowly, fishtailing at every little bend in the road, I pass white fields and black stretches of forest newly frosted with glinting snow and the occasional house, each one spaced well apart from the other; each one surrounded by field and forest and an almost maniacal craving for space, for privacy, as if each house, each family, has secrets. A madwoman in an attic. A drooling, blank-faced child in the back room. Bank money secreted in the closet, skeletons in the cellar.

Cruelty hovers in the ice-cold air surrounding these houses, houses that Maggie would have seen when traveling from Hydesville to Albany; icicles hang from the eaves, sharp as knives, forming crystal bars over the windows. Ice has brought down the better part of the ancient oak tree in Mahalia Smith's front yard, leaving glassy lengths of brown branches strewn over the white snow.

Just a few hundred miles to the south, daffodils are blooming and sheep are lambing. Mumbling to myself over this injustice, I recall the joke I heard at the pharmacy the other day: There's two seasons in this town—winter, and road-repair time.

I try to concentrate on the cold and the tricky driving, but little by little my thoughts focus on a steady knocking sound, a *thud, thud, thud* noise my car doesn't usually make.

My hands are too tight on the steering wheel, my foot is too heavy on the accelerator pedal, and the car starts to fishtail wildly, threatening to spin. I gulp in deep breaths of air, to calm down. It works. The car, almost of its own will, begins obediently to follow the black ribbons of straight track in the white road. The near-accident does not happen. But the knocking continues, so I carefully pull over, switch off the ignition, and get out. Silence. I am alone in a white wilderness, the black tracks on the road are the only sign of other people having passed this way. I tip my head up and let snow drift onto my forehead and nose.

It would be useless to raise the hood and try to find the noise, since I know nothing about engines. But a quick walk around the car reveals the source of the problem. The snow-wheel tread has picked up a large stone and is banging it, *thud, thud thud,* as it revolves around and around.

Helen, I tell myself, calm down.

Alicia pulls a pale orange linen dress over her hips and shoulders, disappears briefly in a cloud of sunset-colored flounces, and re-emerges triumphant, smiling like Venus on her clamshell.

"Like it?" she asks, deepening her smile and smoothing the full skirt.

She is in high spirits today. Too high. Still suffering from Jim's betrayal, she's over-compensating to stave off depression. I tilt my head and consider.

"Looks very summery. And just a touch punk before punk went mainstream."

"Perfect."

To avoid my own reflection in the mirror, I look over Alicia's shoulder to the dressing-room wall, to a Victorian print of a guardian angel guiding a little brother and sister over a rickety bridge. It's the kind of print that would have hung over Maggie's bed when she was a child.

Obsession of this sort sometimes happens to writers. When Jude's writing was going well, he started to dream in Latin. When I wrote a book chapter on "Mortality and *The Charterhouse of Parma*," I came down with every symptom in the book, from a flu that resembled jail fever to chilblains and dysentery. Maggie is taking over my life.

"I said, 'Should I get it in orange and blue, or just the orange?' Wake up, Helen. You're fading away. What's so interesting about that tacky painting?"

Alicia frowns and puts her arm around my shoulder, pulling me closer.

"Get both," I say.

In line at the checkout counter, Alicia nudges me and tilts her head at a woman ahead of us. It's the fortune-teller from the psychic fair. Today, instead of ridiculous gypsy garb she wears a tailored suit and white blouse. She is neat, middle-aged, respectable. She looks like a bank teller, efficient, serious, smart enough to hide any eccentricities she might have in order to not stand out in the gray-flannel world of business.

I wonder if she'll say something to us—Hello, how are you? Did my predictions come true?—or discreetly pass us by, pretend we've never met behind closed doors, as therapists and tax lawyers do. Madam Psyche, that was her fortune-telling name, I remember. The ridiculousness of it had reassured me.

Madam Psyche watches with glittering brown eyes as the saleswoman folds and wraps in tissue several pieces from the spring collection. Alicia and I watch Madam Psyche. When her bag is neatly packed and she turns to leave, she pauses. Her eyes find me.

I nod hello.

She frowns and puts a hand lightly on my arm.

I don't like to be touched, at least not in this patronizing casual manner. I pull my arm away, overcome by a sudden and intense dislike for this woman who appears equally comfortable in gypsy skirts and a gray flannel suit. She, like Maggie, is a fraud and a cheat and I have somehow given her permission to enter my life, I have let her take liberties with my rationalism.

"The letter is coming. It will be a letter," Madam Psyche says. Then, with a mundane, bank teller's smile, she turns and leaves.

"She looked better in gypsy garb," whispers Alicia.

The librarian has a stern, pale face dominated by large glasses. She has a wistful smile, though, and when she hands me the pile of manuscripts—the never-published journals of clients and friends, the private diaries that did not make it into Leah's self-serving official autobiography, the master theses on the Fox sisters, and other bits of literary flotsam—she kindly offers me her smile as well as the dusty papers.

"They are fragile," she says. "Turn the pages gently, won't you? And return them on time."

I promise to treat them well, sign for them, and quickly scan the titles. My excitement is dulled with misgiving.

"I may return them ahead of time," I say. I'm no longer certain I want to complete this piece. Not even for that big check Tom has promised.

I take a quick look at the novels on the New Arrivals shelf, then back out into the cold, where I trudge back to my car, snow squeaking underfoot.

Driving home, snow falls so thickly I can see only three feet ahead. There's not enough time to stop, if a deer jumps in front of me. I leave only my toes on the accelerator, slowing the car to a crawl. The odds of running into a deer and going through a windshield a second time are one in several tens of thousands. But odds can be strangely unreassuring.

The worst thing about death is that it leaves so much that will never be finished. Quarrels, debates, promises, errands, movies we had wanted to see together, next year's performance of *La Traviata* . . . things owed the living, now claimed by death. Jude's proposal.

He wanted to marry me, he said at Christmas. Divorce Madelyn, marry me, make us legal and moral, upstanding citizens once again. Jude, under his veneer of liberal intellectual, was staunchly righteous. His upbringing had taken firm root. "I am living a deception," he said. "I am divided, walking two paths at once. 'One man. Two loves. No good ever comes of that,' says Euripides, and I agree. Will you marry me, Helen? If Madelyn and I divorce?"

He was on edge that evening. His research wasn't going well— the book on marital relations in classical Rome had come to a standstill—and he'd wasted a long and frustrating day on campus, trying to battle out a new curriculum for the department, a yearly event the administration had invented to keep the faculty too busy to realize they were underpaid.

It was eight months after the accident. Jude and I had been quarreling about how to spend the evening. I wanted to stay home, he wanted to go to a movie and dinner.

"The scar isn't as noticeable as you think, certainly it isn't noticeable enough to force you—us—into reclusion. It gets old, sitting here," he said gently.

"I like old things."

"You should consider selling this house. You live too much in other people's pasts. You and your mortality statistics," he said.

"Listen to you. You know more gossip about second-century Rome than your own century, and you tell me I live in the past. I like old things. I like this house. I feel safe here."

"What about a nice, renovated apartment downtown, in the old Brick Street schoolhouse? View of the lake. Great balconies."

"Too expensive. The rent would be more than my mortgage."

"The two of us together could afford it."

"What a prim little kiss," he said, frowning. "What's up?"

"You've been separated for two years. This is the first time you've mentioned divorce. Are you sure? Maybe we should talk about it after your book is finished. I want to be certain you're not just using me as an excuse to avoid writing."

"Helen, reading a spy novel instead of Ovid is how I avoid work. I'm talking about marriage. I want you to make an honest man of me."

I wanted it more than I could say. But I hesitated. Fear . . . of what? That he would change, that he would start leaving dirty socks all over the house, be more demanding of me, more critical? That he would get bored? That he would leave me, as he had left Madelyn? Perhaps the fear was not of how he would react to marriage, but how I would react. Suppose I grew even more dependent? Some days I already felt as though I wouldn't even get out of bed, unless he encouraged me. Perhaps, as his wife, I would lose myself completely. Perhaps I just wanted it so much it frightened me.

Jude was offered a three-month residency at the Massimo Institute for the Humanities in Rome, all expenses paid, beginning in the spring. I felt betrayed, when I saw that letter. He hadn't even told me he had applied.

"Everyone applies. I'd never thought I'd get it," he said. "It's besides the point. Of course I won't go."

"Why not?"

I was so afraid of losing him by then that I insisted he go. It was a kind of test, a way of seeing if, once given his freedom, he would return to me.

"You want me to go?" he asked, incredulous, still holding the letter in his hand. His fingers were trembling with emotion.

No, I thought. Please, please, don't leave me. "It will be good for your career," I told him, "and it will be good for me. Think of all the work I'll get done. I'll learn how to take care of myself again." I said. By that time he was chopping wood, fixing broken screens, painting stairs, and even reminding me to pay my phone bill. I could not imagine falling asleep without him beside me, or getting up in the morning and making coffee for one, not two.

"My career isn't everything. What about my personal life? What about you?" he asked.

"I'll be here when you get back. Do you think there could be anyone else? I will wait." I touched my face.

"You think no one else would want you. You're wrong. It's not as bad as you imagine," he said for the hundredth time. "It's barely noticeable."

"I know," I lied.

"You really want me to go?"

"Yes." Another lie.

Two months later, on a cold spring morning, I drove Jude to the airport. Where was Madelyn? I don't recall. She wasn't there.

Jude and I didn't speak in the car. The two months of waiting, of planning the separation, had changed us. I lived under a cloud of regret and fear, now that what I had suggested was actually happening. He was leaving. Jude, on the other hand, was as loving, as considerate and cheerful as ever, but for the first time I sensed that he was holding back. He did not talk about the divorce from Madelyn, or our marriage. He, who of habit had planned even the simplest things weeks and months in advance, now lived from hour to hour. Sunday mornings, he went to mass.

"More research?" I asked. "Getting ready for Rome?"

He smiled.

I blew kisses to him through the security-gate window when he boarded the plane. He wore black running shoes, brown corduroy pants, and the moss-green sweater I had given him for Christmas; his old briefcase was so jammed with papers and notebooks that it bulged at the sides. His hair, grayer now than when we'd first met, needed a trim. His smile was a little uncertain as he waved good-bye because, although he had never said this out loud, I knew he was nervous about flying. I remember all this in great detail because it is the last memory I have of him.

"Take care of yourself," he said. "I love you. I'm leaving most of myself here, with you."

The Swedish composer who occupied the room assigned to Jude at the Institute had decided to stay on an extra two weeks, so when Jude reached Rome he took a room in a small *pensione* on the Palatine Hill, near the ruins of Livia Drusilla's house, circa 50 B.C. He sent me a postcard of the ruins, but not of his hotel. It was old and quaint, he said, but not worth a picture postcard. He sent two postcards from the Vatican, one with a quote from Saint Augustine: " 'Faith is to believe what you do not see; the reward for this faith is to see what you believe.' " He sent a longer letter detailing an audience with the Pope. "It is humbling to be one of hundreds, as happens in these audiences," he wrote. "But there is still a majesty, a sense of timelessness in these rituals, in this personage, that I haven't experienced elsewhere." It was his last letter to me.

On the evening of April 12 there was a kitchen fire in the *pensione*—the fire spread through the ground floor and up the stairs, to the guest rooms, before firemen extinguished it. The *pensione* was destroyed. Jude was killed. He probably died in his sleep, from fumes, and didn't suffer unduly, I've been told. Strange, the things people say to reassure.

~

I did not go to the memorial service that was Jude's burial. The fire didn't leave much. His scorched watch, his teeth, bone fragments. What they sent back from Rome was only a bag of ashes, not Jude.

Madelyn, to her credit, sent me an invitation to the service, trying to make the mistress feel welcome, trying to make peace between us—her phrase, I think. But I couldn't. I've been to those memorials. The deceased's academic department and friends, if there are any, fill the little stone campus chapel with vases of white carnations, choir music, and sermons of praise. Such events always reek of the hypocritical. People who have expended considerable energy trying to ruin your career, or at least make your workday miserable, say marvelous things about you, once you are dead.

It was Jude's turn, and I would have nothing to do with it.

Too often, when I do sleep, I dream that he is not really dead. In my dreams, I will be having lunch with Alicia and look up, and Jude will be there, smiling at me. Or I will be in New York, meeting with the senior editors of *Savant,* and Jude will be sitting in their midst, pushing papers around just as the editors do. Or I will pull back the shower curtain and Jude will be in the shower, wet and frothed with lather and singing "In the Sweet By-and-By." He steps out of the shower, still singing, and takes me in his slippery embrace, covering me with suds, with his wet warmth; his out-of-key singing in my ear turns to a whisper, an urgent plea, a promise, and we fall to our knees, clinging to each other even more tightly for support. I feel the cold tiles of the bathroom floor under my back as Jude looms over me, but the discomfort becomes pleasure. His smiling face is all my Christmases rolled into one more moment with him.

And then I wake up.

They do not come back, they do not speak to us. But sometimes, when my heart is racing and the room seems to be getting smaller, I think: What if he didn't die? What if he escaped somehow, and is playing a joke, or has forgotten us? Come out, Jude, hide-and-seek is over. All, all, all home free. Come back to me, Jude.

And just as I think that, just as the silence and the longing make me feel as if I will levitate out of the chair, float away like a lost balloon into the dark frozen solitude of outer space, the knocking begins again.

Thud. From down the hall. *Thud*. From overhead. From the kitchen, the back stairs. From everywhere, the knocking that has no origin, cannot be traced. My house is alive with it. Do I need to have the house exorcised? Oh, how Jude would have loved that.

CHAPTER NINE

After a year in Rochester giving private sittings, the Fox sisters were in such demand that a public demonstration was called for. Their mediumship, their conversations with the dead, would move from the dark safety of the parlor to a public stage.

They were, by this time, not only delivering messages from dead children to grieving mothers, but also giving advice on stocks and investments. The depression of 1837 was over, and the middle classes were shoveling all they could into the stock market, eager to get rich fast, to take their place in line with the Vanderbilts and Morgans and, of course, they needed assistance, they needed advice. If a medium, with the inhabitants of eternity at her beck and call, can't give insider information, who can?

The sisters' most popular investment advisor was long-dead

Ben Franklin, the father of electrical science. Maggie, in an attempt to compensate for her traditional female—which is to say, nonexistent—education, had been reading history during the rare hours when the sisters did not receive "visitors."

The spirits weren't limiting themselves to investment advice (most of which was bad), but expanding both their repertoire and audience. In October Maggie had a decision to make: Go back to Hydesville, where her father had finished building a new home for them, or stay with Leah and advance the practical joke to a new level, by performing on a public stage? Leah had booked a hall.

Katie, still young enough to be in need of schooling, floats in and out of the spiritualist circle, sometimes spending months in Auburn, at school, sometimes in Hydesville, sometimes with Leah and Maggie in Rochester.

But Maggie has made her decision: no more school, no more Hydesville. And when John Fox builds a new house in Arcadia, hoping perhaps to lure back his wandering womenfolk, Maggie refuses to move there.

The rat cellar or Leah's constant pinchings and orders? Leah's little house had a hall stand and a parlor piano and flowered curtains and closets to hold their new dresses—Leah insisted they dress in a manner that befit their new roles as ambassadors between this world and the next. Mr. Fox's new house in Arcadia would be small and dark and unadorned, except for the large wooden cross and the faded print of the guardian angel. Maggie's pretty dresses would go into the trunk and be replaced by dusty, scratchy skirts and aprons stained with bootblack and chicken feed because John Fox didn't like his daughters gussied up. And there was the mill awaiting her, the fourteen-hour workday and the small envelope of money to be handed over to her father, leaving her with nothing except an aching back and forgotten dreams.

The decision was not a difficult one: Leah was the lesser evil.

So, a note was sent to Father saying that the spirits had ordered her to remain in Rochester. Flowers for the hall were ordered and notices were put in all the local papers. Maggie was going public.

Autumn. Dried leaves rustling on the sidewalk, catching in the trains of Maggie's and Leah's fashionably long skirts. Streets lit by gaslights, the clomping and ringing of horse-drawn carriages as men in top hats and women in trailing skirts arrive at the theater. As Maggie and Leah enter by the side door, a cat howls and noisily tips over a metal bin. Maggie jumps. Leah pinches her arm and whispers something the doorman can't hear. Maggie's face, pale in the gaslight, grows impassive and unreadable as she wrenches her bruised arm out of Leah's grasp.

Already gathered on the stage is a committee of observers who will determine if the sisters are truly in touch with the spirits. The committee, chosen by the spirits who rapped out their names, are believers, and friends of the family: Mr. Capron, who is writing his little book praising the innocent and fair sisters appointed by the Great Spirit to bring truth to the world; A. J. Coombs; Daniel Marsh; Nathaniel Clark; A. Judson.

The members of the committee sit on their uncomfortable ladder-back chairs, squirming in their black flannel suits and beaming with self-importance. These are the appointed ones who, with the help of guiding spirits, will usher in the promised age of peace and prosperity, of heaven on earth. Now that the door between this world and the other has been opened by the Fox sisters, all things are possible. With supernatural guidance, Wall Street will rise for eternity and never fall, heathens in the Arctic and the Amazon will be converted, the South will repent of slavery—all with the assistance of the holy dead. Some of the women in the audience hope the spirits will also usher in Female Rights, a wish not shared by their husbands, for the most part. But tonight, the old world ends and the new one begins. They truly believe.

When Maggie walks onstage in her new pink woolsey gown

trimmed in satin-and-lace flounces, she is a rose blooming between gloomy twigs. Her youth and appearance, her long black hair left streaming down her back, win her yet more converts. Hers is a sentimental age, and youth and charm count for much. Moreover, she has removed her shoes and stockings, and her little white feet peek enticingly from under her skirts. She explains this bold eccentricity with, "The spirits have ordered it." In fact, bare feet make a louder noise when the toes are cracked.

Mr. Capron, nervously clearing his throat and running his finger around the tight white collar of his new suit, stands at the podium and gives an introductory lecture on the history of the Hydesville Rappings and the character of the family, which, he says, is unimpeachable. Mention is not made of Mr. Fox's little problem with alcohol, or of the fact that Leah's absent husband (they are not yet divorced) is a bigamist. Maggie smiles serenely as she hears her beauty, goodness, and innocence praised in glowing hyperbole.

Then the stage is cleared with a noisy scraping of chairs and the clattering of the wooden-heeled boots of the stagehands. They dim the gaslights and leave two chairs onstage, for Maggie and Leah. Leah pats Maggie's trembling hand and gives her a kiss on the cheek, which gesture brings a subdued cheer of support from the audience. Sisterly love is such a pretty sight. Maggie, consummate actress that she already is, successfully hides the shiver of disgust her sister's touch brings.

Mr. Capron and Mr. Coombs, blushing up to their eyebrows, each take out a handkerchief and bind the ankles of the sisters, as it has been nastily suggested by nonbelievers that the rapping is made by movements of the foot. At this show of delicate ankle and alluring bondage, more than a few men in the audience strain forward, trying to see yet more. There are pokes in the ribs, guffaws. This binding of the mediums, most of whom are young and pretty women, will become a popular element in the demonstrations of mediumship.

Thus bound, and a little frightened because they have never yet performed before so many at once, nor in such a large space, Leah and Maggie sit, breathing heavily with fright so that the lace on their dresses flutters and stirs. They stare out, past the row of uniformed policemen sitting in the front row: Not all the members of the audience have come hoping to speak with little dead Jimmy, to find out if railroad stocks will continue to climb, or to discover where Aunt Jessie hid her will. Some have come armed with firecrackers, rotten fruit, and wads of paper wrapped around dog shit. There is even, the sisters have heard, a warmed barrel of tar and a sack of chicken feathers awaiting them outside the theater.

Maggie and Leah perspire in the heat of the gaslights. Their faces are very pale under their heavy coils of black hair. Leah wishes she had thought to use some Godwin's Rose Cream and powder. Maggie, perhaps, is wishing she were back in Hydesville. The handkerchief binding her ankles is tighter than she had imagined it would be, during the practice sessions. Will the knockings be loud enough to fill this large hall and convince the crowd?

Long moments pass in hushed silence. Women in the audience begin fanning themselves; the men shift back and forth on the uncomfortable chairs, clearing their throats. Just as the audience is growing a little hostile, a soft rap is heard. Leah looks at Maggie, who is frowning with exertion. She's done it. Even with bound ankles and stage fright, she's made the spirits speak.

The tapping grows louder, more insistent. The audience, as one, sits forward on the edge of their seats, mouths open in awe of God's telegraph. Leah, who has by now learned some of the technique, joins in, and her softer rappings echo to the robust noises of Maggie's spirits.

Mr. Capron opens his arms wide, palms up, and murmurs a grateful and undoubtedly relieved amen. "Amen!"

Now that the spirits have announced their presence, Maggie

and Leah are ready to act as mediums for select members of the audience. Hands go up; handkerchiefs wave as their owners vie for the mediums' attention. Joyous weeping is heard from some females in the audience and, later, some will claim they heard the sounds of angel wings overhead, and felt the warm breath of a dead beloved brushing past their face. Corinthian Hall is crowded with the living, and with the dead.

A few members of the audience are invited to bring forward their questions, written on little folded cards. Most of those chosen are women, many are wearing black to show they are in mourning, and they all have radiant expressions. They are eager to speak with the dead.

Maggie and Leah, perspiring from the effort but smiling in truimph, answer questions with the spirit alphabet: They call out the alphabet and the spirit raps when they get to the letter it wants. It is a tedious way to deliver a message, requiring a long time even for as brief a message as, "I forgive you, Betty," or, "Go to the Temperance League, Eugene."

The amount of time spent waiting for the message to be completed, trying to guess in advance, probably added considerable tension to this game and may have helped compensate for the fact that Maggie and Leah, though they had access to ample gossip of many of the families in the audience, had to answer questions from strangers as well, and they had no idea what to say. Consequently the responses from the spirit were "not altogether right nor altogether wrong," as one writer tolerantly reported in the morning edition.

However, the evening was a tremendous success. They turned a profit and made friends and supporters.

Maggie sleeps well that night, confident that she has made the right decision, that a little exaggeration, a few white lies, some shams and counterfeiting, are worth the prize: coins clinking, dollars rustling. The price of a ticket to her future, where bands will play every night of the week and handsome young men of good families will line up to dance with her.

The act is repeated for the rest of the week, in the Corinthian Hall and then in public rooms of the Rochester House and the Temperance Hall. At the Rochester House performance another element is added: A gentleman holds Maggie's ankles so that her feet must remain flat on the floor. Maggie blushes prettily as her little feet and ankles are taken captive, and the audience titters. But the spirits come anyway. (Later, in her confession, Maggie will reveal that Leah's Dutch servant girl was upstairs, directly overhead, tapping on the floor with a little hammer whenever she heard Maggie call on the spirits.)

Fraud is suspected, of course. But it isn't proven and too many people are more than willing to believe. Crowds line up. A quarter a head. Maggie's public life has begun.

CHAPTER TEN

*L*ast night I dreamed of Jude, of his arms around me, and was awoken, in flagrante delecto, as the Victorians put it, by the knocking noise.

Determined to track down the noises, I went to the nursery, piled together a nest of cushions and sleeping bags, brought up a basket of reading I needed to do, shortbread cookies, a thermos of strong coffee, and a storm lantern, since the overhead light in that room does not work, and prepared to camp there for the rest of the night, to see . . . what? The hole I battered in the wall is simply a darker version of night, black and gaping and empty. Once I entered that room, the knocking stopped.

I sat on a cushion on the floor, and by candlelight re-read Leah's journal, searching for the breadcrumb trail of lies in her obviously fabricated story. The autobiography begins, as such stories must, with her too-detailed history of their many psychic aunts, the grandmother who predicted deaths, the uncle who read thoughts—a full lineage of invented mediums who give more credence to her own Spiritualistic claims. It is tedious reading, as Leah shows little imagination . . . until it comes time to explain some of the communications that get rapped out.

There are mistakes in her messages from the dead, sometimes because information gets confused. Did Mrs. Bonnet have three husbands or four? The bribed maid can't remember. Does Horace Liverwright like to invest in railroad or salt-factory shares? Which was the company that failed last year? Sometimes the mistakes come deliberately from Maggie, when she is in a playful mood. *Your loving mother says not to worry, wandering Jimmy will come back to you. You say he married Alice Stokes? Ahhhh . . . well, never fear. Jimmy will be yours in heaven.*

Leah's explanation for those confusions is ingenious, a true brainstorm. One rainy afternoon, sensing that too many messages had gone astray and that Mrs. McEvedy—a plump and free-spending butcher's wife—was becoming a little cranky, a little skeptical, Leah cues Maggie to rap out the the letters *B-A-B-B-X-Z-B*—obvious nonsense. Maggie, puzzled, does so.

Leah, smiling indulgently, pats the table as if it is a child's head. "Ah," she sighs. "That message would be from little Johnny Story. He died before he could learn to read. It is difficult, is it not, when an illiterate spirit comes through?"

Leah invents other spirits, pranksters who do not care about such matters as truth and correct details or even the feelings of the sitters. They are not devils, exactly, they are merely the practical-jokesters of the spirit world and they make fine scapegoats for any number of problems during the sittings. ("The Spiritualist is bound to conclude that the entities with whom the Fox circle were at first in contact with were not always of the highest order. Perhaps on another plane, as on this, it is the plebeians and the lowly who carry out spiritual pioneer work in their own rough way," suggested one of the believers, Arthur Conan Doyle.)

The doctrine that spirits can be mischievous and create trouble will be an especially important one in Maggie's later life, when certain actions on her part will require considerable explanation.

Did Jude know about little Johnny Story? He must not have, or he would have told me. Think of the puns, the new myths my playful Jude would have made of that tale: "Can't work today. Little Johnny Story stole my pens." Or, "Look at the typos on this page—they must have hired little Johnny Story as the type-setter." "A broken cup? Little Johnny Story did it."

I was deep into Leah's journal, oblivious to the dusty dis-comfort of my surroundings, when I realized I had been half lis-tening to the now familiar knocking for several minutes at least, hearing them at the back of my thoughts even as the active part of my mind concentrated on Leah's ungrammatical sentences, and that middle ground of the mind, where memory exists, re-played videos of Jude.

The raps were clear, staccato, and irregularly timed. There was no scratching that would indicate the presence of an animal, just the clean percussion of the light rapping. If the noise once had been in the wall, it was no longer. It was in the room, now, freed. I aimed my light in the dark corner where the noise seemed to be coming from: peeling yellowed wallpaper, an old framed etch-ing of Penelope dreaming of Ulysses . . . but nothing that would make noise.

Yet the noise continued. One rap would be followed by a series of fourteen, then two, then six, then again just one. There was no pattern, no regularity. Sometimes, the rapping would seem to move to a new location, as if it were restless. I would move the light to the new spot, and always, there would be nothing. Once, I thought the wall behind my back was moving, throbbing. It was me, trembling.

About two in the morning, the tapping stopped. Exhausted and light-headed with fear, I sought my bed. The house was absolutely still then. All I heard was the grieving, moaning wind in the pines. I dreamed that Jude was standing outside, in the cold, looking up at my dark window. I have never felt more alone.

Can a mind, a personality, exist without a body?

Sometimes I will see a new style of men's blazer in a store and think, He'd like that cut, but not the color—or, He'd be disappointed to know that Kloffer's Bookstore is out of business. *Matter is just locked-up energy,* Alicia said once. What happens when that energy is freed? Is the mind more than the electrical wiring of the brain?

But there are more immediate matters to consider. How to fix that hole in the wall, for one.

I can destroy a wall, but I have no idea how to make it whole again. Sheetrock, the builder's equivalent of the plastic webbing surgeons now use to hold delicate organs, internal wounds, together, will be required. This is a lesson I learned once before, when I put Jude on the plane to Rome: It is easy to break things apart, but not so easy to put them together again.

There's a whole page of independent contractors in the yellow pages. The fifth number I dial is answered by a person, not a machine. Douglas Howard's voice is pleasant, professional, indifferent.

"Can you fix a hole in a wall?"

"Probably. How did the hole get there?"

"Sledgehammer."

Pause.

"Look, it's one of the old houses on Piety Hill," I say, as if suddenly-appearing holes in walls is one of the recurrent problems of most old houses. "Number 423. My name is Helen West. Can you come out?"

Another pause. "Tuesday soon enough?"

"Tuesday's fine. The hole's not going anywhere."

He doesn't laugh. Jude would have.

Tuesday. Two days. Meanwhile, Mrs. Saunders comes this afternoon. She'll see the hole—she insists on dust-mopping even the unused rooms. I will be hard at work when she comes. I'm not in the mood for explanations. I don't think Mrs. Saunders is the kind to believe in little Johnny Story.

"Cool," says Tanya next day when I tell her how Maggie appeared onstage, cracked her big toes, and pretended she was speaking with spirits. It's Sunday morning, and Tanya and I are sitting in the kitchen alcove, drinking coffee and slathering cream cheese on the bagels she brought.

Tanya is a student at the university. She's tall and lanky and dark-skinned, and has just a remnant of a lilting Jamaican accent in her voice. I've known her since she was a knobby-kneed little girl, when she used to come here with her mother, Mrs. Saunders.

Now Tanya is grown and no longer at all impressed by me (in fact, I sense she pities me a little, for my lack of gentlemen callers, as her mother would say), but she still comes occasionally to drink coffee with me at the kitchen table and tell me the gossip from Downstate Medical. Tanya, too, is interested in mortality statistics, but as a way of describing the needs of the future, not defining the past.

That is one thing my century owes Maggie's: This intelligent young woman, who might have been a slave in Maggie's time, will be a neurologist in a few years, due in part to the Spiritualist movement of the nineteenth century and its close ties with the abolitionist movement. "Spiritualism," because it was unorthodox, anti-establishment, and heavily weighted toward what Jung would later call "the anima," the feminine soul, soon became a catchall for many other heresies of the time: Female Rights, abolition, the labor union movement, and universal education. Some of the most prominent names of the time would become Spiritualists, or at least dabble in it: Abraham Lincoln (there is a legend that Lincoln's Emancipation Proclamation was dictated to him during a séance), Horace Greeley, Victoria Woodhull, Harriet Beecher Stowe, Robert Hare, Judge John Worth Edmonds, Jenny Lind, Edgar Allan Poe, Elizabeth Barrett Browning. I must not disdain Maggie too much. She opened a floodgate.

"So even though they were frauds, they accomplished some good," Tanya says, pouring a large dollop of cream into a fresh cup of Godwin's Special Mocha Blend. Is this the same company that used to make Leah's rose cream? I'll have to check on that.

"But they lied and cheated. Does the end justify the means?"

"Get over it," says Tanya. "It was harmless fun. Turning out the lights and scaring each other. Kid stuff."

"They trivialized death and loss. They created mass delusions. That's not harmless."

Tanya stirs her coffee and doesn't look at me.

We chew in silence for a while and then Tanya makes a certain movement of her head, a kind of dip and nod that I've come to know as her indication that now she's getting down to business.

"Tell me about the hole in the wall," she says.

"Does your mother tell you everything?"

"Absolutely," she grins.

"There was an animal trapped in the wall," I say, hearing the defensiveness in my voice.

"How could you tell?"

"It kept making noises, like it was trying to get out."

"And now the noises have stopped?"

"It's moved to a different part of the wall, that's all."

"Uh-huh," Tanya says. She stirs sugar into her coffee and passes the sugar bowl to me. "Fugue state."

"What state?"

"Between wakefulness and sleep. The mind is alert, but the

unconscious is also rising to the surface. The barrier between the two begins to dissolve. You have waking dreams."

"You're telling me I'm hallucinating."

"It's a possibility."

"Tanya, the noise is really there. I hear it."

"Uh-huh. Does it seem to follow you sometimes?"

"What a silly question," I say, blushing as I remember the incident in the car.

"Sleeping problems? Yeah, I can tell by your face. And drinking, too. Can tell by that half-empty bottle on the counter. Let me know if the hallucinations get worse. I've got you pegged for auditory rather than visual hallucination. You're just the type I researched last year in Abnormal Psych: verbal, ambitious, workaholic. Joan of Arc type. She heard things, too. Try and get more sleep. And remember that the auditory hallucinations can become visual. If they do, just take a deep breath and keep telling yourself they're not real."

It's not real. What a consolation that will be at three in the morning when I wake up and hear the knocking in the wall. Now I don't want the noise to stop; not until I find out what it is . . . that it is . . .

CHAPTER ELEVEN
New York City~1850

$\mathcal{A}$ spouse. Husband. Groom. Leah probably mumbled those words instead of counting sheep when she had insomnia. A man to stand between her and the hazards of a cruel, unpredictable world, to hold and cherish and protect and provide for her—that's what she needed.

After the public career of the Fox sisters began, Leah told her new friends that she had been a child bride but had not been a wife to her husband, had not known him in *that* way, she would explain with a blush. She had been too young. Her daughter Lizzie added some confusion to that story, but it's clear that Leah did not intend to spend her future as a spinster. Her virginity, the Victorian bride's gift to the groom, had regenerated.

On Leah's nightstand rested a smudged, dog-eared book: *The*

Wealth and Biography of the Wealthiest Citizens of the City of New York, 1846 Edition. The book provided detailed biographies of the 850 richest men in the city, their fortunes, and how those fortunes were acquired. Heirs and lawyers, newspaper publishers and landlords, wholesalers and iron merchants, lottery organizers and snake-oil merchants. John Jacob Astor was listed, as well as William Dodge, James Lenox, Pierre Lorillard, John Pierpont Morgan, and P. T. Barnum. To be listed in the book, the gentleman's assets had to be worth at least $100,000.

At the time, a well-paid laborer earned two hundred dollars a year. A mill girl, working fourteen-hour days, six days a week, earned seven dollars a month. Then, as now, there were rich and there were poor, and Leah knew which was better.

Picture older sister Leah in bed, mouth slightly puckered, black brows lifted in awe as she thumbs through that book, daydreaming about its contents the way she daydreams over the stylish dress patterns in *Godey's Lady's Book.* She'll have that one, please, the widower railroad tycoon with the twenty-bedroom summer home in stylish Saratoga. No need to wrap him. Leah, absorbed in her daydreams, turns a page of *The Wealthiest Citizens of the City of New York* and reads through the *L*'s. Maybe a banker would be nicer.

First, though, she must get to New York. That will take money. She will earn it the new-fashioned way, the respectable way: She'll hoodwink the gullible masses . . . with the help of the greatest hoodwinker of all time.

Strangely, Jude enjoyed the story of Maggie Fox, but never had cared for Phineas Taylor Barnum, the king of humbug. P. T. Barnum and the Fox sisters had much in common: those young women made religion into entertainment, and he made entertainment into the new American religion.

When the Fox sisters went public in Rochester, P. T. Barnum was reconnoitering New York State, sniffing out fresh talent. He'd spent several years touring the United States and Europe with

General Tom Thumb, building the American Museum in New York City, and amassing a fortune that was huge even by Victorian standards of greed and ostentation. The public loved to be fooled; that was his motto, and he would not disappoint them or let them down.

About the same time the dead began talking in upstate New York, courtesy of Maggie, Katie, and Leah, P. T. Barnum exhibited to a credulous public a moldering, stitched, and stuffed corpse known as as The Feejee Mermaid, which would become one of the biggest attractions in nineteenth-century America.

I've seen pictures of the Feejee Mermaid. It looks just like what it is: the top of a monkey sewn to the bottom of a fish. No one could have been fooled by it. Yet people lined up to pay the larger percentage of a day's earnings to view it; they claimed to believe in it. If there is a thin but all-important line between faith and credulity, as Jude maintained, then that line is too slender for many of us to see. We cross over, we are easily taken in by the Barnums and the Maggies of this world, by the photographers of fairies and sighters of aliens, by the farmers who mow mazes into their cornfields, by the talking statues and bleeding crucifixes of our churches. We need the miraculous in our lives, we crave it, we suspend all our reason and the testimony of our senses to allow it. Without the miraculous, life is bland and frightening because only a miracle can protect us from life's ultimate injustice: We must, someday, die.

How rare, though, are true miracles, and P. T. Barnum knew this better than most since he was himself a master of the faked.

A sunny afternoon in the Rochester New York Bandstand Park, two young girls, longhaired and slender in their gingham dresses, stand there, hands in front of their blue-sashed waists, and eyes lifted upward. Like angels. Maggie and Katie have been reunited, since Mrs. Fox has once again left Mr. Fox and decided that the devil she gave birth to, Leah, is better than the devil that drinks.

P. T. Barnum, his nose twitching like a hound's, his eyes open to all possibility, fresh off the Erie Canal barge boat that has brought him inland and upland in search of the new and the wonderful, stops before the bandstand. He listens to Leah's pitch, the promised conversations with the dear departed, the advice from Benjamin Franklin or George Washington. He looks at the girls, and for the first time since the English government has refused to sell him Shakespeare's birthplace for export to America, he feels that heart-pumping rush of victory.

"Tell me, Madam, how these little girls converse with the dead?" he says, taking Leah aside and pushing close to her, so close they can whisper

"Many ways, sir. They can make the dear departed tilt tables, or carry lights. They are practiced in automatic writing, and can make messages appear on chalkboards"

Leah smells money and opportunity. P. T. Barnum wears a stylish coat no Rochester tailor could have cut; his cigar has a Cuban band. She drops him a curtsy.

Barnum tilts his head back and grins.

"My card," he says, taking one from his pocket.

It is a beguiling thought: Maggie, Leah, and Katie and the Spirits in ring number two, with dancing elephants to the right and the Tanzanian Wolf Man to the left. The greatest show in both worlds, because by then the sisters were claiming to live in both this and the spirit world, the way Alicia's first husband had been bicoastal.

The Fox sisters become somebodies, with the patronage of great personages like Judge John Worth Edmonds of the New York Court of Appeals, and Horace Greeley, editor of the *New York Tribune*. Greeley, who had just lost a dear son, received a letter informing him of the sisters. The letter, long since destroyed, may or may not have come from P. T. Barnum, who may or may not already have been garnering advance publicity for the residency of the Fox sisters at Barnum's Hotel.

~

Zinnias are blooming in minuscule city gardens and window boxes when the Fox sisters arrive in New York in June of 1850 after a two-day journey by barge, coach, and train. But Maggie has no eye for commonplace posies; instead she gawks at the brightly painted signs, the carriages, the traffic, the shop windows, the fancy ladies and imposing gentlemen who rush by. The new buildings are so tall they block the sky, and Maggie's neck hurts from looking up. A gray twilight has already descended on a city already gray from soot and coal dust. Maggie finds it exciting and, therefore, beautiful.

The newly arrived group from Rochester stands stunned and exhausted, a *tableau vivant* that could be aptly titled, *The Country Cousins Come to the City*. They are a confused grouping, and unspeakably rustic in their quaint, dated country fashions: Leah, Maggie, Katie, Lizzie, and Mother huddle together on the sidewalk, the wide bells of their crinolined skirts jostling against each other, while off to the side, eyeing every passerby with the suspicion that is the hallmark of his trade, stands their hired bodyguard, the only element of sophistication in the *tableau*. Threats have been made against the Fox sisters; bricks have been thrown through bedroom windows; dead flowers have been left on the doorstep. *You are harlots,* stated one hate letter, *poking into where nobody should go. Let the dead rest in peace.* Leah has saved the letter, counting it as one more piece of fan mail.

Next to the bodyguard is one Mr. Brown, Leah's new husband, married hastily and unwisely during her recent tour of upstate New York. He had had the manners and wardrobe of a gentleman; she had believed he was wealthy. That information was seriously incorrect. He has one suit and his politeness is not a result of breeding but of the weakness that accompanies a long illness. He is unemployed and without income; he is another mouth to feed, another body to clothe.

They are all tired and dusty and smell of barge grease. Little

Katie is sleepy-eyed and complaining as they excitedly count their suitcases in front of Barnum's Hotel, corner of Broadway and Maiden Lane. Twilight closes in more fiercely, robbing the city of all color, and the streetlamps have not yet been lighted. The street is becoming sinister, but Leah will not let the coach driver go until all the packages are found and accounted for.

Leah's face looks foxier than ever. Using one arm, she waves away the grubby Irish street children who dare come too close to those bulging portmanteaus. Under her other arm, hidden by her brown sprigged cape, is her worn copy of *The Wealth and Biography of the Wealthiest Citizens of the City of New York*. Page corners have been turned down. Mothers' maiden names have been memorized. Mr. Brown now coughs constantly. He is thin and pale and bent over with fatigue. In the not-too-distant future, Mr. Brown will be sent packing, and Leah will be free again. She intends to do much better on her third matrimonial try.

Mother Fox, more gaunt now than she was a year ago, looks perplexed. Leah convinced her the two girls would need their mother in the city, else they might be deemed of low character and beneath the notice of respectable families. In fact, Leah suspects Maggie is going to be more troublesome than ever, and will need the extra supervision Mrs. Fox will provide.

Maggie looks happy and sad at the same time, a combination that adds an appealing mystery to her dark loveliness, and is no little factor in her popularity—for popular she is, the darling of the East and the West as well. Her likeness has been printed in many, many newspapers, along with glowing and inaccurate accounts of her wonderful doings with the spirit world. A spiritual radiance overlays the rugged strength of her long nose and full jaw. Her belief in spirits is no greater now than it was two years ago when she first dropped apples tied to strings out of her bed to frighten Father, but her belief in herself stretches to the Pacific Ocean and back, though uncharted wildernesses of psyche. She can have anything and be anything. She is fifteen, and famous.

Her face is turned up, sniffing the city air. The corners of her mouth curl and dimple in a satisfied little smile. She is far from Hydesville and Mr. Fox, far from the dark cellar and the chicken coop and the chores and the rats. She can't imagine being farther away than this. She is on the moon. On the moon she can be anyone she wants.

Maggie has fallen in love for the first time, with a city. She will fall in love just once more, with a man. Both affairs will be disastrous.

She, too, has a book under her cloak, a forbidden, secretly acquired copy of *New York by Gas-Light,* by one George G. Foster. Maggie has read of the Bowery Theater, the gents of the East Side, prostitutes, oyster bars, billiard saloons, ice-creameries, dance houses, opera houses, shilling concerts, picture galleries, grand balls, and all the other amusements not found in Hydesville or even Rochester.

She plans to visit them all, to see them all, from the spires of St. Paul's Church to the balcony of Barnum's American Museum to the mansions of Gramercy Park to the National Academy, where Hiram Power's statue of a female slave is on display, despite much public protest and clamoring over morals and family values. It is the first time the people of America have been able to view, in public at least, a life-sized sculpture of a nude woman. The line to view it begins at dawn and stretches round the block until closing time. It is almost as popular as the Feejee Mermaid.

"Eight. Nine. Ten. All here. You may go," Leah finally says to the driver. He grins and tips his hat in a sly manner then flicks his whip at the tired horses who appear to have taken a brief nap while these country-bumpkin ladies sorted themselves out.

"It doesn't look quite . . . genteel," Mrs. Fox whispers to Leah. She hangs back as the others begin to climb the front steps of the hotel. The gaslights have been turned on and Mrs. Fox, dressed in subdued browns and blues, seems to grow wispier, ghostly, under the thin light. Leah appraises this effect and decides that Katie and Maggie should have dresses made in that pale blue; it makes such a pretty yet eerie sensation.

"Mother, it's quite genteel," Leah says, pulling her to the door.

"I don't like it," whines little Katie. "It's too big. I'll get lost. I want to go home."

"The rooms have numbers. You won't get lost," Maggie says, bouncing up the steps and waiting impatiently at the top.

Leah looks up suspiciously at Maggie. "How did you know that?"

At that moment, before Maggie must confess to her secret book, a policeman who has been watching decides to see if perhaps the ladies need a hand and crosses the street, heading for them. This decides Mrs. Fox, who still has a terror of agents and creditors and other representations of authority. She scurries up the step, pushes on the door, and the Fox women, along with pale Mr. Brown and the glowering bodyguard, tumble into the lobby of Barnum's Hotel, into their new lives.

The very next day the sisters begin "receiving visitors." Horace Greeley, flamboyant editor of the *Tribune,* and a willing if not fully-convinced believer in Spiritism, has provided them with letters of introduction and free advance publicity in his paper. (Greeley had a wonderful penchant for novel talent. He once employed, as foreign correspondent, a penniless German named Karl Marx.)

"He (Greeley) advised us to charge five dollars' admission," Leah penned in her journal. "I told him that would be altogether too much; but he feared greatly for our safety, and thought this exorbitant sum would keep the rabble away. I told him I thought it better to follow the directions of the Spirits . . ."

I suspect the spirits agreed with Mr. Greeley on the higher fee. The round table in their darkly-curtained parlor in Barnum's Hotel seats as many as thirty people at a time. There are sessions three times a day.

In one day, the sisters earned twice as much as a laborer earned in a year. The spirits are generous, indeed. Of course, not all that lucre found its way to Maggie's pocket There were considerable expenses: gowns with a suitable dark melancholy to add atmosphere; bribes to various servants hired to ring bells, toss fans into darkened rooms, and perform other actions better kept mum. And, of course, there is Sister Leah's take.

One month later Maggie is sitting in the hotel room she has come to know all too well, with its flowery, flocked wallpaper, dusty lace curtains, bare floors, painted screens, secret-paneled ceilings, the hired room overhead where a maid waits to tap upon signal, the messenger boys who bring the details of the next group of visitors.

Poor Maggie has seen very little of her beloved New York. Leah has imprisoned her and made her a slave to the spirits, and to those who wish to speak with them. She has not been to the opera, an oyster bar, an art gallery, or a wax museum. Boredom and overwork are a dangerous combination in a too-imaginative teenager.

Maggie sits at the large round table in the darkened room, wishing they would all go to the devil and leave her alone. Her head swims with memorized information—the names of dead children and lost brothers, dates of family disasters; the flood, the bad investment, the wife who ran away—information purchased by Leah, who expects Maggie and Katie to make good use of it. The sisters have also worked out a code of gestures, coughs, and sighs.

Memory sometimes fails and the secret code doesn't always work. Maggie is distracted, and when the round-bellied gentleman on her right asks about his wife's health, she doesn't tell him, as planned, that the woman in question is visiting her mother in Baltimore but that she has run off to Scotland. The gentleman tugs at his beard and leans forward, angrily.

"The spirits jest." Leah intervenes hastily, casting a murderous glance in Maggie's direction. Maggie rolls her eyes heavenward and looks penitent. She is not. The next client, a widow, is instructed by Maggie's knocking spirits to invest in a company that went bankrupt a year ago; a dead infant speaks from beyond the grave and reveals he is studying theology at Harvard.

"The spirits are capricious today," Leah explains, rising from the table. "They are playing tricks on us. Remember, there are mischievous spirits, just as there are mischievous people." She moves behind Maggie's chair and, under the guise of a sisterly embrace, pinches Maggie's shoulder so fiercely it will be black and blue for weeks. Katie swallows hard and sits up straighter.

"We will try once more," Leah says, returning to her chair. "Please concentrate. Believe. It is very important that you believe. Dr. . . . Turner? Who would you like to speak with?"

Maggie looks at Dr. Turner. He is middle-aged, but his eyes are much older. His mouth has lines indicating it is perpetually turned down. Maggie, grown out of her own childhood and into dawning womanhood, has a heart. She has learned to recognize the faces of true misery and longing and she opens herself to them. She is, in her own way, a true Victorian woman, soft and sentimental, easily moved to tears, an angel of the hearth, ready to console, to to take to her bosom the sorrows of a dejected world. She will console Dr. Turner.

The séance was attended by a Dr. Rutledge Turner, as recorded in his personal papers.

July 2, 1850

Attended upon the Fox sisters of the Rochester Knockings at their hotel today. They are quite the rage of the city, though I suppose any distraction from the stale news of the Bowery B'hoys and Slaughter Housers would be welcome. Was not eager to attend, but my friend Underhill insisted the amusement would be beneficial for me. Would my dear

111

Jenny have approved? That was the question foremost in my mind. I stick adamantly to the pledge I have made her, to do nothing that would tarnish the perfect love my little wife gave me. Baby is well. She now sleeps through the night.

The sisters inhabit three rooms at Barnum's, one of which is a large parlor outfitted with a huge round table. The sisters sit behind this table, on a large sofa that is draped with shawls, and the room is so dark that the gaslights must be illumined even in the afternoon.

As to their appearance, the mother is a wizened little thing, the kind of dried-up creature my poor Jenny could never have grown to be. The youngest girl is but a child, and sweet and docile. The eldest looks to be approaching middle age, though she strangely refers to herself as a child. Underhill seems taken by her. The Fox sister most in touch with the spirits is Maggie, a young girl of pleasant appearance, though with a sullen mouth. Her eyes were red, as though she had been weeping. I had a sudden impulse to rest her head upon my shoulder and comfort her. I did not, of course.

Fourteen other people attended. We sat in silence for some time, waiting. The eldest sister asked repeatedly if the spirits were present, but no knockings answered. It seemed to me she looked with some hostility upon her younger sister, Maggie, who sat red-eyed but with a slight smile upon her pretty face.

After some fifteen minutes of this, Maggie gave a little start. "Ah! The spirits are here!" exclaimed the elder sister. "Have you a message for someone present? Will you give us his name?" she asked, thus initiating a time-consuming process of one knock for *A*, two for *B*, etc., which is, I understand, the common method by which the spirits speak. Several messages were delivered by this long process, all of them highly inaccurate, judging from the response of others gathered at the table with me.

At the end of a long and unsatisfying hour with these mediums the rapped alphabet produced *T-U-R-N* and I realized the message was for me. Questions were then asked, and answered by a knocking in the affirmative or negative.

"Is your name Jenny?" Mrs. Leah Brown asked of no one in particular. Knocks answered her.

Yes.

"Have you a message for Dr. Turner?"

Yes.

"Were you his wife in this world?"

Yes.

"Do you await him in the next?"

Yes.

I had grown pale enough by then that Underhill thought it necessary to interrupt.

"How do we know this is the spirit of Mrs. Turner?" he asked.

Mrs. Brown turned a cool gaze upon him.

"Ask her a question," she said.

Underhill thought for a moment, then asked what age she had been when she passed on. Twenty-six knocks sounded. Jenny, indeed, had been but twenty-six when she died. "How many children did she have?" "One." "Of what did she die?" "Childbed fever."

"Jenny," I called. "Is it really you?" I rose from my chair and at that movement there was a great clattering; I was instructed to resume my chair.

"I'm afraid she is gone," said Mrs. Brown. "The spirits are more sensitive than we to physical movements. You should have stayed seated, as we instructed in the beginning."

I do not know what to make of all this. Was dearest

Jenny really there? It did seem as though I felt her presence. However, I would hate to be made a fool in this manner.

Dr. Turner's desire to speak with Jenny will overcome his fear of looking foolish. He will return repeatedly to Barnum's Hotel for sittings with the Fox sisters, and even bring Miss Maggie a little silver bracelet as a present.

He will think of the bracelet when he accompanies his friend Underhill on a little trip to Tiffany and Company. Underhill, a wealthy banker, purchases gold drop earrings for Leah, who has given him private séances. The attendant spirits of those sittings gave themselves nicknames such as Cupid and Love's Answer.

Leah has found her pot of gold at the end of the rainbow, her wealthy protector, eventually to be her wealthy husband.

Maggie—alert to the sexual undertones, the frisson of lust nearly but not yet consummated between Leah and Underhill— grows excitable. There are tantrums and sulks; threats are necessary to get her to sit at the séance table. Maggie senses her impending freedom, her release from bondage. When Leah weds Underhill, the sisters will be separated. Parting is such sweet sorrow.

CHAPTER TWELVE

"I hate it here," Maggie fumed, pulling the brush through her thick hair with such vigor that it crackled and gave off sparks. In the vanity-table mirror she could see her own stormy face, the flowered wallpaper of the hotel room, the wilting vase of white roses, her little sister tucked into bed.

The Fox sisters had been at Barnum's Hotel for two months, giving three sessions a day, approximately twenty-five people to a session, six days a week. As many as thirty-six hundred people could have attended a sitting with the Fox sisters, not including the smaller, private sittings they gave in the later evenings. Maggie had traded one prison for another.

"It's not so bad," Katie said, hugging the new doll Leah had bought for her.

"I want to go to the opera house," Maggie said. "And to the

park, and the museum. I want to eat oysters and wear high-heeled shoes. I want to put my hair up." Leah required them to dress as children, in white frocks with flat shoes and ribbons in their hair.

"I want to go to Water Street and watch the prostitutes dance for the gentlemen." Maggie pursed her lips and pouted at her own reflection.

"Oh, that's wicked!" Katie whispered.

"Someday I will do just as I want."

"Till then, get dressed," said Leah, who had come in without knocking, without a sound, sneaking up on them as was her habit. "We are going to visit with the Greeleys today." Leah was already dressed in her carriage coat and big hat.

"Not again!" Maggie muttered, turning away from the mirror.

"You ungrateful girl! A nobody, a good-for-nothing like you complains about having one of the most powerful men in the country as a friend!"

"He doesn't care about us. Only about the ghosts," Maggie said.

"Get dressed. Or I will dress you myself." Leah was in a particularly bad mood. An early riser, she had already thumbed through the morning papers searching for references to the Fox sisters. Patronage was largely influenced by publicity, and a day with no mention in the papers was a day when income dropped.

She had found the all-important notices: the quarter-page one paid for by Mr. Barnum, announcing that the Fox ladies were in residence at the Barnum Hotel and able to meet with those wishing to speak with the dear departed—she liked that one; "ladies" had a nice ring to it. And there were other notices and comments by various journalists, some respectable and favorable, some not. But she had discovered, for the first time, notices of other mediums announcing that they, too, could open the window into the other world, for a modest fee.

Maggie and her sisters were now notorious, almost as popular as the Feejee Mermaid. They were so well known they already had imitators, and the competition was warming up.

Two years after Katie and Maggie had dropped winter apples on a bare wood floor and called the noise "Mr. Splitfoot," every town in America had at least one medium in its ranks. All over America, and in England, too, ladies and young girls were tipping tables, falling into swoons and prophesying in strange voices, and carrying messages between living and dead as if a biworldly Valentine's Day had been declared. As English mathematician Augustus de Morgan described it, "It came upon them like the small-pox, and the land was spotted with mediums before the wise and prudent had had time to lodge the first half-dozen in a mad-house."

"Greeley. He always lectures," Maggie complained.

"And you yawn, when he's trying to educate you about monopolies, the robbing of the poor, the railroad tycoons, slavery. But what matters is that he welcomes us to his home, to talk with spirits. And, his paper gives us publicity."

Half an hour later, Maggie and Katie and Leah were out the door and signaling for a cab. As Maggie climbed in, Leah saw a flash of color under her heavy coat.

"What's this?" she asked, pawing at Maggie.

"A sash. That's all."

"Scarlet! Like a whore's! Take it off this minute."

"No. I like it. It's pretty. If you make me take it off, I won't go."

Leah frowned and considered. They were already late. She'd take care of this later.

"Drive on," she yelled, tapping at the coachman's bench.

Greeley and his wife had just lost their baby, "Pickie," and his wife was taking it hard. The sittings—Sunday afternoons behind drawn curtains when Leah, Maggie, and Katie "brought Pickie back" and provided news, such as that, in the Summerland, Baby had many friends and pleasures and was sleeping through the night—brought comfort. What harm could it do? Greeley reasoned.

This Sunday they were greeted by Sarah, the maid, and immediately shown to the back parlor. It irked Leah that they had never been shown into the good front parlor. She wanted no less than full acceptance and the respectability that accompanies it, but she could bide her time. Until then, the back parlor would do.

Mrs. Greeley poured tea. Leah saw that there were tear stains on her black bombazine dress, and her hand trembled. Leah's black eyes flashed a silent warning to Maggie. No antics. No jokes. Not for this sitting—or else. Maggie obeyed. After the lights were dimmed, the curtains drawn, the chairs pulled around the round table, Pickie began rapping back immediately. I am so well, Mommy. So happy. My angel plays with me, and keeps me safe. I am waiting for you, Mommy.

Maggie's toe and knee joints were burning from the length of the cracked-out messages. But Mrs. Greeley was smiling. She was content.

After the sitting, when the curtains were reopened, she hugged little Katie and said, "You must come stay with us. How sweet to have a child in the house!" Katie squirmed and Maggie, no longer a child, looked away, self-conscious of her newly-grown breasts, of the innocence she had already lost.

"Perhaps . . ." Leah began, but was interrupted by the sounds of footsteps in the hall. Sarah was showing another visitor into the parlor.

"Mrs. Freeman, ma'am," Sarah announced.

"Oh, Mrs. Greeley! I come with news of such import!" A tall, thin woman dressed in layers of flapping black lace and taffeta fell onto her knees before Mrs. Greeley and grasped her hands. "I know of Pickie. He has spoken to me. I have a message I must deliver."

Leah cleared her throat. For a second, Leah and Mrs. Freeman glared at each other, assessing, judging, deciding.

"A message?" Mrs. Greeley asked. "I have just heard from Pickie."

Mrs. Freeman thought quickly.

"Today, it wasn't Pickie who spoke to me. It was . . . It was Horace."

"But . . . But Mr. Greeley is just outside the door, in his study!"

"Not Mr. Greeley, but his little brother, Horace, who was named for him, and then died. He did have a brother, did he not?" Mrs. Freeman looked bewildered.

"I know of none. We must look into this." Mrs. Greeley pulled a bell cord that connected with her husband's study. He came into the room a moment later, looking angry, distracted, worried. He had been working. He did not enjoy these Sunday disruptions.

"Had you a brother named Horace?" his wife asked.

His eyebrows shot up. "Dead before I was born. I have never spoken of him."

"Praise the saints, then, for he has reached through to me, and given me a message," Mrs. Freeman exclaimed. She fell to her knees again, this time kissing Mr. Greeley's hand in reverence.

"We will leave now," Leah said, rising from the horsehair settee from which she had stared daggers at the newcomer. "Next week?"

"Yes, yes," Mrs. Greeley was already fussing over her new visitor, pulling at her bonnet strings, leading her to a chair. "Come back next Sunday, Leah dear. Sarah will show you out. Now, Mrs. Freeman, will you take tea?"

"A cemetery," Leah said, when they were back in their carriage.

"What?" Maggie asked, puzzled.

"The cemetery. She must have found the cemetery where the brother was buried. She went to his birthplace. The bitch. Why didn't I think of that?

"You must choose, Maggie," Leah said stonily. "Be a medium or a mill girl. Wear a red sash like a tart, or a white one, for believers. There are girls ready to take your place, and if the act ends, I'll not keep you and feed you."

Back at Barnum's Hotel, Leah takes Maggie back into her sitting room and firmly closes the door. Women's voices rise and fall, plead, weep, command, for the better part of an hour. When the two Fox sisters emerge again, Maggie is pale and silent and Leah is triumphant. Maggie has removed the red sash she wore as a badge of rebellion and now is all in white, as Leah requires. She has loosened the black hair she twisted on top of her head, and wears it flowing virginally down her back, as Leah requires. Maggie's eyes are lowered to the floor and her voice is soft. She speaks when spoken to.

The battle is not without some losses for Leah. For submission, for cooperation, Maggie will be allowed to go to the ice-cream parlor on Sunday and hear band music in the park on Friday; she will have one afternoon and one evening a week free for elocution and piano lessons.

And Maggie's surrender to Leah proves far less than complete. The emotional and physical distress of her situation, the long hours and lack of exercise and fresh air, the inner conflict, leads to the Victorian woman's ultimate recourse when all other chance of rescue has disappeared: Maggie develops headaches and swoons. "I can't sit tonight," she tells Leah one rainy night, putting her hand delicately to her forehead. She is pale as a blank sheet of paper, and all day has been unable to eat anything but calf's-foot soup.

"Oh, yes, you can," insists Leah. "The money is already in the bank. I'll not give it back."

Leah, desperate for a respite from this constant struggle with her obstinate younger sister, hesitates a moment, then takes from her mahogany cosmetic chest a small glass vial with ruby-red contents. She pours three drops into a glass of water. "Drink," she orders. "It will make the headache go away."

And for the first time, Maggie drinks a laudanum cordial. The tincture of opium settles over her pain and discontent like a fur rug, stilling all sensation except that of warmth and comfort. She slips into the laudanum mood, a place where, before the addiction sets in, the world is warm and welcoming and filled with joy. The uncomfortable horsehair settee becomes soft as a cloud. The red of the curtains and the green ferns blaze in musical vibrations. The heart opens and inhales into itself all the love the world has known since Eve first kissed Adam. Fairies dance in the hearth. Maggie has been initiated into one of the most prevalent rites of Victorian womanhood: opium addiction.

"Certainly, opium is classed under the head of narcotics," writes Thomas De Quincey in *Confessions of an Opium Eater*. "But the primary effects of opium are always, and in the highest degree, to excite and stimulate. . . ."

That evening, quick-witted and more imaginative because of the opium, Maggie gives her most convincing performance yet. Not a name, not a date, is wrong. She reunites Miss Agnes Withiam with her dead fiancé, Paul-Albert, who says that not even the angels are as beautiful as his Agnes and that he awaits her with joy. Maggie receives a message of comfort from Baby Anne and gives it to Mother Connelly, who is relieved to hear that in heaven her baby isn't being forced to eat the hated sieved peas. Maggie tells Mr. Arbor that his dairy company will do better if he fires his lazy secretary who is also stealing and replaces him with a Mr. Corwin, currently unencumbered by duties elsewhere (this advice is courtesy of that old penny-pincher Benjamin Franklin, and particularly pleases Leah, who sat for Mr. Corwin the night before and promised him employment in the near future).

Gaslight makes shadows flicker in the dark room, and sorrow brings those shadows to life for the sitters; opium makes fantastic scenery in Maggie's thoughts and waters the desert of her mind. The opium brings another gift. She can believe. It's not just trickery. Paul-Albert and Baby Anne and Ben Franklin were in her sitting room. They spoke.

Spiritualism, for Maggie, is no longer a schoolgirl's practical joke. With the help of opium, she can hear the voices of the dead; Maggie will now move in a never-never land where truth is as unsubstantial as doubt.

Despite the lovely laudanum haze, tensions between Maggie and Leah continue to escalate; there are shrill quarrels, hair-pulling, rough slaps. Maggie and her mother pack their battered portmanteaus and leave New York. Leah slams the door after them; they were getting in the way anyway. Banker Underhill was starting to complain about them, and *he* is the higher goal, not Spiritualism.

Maggie leaves Leah once again and wanders with her mother in upstate New York. She gives sittings and public performances by herself, and looks into the strangers' eyes for what she cannot name. Mrs. Fox, if pushed, would call it peace, or at least stillness. The past three years have exhausted her. She wants to unpack her suitcase and stay . . . But where? Hydesville, with Mr. Fox?

Maggie, too young still to value peace and stillness, catches herself looking into crowds and daydreaming, thinking, Could I love him? No, too fat. Him? No, too skinny.

Then Maggie and her mother, on a whim, travel south, to Philadelphia. She doesn't yet know it, but this very proper city is the home of Elisha Kent Kane, the explorer who will map Maggie's conscience and chart the undiscovered land of her most secret thoughts.

"It is easy at all times to create a sensation in Philadelphia," Maggie wrote, many long and sad years after her arrival there.

What a city she chose for her first and only love affair! Did she really believe she could win over those blue-blooded, stiff-backed matrons of prim, snobby Philadelphia, those harpy guardians of her beloved!—she, a coarse country girl who performed in public with her feet bare and white ankles flashing, and who spoke with ghosts?

She is sixteen. Doors are still opening for her. None has yet been slammed in her face. *There's a first time for everything,* her father has warned.

The love affair has been written about by several historians; the details are there, the dates, the tokens, the first meeting, first quarrel, first mention of Dr. Kane's so-very-respectable family. This affair will be the stuff of Victorian melodrama. Like Maggie herself, if it hadn't actually happened, someone would have invented it.

Maggie is no longer a straight and skinny farmgirl. Her chest and hips swell and curve; her waist is stylishly pinched. Her black eyes are large and shining. Her red mouth is full. She is beautiful, but not in the approved way. In one of those dreadful dime novels Victorian booksellers kept in the back room, she would be the femme fatale, the wrong woman for the right man, the Veiled Lady who must go over the cliff, or to Havana, or to the insane asylum, so that the true lovers can finally be happy together. Maggie is not the right type for a happy ending.

She seems a bit young for such sinister passion. There is still innocence in those dark eyes. She has not been kissed by anyone other than her parents and sisters. But according to Victorian standards, she is fruit ready for the harvest. Edgar Allan Poe fell in love with his cousin Virginia when she was eleven years old; in many households, daughters were engaged by the age of thirteen, and the average New York City prostitute of the times began walking the streets at the age fourteen. Childhood was short in the 1850s. Maggie's is about to end.

She's ready. Leah has kept her shut up in hotel rooms and apartments for much of the past three years. But even though Maggie couldn't go to the world, the world came to her, in the form of clients. Like a king indoctrinated by hand-picked and narrow-minded ministers, like a sultan cultivated in the hothouse climate of a harem, she has received an education of sorts.

Observant of those ladies who called on her and came for sittings, she knows how to crook her little finger over her teacup, how to smile with closed lips rather than laugh aloud, how to keep her voice low, how to shed tears on demand, how to swoon. She knows the styles being worn in Paris and the names of journalists in all major American cities. She can say "please" and "thank you" and "do come again" (but no more than that) in four languages. She knows that *artistes* (always pronounced the French way) and intellectuals favor abolition, while the capitalists condone the continuance of slavery, even if they don't say so in so many words. She knows that a lady never slurps the tea out of her saucer, that "ain't" is frowned upon by the educated, that limbs should be crossed only at the ankles, never the knees.

In fact, in the Union Hotel suite in Philadelphia, in the stormy autumn of 1852, she is curled up on the sofa in the parlor, frowning over a German grammar. She chews the tip of her pen and grimaces, determined to master this language of fashionable ladies.

This wet and dreary morning, this moment, is the closest Maggie will come to happiness. Years after, she will look back at this instant in time and see that this was where her destiny offered a forked and treacherous path. Which one to take? This is the kind of moment that leads to regrets and bitterness, though, of course, one can't know it at the time. The moment slides through time as easily as the ones that go before and after, yet it is different. A single proton can live for tens of billions and billions of years— almost as long as a regret.

Maggie, though she is grimacing, is happy. Elder sister Leah, she of the pinching, slapping hands, is gone; only Mother is here, and Mother doesn't want her daughter to be a performing monkey, as greedy Leah does. There are no more sittings scheduled three or four times a day, every day but Sunday. Maggie sits for her clients once a day at most, just enough to keep the hotel bill and seamstress and hairdresser paid. And there is money in the bank. Not as much as there should be; Leah took more than her share. But tucked inside Maggie's new lavender lace reticula is a little book with handwritten entries, and they add up to a sum that makes Maggie smile when she thinks of it. She is safe—from what, she isn't certain, but that is what she will think when she looks back at this moment: I was safe, then.

A single knock, and this serene moment landslides into history.

"Open the door, Brigid," Maggie says impatiently, not looking up from her book. She is between sittings; this is her quiet time, her only chance during a long day to relax, to daydream, to prepare for a future she cannot yet imagine. Some of the second sitting guests were so entranced with their messages from the Summerland that they have overstayed, ignoring Maggie's yawns and hints, pretending to be entertained by Maggie's mother, who insists on talking about her farm upstate. Now, who has else come to disturb this time?

Brigid, the first of many in a long string of Irish maids, opens the door. It is late afternoon. The gas lamps in the hall have already been lit. The man standing in the doorway, before the lamps, casts a shadow that ends right at Maggie's bare toe.

Maggie looks up from her dog-eared grammar book. Curiosity enlarges her already large eyes. She is still chewing on her pen, still curled on the sofa, long legs tucked under frothing skirts and petticoats. Her young body tenses with expectancy. Did she somehow see his arrival in a vision? Why did she rent the bridal suite of the hotel?

This is how Mr. Elisha Kane sees Maggie: childish, perplexed, just emerging from the chrysalis of innocence, an exotic butterfly waiting to be named, a land waiting to be claimed, a virgin ready to be taken.

He has come because he is curious. He wants to meet this imposter, this liar, this fraud from New York who claims to speak with the dead. Philadelphia is speaking of her—in lowered voices and with a disapproving wag of the head, certainly, but speaking nonetheless—and he wants to see with his own eyes this virago of tricks, this monster of female wiles and deceit.

Kane, thirty-two years old, wealthy, well-bred, handsome, already famous as a naval surgeon and Arctic explorer, is not without ego. For the past week this feminine upstart from upstate has had more column space in the Philadelphia papers than he has.

"I . . . I have the wrong room, obviously." Dr. Kane blushes, stammers, backs away into the hall. This room, with the young virgin on the sofa with her schoolbook, the old mother in the rocking chair, the polite and silent women guests sitting on assorted chairs, looks like a tea party, not the expected den of iniquity.

"No, no," says Mrs. Fox. "This is Margaret Fox, my Maggie. This is the party for which you seek," she says, trying to sound elegant and instead sounding foolish.

He has seen Maggie. She has seen him. He comes into the parlor. The door closes behind him.

CHAPTER THIRTEEN

$\mathcal{Y}$our youngest brother has died. Are you here to speak with him?" Maggie asks, closing her book and sitting up straighter.

"And how do you know that? Have you had a vision?" He is already on the defensive. Mediums are charlatans, and this young virgin claims to speak with the dead, therefore . . .

"No. It has been in the papers." Maggie smiles and points to the pile of yellowing dailies in the corner. "Please, sit down, Mr. Kane."

"You know me?"

"I know of you."

"And I, of you."

They continue to stare so intently at each other that the other visitors grow uncomfortable. "She's not a lady. You can just tell," one of those visitors will whisper later to her friends. "You should have seen the way she looked at him! Bold as brass, she was."

This is what Maggie sees, what she knows from reading the papers: a man blessed with physical beauty, wealth, and virtue . . . but not good health. Elisha Kane is tall, but too thin and pale despite his strenuous outdoor life. He has had several attacks of rheumatic fever, which have left him with little regard for mortality. At any moment, without warning, his ravaged heart could stop beating. He has defied rather than pampered that heart, circling the world and contracting and recovering from the diseases of travelers—malaria, typhus, dysentery, scurvy—with a bravado that stronger men envy.

He has sailed to the mysterious Arctic, searching for (and not finding) Sir John Franklin, who disappeared without a trace into that frozen wilderness seven years ago. He has slept in a tent with sled dogs for warmth, on the cold whiteness of Beechey Island, and seen the skyscraping pinnacle of ice that marks the entrance to Baffin Bay.

Kane is feverish with ambition. Of the two secrets of the Earth which obsessed his generation—the source of the Amazon, and absolute North—Kane has chosen the wintry one, not the fetid tropics with their rainforests and obscene lusciousness, but the frozen pole whence all flows South. But first, because gentlemen do such things, he must find and rescue Sir John. Even now, as he studies Maggie Fox, his secretary is recopying a letter to the Secretary of the Navy, John P. Kennedy, asking for funds for a second expedition. Kane's stay in Philadelphia was meant to be a short one.

He is already reconsidering the length of his visit. He sits in Maggie Fox's parlor, feeling the tightness build up in his chest, feeling as though he's shipboard during a storm and can't get secure footing.

He doesn't know what to do with his hands. The maid has taken his hat and cane, so he can't fidget with those. He sits bolt upright on the offered chair and puts his hands over his knees. The girl is looking at them. He is proud of his hands. They are long-fingered, elegant, strong. He blushes again, suddenly feeling as exposed as if he were naked, because of the way she is looking at his hands. He wants to stroke her dark, lustrous hair, that dewy forehead.

Dr. Kane, at this moment, has an understanding with another young woman, a woman selected by his mother who fits nicely into a drawing room, who is pretty but not seductive, who has been trained to run a household, not to hoodwink crowds. This young woman will be disappointed by him in the very near future. The word "jilted" will never be used, for both parties come from good families, but jilted she will be.

Maggie and Kane talk in short bursts of revelation as they devour each other with their eyes. He tells her that icebergs remind him of Greek architecture; that frostbitten fingertips turn black, as if they have been burnt rather than frozen, thus proving once again that opposites are, in fact, the same thing.

Maggie plays none of her tricks on Elisha Kane. He is not a believer. He is not a dupe. He hates Spiritualism and Spiritualists. He hates Maggie. And he cannot go away from her. True North is buried in her heart, her secret thoughts. Her little white body will become his new destination.

After that first visit, he comes to the bridal suite of the Union Hotel twice, thrice a week. He sends Maggie gifts, and takes her riding in his cousin's carriage. He is careful to stir no hint of gossip, to give no proof of bad behavior. The gifts are first presented to Mrs. Fox, who accepts or rejects them in her daughter's name. (She accepts everything, even the expensive gold necklace she should have refused.) The carriage is open, and Maggie never leaves the hotel unescorted. Kane never visits the bridal suite without another friend in tow, to protect what is left of Maggie's name and reputation.

Elisha Kent Kane is a man of passion and of quick decisions, a man who finds life bearable only if it has direction, a course, a mission. Sir John Franklin could or could not be found, and that ended that mission. He would need another, and beautiful, wayward Maggie is the perfect challenge. Kane has already decided that Maggie will be his wife.

There will be conditions, of course.

Photos of Elisha Kent Kane show a serious young man with a fashionably bushy dark beard, large, candid eyes under black, arching brows, and a broad forehead made larger yet by a receding hairline. He is both poet and outdoorsman. There are contradictions in the beauty of the eyes, the ruggedness of the beard. There are questions forming behind that high brow.

Kane has a querulous mind, as do most explorers. It is the constant complaining of his own thoughts that drives him to discovery. Maggie will discover that, later. She first notices about him those things that young girls of the nineteenth century cherished: his respectability, wealth, breeding, sense of adventure, the dauntlessness and sophistication that travel provides. His suits are well-cut and made of expensive fabric. His voice is without accent. Maggie's world has expanded; she recognizes quality. But Elisha offers something more, an honesty and a self-confidence that have been sadly lacking in her world. Elisha alone sees her for what she is: a young girl making her own way in a hard world. A fraud. He is not taken in by the rappings, the table-tilting, the mysterious lights in the darkened room.

"Have you no conscience, to deceive grieving mothers and widows in this way?" he asks her on several occasions.

Yet, he forgives. He knows life is hard. She has had none of his advantages, unless you count a trip to Buffalo as travel, or Miss Singleton's one-room schoolhouse as education, or a religious hysteric for a mother and an alcoholic father as breeding.

He knows that when Maggie looks at him she sees an heir to a wealthy family—safety. Fears about fourteen-hour shifts in a mill, the farm with its chores at daybreak, hens to be fed, butter to be churned, hay in the field to be turned, would never again hover over her future like a bird of prey, should she become Mrs. Kane.

A husband also represented a kind of danger, however. Suppose, as her husband, he fell out of love, or his love grew possessive and violent. He might beat her. He could send her to an institution for hysterical females. He could just wear her down, word by word, action by action, like water and wind eroding rock, until she was simple with despair, like her mother. Women had to make difficult choices in Maggie's time.

What decided Maggie in favor of Elisha was the simplest part of this equation.

"I love you," she whispers to him during their fourth carriage ride together. Their chaperon, his brother John, turns away and pretends not to hear the girlish voice whispering in the darkness. John is embarrassed for his brother. And yet there is something very appealing about Maggie. Beneath his embarrassment is a different emotion. He will not give it a name, but later that evening, in his bed, he will touch himself and think of Maggie.

"I love you," she repeats, pressing closer to him and putting her head, feathered hat and all, under Elisha's chin. "Do you love me, Mr. Kane?"

Elisha catches his brother's eye. They look at each other, watching their faces grow light and dark again as the carriage rocks along from lamppost to lamppost. John sees such sadness in Elisha's face that he can no longer bear it; playfully he pulls a feather out of Maggie's hat and tickles her chin with it.

Her love, too, is tinged with sadness. Her lover is frail. Even one flight of stairs tires him; back at the hotel he climbs up to her suite, then stands exhausted before her door, panting, one hand over his chest. She can hear the small wind of his breath, and it makes her clutch at her own heart in fear and sympathy. If he had been a simple farmboy, he would not have lived to adulthood. To

Maggie, Elisha represents in every way *the other,* for "the other" is also about miracles, and his very life is a miracle.

"Very pretty," John says as they walk into the night. "But . . ."

"She has youth and health," Elisha says. "She will do in a drawing room, too, once she learns about fish forks and the etiquette of calling cards, and I have weaned her away from this squalid business of hers. Maggie will look good on my arm, look good at the buffet table . . ." And look even better in bed, he does not say.

But Elisha's affection is not shallow. He sees deeper things in Maggie, things that sometimes make him think that if she had been a man, they would have been great friends. She is daring and adventurous. She, no less than he, is an explorer—but in his case the frozen world of the Arctic exists, and her world of spirits does not.

There is no such thing as a true opposite; beneath opposition lies similarity and an invisible glue holds the universe together. What appears separate is in fact already unified. Maggie and Elisha are already united.

"But Mater," says John.

Ah, yes. There is the little problem of Elisha's mother, Mrs. Kane, known for her splendid late-season dinners and the exquisitely subdued taste of her house decor. She, like her rich, well-bred peers, has vases of peacock feathers in the hall, but so situated that the visitor never even notices them. Can Maggie ever learn such subtlety?

Mother Kane swoons when she sees the first newspaper account about her son paying a visit to the infamous Fox sister, now staying in the gaudy bridal suite of the Union Hotel and giving readings for a dollar a head.

"Now, Mother, stay calm," says her husband, waving the smelling salts under her nose. With his other hand he rings a bell, and two little frightened maids, dressed all in black-and-white, with lace caps restraining their curls, hurry in to straighten the breakfast tray and refill the tipped teapot.

"Mr. Kane, you must put a stop to this," Mrs. Kane declares, rather forcefully for a woman lying supine on the fainting couch in her bedroom.

Mr. Kane screws the top back onto the smelling salts. "Mother, he is a grown man. We must trust in his virtue and common sense. Besides, he sails in four months. What can happen in four months?"

"Thank the good Lord he sails soon," sighs the mother, who just the day before had been pleading for the hundredth time that her son cancel this dangerous trip What were icebergs and Indians (all wildernesses had Indians, why not the Arctic?), compared to the wiles of a fallen woman? And any woman who performed in public, in a hotel as did this Fox tart, must be very, very fallen. There were words, not used, of course, in a respectable household, to describe Maggie Fox. "Adventuress" was perhaps the kindest.

Mother Kane, this is what can happen in four months:

Elisha, enthralled, visits Maggie three, sometimes four times a week. Sometimes he comes for the public sittings, at which time he steels his face to the disgust he feels listening to Maggie crack her toe joints and receive and pass on messages from the Summerworld or wherever the spirits dwell. He passes little notes to her: "My Sweet Maggie, how long is this charade to continue? You cheat these people and us, of happiness, with these tricks. I could never love and respect a woman who so ruined my peace of mind with her trickery and deceit."

But he does. That is the strange thing. He does love; he even respects. She is an explorer—misguided, yes; off course, yes; searching for lands that don't exist—but an explorer, nonetheless.

And she is glorious. Her thick, lustrous hair, dark, exotic eyes, little pale hands, wasp-waisted figure . . . The magnificent way this young girl of sixteen controls a crowd, sways minds to believe

133

her, and in her—those are not talents to be scorned, however misused. Sometimes he feels the power that comes from her, feels the desire to believe, to be swayed, to let her gentle voice guide him into the dark unknown. But he wants more than the clamoring crowds. He wants all of her, not just that public person.

Most often he calls on her between the public sessions. They are never alone—he is careful about that—but they are less distracted by the outside world when it is only the preoccupied, knitting mother (*click-clack,* go the needles, over and over, like creaking insects) who sits in the room with them. They speak with their eyes, with the slightest pressure of their fingertips touching. He kisses Maggie's hand in greeting and farewell, placing the kiss in the warm scent of her palm and sealing her fingers over it.

He sends her gifts: lace handkerchiefs, mittens, books he wants her to read. For Christmas, he sends her an ermine hat. The white fur haloing her dark hair is bewitching.

He grows incautious, takes her driving in a closed carriage, alone.

He'd had a dream, the night before: Ice was enfolding his ship in a death embrace. He could hear the wood creaking, straining, threatening to crack and splinter. All about him was frozen whiteness, without house or tree or even mountain. Just whiteness, and the crackle of ice, like Mother's good crystal breaking.

"Don't go," Maggie says, when he tells her this dream. "Please."

"Have you really a heart, Maggie of the Spirits? And is that heart mine?"

"It is."

They listen to the *clip-clop* of the horses' hooves on the cobblestones and press close to each other. She unties the huge blue bow under her chain and takes off her bonnet so that he can bury his hands in the warm blanket of her thick hair. It is late December. It has snowed the day before and the city of Philadelphia is decked out like a bride, all in white. In the frozen Arctic, the two knees of ice in Baffin Bay tighten virginally against each other, closing off the bay. In the spring thaw, the icy, white melting legs of the bay will slowly open to the explorers like a dutiful, chaste bride.

Elisha broods in the carriage, inhaling the scent of Maggie's perfume and thinking how easily ice can smash a wooden ship, how easily a virgin can break a man's heart. He shivers, and Maggie presses closer yet, to give him warmth. She tilts her face up to his. His beard tickles her; she laughs and pretends to pout.

He is older. He is well-bred. He should know better. But in this closed carriage, in this embrace, there is no age, no class, no weak veneer of manners, only a man and a willing woman.

"Forgive me, forgive me," he whispers as he unties the laces of her dress to reveal her white, raspberry-tipped breasts. She reclines on the cold, tufted leather seat of the rocking carriage, smiling dreamily, stroking his face, whispering words he cannot hear. Kneeling over her, he reaches under the froth of skirts and petticoats and finds the smooth coldness of her thighs. She pants as if she has been climbing stairs, and twists under him. Her knees lock around his hips. At the climax it is not young Maggie who swoons, but Elisha. His heart hammers in his chest, his vision turns red then black, and he falls into a darkness he never before knew.

Maggie calls to him. She covers his face with kisses. Wetness. She is crying. Maggie of the Spirits is crying. He has conquered her twice.

CHAPTER FOURTEEN

The recurring dream of the months following Jude's death has begun again. Jude is not really dead, he was not in the *pensione* when it burned, he escaped down the back stairs. I go into my kitchen and he is standing there, pouring a cup of coffee, looking the way people look when they have been traveling for a very long time, disoriented, disheveled, alien, happy. He puts his arms around me and kisses me and we make love right there, in the kitchen.

I had the dream last night. I fell asleep just at dawn—birds were beginning to twitter, gray streaked the sky—and the dream began immediately. In the dream I am deliriously happy. It is when I awake that the nightmare begins: devastation, shock, grief . . . all over again.

In last night's version, he has grown a beard and looks somewhat like Elisha Kane. In real life, of course, they were nothing alike. Jude, even with his paleness and middle age, had that Viking robustness of good health that I'm certain Elisha, thin and ascetic, never enjoyed. Yet in the dream they look alike. They merge into one being and both sides of Jude, the fair and the dark, love me till I am weak. I awake trembling with desire.

When I am calm again, I go to the worktable and begin sorting notes on Maggie and Elisha.

Now, I look out my window over the snow-covered fields and there, in the middle of all that cruel, pristine whiteness tainted red from the dawn, is a stag. He is lean and muscular and almost six feet tall at the shoulders. He stands watching the house and sniffing the cold, dry air with his black nose.

It's rare for stags to come into the open like that. Rare, and somehow unnatural and frightening. I have a sudden impulse to go to him, to rest at his feet and see if he would put his head in my lap, as unicorns were said to do with virgins.

In older usages of the word, a "virgin" was simply an unmarried, still-young, or at least youngish, woman. Jude sometimes called me his virgin, on lazy, peaceful nights when we lay before the fireplace, his head in my lap. Remembering this, missing it the way starving people miss food, I lean my head back into the chair. My eyelids feel heavy. Shooting stars dart against a red background and then I fall into darkness. An hour later, when I wake up, winter sun, without warmth, glows through the windows.

The house is filled with the knocking. *Rap. Rap. Rap.* It makes the old windows tremble in their sashes.

I jump up, turn in all directions like a cornered animal. Then I laugh. Jesus. It's the front door. This is Tuesday. The workman is coming to patch up the wall.

" 'Morning" he says. His lips are white with cold and a layer of errant snowflakes coats his shoulders. He's obviously been standing out here awhile. He stamps his feet and jams his hands under his armpits for warmth as I fumble with the door chain. A green-and-orange-checked hunting cap with earflaps is pulled down low on his head, and under that cap are gleams of black hair, reminding me of the fortune-teller's prediction that I would meet a stranger. But not even the wildest imagination could describe this hair as red—nor him as unattractive, despite the ridiculous hat. The fortune-teller got this one wrong. I rack my brain, trying to remember his name as it had appeared in the yellow pages. Douglas, that was it. Douglas Howard.

"I'm sorry I kept you waiting. Do you want a cup of coffee or something before you start?" I offer an apology, to placate him. His goodwill is important. Contractors around here don't like to work on houses like mine. They are too old, too run-down, too risky. And many of their owners are proud academics who believe in perfection, especially from other workers. It makes for a nasty mix, one that often results in lawsuits.

He softens at the offer of coffee. The corners of his mouth turn up. "Maybe just a quick cup." His grin is friendly. "I've got other calls after this." He comes in and I close the door behind him, taking his hat and coat. His eyes go to my face, to the scar, and a little frown of curiosity forms between his eyebrows.

"Car accident." I answer the unspoken question. He looks away, as all others do, no longer knowing where to look when he looks at my face. Most people stare at the tip of my nose, which makes them a little cross-eyed.

In the kitchen, Douglas drinks the coffee I pour for him, but does not sit at the table with me. Instead he leans against the warm stove, his hips resting almost at the very top of it, his long legs stretched slightly forward. He's young . . . well, younger—late twenties, early thirties. There is humor and intelligence in his face. A doctoral candidate from the university? I ask him.

"I have my degree," he says. That's all. Strong, quiet type, apparently. He seems a little nervous. So am I. I remember last night's dream, how the black hair of Jude/Elisha fell across my chest as he leaned over me.

Douglas looks strangely at home in my kitchen, sprawled and vaguely smiling, gulping his coffee. The color of his blue workman's pants are the same background blue used on Jude's last book, the one published posthumously.

"You live here alone?" he asks, already knowing the answer. "Big house for one person."

"I like a lot of space around me. And I need a lot of storage room. Books."

"I'll say." He picks up one from a pile on the counter next to him. It is Sir Richard Burton's translation of *The Arabian Nights' Entertainment,* a volume I keep in the kitchen for insomniac nights when I make chamomile tea and and read here, waiting for dawn.

"I never read this. Any good?" he asks.

"If you like that kind of thing."

He puts the book back down exactly as it had been on the pile. We drink our coffee in silence. The wind, which has been steady all day, grows quiet and in its place I hear the faint tinkling sound of sleet and frozen rain beginning to fall. Soon, the bare tree branches and even the brown, tilted stalks in the meadow will be coated with ice. Soon the world will be a beautiful, fragile piece of crystal, ready to drop, ready to be broken.

Douglas puts his mug down.

"Some winter, isn't it?"

"A bad one," I agree.

"Time to get that Sheetrock up. I'll tape and spackle today, but I'll have to come back later for the paint job. Got a color in mind?"

"I'll pick one out. Up the stairs and to your left. Third room down."

I follow behind, feeling a little uneasy. It has been a very long while since a stranger has been in this house. Douglas Howard glances at the hall ceiling, where the paint is flaking, and at the wood risers of the staircase, scuffed with the footsteps of a hundred years. He is judging the house, and its condition. The atmosphere in the house changes. It doesn't like being judged. It feels colder than normal. I shouldn't have called the contractor. But it's too late. We're up the stairs, outside the room where the noise comes from.

"This it?" Douglas asks, stopping in front of the door.

"This is it," I say, avoiding his gaze.

We go inside, where pale light shining through the two-over-two windows casts a vague shadow of a cross against the bare wood floor. Motes float in the light and when I look through them to the wall I have a sense that the old, faded hot-air balloons of the wallpaper are moving, ascending. The house is very quiet. It's holding its breath the way children do when they must have an injection or hear bad news.

Douglas noisily puts his toolboxes down, breaking the silence, and looks around. He's a large man; his presence fills the room, overwhelms it. He stomps to the damaged wall and appraises it with a knowing eye.

"Quite a hole," he says, running his finger over its raw edge. He turns and looks at the sledgehammer still lying in the floor, and then at with me with a different expression on his face: wariness, even a little suspicion. Does he take me for some kind of violent maniac? A house-wrecker?

"There was an animal trapped in the wall." My voice is defensive and small.

"I see. Did you get it out?"

"No."

His straight, black eyebrows shoot up.

"Right. Well, no serious harm done. This isn't a supporting wall. Definitely put in after the main house was built. Interesting room," he says. He strides to the window. "There used to be bars here."

"Really?" Standing next to him, I run my hand over the bumps I see now for the first time—ragged, sawed circles, painted

140

over many times but still not quite flush with the wood. It suddenly strikes me as cruel, this room, with its symbols of freedom, the balloons, and the barred window making it a prison.

"Don't read too much into it," Douglas says, glancing at me. "It was the nursery, I'd say. The nanny didn't want the kids falling out the window. That's all. Common enough. What I don't understand is why the room hasn't been used. Not in decades, I'd say. The house is so big. Who needs so many rooms, these days? Cheaper to close the door than try to fix it up." He answers his own question. "I've got Sheetrock and plaster in the truck. I'll go get it and get started on this wall."

"I'll just be in here"—I point to my workroom—"if you want anything."

At my desk I pretend to work but instead rest my chin in my hands and simply stare out the window, thinking of nothing, listening to the sounds of banging, sawing, taping, coming from the nursery. It is strange, having another living presence in the house.

Finally I reread my last pages about Maggie, wondering what Tom, my editor, would think of them, worrying that the magazine might find them too racy, yet knowing they aren't passionate enough. The simple declarative sentences can't begin to describe the sexual union of Maggie and Elisha in the carriage: damp flesh slapping against damp flesh; her breath-catching awe the first time she touches the silky underside of a penis; Elisha's desire to put his mouth to those unseen places of hers; to do things to this tender girl that gentlemen only do with prostitutes . . .

Quiet. The house has grown quiet again. Then, footsteps descending the stairs. I follow.

Douglas stands at the sink, running water over his hand. Pink water flows down the drain.

"It's nothing," he says. "Little cut, that's all."

"Let me see." I take his hand and turn it over. It is large and callused and slightly freckled. It is warm. A ragged red line appears in the delicate flesh between the thumb and forefinger and a drop of blood splashes into the sink.

"Wash it again and I'll get a bandage." I reach over his shoulder for the cabinet, where I keep a first-aid kit. After the accident Jude and I stashed them in various locations throughout the house, as if Band-Aids and travel-size packets of aspirin could protect us from further disasters.

"It's nothing," he says again, but he stands obediently still as I wash the cut, smear antibiotic cream on it, and then wrap it with gauze. I feel his warm breath on the top of my head, feel the heat radiating from him, smell his sweat and aftershave. After his hand is bandaged we stand like that for some time, silent, his hand in both of mine. His other hand reaches up slowly and rests on my hair. We stand still, barely breathing, frozen as deer caught in the oncoming lights of a car.

He moves first, lowering his head closer to mine. I feel his breath on my face. We are so close I can see the thickness of his eyelashes. I step closer to him and tip my head up to him. His lips are in my hair, on my forehead, on my mouth. They brush tenderly against the scar. Only Jude has kissed that place before.

"Lay down," he whispers. His voice is husky but certain.

Together we fall to our knees on the kitchen floor, as if for prayer. He puts his hands on my shoulders and gently pushes me onto my back. I lay still, watching, as he unbuttons my sweater and tugs at my jeans. Then his hands, warm and authoritative, are on my bare skin and my eyelids fall, my eyes seek only the red-and-green sparks of inner vision, the private fireworks of passion. I move under him, remembering this dance of flesh on flesh, this sweet quarrel of hard thighs between mine. He bites my lip and moans.

"Jude," I whisper.

Douglas tenses. He lets his breath out in a low, sibilant hiss. He moves off me, gently, rests beside me on the cold floor. His hand touches my face, the scar.

"Douglas," he says. "I am Douglas, not Jude."

"I'm sorry. I'm really, really, sorry." I stand and pull on my jeans and sweater and turn to look out the window so that Douglas does not see that I am crying.

CHAPTER FIFTEEN

Something has begun. I feel it in the air, a subtle shift, a change of emphasis, of the way the cold winter light pierces the windows but fades away before it can cast shadows.

And two very strange things have happened. The day after Douglas was here, when I was working, I could have sworn someone was in the house with me.

Footsteps paced back and forth between the kitchen and the hall. The back door opened and closed. Voices whispered angrily. I thought the oil man had come and was complaining about something, as he had done once with Jude. Mrs. Saunders, coming ahead of schedule as she sometimes does, dropped her purse on the floor; loose change rolled across the floor.

I caught words—". . . think only of yourself, your needs . . .

self-pity . . . we will die of it . . ."—answered by a woman's voice. "No . . . I care too much . . ."

Mrs. Saunders and Tanya were quarreling in the kitchen. It had happened before.

Or that was what I thought I heard. I kept working. When I finished the chapter and went down for a cup of coffee, they weren't there. Nor had they been there. Dirty dishes were in the sink. Breadcrumbs littered the hall rug. Nothing had been touched. And I remembered then. The words were from a quarrel I had had once with Jude. And a copper penny lay on the floor by the back door. I picked it up. It was an Indian head, minted in 1864. A collector's coin. Jude had shown me one like this.

Second strange thing: Tom Riley, my editor at *Savant,* called to ask if he could spend a couple of days at my place. He has to be in town for a gala reception at Eleusis University Museum to honor Mrs. Gerald Lister's collection of Indian miniatures. *Savant* is doing a piece on the collection. Or so he says.

I think he's come to check up on me and my progress on the biography of Maggie. *Savant* wants this article. Intellectual as the magazine may be, it is not indifferent to trends and anything that sells, and the news is filled with tales of the supernatural: children in New Jersey worshiping the devil; survivalists in Montana preparing for the end of the world; a TV series about guardian angels. If Margaret Fox were to come back, she'd be in business all over again.

According to some, she never really went away. Are you out there, Maggie, floating in space, your fraudulent molecules dancing this way and that? Are you in my house? Or am I just going crazy?

Loneliness is something we are educated to. Preparing for Tom's arrival makes me realize that I must now, once again, learn society and the simplest needs of others. Clean sheets. Cream for coffee. Guest soaps. I feel like a child trying to remember lessons in etiquette.

~

The day of Tom's arrival dawns mild and sunny, as if Eleusis wants to show off for visitors. The first tentative birdsong of spring twitters in the dawning, and some of the snow is even beginning to melt. I can see black road and green pines in the background framed by my bedroom window; in the foreground, diamond drops shimmer off the melting icicles that fringe the roof.

I pick Tom up at our small local airport, careful to dress in jeans and flannel workshirt, no makeup, a bag of suet from Agway on the floor of the car. Country style. When people from New York come to Eleusis, this is what they expect, a kind of show-and-tell for city slickers. Tom, too, is wearing jeans and flannel, except his are brand-new—just unwrapped from Barney's, I'd guess—and they creak with fabric sizing as he lifts his suitcase and laptop into the trunk. The hug he gives me is a little too tight, lasts a little too long. He is concerned.

He has looked better himself. Perhaps New York, the stress of his job, is finally getting to him. His hair, which used to be black and thick, is going gray and thinning on top. His face is white and puffy. Circulation problems, Tanya would say. Heart-attack candidate. He moves stiffly, like a person used to sitting for long stretches of time, like a person who has forgotten the other movements, the other postures of the body, and looks so out-of-place in his new expensive country clothes that my heart, closed to emotion for three years, opens a little for this old friend. I give him two kisses on the cheek and one on the forehead, for protection. Age is stalking him.

Tom and Jude were undergrads together at Harvard. They marched on Washington together during Vietnam, smoked joints at the same parties, argued about Pynchon and Gide. Their friendship survived graduate school, different careers, incompatible wives, bouts of alcohol or drug abuse. When Jude died, I think Tom mourned as much as I did. We used to call each other late at night, crying, talking for hours about Jude, just for the pleasure of hearing his name said aloud.

"Good flight?" I ask, taking the smaller bag he has pulled off the luggage belt.

"No such thing. Only quick ones. It's pretty up here. White snow. In New York you start to believe that snow starts out brown."

"Well, you get a lot less in New York, too. See how pretty it looks at six in the morning when you help me shovel out the driveway."

"I'm here for R and R. Wake me at noon. With a breakfast tray."

"Not likely. You could use some exercise, I think."

I drive him past the village green, which is now, of course, white but littered with snowpeople from the village snowperson-building contest, and a whole kindergarten of children bundled in red and yellow snowsuits, so that it looks like a modern book of hours, a busy illumination of the joys of the season. We pass the vet-school pasture, where horses stand picturesquely in snowy fields, their breath casting white plumes into the cold air; the shopping commons, littered with students and professor types. I stop at the health-food store opposite the Firehouse Theater and pick up some organic tomatoes, California strawberries, and hormone-free milk with thick cream floating at the top.

"This is the life." Tom stretches as though just waking from a long nap. He said this last time he was here, but he knows and I know he would never trade his apartment in SoHo for a little Greek Revival house in Eleusis, or anywhere else, for that matter.

"If you like this kind of thing. No Russian Tea Room or all-night jazz clubs here, though," which is exactly what I said last time.

Tom laughs tensely and pokes around in the grocery bag.

"I've invited a friend for dinner with us. Do you mind?" I ask.

"Alicia Vaclav. Physicist and professor at Eleusis U. Well-known in certain circles."

He grimaces. His live-in love for the past decade had left him six months ago. No reason, she said; just needed a new beginning when Tom seemed like an old ending. He has sworn off women.

"She's a friend. Really. No expectations. No fix-up."

He relaxes and curiosity lightens the dark eyes of The Man Who Has Sworn Off Women. He wants to ask questions—How old is she? What does she look like? Is she claimed, or free?—but is too well-bred . . . or too injured.

"See for yourself," I say, answering the questions he will not ask.

By now we're bouncing and fishtailing up Piety Hill, past the acres I bought along with the house, the empty meadows and fields buried under snow. It's white and open all the way to the green edge of the pine forest, and the sky overhead is the color of old pewter. We round one more curve in the road and my brooding, turreted house comes into view, lovely and lonely. It's a Currier-and-Ives print, a scene from *Doctor Zhivago,* and all at once, seeing it anew as Tom must be seeing it, I fall in love with it all over again. Why didn't Jude grow to love the house, as I did?

"All that gingerbread woodwork around the porch and windows. It looks like a wedding cake," Tom says.

"That was the idea. A house this size, in mid-Victorian America, was actually called a cottage. It was built for newlyweds. Ironic, isn't it? It's big enough to house a Fourth World village."

"So," he says, as we unload his suitcase and briefcase and my groceries. He is forcing a tone of easy casualness into his voice. "So, are you going to the ceremony next month? To Jude's memorial? Madelyn called to be sure I was coming."

"No. Jude would have hated the whole idea," I tell Tom.

"I'm not so certain of that. He liked being the occasional center of attention, and the ceremony sounds like a good way to say

say good-bye to the past." Tom struggles up the driveway behind me, trudging through calf-deep snow in his city shoes.

"He was shy and he didn't like speeches."

By now we're in the kitchen, stamping snow from our feet and struggling out of coats.

"It's freezing in here. Don't you have any heat?" Tom complains.

"It's been a very cold winter. Put the water on, I'll make coffee."

We dedicate the rest of the afternoon to going over the manuscript, at least what I have so far, and my notes for the rest. Tom's suggestions and criticisms are, as usual, painfully acute and sensibly helpful. He crosses out entire paragraphs, then inserts asterisks where I need to elaborate. He is particularly pleased with the material from Leah's diaries, and makes a note in his datebook to contact several photo archives to see if any of the Fox family photos have turned up in their files.

At the end of the afternoon he gives me a pat on the back, some editorial words of encouragement, and a push toward the kitchen to prepare dinner while he fumbles into Jude's old down-filled jacket and rubber boots, which are still in the mudroom.

"It'll be dark sooner than you think," I warn him. "Don't get lost. Take the deer trail as far as the creek, then turn back and come the same way." He raises his eyebrows in protest, but says nothing.

Standing at the sink, I watch him through the window, a large man struggling through ice-covered crusts in the snowy field, and my heart tumbles. From the back, from this distance, he could be Jude. On the counter are the ingredients of Jude's favorite dinner, northern-Italian style: arborio rice for a risotto Milanese; thin veal cutlets marinating in Marsala wine; radicchio and baby artichokes to grill with olive oil and garlic and lemon; strawberries with sweetened mascarpone for dessert.

I look at the food and back out the window at the figure of

the man growing smaller and smaller as he walks away from the house.

Who is the greater fraud: Maggie, who pretended the dead came to speak with the living, or myself, who refuses to admit death at all? Jude's hiking clothes are still in the mudroom, his bathrobe still in my bedroom closet, his back issues of *Humanist* in the parlor.

Admit it, Helen. You're hoping Jude will come back, just long enough to say he forgives you. You want to make that leap of faith that Maggie's followers made.

Suppose, for instance, that you are climbing a mountain, and have worked yourself into a position from which the only escape is by a terrible leap. Have faith that you can successfully make it, and your feet are nerved to its accomplishment. But mistrust yourself, and think of all the sweet things you have heard the scientists say of maybes, and you will hesitate so long that, at last, all unstrung and trembling, and launching yourself in a moment of despair, you roll in the abyss.

That's how William James described the leap of faith. I am on that mountain. There is no escape. And my feet are rooted to the ground and I am clinging to all the sweet things that scientists say of *maybes*.

Still standing at the sink, watching out the window, I start to shiver uncontrollably. This house is so cold.

At dinner Alicia is strangely shy and reticent. She and Tom cast sidelong glances at each other but address their comments to me rather than each other. This restraint is not due to a lack of interest on their respective parts; indeed, I see lust in their eyes and the modest conversation is because they are trying to control it. For my benefit. For poor Helen.

Candlelight shines on the golden bottle of Frascati, the fourth that we have opened. Bread crumbs and damp, puckering spots of spilled wine mar the yellow damask tablecloth. I usually like this stage of a meal, when the formal arrays of food have been breached like castle walls and politeness has given way to a more boisterous style fostered by good wine. I am lighthearted from wine and not enough sleep; tomorrow I'll have a headache, but tonight I will be merry. Or, I would like to be merry. In fact I am sad. The sexual tension in the air is almost palpable and I feel like an outsider in my own home. Three's a crowd. I have a sudden, unbidden image of Alicia and Tom coupling. I shake my head to chase it away.

"How is Maggie coming along?" Alicia asks, too brightly.

"I'm up to her sex life. Victorian repression, unrequited passions, the usual," I say, pushing an olive pit around my salad plate.

"Do you think sexual repression had anything to do with all those strange fantasies of hers?" Alicia asks.

"Probably a lot. Listen to this . . ." I pick up a book next to my chair. I have books all over the house in various positions of use and disuse. I thumb through this one, a silly Victorian novel I've been reading for background material, and find an excerpt:

" 'From her despair there was but one refuge. She could appeal for help now only to the source of her terrors. The fact, hemming her inexorably in, pressed upon her excited brain with a strange benumbing stress, in which there was yet all possible keenness of pain. Presently, it seemed as if she shrieked out with a cry that rang through the house.' "

I put the book back down and wait.

Alicia grins and fidgets with the stem of her wineglass. "Sounds like a great description of multiple orgasm."

"It's a romantic novel. That scene describes a young girl who is a medium. She has just argued with her father."

"Kinky," says Tom.

"Not to them. From what I've read, I'd say Victorian women spent an unusual amount of time in a state of unfulfilled sexual arousal. Maybe it was the corsets. And the drinking . . . they spent a good deal of money on patent medicines, most of which were pure alcohol with opium mixed in for good measure. The Fox sisters, especially Maggie, drank quite a bit. She also helped herself to an occasional dose of opium, when she had trouble sleeping. The Victorians weren't quite as hung up on recreational drugs as we are." I stand and clear the salad plates.

"Lucky Victorians," says Tom.

"No, not lucky. You wouldn't want the rest of it. For one thing, you'd be dead in a year or two. You're just about at the end of the lifespan of the American Victorian male."

"Well. Here's to the late twentieth century." Tom lifts his glass and winks first at me, then Alicia. Alicia winks back.

Over coffee, Alicia announces that she has brought a Ouija board with her. "For research purposes. Let's see if Maggie will speak to us," she says.

It's nine o'clock and snowing thickly outside. We've all had enough Frascati and Marsala that this seems a fine and amusing idea.

"In the parlor," I say. "We'll set up a card table and I'll show you some of the tricks I've learned, how Maggie and her sisters duped the crowds. When Maggie went to New York her patrons were none other than Horace Greeley and P. T. Barnum. If you two will be so kind . . ." I point to the kitchen. "Give me fifteen minutes to set up."

Tom and Alicia disappear into the kitchen. I hear the sound of water running, dishes rattling. Another mental image: Alicia at the sink, her hands slippery with water and suds, Tom standing behind her, pressing against her . . . as Jude used to do with me, trying to tease me away from the dishes, the cleaning.

I blink hard and go into the dark, empty parlor. Sometimes I think I can still smell Jude's aftershave when I first step into this room. Sometimes I think I see shadows moving in the corner of my eye.

The hearth is cold, as it has been since his death. On the carved Gothic mantelpiece is a photo of Jude standing in front of the house. I used the telescopic lens of my camera, so the photo has preserved the smallest details: the shadow of his eyelashes on his cheeks, the childhood scar near his right ear, the slight, sexy space between his front teeth. His expression appears to change sometimes. Tonight he looks pleased, maybe because his old friend Tom is here.

In five minutes I've arranged the table and lowered the lights and pressed a few dials and knobs, tied a few strings. "Ready!" I shout to the kitchen.

"Hey!" says Alicia, as she comes in, wiping her hands on a towel. "New table?"

"Found it at an auction. Like it?"

Tom runs his fingertip over the rough, age-darkened wood. It's a small table, barely large enough for four. "Nineteenth century," he says. "Imitation Shaker style. Probably just an old farm table."

"Right," I say. "Be seated, please."

"If I can find my chair," complains Alicia. "It's dark in here."

"It's supposed to be."

"Here," says Tom, pulling out a chair for Alicia. He sits opposite her. We make a triangle seated at a square table. It will have to do.

"Relax. Take a deep breath. Hold it. Let it out. Another deep breath. Put your hands on the table. Empty your minds."

They are both a little tipsy, a little tired, which suits my purpose perfectly. I let them sit in the dark silence for as long as I think they will stand it, ten minutes. It is so quiet we can hear the candles sizzle and spit. They are tense with anticipation. This was one of Maggie's techniques. Don't rush. Let the excitement gather. Make them wait long enough and they will believe something happened, even if the medium does nothing at all.

"Is there a spirit present?" I ask, using my softest voice.

Three knocks answer me, dull but loud thuds that seem to sound from all around us.

Alicia almost jumps out of her chair. Tom, who has closed his eyes, opens them and stares wildly at my hands, which are flat on the table.

"It's all right," I say in my most soothing voice. "Relax. It's all right. Close your eyes again. Listen carefully, for the spirits speak with gentle voices." His eyes close again. Alicia settles down; her eyes close, too.

"Is there a message?" I ask of the room.

Three more knocks.

"Is the message for Tom?" Silence.

"Is it for Alicia?" Three knocks.

"It's for you, Alicia," Tom says. She laughs nervously, but she is visibly trembling.

"I'll use the spirit alphabet to name your visitor," I tell her. "One knock for *A*, two knocks for *B*, up to twenty-six, for *Z*."

By the time we've knocked out *S-Y-L-V-I*, Alicia is giggling again.

"Oh, Lord," she says to Tom. "It's from my dead cat."

Laughter ends the séance.

"Admit it," I say, rising from the table and turning on the light behind the sofa. "You were ready for a message from the other side. If I had knocked out a message from your mother, this would not have been a joke. You would have listened. You would have wanted to believe, even if you could not."

"How did you do it?" Tom asks. He tilts the table, looking for wires.

"Not underneath. Inside." I show him the knob on the side, located just at the sitter's knee level, and how the knob is tied to a wire, which is tied to a hammer inside the hollow center strut.

154

The slightest touch of the knee produces a loud, convincing knock.

"Is this how Maggie did it?" Alicia looks disappointed. She wanted to believe. We all do.

"This is one way. There are any number of ways to produce knockings. Sometimes she used her toe joints. During tests, when her feet were held, she bribed servants to hide in an upstairs room and make the rappings for her."

"And they never told?"

"They were probably well-paid, and probably threatened within an inch of their lives. They'd be too afraid to give it away."

"You had me fooled for a moment," Alicia says.

"You mean you thought a spirit was here?" Tom uses his deepest voice, the voice a man uses when he needs to convince the womenfolk that he wasn't fooled, he wasn't impressed. He was.

"Not exactly. But something—otherworldly?—seemed to be going on. At least, something was happening that I could not explain."

" 'What was incapable of happening never happened, and what was capable of happening is not a miracle. There are no miracles.' Thus spake Cicero, and thus agrees Helen. Where's the Ouija board? I haven't seen one since my last junior-high pajama party."

Tom pours cognac for us as I light more candles; they throw flickering shadows across the walls and over Alicia's hands as she sets up the board. When she has finished, she tilts back her head and drinks her cognac. Tom cannot take his eyes off her.

"Okay. We join hands and sit quietly for a moment," she says.

Tom takes her right hand, my left hand. I close my eyes, but before I do I see how he furtively strokes her fingers.

We sit still for a long while, eyes closed, listening to silence, to our own heartbeats. The night is quiet. Outside the small circle we make with our connected hands, all movement seems to have ceased. We have become the center. The air in the room changes, grows thicker and more restful; the curtains no longer flutter in the cold drafts; they are still as the carved folds of Greek statuary. Even the wind dies, in our lexicology. A bubble of well-being starts to grow within my chest. It grows until it takes me over and I am made light by it; I am as transparent as a saint, taken over by an unexpected joy, the way I was on days when Jude arrived unexpectedly, bearing a duffle bag that meant he would stay the night.

Alicia starts to speak. Her voice is soft and low and solemn.

"If there is a spirit who wishes to join us, do so now," she says, eyes still closed. "We welcome you. Come. Speak with us."

We sit another moment. Alicia repeats her invitation. "Come, spirit, and speak."

There is no rustling of curtains, no flickering of the candles, no unearthly sighing, no special effects of any kind. Yet the atmosphere seems different and now we open our eyes and drop hands.

"Right hands on the pointer," Alicia says. "No pressure. Just fingertips."

I can't help myself. I giggle. Tom presses his lips together to hide a smile, but Alicia makes a face at us.

"Spirit!" she calls to the room in general. "Are you there?"

Nothing. The pointer stays in the middle of the board. Alicia sighs. Tom clears his throat. Then, without warning, the pointer moves quickly, in a straight line. It lands on *Oui*.

"Oh, good," says Alicia gleefully. "Are you from the land of the dead?"

The pointer is motionless for several minutes. My wrist begins to ache. Then the pointer wanders back and forth across the board, touching *Non* and some letters, and finally stopping at *Oui*.

"It seems somewhat indecisive about that," says Tom, smiling.

"Hush," says Alicia. "Spirit will you name yourself?"

With a scratching sound, the pointer leisurely spells out a *J* and a *U*.

"You're guiding it," I say to Tom and Alicia. They both deny it.

"What is your name?" Alicia asks.

The pointer moves slowly, again landing on *J*.

"Stop," I say. I take my hand off the pointer and stand up. "This is silly. No more."

"Time for some music," Tom agrees, standing and moving over to the stereo system in the bookcase.

"We were just beginning," Alicia protests.

"It's silly," Tom agrees. "Drop it." He looks tired. He puts a Schubert tape in the deck, then pours himself another large glass of cognac, and one for me. The Ouija board sits abandoned on the table, the pointer still on *J*—*J* for Jude? Helen, the dead do not speak.

Tom sits next to me on the sofa and considers the board. "Helen's parlor tricks are better than yours, Alicia."

"Yes, well, she's had more practice, with all this bizarre research she's doing," Alicia says. There is an edge to her voice.

Later, upstairs, I lay awake, sleepless, staring out the window. The new moon is thin and sly as the Cheshire cat's smile. Sighs and groans and the creaking of bedsprings wash down the hall, under my door, to lap at and tease my ears. They come from the guest room, Tom's room. Alicia is spending the night. "The roads look dangerous," Tom had told her. "Better stay here." She didn't argue.

I can't sleep, of course. The house feels so different, with Tom and Alicia here. And the sidelong looks they kept giving me—that awful mixture of pity and skepticism. I drank too much, and my thoughts are not a hospitable place at this moment. Time to retreat. Go back to Maggie's world. Check up on her.

On tiptoe, trying not to distrub Tom and Alicia, who seem finally to be asleep—at least, that creaking of the bedsprings has stopped—I go to my workroom. Press a button. A whir, a click, and the greenish light of my PC terminal glows in the night.

CHAPTER SIXTEEN

$\mathcal{E}$lisha sat in his study, enjoying the roaring fire, the snifter of brandy, the mastiff snoring and twitching at his feet, the evening edition opened on the side table, waiting to be read. He was about to embark again for the wilderness, for the savage cold, for a world of tents and snarling sled dogs, and these simple pleasures would be denied him for a long while. He wished Maggie could be with him in this pleasant room, but there were two impediments: his mother downstairs in the music room, her thin voice quavering through a *lieder;* and Maggie herself, who was at her hotel, "receiving," as she put it, like a hired woman, but worse—she sold her soul, not her body.

How could he ever make Maggie fit into his world of high-ceilinged dining rooms, butlers, and upstairs maids? That would be more difficult than any journey to the Arctic. Elisha watched the flickering flames in the hearth and felt himself torn between his old life, the life of comfort and respectablity and fame, and the new life he contemplated, of passion and notoriety. For a union with Maggie Fox of the Spirits would make him notorious, if he did not learn to control her, to shape her.

First, his "understanding" with Dora must be broken off in a way that would leave her reputation unscathed; any hint of scandal would ruin her chances for other respectable suitors. For a second or two he allowed himself the luxury of jealousy and brooded over the question of who would, in the future, escort his gentle-eyed Dora into dinner, and then up the stairs into the matrimonial bed, his no more. He belonged, body and heart, to Maggie now.

He penned a letter to Dora, saying simply that he did not deserve her and could not, therefore, claim her. She should tell her family that she had, for reasons she could not state, ended their engagement. Her family would assume she had learned something devastating about him, something that put him beyond the pale of acceptability—syphilis, a mistress, gambling debts, a mulatto grandparent. And for the time being, at least, he must allow them to believe as they wished, for Dora's sake.

Dora would behave decently. She would read the letter and calmly fold it into quarters and stick it up her sleeve, to be disposed of quietly upstairs, in her bedroom fireplace. She would rearrange the napkin on her lap and not allow even a frown to indicate distress, much less tears.

Her mother was not quite so agreeable. "Why are you breaking the engagement?" she screamed, and Dora put a finger to her lips to indicate they must not speak loudly. Servants were in the hall.

"He bids me be silent. There are to be no rumors. For his sake."

Her mother nodded and assumed what she had been meant to assume: bad blood or bad debts on the part of the would-have-been groom. Oh, poor Dora!

"Of course you will not wed him," Dora's mother quickly agreed. "Does anyone else know?"

Dora's eyes shimmered. "This summer I will go abroad, Mother."

Elisha's mother, on the other hand, cried and swooned and took to her bed. She threatened to die of heartbreak, of shock, of shame. Elisha, fearless and hardened to the fact of his own impending death, the probability of his enjoying a very short life, flinched before his mother's grief, but would not change his mind.

A third impediment arrived in January. Leah, tired of New York, or so she said, materialized unannounced in Philadelphia with her trunks, hat boxes, maid, and bodyguard. She took the rooms next to Maggie's at the Union Hotel.

"I have missed my little sister!" she exclaimed, bursting in one evening as Maggie and Elisha were sitting quietly in front of the fire. Mrs. Fox was already in bed.

Maggie, startled, looked up at Leah with stormy, frightened eyes. Elisha, ever the gentleman, rose to his feet and made a little bow.

Leah and Elisha were the same height and eye-to-eye. Each sized up the other. Elisha, with the well-honed instincts of an explorer who must quickly judge if the smile on the stranger's face is sincere or cunning, if the clouds overhead bid ill or well, took an instant dislike to Leah, and she to him. Both recognized the enemy.

"Oh my dear, dear sister," cooed Leah, bending and pinching Maggie's face between her kid-gloved hands. Leah's clothes were new and expensive but gaudy; her bosom dripped with gilt jewels. Elisha's eyes narrowed in judgment.

Sister? Oh, yes, there were three of them: Maggie, Katie, and Leah. He had been so absorbed in his Maggie, he had forgotten there were two sisters in New York. Future sisters-in-law. More

160

unpleasantness. Well, he could take care of that. Once wed, Maggie would sever ties with her family, of course. Except the mother, who seemed harmless, and a girl needed her mother.

"Go to bed, Maggie," Elisha said. "You look tired."

Maggie opened her mouth to protest, then closed it without saying a word. She made a clumsy little curtsy and went to her bedroom without looking again at Leah or greeting her.

The door was too thick for her to hear the conversation between Leah and Elisha. Voices rose and fell. Eventually a door slammed. Later, a second slam. Maggie felt the emptiness of rooms that no longer contained Elisha, her beloved. He had left without saying good night, without so much as a kiss.

But next day, Leah was gone.

"When I return from the Arctic, we will wed. Not before," he whispered in her ear.

Maggie was tired. The afternoon séance had taken longer than usual; the parlor of the Union Hotel bridal suite was busy with men pulling on their gloves and women arranging their hats in preparation for departure. There were only six people for this sitting, though, where previously there had been twelve and even twenty. Philadelphia was wearying of this new fad, and Maggie recently had been making some progress in her studies.

"Yes, dear," she sighed. Her eyes were large and luminous, thanks partly to the dose of laudanum which had become an almost daily ritual.

"There is much to arrange. And you are still young for the responsibilities you will face as my wife."

He said "young," but she heard what he didn't say. She heard the doubt and answered in a way she thought would please.

"I will study diligently." She pointed at the dog-eared German grammar resting on a sofa pillow. She smiled, and his doubts melted.

~

But doubt soon returned, and in such strong measure he wished he had never taken that carriage ride with Maggie Fox. Three weeks after Leah's visit, he stomped into the bridal-suite parlor well past acceptable hours for calling on a single woman, even one chaperoned by her mother.

Maggie, thankfully, was not receiving that night. She sat in the semidarkness with her mother, knitting, two farmwomen still accustomed to frugality and not wanting to waste the oil in the lamps.

He lit the lamp nearest her.

"Read it," he said, throwing the newspaper in Maggie's lap.

"I never read newspapers," Maggie lied. The stern, straight line of his mouth, the tilt of his head, frightened her.

"Read it. You may find it amusing."

The article was not difficult to find, since the headline was two fingers high: "HEIR FOUND DEAD," with its almost-as-large subheadline, "Put Pistol to Head After Consulting Leah Fox of the Spirit Rappings."

The facts were sketchy but the enterprising journalist managed to describe the death scene in lurid, copy-selling detail. The young man was scion to a New York industrialist and had entered his father's firm the year before. He was engaged to be married to a charming young person and all of his acquaintance had believed him to be of cheerful mind and anticipating a happy future.

On the evening of January 28, for a lark, he had visited Leah's public rooms with a small group of other young men. The spirits were unwilling and uncooperative that night, except for one, a Mr. Corcoran, who rapped out his name through Leah and then indicated that he wished to speak with the young man alone. The others shuffled into the hall, leaving the unfortunate young man alone with Leah and her conjured spirit. It never occurred to the friends in the hall (so they told the reporter) to eavesdrop through the keyhole. No one knew what Leah had said. But, the night after the séance, an upstairs maid had gone into his bedroom to light the evening fire, as usual. She discovered the young man dressed for dinner, but with red splattered on his shirtfront and on the imported flocked wallpaper. The pistol was still enclosed in his fingers, but his brains, the article went on to say, were no longer contained within his skull.

Maggie put the paper in her lap and folded her hands over it. She looked pleadingly at Elisha. He would not look at her. This was the very thing his mother had warned him to expect, the thing he himself had most feared from such a family. "Notoriety! Scandal!" he yelled, thrusting his fists into empty air. He had never yelled before. She cringed. The lamp flickered and cast menacing shadows. The following silence pressed against them like a cold avalanche.

They could hear footsteps and a woman's laughter in the hall. Outside, it was snowing again. Far to the north, Baffin Bay, pure and white and cold as the virgin of a Victorian gentleman's dreams, waited.

"I must leave you," he said.

"Go, then. This was none of my doing." Maggie crushed the newspaper under her slender foot and resumed her knitting with a cold-bloodedness that sobered him.

Maggie didn't know how a lady handled herself in such circumstances. Did ladies cry and swoon? Smile brightly and say, *It doesn't matter, they have a Friday-to-Monday at Mrs. Wortley's country house coming up soon?* Throw herself at his feet and beg for mercy? Does a lady accuse, or sit silently? What in hell had his Dora done when he retracted their little understanding? Maggie was in a foreign country and did not know the customs.

Elisha, helpless before her indifference, stormed out.

A week passed, with no message, no visits. Maggie, terrified, sent a letter to his house, begging him to come to her, since she could not go to him; the door would never be opened to her at that house. He did not answer. Her stylish new dress began to hang loosely; she grew pale. She slept too much, and always with the help of laudanum or whiskey or, most dangerously, a combination of the two. And finally, she fled.

At the end of January 1853, Mrs. Fox and Maggie left Philadelphia and returned to New York City.

CHAPTER SEVENTEEN

At dawn I wake to the sounds of birds chirping. My head rests on an open book, my neck and shoulders cramped from having fallen asleep at the desk. A screen-saver pattern of water drops plays across the computer screen.

I press the RETURN key to see if the text I wrote last night has been saved, or if I fell asleep in midsentence.

. . . *returned to New York City,* flashes on the screen.

The house feels strange as I swim up to full, alert consciousness. I am not alone. Someone else is in the house, the very air feels different. And then I remember. Of course I'm not alone. Tom and Alicia are here. A soft, rhythmic creaking of bedsprings fills the house. Locked in each other's arms, as the Victorians would say. Jumping bones, as the university students say.

The creaking grows louder and irregular. Is it Tom and Alicia?

The noise seems to come from the old nursery, not the guest room. Well, I can't barge in on them to see if they are the source of the disturbance.

As quietly as possible, I rise, pull on jeans, socks, a heavy sweater, and creep downstairs to the kitchen. Silently, as in a pantomime, I make coffee and toast. It is odd to have to be quiet in my own home.

I pull my chair closer to the table, and randomly select a book from the pile. It's a thin volume of Christina Rossetti's poems, and the page automatically turns to "The Convent Threshold," one of Jude's favorites.

> I tell you what I dreamed last night
> It was not dark, it was not light,
> Cold dews had drenched my plenteous hair
> Through clay, you came to seek me there.
> And "Do you dream of me?" you said.
> My heart was dust that used to leap
> To you; I answered half asleep:
> "My pillow is damp, my sheets are red,
> There's a leaden tester to my bed:
> Find you a warmer playfellow . . ."

The furnace kicks on, rumbling like a big friendly cat, offering little currents of warmth in the ocean of cold. I try to absorb myself in the poem, but few things aside from Maggie truly absorb me these days. My brain has become layered and fragmented; I am waiting. For what, I don't know. The time passes slowly, tick by tick, till dawn silvers the sky and then rouses the winter birds who brawl at the birdfeeder like peasants demanding their due from the lord's feasting table.

Just as I finish scooping more seed into the feeder—I can do this from indoors, by leaning out the open window—I hear a tapping. It's louder than it has ever been before, so loud the window rattles. The noise? Now, with others in the house who might hear?

Panicked, I jump from my chair and look wildly around, willing the house to be quiet. The tapping continues. My eye catches a shadow.

It's Douglas at the back door, knocking and waving.

"Didn't mean to scare you," he says, coming in. He spends quite a few moments wiping his boots on the mat so he won't dirty the floor. He is so intent on this courtesy that we don't make eye contact: His eyes are on his boots, my eyes are on him.

"Didn't scare me," I say. "I was just feeding the birds."

His feet finally dry, he ambles over to the kitchen table.

"Coffee?" I offer. He accepts a cup and sits down, opposite me. It is my turn to smile. He is trying to act comfortable, at ease, and failing. Douglas has been thinking about me.

"So. Is this a social call?" I look at him over my coffee cup.

"Yes. No. Sort of. I can't find a level. Thought I might have left it here, upstairs in the room."

"I don't remember it. But of course you should go up and look for yourself."

"Thanks. Soon as I finish my coffee."

We sit in nervous silence, both of us sipping coffee and looking too intently out the window, watching the cardinals at the feeder. The morning is so cold that frost still etches the sides of the windowpane, framing our view of the feeder and birds like a fancy Christmas card.

"I'm sorry," I tell him. "About calling you . . ."

He puts his hand up to stop me. "I understand," he says. "Someday you'll have to tell me about it."

"You wouldn't be interested."

"Maybe if you talk about it . . ."

Douglas is just beginning to relax, to feel the ease he tried to counterfeit, when we both hear heavy footsteps coming down the stairs.

167

A moment later Tom ambles into the kitchen. He is wearing pajamas and a bathrobe and it's quite clear he spent the night.

Douglas's eyebrows shoot up. He blushes and stumbles to his feet.

"I'll go look for that level," he mutters, shooting out the kitchen and upstairs before I can say a word.

Tom pours himself a cup of coffee and shrugs.

"Did I interrupt something?" he asks.

"I don't know," I answer.

A minute later Douglas comes back down, empty-handed. "Must have left it somewhere else," he says. His face is pale and icy as the snowy meadow outside the kitchen window. Without another word he lets himself out the door and a moment later his truck roars and skitters down the icy drive to the road.

"Guess I did," Tom comments.

I stare after Douglas's retreating pickup truck.

"Who was he?" Tom asks, pouring himself some of the Godiva Special Blend.

"The handyman. No jokes, please."

"Young. Good-looking. I sense hope for you yet, Helen."

"Don't. It's nothing."

Tom has his notebook sticking out of a bathrobe pocket. It's to be a working breakfast. I fry him some eggs and ham while he goes over a brief list of other points he wants me to think about for the biography.

"And the deadline. Three months from now. That way we can run the piece in the February issue. Think you can handle that?" There's egg yolk stuck in the corner of his mouth. I reach over and wipe it away. Déjà vu. How many times did I do that for Jude?

"No kid gloves, Tom. Stop acting like I'm going to go to pieces if someone looks at me cross-eyed. Three months is plenty of time," I say.

"Between you and me, you're not looking well. The circles

under your eyes reach to your knees, and you're jumpy as hell. I feel I owe it to Jude to say this, Helen: You're a mess. You're not taking care of yourself."

"Thanks for the vote of confidence."

"I spoke as a friend, and you know it."

"I'll be okay. In a couple of weeks. After the anniversary of Jude's death. This is a bad time of year for me."

"Keep in touch. Call every week. Or I'll call you." Tom reaches over and takes my hands in his.

"Right." The mood, thank God, quickly changes. It's difficult to be morbid in a country kitchen that smells of ham and eggs. We both laugh and Tom gives me a chaste kiss on the forehead.

Alicia drives him to the airport. No need for me to go out in the cold, they say. What they don't say is that they want to be alone. I think when Tom next comes to Eleusis, it will not be my house he stays at.

Tom waves from the car window and I wave back. I watch Alicia's red sports car skid down the drive, taking him away, then go and sit in the cold parlor. The room still smells of last night's meal; the table we used for our games is pushed against the wall. The house is silent.

Two days later—two days of pacing and roaming through unused rooms, rearranging drawers, cleaning windows, doing anything that does not require thought—two days later I am sitting there again, feeling like a river that has run itself dry.

I would very much like to sleep. It is two days since I even pretended to go to bed, to sleep. I rest my head on the soft back of the sofa, pull a blanket tighter around my shoulders, and close my eyes. They won't stay closed. They spring open of their own accord and look out the window.

The stag is here again, standing in the white field. He kicks and scrapes at the snow to reveal the grass underneath, and with the grace of a fallen king lowers his head to the ground. He stops his foraging and looks up at the house, at the window where I sit, framed by electric light in the darkening afternoon.

Only a virgin can catch a unicorn. She must sit in the millefleurs-tapestry field of spring and let the animal put his head in her lap. Then, the hunter jumps out from behind his concealing bush and slashes the animal's throat. Virgins are dangerous things.

The Romans, on the other hand, found them to be somewhat foolish. They carved life-sized stone phalluses on which virgins could deflower themselves, saving their husbands-to-be the effort. Or so Jude said. He called me his virgin, sometimes, when he was in a teasing mood—a virgin deflowered by the stone men I had known before him.

When I open my eyes again, it is dark.

Groggily I raise my head from the sofa. My neck and shoulders are stiff with pain from sleeping in a half-sitting position. I hear footsteps in the kitchen down the hall and smell ham and eggs cooking and think, How nice, Jude is making us some supper. I'm famished.

But then consciousness arrives like an unwanted houseguest. No one is in the house but me.

Do houses have memories? Is the house trying to play back for me some earlier, more precious reality than the one I have awoken to?

Slowly the enticing odor dissipates. I smell old house, musty books, nothing more. But the footsteps continue. Back and forth. Back and forth. I listen harder, squinting with the effort. They aren't footsteps.

Tap. Tap. Tap.

It's starting again. The animal in the wall.

"Speaking generally, it seems to me that the difference between what we call the natural and the supernatural is merely the difference between frequency and rarity of occurrence," wrote Victorian ghost-story author Jerome K. Jerome. This tapping in my house is no longer a rarity. I suppose that means it is not of supernatural origin, at least according to Jerome's theory, which would have a perfectly natural blue moon (a full moon occurring twice in one month) be a supernatural occurrence, and untraceable tappings at night be of natural origin simply because they happen frequently.

I'm wide-awake. Resigned, I pull myself out of the leather chair, my body feeling heavy and wooden. The blanket I draped over my shoulders falls to the ground, and a wave of cold air slaps at me. Gooseflesh rises on my arms and thighs. The cold is unremitting and punishing and invariable. The two hours of melting mildness we experienced on the morning of Tom's arrival will not be repeated until the first day of spring, and, oh, how I long for spring, for warm mornings and chirping robins and daylight that lasts past the supper hour . . . for the biography of Maggie to be finished so I can throw her out of my workroom, my life.

Shivering, I make my way down the black-shrouded hall to the kitchen. The tapping continues through all this, growing soft and loud, quick and slow, but never stopping, a Morse code from my worst nightmare, a door-knocking from a visitor I don't think I want to meet. "Please stop," I tell it, but it does not. I make myself a cup of tea and pretend my hands are not trembling as I carry it back to the parlor, to the sofa in front of the cold hearth.

I pause going through the front hall. There, the tapping can no longer be heard. And there, barely visible in the dark, I see something moving across the floor. Small, slow, rounded, the color of shadows. I rub my eyes. This can't be happening.

It's a turtle. I close my eyes tightly, open them again and the turtle is still there, moving slowly, clumsily, across the worn carpet toward the front door. No, not the front door. Toward another small shadow immediately in front of the door. I hold my breath and blink.

The turtle is gone.

Hallucinations, Tanya had said. *Watch for them.*

My knees are quaking and I want to sit, but I'm not near a chair and if I collapse on the floor I'll never get up again. The turtle has disappeared, but the object it was heading for is still there. Carefully, like an old woman walking on ice, I go to the front door and bend down toward that shadow.

The shadow is real, it has substance. It is cold to the touch, has angles my fingers can discern, texture.

It's a small box wrapped in brown paper. The light from the hall struck it in such a way as to cast a large, elongated shadow behind the box. It has fallen and bounced three feet out from the the letter slot. The mail carrier, who normally leaves the mail in the box at the end of the drive, must have left this yesterday. Time for a shot of scotch in my cup of tea. Back in the kitchen, with the bottle at my elbow, the fear becomes palpable when I recognize the handwriting on the box's label.

It is Jude's handwriting and the return address is the hotel that burned.

I sit and stare at it for a very long time, not conscious of thinking or remembering, or even of time passing. Finally a smell of scorching forces me to move, to function. The kettle, put on for a second cup of tea, has boiled dry. I turn off the stove, take the kettle off the burner and remember to rest it on a trivet so its burnt bottom won't mark the counter. I'm proud that I have thought to do this, to protect the butcher-block countertop. It is almost dawn. Hours have passed. How? I did not feel them passing. Have I slept?

With clumsy fingers, I tear the string and tape on the package in my lap. Distant churchbells sound. Sunday? During the plague in thirteenth-century England, the church forbade the ringing of bells to mourn the dead. There were too many. The constant clanging hurt the ears, and the incessant reminder of death led to licentiousness in the parishes: *Eat, drink, be merry.* During the French Revolution, however, people were encouraged to ring the tocsins day and night. And for the very same reasons. Licentiousness is an enemy of law and order. Headaches and panic reinforce revolution.

Neurasthenia. That's what the Victorians called it. An inability to control racing thoughts. Dread of things to come.

How can this package be here? Jude is dead.

I open it slowly. Inside the small box is a layer of cotton, and under the cotton a gold ring set with an exquisite cameo. It is not the traditional white silhouette of a woman, this cameo shows the two profiles of a man and woman, facing each other, their high pompadours and softened chins reflecting the styles of the eighteenth century. Jude and I in dress-up-party fantasy. Once we went to a Halloween party together, dressed as Marie Antoinette and her lover, Count Fersen. He must have been thinking of that night when he bought this.

But that party was five years ago and he has been dead for almost three years.

I finger a folded paper that has been slipped between the layers of white cotton, then reluctantly open it.

Helen,
It is lonely here, away from you. I think of you more than I should. Regards to Tom, when you speak with him.
Love,
Jude

No date. The lack of specific details make it possible for this letter to have come from anywhere, any time. It is not Jude's usual style; he was a master of detail. I'm shivering. I pull my sweater tighter across the back of my neck and sit motionless, except for the shivering that will not stop.

The dawn grudgingly turns to full day; in the stronger light from the window over the kitchen sink, I turn the brown wrapping paper over and over. The stamps are Italian, but the postmark is unreadable.

Italian mail is slow, I realize, but this is ridiculous. This is impossible.

"Jude sends his regards to Tom," I say when Alicia phones that night.

A long silence. Then, "Run that by me again," Alicia says.

"Jude sends his regards. I just got a letter and a present from him. Italian cameo. Quite lovely."

"Helen, I'll be right over."

Half an hour later her red Mazda is roaring up the drive. How she manages in all that snow, I'll never know. I don't think she even has snow tires. For some reason, this thought makes me laugh. I'm still laughing when she charges through the kitchen door, her forehead corrugated with concern.

She hugs me but says nothing; even puts her finger in front of her lips, schoolmarm style, to indicate I should not speak yet. She puts on the kettle, pulls a box of Stella d'Oro cookies out of my cupboard, arranges them on a tray, hesitates, then fetches the bottle of scotch and puts that on the tray, too, next to the teacups.

I go into the parlor to sit in front of the cold, empty hearth.

Something has changed, is different. I decide I will not tell this to Alicia, but I am losing my physicality. I can't influence inanimate objects the way we are supposed to be able to do. I can't arrange teacups. Sometimes, when I'm typing, I hit the keys but the mark doesn't register. When I try to shovel snow from the sidewalk it just falls right back in place. When I take the glass of brandy, will it slip and fall through fingers grown transparent and useless? Of course, on the subatomic level, there is no such thing as an inanimate object. Everything is movement; unpredictable movement, at that.

"Jesus," Alicia says, looking at me. "You look worse than ever. And you're talking to yourself."

"I'm not sleeping well," I admit. "Here's the package."

"Pretty." Alicia fingers the cameo, admiring the workmanship. "Now show me the letter."

I hand it over. She reads it thoughtfully, several times.

"You're sure it's Jude's handwriting?" She hands the paper back.

"Absolutely. I know it as well as my own." I am, at this point, quite pleased with myself. The glass of scotch is in my hand. It has not slipped through my fingers. They have not grown transparent. But just as I'm about to sip it, Alicia takes the glass away.

"No scotch," she says. "I'm going to give you one of my sleeping pills instead—you can't mix them with alcohol."

"Fine. Whatever. What do you think of the letter? Nicely affectionate after three years' separation, wouldn't you say? Is there an equation yet to define the afterlife?"

"There is an explanation, Helen. Come back from the deep end. I don't think you should even go wading up to your ankles right now. It got lost in the mail. That's all."

"Three years lost?"

"It happens. There was a piece in the news last week about a postcard dated 1921 that someone just received. Really. They figure someone bought it at an antique store then slipped it into a post box for laughs. It so happened that the person it was addressed to was still alive and living at the same address."

"The fortune-teller said I would get a message from someone I love."

"Ah, the fortune-teller. I'd hoped you'd forgotten that. So, people get messages from people they love all the time. Coincidence."

Alicia collects the teacups and takes the tray back into the kitchen.

"Now," she says with authority, "into your PJ's and into bed. Then I'll give you a pill that will guarantee a good night's sleep."

As I lie in bed, already starting to feel sleepy, Alicia sits near me in a chair and holds my hand, mother-and-child style.

175

We stay still, my hand in hers, for a very long time. I hear a clock ticking, a drip somewhere.

"What is your worst fear, Helen?" Alicia finally asks. Her voice is very quiet.

"There are so many. How to choose?" I try to laugh again, but am too tired. My words are slurred. I'm dropping off, going over a cliff.

"Seriously. Tell me."

"My worst fear . . . Let's see . . . that Jude, with his last breath, did not forgive me for packing him off to Rome. He didn't want to go, you know."

"Poor Helen. I am afraid of being alone," she says after a while. Her voice is soft and low, the kind of voice we used when we were teens, kneeling in the confessional. "Really alone, not just alone for a night or a week or a year. Forever alone."

I nod, or at least try. The whole world shakes with just the slightest movement of my head.

"Yes, 'alone' is a fear, too," I whisper back.

"I liked Tom. A lot. Thank you." As if he were a gift. A package sent from Italy that arrives too late. I want to say something, but can't. I have slipped down a long black tunnel and landed somewhere warm and soft and dark. Sleep.

CHAPTER EIGHTEEN

The sleeping pill, supposed to last for eight hours, lasts for four. Tanya has warned me about this. "Most sleeping pills," she lectured at our last coffee klatch, "are more wishful thinking than anything else. Sure, they can knock you out, if they're strong enough. But they won't keep you out. Only peace of mind allows us to sleep through the night."

It is two o'clock in the morning. Pitch-black. Cold. I can feel how empty the house is. Nothing. No tapping. No footsteps. No smells of cooking. Absolute solitude. Where is Maggie?

Back in New York, with her mother for company. Longing for Elisha.

"Cheer up, Maggie dear. There's plenty of fish in the sea. And richer, too. Just look at the ring that Mr. Underhill gave your sister Leah. There must be a hundred garnets and diamonds on it."

"It's gaudy," Maggie said, glaring at her mother. "It looks like a cheap bauble from Woolworth's." That was what Elisha had said.

"I don't know about Woolworth's. Leah did say it was from Tiffany's, I believe."

"I'll take this room for my own," Maggie said, pushing open a carved door and looking into their newly rented and furnished rooms on fashionable Twenty-sixth Street. She walked to the window and threw it open, sniffed at the wintry, coal-tainted air, and tossed her hat on the bed. She did not want to talk about Leah's ring, nor the way Underhill looked at Leah with those adoring, puppy eyes, as if she were perfect, as if she shat gold, Mr. Fox would have said. As for Spiritualism, the sittings amused Underhill; the money and gifts Leah received were her pin money. What harm was done? he asked jovially, slapping his knee.

Elisha, in comparison, had been critical of everything Maggie did: How she held her fork, pronounced her "thank you"s, dressed her hair, where she bought her gloves. And Spiritualism, her livelihood, he classified as fraud of the worse sort, and she, a lower being because of it. It occurred to Maggie that a banker husband such as Underhill might be an easier prospect than an explorer. Yet when she slept, it was Elisha she saw, Elisha she wanted.

"It's the bigger room," her mother said doubtfully. "I'm not sure you should have the bigger room. It's surely bad enough you won't share a room, as a daughter should."

"It's my money, earned by me. I'll take this room. Yours is across the hall. If you don't like it, go stay with Leah."

"Now, now, Maggie. This'll do fine. Remember, the Bible says to 'honor thy father and thy mother.' "

"It don't say anything about who gets the bigger room."

Maggie paced, assessing the new plush sofa, overstuffed in blue-and-white-striped silk, the red flocked wallpaper, the crystal prisms dangling from the gas sconces on the wall, and thought, Perhaps I don't need Elisha.

What is love to a tough farmgirl who can wring chicken necks, tar rats, drown kittens? Surely the thrill she had felt whenever Elisha came into a room could be throttled, starved, or drowned out of existence.

"Isn't it grand for our Katie?" Mrs. Fox asked, unbuttoning her thick gray cape and carefully draping it over a chair.

"Grand," agreed Maggie through clenched teeth.

Katie, thanks to Horace Greeley's patronage, now spoke French and some Italian; her table manners were exquisite, her clothes subdued and perfect. She still held séances, too, but only for friends, and friends of friends, never for the general public. Maggie felt common and cheap next to her little sister. Their reunion had been tense.

Maggie felt herself thinning at the edges, blurring.

She had even considered purchasing one of the new special tables "to the trade" made by Hiram Pack, cabinetmaker at 488 Pearl Street in New York, a special table with a built-in secret knocking mechanism operated by a slight movement of the knee, in case her joints gave out, so defeated was she feeling. But in bed at night, practicing, her raps were loud as ever, so the table hadn't been needed.

Late winter in New York was gray and dismal. The newspapers were filled with the same old stories. The Butcher Boys and Bullies were beating up the Irish. The Buckoos and Swamp Angels were beating up Jews and Germans; the Slaughter Housers beat up anyone who trespassed on their tenement territory. The Five Points roiled with nightly riots. Prostitutes were rounded up by the police or knifed by madmen. Abandoned children huddled in doorways, and if they were old enough (to handle a broom, use an axe), the Children's Aid Society sent them out West on Charles Loring Brace's Orphan Train. The armed camp of squatters living in the wilderness that was to be landscaped into Central Park still refused to leave.

Maggie felt indifferent to it all, even to the ongoing problems with plans for the new St. Patrick's Day parade ("an insult to patriots and real Americans!" the papers shouted), the success of Miss Stowe's book-turned-play, *Uncle Tom's Cabin,* and the scandal over the slave market at Sweet's Restaurant at Fulton and South. (When a slave trader flying the colors of the New York Yacht Club was discovered carrying slaves, that member was merely, and rather reluctantly, asked to return his key. Duty required no more.)

Maggie even ignored the new exhibit at P. T. Barnum's American Museum: *Ali Baba and the Forty Thieves.* Barnum had hired additional bodyguards, as the wax figure of Ali Baba bore a striking, and by no means coincidental, resemblance to a man whose name already was a household curse—William Marcy Tweed, the politician who would eventually rob New York City of one hundred million dollars, at a time when laborers earned five dollars a week. Tweed was already billing the city for dinners at which each man supposedly consumed ten cases of champagne, fifty pounds of beef, seventy loaves of bread, and a hundred cigars, and Katie's patron, newspaperman Horace Greeley, was hot on Tweed's trail.

Maggie, lost in a twilight of lovesickness and misery, paid no attention to the riots, the theater season, or Tweed. She should have. Tweed knew her name.

And Tweed kept lists. Tweed extorted, robbed, blackmailed. Tweed's "rent collectors" kept track of Maggie's name in the papers, and bided their time.

Meanwhile, unaware of the vultures waiting for her to falter, Maggie brooded in the afternoon and tossed and turned at night. She felt as if a part of herself had been amputated.

Elisha, shivering in damp Boston during a prolonged lecture tour, was equally miserable. His conscience was pricking him, and men like Elisha Kane listen to their consciences. Maggie was so young and he had been so hard. He had used her, loved her, and left her. He had railed at her for her public life, for taking money from strangers, for becoming notorious. Was he, traveling from lecture hall to lecture hall, pleading for money for his expedition, much better than Maggie? Finally, missing the smell of her hair, her skin, he wrote to her:

> *When I think of you, dear darling, wasting your time and youth and conscience for a few paltry dollars, and think of the crowds who come nightly to hear of the wild stories of the frigid North, I sometimes feel that we are not so far removed after all. My brain and your body are each the sources of attraction, and I confess that there is not so much difference.*

He sent a prophetic warning to Katie:

> *I know you have a tender heart; but practice in anything hardens us. You do things now which you would never had dreamed of doing years ago, and there will come a time when you will be worse than Leah; a hardened woman, gathering around you the victims of a delusion. The older you grow, the more difficult it will be to liberate yourself from this thing.*

His fever returned, and his cough. He was losing weight at a time when he should be should be fattening and strengthening himself for the northlands. Maggie was so strong. She could lift heavy suitcases, could climb six flights of stairs without pausing in her conversation. She never had the flux or the fever. He missed her strength the way paupers miss a rich and absent relative, hoping some of the wealth will rub onto them.

Maggie's return letter to Elisha was cunning. She had been invited to Washington, she informed her sickly beau. Some senators, a Charles Sumner of Massachusetts, Tallmadge of Wisconsin, had taken an interest in Spiritualism and wished to meet with her. Oh, and Maggie missed her dear Elisha very, very much.

The pain in Kane's chest thickened and spread tentacles into his groin and head.

"Jealousy," wrote Elizabeth Bowen, "is feeling alone against smiling enemies." Not only was Maggie going to a city populated largely with men of dubious virtue—how little things change!—but she would be hobnobbing with those very men who were scratching their heads and hesitating about financing Kane's expedition to the Arctic. She would be meeting with the president's wife!

Elisha choked on jealousy and sent Maggie a thoughtful letter, warning her not to recite any spirit jokes before the Washingtonians, as they had little humor, never to go out alone, and to have no social contact with the members of Congress, who were known for their vulgarity—politicians were men of easy, and often no virtue.

Her subsequent letters from Washington did not reassure him.

Last evening I saw a large company of officers. I believe they took me for the spirit, for they looked at me so incessantly that I nearly fainted; and I heard one gentleman ask his friend sitting next to him whether Miss Fox did not attend the ball. . . . He said if it was not myself it must certainly have been an apparition. He was a Frenchman.

Elisha Kent Kane arrived in Washington two weeks after Maggie, cutting short his lecture tour.

A cold early spring evening in 1853 at Mrs. Sullivan's Boardinghouse for Ladies in Washington, D.C.

The lamps are lit and a Miss Emmeline Badger sits prettily at the piano, playing a Glinka polka. The parlor is overflowing with young women wearing their brightest colors and fullest skirts. Hovering like black birds of prey over these dancing maids are assorted members of Congress. Sherry has been poured into etched crystal glasses. The fire roars in the fireplace; the polka rattles the windowpanes.

Mrs. Fox, still knitting, sits on a settee, tapping her feet and humming. Her daughters Katie and Maggie are, in her opinion at least, the prettiest girls in the party. Several male visitors, judging from the look in their eyes, seem to agree. Leah is in New York which is just as well; everyone breathes a little easier when Leah isn't around. One man—a senator, he says, though in fact he is an aide—is holding Maggie's hand.

A knock sounds at the door, but can't be heard over the thump and tinkle of the piano. Mrs. Sullivan, broad in the hip and red-nosed from sherry, senses rather than hears the visitor, and opens the door to him when he knocks the third time.

A cold breeze makes the lamps pause and flicker. Miss Emmeline's hands hesitate over the keys, and the music, too, pauses.

Maggie looks over her shoulder and sees Elisha standing in the doorway, watching her. She drops her dancing partner's hand and moves slowly, as if underwater, toward Elisha.

Maggie sees the face she has longed to see for weeks, the face that floats in her dreams, both day and night. This parlor is now the true center of the world, of the universe, because this small, pale, fragile man is here, and all the colors of the world seemed to have gathered around him.

She goes to Elisha and puts both her hands in his. She leads him into the parlor. Their eyes have locked and will not let go. The courtship is over. They cannot live without each other.

Four days later there was a wedding of sorts, back in Mrs. Grinnell's New York townhouse.

The candles in the borrowed parlor flickered, casting venomous shadows into the deeply tufted chairs and sofa. The rug, wallpaper, and cushions were patterned with livid, overbloomed roses. Over the arched doorway hung an embroidered motto: *No Cross, No Crown*.

Her silk gown rustled as Maggie slowly descended the stairs into Mrs. Grinnell's parlor. Elisha stood at the bottom, waiting. His keen eyes took in the vision: her gleaming black hair piled on top of her little head and held in place by a wreath of flopping silk flowers, the Paris gown in the latest cut, off the shoulder, tight at the waist, gathered in the back. Maggie didn't know that a Knickerbocker lady would have put that dress away for two years before wearing it, that a lady never dressed au courant; it was vulgar. Elisha's eyes ran the length of her figure, and he smiled nervously.

In the parlor, she stood among the rosewood settees and tables cluttered with Chinese-export figurines, and put her hand in Elisha's. They pledged themselves to each other in front of brother John. John's face, like Elisha's, was grim.

Maggie and Elisha exchanged rings, and promised eternal loyalty to each other. "For richer or poorer, in sickness and in health," Maggie whispered, happy for the first time in months.

Not present at this little ceremony were mother or father— neither Elisha's nor Maggie's—or a minister. Even Mrs. Grinnell was out for the evening. John was the only witness of this exchange of vows. Elisha had wanted it that way.

"The other ceremony will come later, dearest Maggie, when I have returned from the Arctic with Sir John Franklin. Then, my family will deny me nothing," Elisha whispered, taking her hand and twisting the new ring on her finger. He coughed several times, interrupting this promise.

His fever had worsened. His face was patchy red-and-white, like a consumptive's. Coughing spells doubled him over with their intensity and frequency. He didn't look strong enough to go shopping on Saturday, but in less than a month he would sail for the Arctic.

When he comes back—he will come back, Maggie promised herself—he will introduce me as his wife, and somewhere, sometime, there will be a real wedding with a minister and an organ and real white lilies, not just the ones figured on her dress. There will be six children, and a house in the country and a new brownstone in New York. When my hair starts to turn gray, he will buy me a necklace set with a dozen diamonds to cheer me. This is my happy ending.

Elisha and Maggie kissed. Then he gently pushed her away. Mrs. Grinnell would be home soon. The honeymoon, like the minister and organ music, would come later. Maggie was bundled into a public coach and delivered back to her mother and her rented rooms on Twenty-sixth Street.

In May, tulips and daffodils were blooming in city flower boxes. In May, the housemaids of the city draped every railing and windowsill with carpets, to rid them of winter's mustiness, and gay rugs snapped in the sweet breezes like flags on sailing ships. The air whispered of adventure, new beginnings, and afternoon picnics. The sun aroused the skin to new and pleasant sensations, like the touch of one's beloved. In May women strolled in their new, bird-bright spring dresses, and the dray horses of the milk and vegetable carts sported daisies behind their ears.

In May, just when New York is at its most charming, Elisha Kane sent his young bride away from the wicked city, to a school for young ladies.

He chose a very proper, very conformist institution just outside of Philadelphia. Maggie was given a white pinafore to wear over her frocks, a pile of books, a new pen with a set of gold-plated nibs, and a blue leather blotter.

She opened these gifts from Elisha while still in her rented rooms at Twenty-sixth Street. Cohabitation, like her formal introductions as Mrs. Kane, would begin when Elisha returned from his expedition.

Dressed in a daring red frock with black lace mittens (she had been to the theater that afternoon to see *The Drunkard's Progress*), she held the white pinafore to her shoulders and forced a smile.

There were footsteps on the hall stairs: Mrs. Hammel (surely the "Mrs." was an honorary title) was going upstairs with Mr. Hammel, a bank clerk who habitated with the Mrs. only one weekend a month. After their door closed, Mrs. Hammel would sing and play her little parlor organ for him, and then footsteps would cross overhead to a different room, the bedroom from whence would begin a rhythmic *tap, tap, tapping* that insinuated itself through the floorboards and into Maggie's parlor below.

"Listen, the spirits are talking," Maggie giggled when she heard the familiar sound of a headboard knocking against the wall.

"Ladies do not hear such noises," Elisha said sternly.

She fingered the stiff, white pinafore, and wondered if she should laugh or cry. Both seemed in order. Mother decided the issue: Mrs. Fox, sad to lose the companionship (and the income) of her favorite daughter, cried, and Maggie laughed until Elisha shook her by the shoulders to make her stop.

CHAPTER NINETEEN

$\mathcal{T}$he bitter March wind wails and the house creaks in protest. The windowpane is icy to the touch. Winter. The winter that will not end. According to the calendar it will be spring in two weeks. Eleusis' weather defies the calendar.

I feel better, though. Soldiers in the trenches in France got by on two hours' sleep. I can make it on four. The floor is not as steady as I prefer, however, when I plod into the waiting kitchen, the waiting kettle, the waiting table where I wait for dawn.

The book looks small and fragile on the large oak table, resting beneath the flowers Tom bought for the dinner party. An avalanche of shriveled, browning rose petals has half buried it. I pick it up and dust away the shattered flowers: Tennyson, most beloved of the Victorian poets. Steam from the coffee cup rises and warms my face as I open the book to "Maud."

. . . I thought the dead had peace, but it is not so;
To have no peace in the grave, is that not sad?
But up and down and to and fro,
Ever about me the dead men go;
And then to hear a dead man chatter
Is enough to drive one mad.

I put the book back on the table and pour another cup of coffee, then thumb through the book, looking for something more amusing. I haven't read these poems since an evening long ago with Jude, before death, before partings when, innocent of such griefs, we could afford to sentimentalize the unknown.

A thought pricks the back of my consciousness. I reread the poem, then stand so quickly my chair falls backward, clattering on the floor like dry bones, but the noise barely reaches my ears. I have just remembered something else.

I did not leave this book here. I had been rereading one of my favorite travel books of India. I did not put this book here. And the bookcase is six feet away. It couldn't have fallen to the table.

I felt so alone before, and now it feels as though the house is filled with unknown, frightening presences and unexplainable events. My solitude is crowded, not peaceful, and I feel in great need of an ally.

Douglas's card is stuck on the wall with a thumbtack, layered on top of a jumbled mass of cards for my hairdresser, dentist, plumber, lawyer.

As soon as it is daylight I dial the number on the card. Douglas is a laborer; he should be up by now.

The phone rings six times. He answers on the seventh. His voice is sleepy, slightly irritated. I can't stop myself from wondering if he hasn't slept well; if he has slept at all. Perhaps he has a girlfriend there with him. Maybe she's sitting at their table, next to him, her fingers playing in his tousled hair, teasing.

"Helen West here. Am I interrupting?"

"Interrupting? Only my sleep. What time is it?"

"Seven. Too early? It's too early. Sorry." My voice falters. "I'll call back later."

"Wait! Don't hang up!" He's yelling. Then his voice grows softer. "Don't hang up," he says again.

"Okay. I'm not hanging up." I lean against the wall. Suddenly, the reservoir of strength insomniacs carry in the pit of their stomachs is depleted. "Come for lunch?" I ask. "I could use some company."

"What time?"

"One."

Sitting at the window, waiting for Douglas, I saw the stag again. He came and stood in the middle of the back field, looking toward the house. He seemed sad. I blinked, and he was gone. There were no hoofprints in the snow, where he stood.

In one week is the anniversary of Jude's death. Reality seems to be in a state of flow, constantly shifting and redefining the sharp-pebble shores of what is, and what is not.

Douglas arrives, not in his pickup but in a little red Toyota that skates over the snow and ice and then gets stuck in my driveway. He comes in without knocking, shaking snow from his shoes and dark hair. He's wearing shirt, tie, blazer, corduroy trousers. I'm in jeans and a sweater, feeling out of place and shy in my own house.

"Smells good." Inside the kitchen, he sniffs and smiles. He is careful not to stand too close to me, to make no claims.

"Curried chicken soup. To be followed by an omelet, salad, and apple cake. Do you want coffee now, or a Bloody Mary?"

"Bloody Mary. In a minute. First . . ." He takes a step closer and lightly puts a hand on my shoulder to make me stand still. I realize I've been walking on my toes in nervousness, jumping around the way kids and maniacs do. His hand is warm, even

189

through the thickness of my sweater. His touch sends electricity through me. "What's up?" he asks. "Are you all right?" His smile makes me feel younger than I have felt in a very long time.

"I'm fine. Let me make us a couple of drinks, and then we'll eat. After, we'll talk. I need food."

I make the Bloody Marys strong. Douglas winces when he takes the first sip of his, but he pretends to enjoy it. We eat quickly, at the kitchen table, not fussing over the meal, not pretending that food was the point of this get-together. I am a competent cook, can be a great one when the occasion requires, but no woman who is just beginning to believe that her house is haunted can be blamed for being a little too preoccupied to have seasoned the soup just right.

The meal gives me time to observe Douglas, though. He eats well, with relish, with enjoyment, but always observing those small rituals we call table manners. I have a sudden impulse to explain to him about Tom and Alicia—that Tom is not my . . . My what? What words would this younger man use? Boyfriend? Lover? Significant other? I keep quiet.

After lunch, Douglas helps with the dishes, washing while I dry and put away. He knows just the right amount of soap to put in a sink of water, can stand steaming-hot water, not just luke-warm. I wonder again if maybe he lives with someone, perhaps a career woman who demands he put in equal time with the housework. The question comes, but not the right words for it. Twenty years ago I would have asked if he was married. Ten years ago, if he was with someone. Now how is it expressed? I have forgotten this part of my own language, those words we use to define intimacy. I am a stranger, a foreigner poor in the coinage of the realm, staring at Douglas's straight back as he stands at the sink, at the way he has tied a dishtowel around his narrow hips. Does he feel my eyes on him? He shifts from foot to foot as he works.

When the dishes are finished we go into the parlor; he looks around for logs to put on the cold hearth. I remember now why I never invite strangers to the house. Explanations.

"I don't use the fireplace," I explain.

He taps at the mantel, the chimney. "Looks sound to me," he says.

"It is. At least as far as I know. That's not why I don't use it. I don't like open fires. Flames." He says nothing, but a flicker crosses his face. I wonder how much he knows about me, about Jude. This is a small town. I feel foolish. I wish now I had not called him. But Douglas sits on the sofa facing the cold hearth as if that was what he had planned all along. Nothing strange here. No, ma'am.

"You sounded upset on the phone. What's going on?" His voice is kind yet stern, like a gentle father giving instructions on how to ride a bicycle. Do this, and you won't fall off. But I am falling off.

"I just . . ." And then I have no words. Why did I call him? I don't know.

"You're still hearing the noise in the wall," Douglas says.

"Yes. And more. Books moving themselves around. There was a book on the table, there. I didn't put it on the table. How did it get there? I hear people talking. Sometimes I have a feeling that someone else is in my workroom with me, though I'm alone. The usual." I try to laugh, make a joke of it. But Douglas is frowning and looking much too concerned.

"Helen, old houses make noises, and this is a very old house."

"I've been a little stressed lately . . ."

"Not sleeping, either, I'd say from the circles under your eyes."

He traces his finger along the scar, as Jude used to do.

"Old houses make noises," he repeats. "Mice and squirrels run around in the attic. Branches tap against the roof. You should have some of those trees trimmed, by the way, or you'll get bugs in the house. Beams creak when the temperature changes. Faucets drip. The water boiler switches on and off. The furnace makes creaking noises like footsteps. You have an interesting house, by the way. Did you know it was a brothel during the Depression? And a gambling house. It was originally built in 1852, as a summer house for the Barwell family.

"Under the coats of paint on those stair treads"—he nods backward, toward the hall stairs—"you'll find top-grade oak. The stained-glass window in the dining room came from Paris. There used to be a stable out back, but it burned in 1916, and the family built a new garage instead of rebuilding the stables."

"You know an awful lot about my house."

"I'm interested in architectural history, and local history. It's all on file, down at the county library."

We sit in silence for a moment.

"You're a writer?" he asks, already knowing I am.

"Journalist."

"What's your specialty?"

"Death. A different kind of architecture."

Douglas sips his drink and frowns.

"I write about death. Mortality statistics. Disasters. Gloom and doom."

"That's what you remind me of," he says. "A woman I knew. A nurse. She worked in a cancer ward, with terminal patients. She was always alone, even when she was surrounded by people. Apart. You're like that."

"I did a story once on a village in southern India, where every other child died before a first birthday. I interviewed a young woman who had lost all five of her children, and then her husband, too. The other people of the village would not go near her, not even her own mother. 'She smells of death,' one of them told me."

He picks up my hand and kisses it.

"Tom's my editor. He spent the night here, with my friend Alicia," I say.

Douglas smiles. "Thanks for telling me that. And that explains how the book got on the table. Tom put it there, you just didn't notice it before. Rule out the impossible, and what's left, no matter how improbable, is the solution. Or something like that, according to Sherlock Holmes."

"Did you know that Conan Doyle was one of Maggie Fox's strongest supporters? So much for the man who invented the master of reason and deduction."

I can tell from his expression that Douglas has never heard of Maggie Fox. I tell him the basic events of her life and her role in the Spiritualist movement. When I finish, he is looking at me as if all has suddenly been illuminated.

"Don't look at me like that," I say, keeping my voice low and calm.

"Like what?"

"Like I belong chained in an attic. That's what they used to do, you know. A woman would become a problem of some sort and they would say she was deranged and lock her away. Dr. G. Fielding Blandford locked away seventy-eight percent of all female patients brought to him in London in 1885. Charcot in Paris committed half his female patients. He sold tickets to the public, who would come and watch the madwomen of the Saltpetrière. It was quite a show."

"You need a good night's sleep," he says. "And some distractions. Have dinner with me on Thursday. I'll come for you at seven."

I am the place, the universe, where Jude still lives. Love and death are places. We give the intangible three dimensions, define them, make them real; when in fact they are mere wishes circling an eternity of nothingness, atoms without a nucleus.

As for ghosts, for souls lingering on earth at the scenes of their crimes or scenes of their loves, that is a gothic notion, surely, and rationalists steer clear of such notions. But how did that book get on the table, opened to Jude's favorite poem? Tom does not read poetry.

Reality is starting to disintegrate. Parallel universes are forming and spinning out of my thoughts; molecules of dust are longing for each other, reassembling, plotting resurrection. There are no more absolutes. Even numbers no longer reassure me. What if I add a column of figures and end up with a color instead of a sum? And where is spring?

Work, Helen. You are alone. The house is empty.

But just as I turn on my computer the phone rings. "How's the manuscript coming?" Tom asks in a forced, cheery voice.

"You'll have it by deadline."

"That wasn't the question. I can always use it in a later issue, if you need more time. I asked how the work was going. No more eerie, weird stuff happening? Alicia told me about the package you got from Rome. Some mess-up, huh?" He laughs—ha, ha.

I decide not to tell him about the poetry book, the noises, the sensation of being watched.

"No, no more weird stuff. Maggie's bio is turning into a love story. That's about as weird as it gets."

"Love story? Remember the audience, Helen."

"Right. No licking of nipple or navel, no moistness between the thighs."

"You know what I mean. Facts."

"Tom, I'm writing about an alcoholic, overly imaginative young woman who invents a new religion based on speaking with the dead, and you want me to stick to the facts?"

"Do your best. I trust you to eliminate luridness at all possible opportunities."

"Right."

"I'm coming up to Eleusis on Saturday."

"To see Alicia?"

"No, to stay with you. It's the anniversary. Jude's death. I want to be there."

"No. I mean, not a good time." I'm always alone on the anniversary, and it seems this year especially I should continue that tradition.

"Why?" Tom wants to know.

"Come next month. For spring."

I hang up, go into the kitchen, and pour myself a cup of coffee. The cardinals are at the birdfeeder outside the window. Mr. and Mrs. They always come in pairs. Candidates for Noah's Ark, I suppose, ready for the day of destruction, suitcases packed, boarding passes in hand, in case the millennium brings another flood, though I understand this time it is to be fire.

Ends of eras are unnerving. They are corners we are about to turn, blind corners around which we cannot see. We don't know if we'll encounter a hungry lion or a purring housecat. Our hard-earned self-confidence, what the rationalists and philosophers of the Enlightenment termed "reason," devolves back into the atavistic fear of the dark and its lurking monters. In Maggie's early years, there was a succession of religious fanatics who preached the world was going to end at any time, the sooner the better. In a way, they were right. The industrialization of America ended one form of their world; the Civil War ended another.

The phone rings a second time. I let the answering machine pick it up, and listen to the message. Alicia. She wants to talk. She sounds happy and pleased with herself.

"Call me," she says.

I don't. Instead, I return to my desk, to Maggie's story.

CHAPTER TWENTY

On May 30, 1853, Dr. Elisha Kent Kane sailed out of New York harbor to begin his second voyage to the Arctic.

Women in floppy picture hats and men in pale checked spring suits waved and shouted. Little boys in short pants waved little flags. Guns saluted. But Maggie was not there. Maggie was in the country, at Mrs. Turner's Academy for Young Women, in her white pinafore. Alone. She had abandoned Mother, said good-bye to Katie, and broken completely with Leah, who had tried to command her to stay in New York, had forbidden her to go to her school.

Alone, in a place where the squirrels were the most interesting thing to watch and some of the other girls still believed that babies appeared in the cabbage patch.

Alone, where there were no theaters, no Barnum's American

Museum, only the school library (which did not allow Jane Austen novels or even explicit biology books) and Sunday service (which lasted forever).

Alone, with no adoring men (many of her clients had been men, and certainly Elisha had not been the only one of his sex to notice the suppleness of her waist, the seductiveness of the shadows around her dark eyes). Alone, with no clients at all, male or female, no reassuring feel of money being pressed into her palm, no grieving mothers, no mourning widows shedding tears of gratitude for Maggie's intercession into the affairs of the recently dead. Alone, because her husband's family denied her existence and the other schoolgirls were, naturally, terrified of her.

It was as bad as Hydesville.

Worse, because she had eaten of the apple. She had been to the city, enjoyed its pleasures, acquired a modest fortune, fallen in love, felt for the first time the sweet gust of a man's breath mixing with hers as their bodies met at knee, hips, breast, and mouth.

All that had been given up so that she might better conjugate verbs, practice several clever ways of folding table napkins, and learn to walk without wiggling, for those things were the basis of respectability.

No Cross, No Crown.

For Elisha, she wore the hated schoolgirls' frock and collected seeds from the browning flowers in the summer garden for her botany class. She, with the other schoolgirls, carved pumpkins for Halloween as Miss Tuttle, inspired by Maggie's bold eyes, delivered a somewhat racy lecture on pagan mythology (she was reprimanded for that faux pas by the head mistress after supper). Maggie choked on bland pasty pudding (so good for the digestion!) as Reverend Smith read weekly from Corinthians (so good for the soul!).

All for love.

The first few weeks, she received letters from Elisha, who sent them to her by way of ships heading south as he headed north.

197

They were not the love letters she hoped for. Filled with dire warnings and lessons and preachings about the evil of her former life, they could have been written by a father to a child, by a minister to a parishioner. She knew quite well he found her breasts beautiful. Why did he not say so, instead of going on and on about the wretched evils of Spiritualism and of a life lived too publicly?

Soon even those lacklove letters ended, as Kane's expedition moved inexorably north, past civilization, past what is known, into Ultima Thule, where the world ends. Baffin Bay would be his bride now.

When the letters stopped arriving, Maggie went into a swift and dangerous decline. Not even a young woman of her robust constitution could survive such a determinedly wholesome regime of fresh air and womanly education and character-improving ad- monitions.

She stopped eating. She began, for the first time in her brief yet busy life, swooning in earnest. She would not get out of bed, not even for her French lesson. The squirrels she had thrown seeds to in the autumn now tapped at her window in early winter, and she gave them not so much as a smile.

Mrs. Turner had "lost" two girls in five years. One fell in the river (jumping in fully-clothed and with rocks weighting her pockets); another had pined away (refusing food, and when they had forced bread pudding down her throat she stuck her finger in her mouth and gagged it back up). Both events had been grievous for the school's reputation, and disaster only nearly averted by large amounts paid to the press to kill the stories.

Would Maggie be the third? The headmistress, more afraid of bad publicity than of death itself, decided something must be done.

Dr. Edward Bayard was sent for. It was a propitious choice for everyone involved. The doctor was brother to Senator James Bayard, and had met Maggie during her stay in Washington, D.C. He knew exactly what ailed the young woman and was not mean-spirited enough to deny it to her.

"She needs a change of scenery," he said sternly to Headmistress.

"Oh, yes, I'm quite sure that's exactly what she needs. I'll have her trunks packed immediately," agreed Headmistress, for whom Maggie was now a Problem rather than a Student.

Maggie, pale but smiling wanly, was transported back to New York, to remain a houseguest of Mrs. Ellen Walters, sister of New York Congressman John Cochrane, until her mental disquiet should pass.

She had made no friends at the school, so no one regretted her going, although the girls' letters home grew suddenly tamer and more judicious now that the young Spiritualist was gone: Prudence stopped having visions of Christ; Amarilla stopped writing poems to her dead brother. The little schoolgirls slept better.

Maggie, back in New York in Mrs. Walters' palatial and stylish home on Clinton Place, slept little.

For a while, she kept her promise to Elisha to hold no sittings and conduct no communications between this vale of tears and the Summerland, no matter how badly the spirits wished to speak or their earthly friends longed to hear them.

But she had not promised to give up dancing and card parties. She hadn't promised not to tell stories of the many times when she had conversed with the dead, when her sister's house in Rochester had vibrated at night with the sound of blood being poured from buckets and dripping down stairs, when lights from the nearby graveyard flew through the air and through their rooms, waking them, as invisible hands pinched and pulled at them, and turned over chairs and smashed plates against the wall.

Fans fluttered with the speed of hummingbird wings, then

stilled completely as Maggie spun her tales; gentlemen cleared their throats and made small, knowing noises but soon were as drop-jawed and quivering as their lady companions.

Mrs. Walters' Wednesdays-at-home were the hit of the season, and Maggie gained back the weight she had lost; her skin glowed again, despite the constant ache for Elisha. She was conscious of waiting. Time would pass. He would return. Surely he would return.

She was unaware of danger. But her name in the society column was drawing attention. She was making enemies. Leah, Tweed, and Mrs. Kane had her name; they had fixed it with cold eyes, burnt a candle of ill will before it, hexed it. They were letting the calf fatten itself for the slaughter.

Stare at whiteness long enough, and you begin to see all the colors that aren't there. Snow, for instance, is not really white. It is pink or gray or blue or lavender or green. In the shadows, it becomes its own opposite, black. True whiteness does not exist. It is an absolute and, like all absolutes, becomes meaningless when you are hungry, or cold, or exhausted, or feverish.

"He's feverish again," said the first mate, leaning over Elisha.

"Was I talking in my sleep?" Elisha mumbled. He tried to sit up, but could not. He must. To be still is to die. Life is movement. He must move. "Not feverish," he insisted. He rose up on elbow, then buttock, then knee, then feet, his thick furs cushioning his bony limbs against the impact with the hard, frozen wood. He leaned over the railing of the *Advance* and saw, in the unmoving white vastness, all the colors of the world.

Elisha Kent Kane, ship's surgeon for the Second U.S. Grinnell Expedition led by Lieutenant Edwin De Haven, had sailed to Greenland, then skirted the huge, wheeling ice packs of Baffin Bay by hugging the shore, always moving—the ice pack would crush them like a toy boat if they were to get caught in that immense white, creaking, false land of ice—past Cape York of

Melville Bay, into the miracle of the northern waters which are paradoxically, ice-free, and as false as false spring, for past Melville Bay the ice appears again, blocking, jamming, pushing, bullying. One day, Kane recorded their progress as half a ship's length. Icebergs large as the Parthenon bore down on them.

It was, for them, a summer of white snow and pastel ice, of wind and storm, and deep silence that made all the more alarming the irregular, always unexpected, immense booms of calving icebergs and cracking ice sheets. The loneliness, the space, the solitude, the silence, were hallucinogenic. The sailors sang and talked to themselves constantly, trying to fill the unfillable silence.

But when they found Franklin's winter encampment on Beechey Island, hope shriveled. Franklin and his men had disappeared. Search as they might, they found no other sign of them.

By September, other things had gone wrong in addition to the failure to find Franklin. The weather turned, and the *Advance* and her crew drifted helplessly past Lancaster Sound and back into Baffin Bay.

At the end of autumn the expedition had reached eighty degrees latitude 35' north. This was the farthest north an expedition had ever wintered, and they reached it just as the ice was closing in, capturing the ship in a long, deadly embrace.

De Haven and Kane set up winter camp in a shelter harbor they named Rensselaer Bay, in memory of the Kane home, made unbearable and sold when Kane's fifteen year old brother had died. The echoing solitude of the frozen north, the whiteness, kept Kane in constant memory of those he had lost. He ached for Maggie, just as the rest of the crew shivered in their hammocks and thought of loved ones at home. Fearing a diminishing morale and strength for himself and the others, Kane established a vigorous regime of exercise for the crew; he checked regularly for signs of scurvy. He started a ship's newspaper and a theatrical society to keep his complement of eighteen busy. He enforced a strict schedule of activities, even though the days were as dark as the nights and without a good watch you couldn't tell noon from midnight. When you are frozen into the ice and can go neither forward nor backward, when day and night are equally dark, time no longer exists. Some of the men were having visions; others reported they could no longer dream when they slept.

Supplies ran low, so the sailors dined on the rats which overran the ship. Tempers shortened and flared. Memories blurred, especially memories of seventeen-year-old brides who might never be seen again.

During the long day-nights, occasional sledge parties ventured up the coast, but the scouting expeditions grew less frequent as the dogs, by twos and threes, succumbed to the foaming and convulsions of an illness the Eskimos called *piblokto*. Kane's favorite dog, Tiger, fell dead at his feet. He watched its last feeble twitchings and whinings and then let the remaining half-starved dogs tear it to pieces. It was no longer a pack mate, it was a carcass, food.

Once, an Eskimo hunting party found them; they stared at the inept monstrosity of a ship, tilting in the ice like some wounded, dying ocean beast. They waved and left a gift of whale blubber, which the sailors wolved down, raw, and then gagged back up.

Sometimes Kane lay in his tent, listening to the wind and hearing in it the voices of Maggie's spirits.

They had not discovered the long-missing Sir John Franklin, or his ship, or his crew—they had vanished into the nothingness that was trying to swallow them, too. The ship was locked into ice, it could go neither forward nor backward, not up or down. Entire seasons passed: autumn, winter, spring, summer, another autumn and winter, all marked by ice, snow, the occasional cracking of calving icebergs, and the ship stayed locked tight in its deadly white embrace. Fuel ran low, and they resignedly began to hack at the ship for lack of other wood. By their second spring, the entire upper half of the ship had literally gone up in smoke.

Still, the ice held her.

Kane gave the command to abandon ship.

The crew, exhausted, frozen, scurvy-ridden now, scrambled into the long boats and took to the ice-clogged sea, sometimes carrying the boats over ice, sometimes rowing through narrow stretches of open water. When they reached land they marched for months through Greenland's northern coasts, finally arriving at the settlement of Upernivik. It would be another six months before the relief party sent to rescue them would lead them into New York harbor.

Two years is a very long time for a young woman.

Twice, cherry blossoms opened, then spent their petals on the sidewalk, then their withered leaves, and then sparrows shivered in the bare winter branches. Twice the orchids in Mrs. Walters' sunporch sent out long, snaking stems that bent under the weight of waxy magenta flowers. Twice a Christmas tree was put up in the front parlor and guests invited for eggnog. Two New Year's Eve parties, eight formal balls, forty-eight dinner parties, six Friday-to-Mondays in the country, one trip to Hydesville to see her ailing father. When she got there, they had nothing to say to each other. She had wanted to be gentle and forgiving with the old man. But in her father's presence she was eight years old again, and she hated him. She gave him some of her laudanum pills for the pain, then left on the next public coach.

Maggie waited. Days passed. Seasons passed. The news finally came on an autumn day in 1855 that Elisha's ship was nearing New York.

Maggie's eyes were darker, and sad. She was quieter, gentler. She had her first regrets, memories of days she wished she could live over, redo. She remembered the little girl who had dropped apples on a farmhouse floor and named the noise "Mr. Splitfoot," and she wanted to shake that little girl, make her promise never to do it again. She had been naughty and deceitful. She had blasphemed, and surely there was a place in hell awaiting her.

But look where deceit had got her: She was in New York, the belle of the season, waiting for her husband, the famous explorer, to come home to her. She was joyously happy. Even waiting no longer seemed burdensome, since it was Elisha the beloved she awaited.

Maggie longed to hold her husband in her arms, to comfort and be comforted. She was incomplete without him.

When a gun salvo announced the arrival of Elisha's ship in New York Harbor, she flew into the hall, into her coat.

Mrs. Walters pushed her back into the parlor.

"Wait here," she advised. "There will be such a mob at the harbor you'll not even be noticed." Or worse, she didn't say, he'll look away, purposely not see you. There had been no letters from Dr. Kane for many months.

Something unpleasant was afoot, and unpleasant things should occur in private parlors, not in public, was Mrs. Walters' firm and wise belief.

Maggie had broken promises. She had acted imprudently, gone riding in carriages, danced too frequently at parties, conducted séances and sittings when she grew bored with her German grammar book. Maggie had given Mrs. Kane all the ammunition she needed to ensure the girl never officially joined the family.

Maggie, still in her coat, sat back down and waited, as Mrs. Walters had ordered. She sat by the window, staring out into the dark autumn night. Elisha did not come. He did not even send a message.

The next day Maggie went for a long walk. Surely, if she was out, he would call for her, she reasoned with farmgirl superstition.

When she returned, she learned someone had called for her, but not Elisha: a lawyer, asking for the return of all the letters Dr. Kane had written to Miss Fox. Miss Fox, he said. Not Mrs. Kane.

"Of course, I didn't give them over," Mrs. Walters said, wiping her streaming eyes. "You might want to sell the letters, if you need . . ."

Maggie, wet-eyed, looked hard at her. "Never. I will never sell them."

Elisha finally called upon the Walters household at nine the next morning, two days after his homecoming. By that time Maggie was in such a state of misery she refused to see him.

He insisted. He stood at the bottom of the stairs and yelled up at her, commanding, pleading with her to see him. He was prepared to forgive, and start anew . . . under modified circumstances.

Maggie, dressed in a virginal white morning gown, pale, her dark hair loose upon her shoulders, wide-eyed with tears, laudanum, and fright, a very picture of wifely grief, crept down the stairs and into his opened arms.

How thin his arms felt, how dark were the shadows under his eyes. In his frailty, she saw the mortality of her own dreams. But love, for women like Maggie, is a door that opens only one way; once through, you can't go back. Her future was already written. She would not struggle against it. She put her arms around him and leaned her head against the scratchy wool of his coat.

"Maggie." He held her close and pressed her face tightly against his chest so that she could not look up at him. "Maggie, Mother is insisting that you sign a paper stating we never were, and have no intentions of, marrying."

He avoided looking at her as he produced the paper, written in formal script on heavy paper, from his overcoat pocket. There was a large mark at the bottom, where she was to sign.

Maggie pulled away and looked at him through a curtain of dark hair that had fallen over her face. She stared, and he grew uncomfortable. Something in her face reminded him of the madwomen he had visited in the Boston hospital.

"Sign, or we may never see each other again," he said.

"Should I use my own blood to sign the pact?"

"Don't be melodramatic. Ink will do."

"Is this what you want?"

"It is necessary."

She hesitated long enough that the pen in her hand dripped and indigo blue ink splattered the document, ruining its pristine, officious neatness. There was a moment of blackness when she almost fainted; then, she signed. She would do what she must to be with him. Her love was stronger than his.

If the Kane family thought this document would put an end to the rumors and gossip, they were gravely mistaken. If anything, it intensified them. Were Maggie Fox of the Rappings and Dr. Elisha Kent Kane of the Arctic engaged? Most papers in the United States had an opinion and supposed inside information, and printed it.

The notoriety, the scandal, did not go away, but intensified.

Horace Greeley tried to restore some balance in one of his own editorials: "What right has the public to know anything about an engagement or non-engagement between these young people? Whether they have been, are, may be, are not, or will be engaged, can be nobody's business but their own. . . ."

Months of quarrels, separations, brief and tenuous reunions, followed Kane's return to New York. Realizing that the promised wedding was not to be, Maggie returned to her mother and the two rented a better, larger apartment on East Twenty-second Street with the help of Leah. She had been waiting and watching.

But now Kane was back, and his promises were empty and his love flawed. Patient, cunning Leah, slowly, cleverly, worked Maggie back into the fold of Spiritualism, one client, one sitting, at a time: "Just a few minutes with her, dear sister. She is so distraught. A few words would mean so much to her, and what's the harm? She's very wealthy and you do need a new coat, you know. The good weather won't hold forever."

"Maggie, you will destroy us," Elisha protested when he learned that Maggie was holding public séances once again. They had made up the quarrel—Elisha had even torn up the paper she had signed and, in a gesture even more indicative of bravery than his voyage to the Arctic, had informed his mother that he would call on Maggie Fox three evenings a week. With or without her blessing.

"Without," his mother had said.

"We need money," Maggie said. "I will earn it." Elisha couldn't argue with that. The advance that Elisha had been promised on his book was not forthcoming, and he had no money of his own, no funds that were not provided by the family, and the family was not willing to provide for Maggie.

Sensing his mood was dangerously low, Maggie tried to cheer him. She let him select the furnishings for the new rooms—they were much more subdued, more expensive than her taste would have allowed—and let him choose her maid as well, a quiet Irish girl who kept her eyes lowered and the rooms faultlessly clean.

The new apartment had a well-furnished parlor on the third floor set aside for Maggie's exclusive use. Here, on the rosewood settee, Elisha came to call and sometimes work, when he had lectures to prepare and book chapters to ponder. He and Maggie spent hours alone together, behind the locked door.

When Elisha wasn't visiting, clients were. The parlor became Maggie's "sitting room," where visiting spirits tapped out messages to other, more fleshly, and still-mortal visitors.

Maggie was a working girl again, despite Elisha's continuing discomfort and hatred of Spiritualism. On days when he did not come to her, he sent chastising letters.

Do avoid the "spirits." I cannot bear to think of you as engaged in this course of wickedness and deception. . . . I can't bear the idea of your sitting in the dark, squeezing other people's hands. . . . The old year is dying; let its spirits be buried with its dead.

But soon both Maggie and Elisha realized there were more important matters at hand than church weddings and spirit rappings. More than the old year was dying. Elisha, after the forced bravado of the journey and its homecoming, was growing steadily weaker; death nipped at his heels. During their embraces on the settee, Maggie listened to his ragged breath pumping through exhausted lungs.

He worked twelve hours a day on the huge pile of manuscript pages he nicknamed "the coffin," describing his arduous expedition, the thickness of the ice in July, sledge-dog diseases, customs of Eskimos, edible roots that grew in the Far North, the color of sunset over a glacier, longitudes and latitudes. He hadn't found Sir Franklin, but this book would help rectify that failure, would grant him a measure of fame. If he lived to finish it.

Doctors advised a change of scenery and Elisha decided on London, where he could visit Sir Franklin's widow. Maggie would stay behind.

She did not beg him to stay, or to be allowed to go with him, knowing it would do no good. Instead she knit warm socks for him, and during his afternoon visits, showered their hours together with the lightning storm of her passion, determined to make him love her with his body, even if he could not be wholehearted about it.

They had a summer together, a summer of slow walks in the park at sunset, of late mornings in bed, Elisha almost buried under his papers and pen trays, of frugal meals of fruit and cheese eaten alone, in the privacy of their rooms. They did not talk of the future.

The night before he sailed for London, Elisha called at East Twenty-second Street, where, standing in front of Mother Fox and Leah, he put his arm about Maggie and announced to them, "Maggie is my wife, and I am her husband." It still wasn't a legal, sanctified ceremony; yet after that evening Maggie openly used the name Mrs. Kane, and kept it for the rest of her life.

In London Elisha grew so weak he could not dress or bathe himself. Maggie read in the New York papers that her husband, near death, was leaving England and journeying south, to Havana, on the advice of his doctors. She received a letter from him, complaining that he hadn't had any letters from her, and she knew that the long arm of the Kane clan was still keeping them apart. She'd written daily to the address he had given her in Havana, but received no answer. Did he get them? Did he write to her, but were his letters to her burned instead of posted?

Terrified, she packed her trunk and booked passage to Cuba.

Too late. The day before she was to sail, the papers announced that Dr. Elisha Kent Kane of the Arctic had died in his mother's arms in Havana, and was now at peace in the Spirit World.

At peace? Maggie did not want him to be at peace. She wanted him here with her, suffering and weeping and regretting and missing and loving. Peace? Not if she could help it. If ever she called anyone back from the dead, she would summon him. No one could come between them now. He belonged to her.

She set out candles and a plate of his favorite chocolates, sherry, a new gold-nibbed pen she had purchased as a coming-home gift. She lined them up on the table and put his slippers by the fire. She put out the lights and sat quietly, in her chair, not his.

"Come to me, Elisha," she said. She had done it for others. She would do it for herself. There must be a way, a real way, not the faking way. It would take time. She could wait. "Come, Elisha," she said again.

He was the stillness, the silence that enveloped her. She felt him, though he refused to speak.

CHAPTER
TWENTY-ONE

What if—just what if—Jude does exist, Jude has been trying to come to me, to speak to me? What if the noises, the books opened to his favorite poems, the smells of his cooking . . . What if Jude has been reaching for me, and I have been turning him away?

What if.

What if I could see him again, talk to him again? What if there was some truth behind Maggie's tricks?

Time to find out. I don't need Alicia's Ouija board. I don't need Maggie or any of her sister mediums. If Jude is here . . . Please be here.

~

I sit in the parlor, before the cold hearth, Jude's old bathrobe wrapped around my shoulders. It is twilight, his favorite time of day. The lights are turned off and I wait as colors and then shapes lose distinction and the room grows dark. I try to empty myself of everything except the need to speak with him. My body becomes one single ache, a single focus, a single need. Jude.

Come to me, Jude. I am here.

The house is silent. I sit without moving, barely breathing, letting the cold and the darkness and the silence enfold me in their embrace. I feel my skin growing thin and then transparent as the darkness merges and separate edges of reality meet within me. All things become possible. Love works miracles. I laugh quietly, remembering that this morning another book had appeared on the kitchen table, not opened for me but with a paper sticking out: a note Jude had written years ago, and on it a translation of part of a Antonio Porchia story: "He who does not fill his world with phantoms remains alone."

Jude, I say again. My eyes are tightly closed. Please, Jude.

And it happens.

I feel his hand stroking my hair.

Jude. I sit still as stone, not daring to open my eyes. Maggie insisted on this: We could speak to them, but we could not see them.

Say something, Jude. Speak to me.

His hand is still on my hair, stroking gently, but he doesn't speak.

I miss you so much, Jude.

His hand wanders to my forehead, touching it.

Let me hear your voice. Let me see you.

The room is warm now. His hand is on my face, touching the scar.

I love you, Jude. A burst of light, of joy, explodes in me. Let me see you, I say. One more time.

Then, his hand is gone from my face and the light inside me darkens. The room is cold. I am alone.

It doesn't matter if it's real or not, because reality itself is changeable; it is as we need it to be, want it to be. If I believe, I can have Jude back. The simple joy of it makes me dizzy. When I begin my next day's work, I am humming to myself, making little dance steps as I climb the stairs. As soon as I finish the word quota for the day, I can sit in the dark parlor again with Jude.

In her rented house on East Twenty-second Street, Maggie did not unpack her trunk or take the white dustcovers off the furniture, but went to her room and shut the door. No one was permitted near her except the maid who brought a daily tray of bread and broth and emptied the slop pail. The house began to smell of seclusion, of death, of grief. Maggie stayed there, shut away, for two months. When she came out, she was dressed in black, the color she wore till her death.

Nowhere in Maggie's memoirs, or Leah's, or any other account of the time, can I find an indication, even a suggestion, that Maggie ever loved again. Why should she? Her love was still with her. She felt him near and eventually, she would convince him to break his silence. Years of helping others feel the presence of their dear departed had left her with a certain knack.

Elisha's mother was not as comfortable with the loss of her son, however. She grew bitter, and blamed Maggie. It was Maggie's fault that Elisha had gone north (to escape her!); that he had not taken care of his health (that she forced him to eat in public places, dance till dawn—none of this was true); that he had wasted his youth in false goals rather than marrying and settling down and leaving her with a grandchild.

When a son dies, a mother must blame someone, after all, so her persecution of Maggie grew heavier, not lighter. Maggie was excluded from the monthlong ceremonies that accompanied the cold body of Elisha Kent Kane on his last voyage from Havana to the family plot. He had become a national hero, and mourners paraded and rang bells for him in almost every city in the nation, but Maggie was not invited to any of the public or private ceremonies.

Mother Kane wasn't finished yet. She hired a writer to do her son's authorized biography. In this biography, paid for by the Kane family, there is no mention of a woman named Maggie Fox. She doesn't exist.

A third blow came the week after Elisha's will was read. Before his London journey, he had drawn up a will which stated that a portion of his estate was to be given to his brother John, who would then share it with Maggie. When he made this will, his estate was negligible. After his death, the two volumes he wrote about his Arctic expedition had proved profitable. In fact, they made a small fortune. But the indirect, unspecific wording of Elisha's will enabled the Kane family to withhold the money that would have been Maggie's, the widow's share. Instead they agreed to let her have the yearly interest on a small account Elisha had set aside for her, on condition—of course—that she never ask for more and that she never publish the love letters Elisha sent her. They bought her silence for a pittance.

Maggie, still locked away in her room where slanting sun, murky as a tea stain, cuts through the lurking twilight, is ill with grief, with longing, with regret. A month ago she had been Mrs. Elisha Kent Kane, busily preparing to be reunited with her ailing husband. Yesterday she had been Mrs. Margaret Kent Kane, his grieving widow. Today she is just Maggie Fox, a farmgirl from nowhere who knew a few tricks and could get some attention.

Remember that Maggie Fox of the Spirits was loved by Elisha Kent Kane of the Arctic, he had once written to her. *Be my brave little girl and let me guide your future,* he had said.

The future is a stuffy, dingy room with drawn curtains.

~

Poverty is worse the second time. You already know what it means, you already know the taste of soup made with salt and potato peels, and the feel of undergarments mended so often they chafe the skin. You remember the smirks and giggles of the schoolchildren of Hydesville who point at your winter coat, which has been cut down from a man's hand-me-down and has tobacco stains on the front. You know the sound of mice scrambling overhead in run-down rooms, the glare of the minister when you have no coins to put in the collection plate.

When Maggie fell in love with Elisha, she had been a girl of sixteen. When she came out of that room, she was no longer young. Years had been spent in loving, quarreling, parting, reuniting, separating, coming together. Her youth was past. Reputation, she had never had.

Maggie pondered the future. *Future,* when she had been Elisha's dear little wife, had been such a lovely, soothing word. Now it was a word as ugly as *corruption.*

After mourning him, she resumed the only business she knew. Announcements were placed in the papers; little cards were sent round to people she knew or hoped to know as clients. "Margaret Fox Kane . . ." (She couldn't help herself; she had to use his name, had to keep that little connection with him, no matter how much the family raved and complained.) ". . . after a long period of disabling illness, now resumes the exercise of her mediumship, begun in Hydesville, on the 31st of March, 1848. Séances held at 231 East Thirteenth Street, New York."

That would put food on the table, and pay the rent. But for consolation, Maggie turned elsewhere: After Elisha died, Maggie Fox, the founder of American Spiritualism, converted to the Roman Catholic faith.

This act of conversion was the part of Maggie's history that had most fascinated Jude. He used to lie in bed next to me, imagining it aloud, the smell of incense, the candles, Maggie reciting

214

from heart the Act of Faith and the Apostles' Creed, the priest's fingers making the sign of the cross over her forehead and chest. To move like that, from the newest religion to one of the oldest, required a mental quality Jude could not name.

"Confession," he said once, sitting up. "That was it. The act of confession, and of forgiveness. That was what she wanted from Catholicism. The confessional was the only place where she could speak the truth, reveal herself completely. That had to be the attraction."

"Do you ever feel the need to confess?" I asked, rubbing his back. His shoulders were in tight knots from the hours he had spent working at his desk that day. The trip to Rome was only three weeks away and he was trying to get a year's worth of unanswered correspondence, research notes that needed to be filed, and incomplete book proposals cleared off his desk.

"What would I confess? That I have loved two women?"

"Only two? How chaste you've been."

"Only two that mattered. No, love is not the sin. But perhaps disloyalty is. Remember the murder of Caesar. His grief was not that he was assassinated, but that a trusted friend took part in the assassination. Disloyalty is the greatest moral fault."

"Even if a tyrant deserves to die?"

"It's not about the tyrant. It's about Brutus changing his mind. Can a man ever know himself, if he is not capable of declaring and maintaining loyalty? And if a man cannot know himself, and be loyal to himself and his opinions, he is nothing. A straw in the wind."

I knew then he was talking about himself.

"Are you a straw in the wind because you love me? Because you no longer love Madelyn?"

His shoulders stiffened under my touch. "Do you ever worry that I might fall out of love with you, as I did with her?" he asked. "That if a man changes his mind once, he will change it again?"

215

"Never," I lied.

His finger stroked the scar near my eye. "This reminds me that I almost lost you," he said. His voice was very sad. "How could a man willingly part with anything, anyone, he has once loved?"

"Lovers part all the time. True lovers come back. Jude, you are a good man. A true one. To thine self. To me."

"Eternity is the problem," he said. "Where time does not exist, where there are no more choices. No more chances."

"Thank God Elisha is safe," Maggie said, peering out the window. It was the spring of 1861, and there was a riot in the street below. Youths marched with placards, calling for an end to slavery, for war, for jobs, for better times. Their shoes and pants were coated with the heavy mud of the March snow thaws, and when they marched, their feet made a sucking, slurping noise that reminded Maggie of the noise boiling tar made. They had been marching all afternoon, growing noisier with the passing day, not quieter. Soon, Maggie knew, the police would come, with their nightsticks and whistles.

"They just want work," Leah said, sipping her tea. "There won't be a war."

"Texas has left the Union. That makes seven states," Maggie said. "Mr. Davis has issued a call to arms. I get a strange feeling when they put a photograph of Mr. Lincoln in the papers. . . ."

"Won't be a war," Leah insisted, echoing her husband's view.

"Perhaps," Maggie agreed wistfully. She thought of the afternoons she had spent with her mother under the evangelic tents, listening to preachers call for reform, for an end to poverty, to hatred, to the evil with which mankind was tainted. Their dreams and promises had vanished like morning mist. The world had neither ended nor transformed itself. The Savior had not reappeared.

"They got us instead," Maggie said, speaking her thoughts aloud, as had become her habit, since Elisha's death.

"What?" Leah asked, frowning.

"Nothing. Just thinking. You know, this March is our thirteenth anniversary. From that night when we dropped apples on the floor."

"When the spirits first spoke to us," Leah corrected. "Did you read about the Hatch girl in yesterday's papers?" Pretty, blonde-ringleted Mrs. Cora Hatch had lectured on Spiritualism at the New York Philosophical Society of Mechanics Institute, and communicated with Mozart, Beethoven, Handel, and other harmonists of the spirit world. She'd been a hit with the crowd, to Leah's distress.

"We really started something, didn't we?" Maggie asked, half smiling.

"I'm sure I don't know what you mean." Leah put her nose higher in the air and glared out the window.

Maggie and Katie had started a macabre celebration of death: ghostly weddings between young women and the spirits of their dead fiancés; unmarried couples avoiding ostracism by claiming that their baby had been fathered on the women by a spirit; husbands who left wives upon the advice of spirits who pointed out true soul mates, who were usually younger, prettier women.

Newspapers were filled with horrific tales of people who had murdered in the name of Spiritualism: Almira Bezely, who killed her baby brother; John Crowley, who killed his mother after a vision of the Summerland; Samuel Sly and Thankful Hersey, who clubbed Justus Matthews to death upon the advice of the spirits.

And the suicides: People were jumping out of windows and walking into deep rivers in their eagerness to be with the spirits.

Worse than murderers or suicides, in the opinion of many, were the Cleveland Spiritualists who believed in free love and built a cathedral for themselves in the shape of a human body, complete with all its orifices. They adopted the free-love platform and worshiped the naked human body because, so they said, spirits preferred unclothed people.

217

In Texas the papers stopped printing debates about Spiritualism because of the gunfights and riots that followed the editorials, so strong were the opinions of believers and nonbelievers alike.

"While some are crying against it as a delusion of the Devil, and some are laughing it as an hysteric folly, and some are getting angry with it as a mere trick of interested or mischievous persons, Spiritualism is quietly undermining the traditional ideas of the future state," wrote Oliver Wendell Holmes in the *New York Tribune*.

"You've had your cup of tea," Maggie said, closing the curtain on the twilight and the rioters. "Why have you come here, Leah? You know Elisha does not want me to spend time with you. If it weren't for you, Elisha and I never would have quarreled. He never trusted you, you know. Still doesn't. Neither do I."

Leah watched as Maggie poured whiskey into her empty teacup.

"Early, isn't it?" she commented.

"Not by my standards."

"All couples quarrel, sister. Mr. Kane merely needed an excuse."

"Which you readily provided. He speaks to me, you know. He warns me against you."

Leah carefully placed her teacup on the table. She had come, as she did every month or so, to ask Maggie to join her in séances. Married to her banker, safe from poverty and hard times, Leah wanted more than wealth, more than security. She craved fame. She held séances and gave sittings, but too often the results were disappointingly predictable and lackluster, no better than a well-rehearsed chambermaid could produce. Leah hated disappointing her friends. She needed Maggie and Katie, who, even if their tricks were a little dated, still were the most famous mediums in the country. People believed them, and in them, simply because they were Maggie and Katie, the little mothers of Spiritualism.

Perhaps Maggie and Katie were more talented because they had started young, when their joints were still supple. Perhaps, like acrobats and ballet dancers, Spiritualists must begin training early in life. Leah had been a grown woman when she learned the rapping technique. The little thuds she made, when she could make them at all, were barely audible. And her other techniques could be bought a dime a dozen: special, rigid shoes that tapped out the most noise with the least movement; telescoping rods for moving objects in dark rooms; trumpets that descended from a false ceiling; hands that crept out of boxes placed over hollowed-out tables; luminous paint that made any mundane object seem otherworldly once the gaslights were turned down.

But these tricks were commonplace. Leah needed Maggie for authenticity. And, it would seem, Maggie was more authentic than even Leah had thought.

"If Mr. Kane speaks with you . . ." She spoke very slowly. ". . . If he does, why will you not conduct séances with me, at my house?"

"He does not approve of you, Leah."

"He is dead," Leah hissed, leaning forward. The feathers in her hat drooped over the teapot and trailed in the sugar bowl.

"I know that," Maggie insisted, moving the sugar bowl out of harm's way. It was of thin porcelain, and if Leah broke it, it would be expensive to replace. She was beginning to horde the china she had bought to please Elisha; inflation was driving prices up so badly she knew her next dishes would be the cheap, thick pottery of her Hydesville childhood.

"Marry again. You've still got your looks," Leah said.

"I don't want to marry again. Go home. I will not sit with you. And you need rest," Maggie pointed out. Leah had not been able to produce an heir for the Underhill fortune. She had tried herbal teas, massage, spending entire weeks in bed, eating oysters by the bushel, to no avail. She and Mr. Underhill took seriously their duty to produce well-bred white Anglo-Saxon Protestant Americans so that the United States would not be overrun by foreigners and Catholics. Of the fact that her own sister, Maggie, had converted to Catholicism, Leah and Underhill did not speak.

In fact, she reflected bitterly, they spoke very little. "Don't worry your little head, it will produce headache," he said, whenever she inquired about his business, his politics, his gentleman's club, his winnings (or losses) at the card table, and the pretty young housemaids who were hired and fired at regular intervals. Perhaps it was through the housemaids (because of them!) that he had learned of Monsieur Desmoreaux's Preventive to Conception, and through their gossip that he had come to suspect Leah of using Desmoreaux's suppositories. It was an unfounded accusation and he apologized as soon as it had been made, yet the charge, the suspicion, hung between them, tainting their intimacy and making Leah constantly self-conscious about the unremitting flatness of her stomach.

"Yes," Leah said, rising. "I will rest. But I will come again next week, or send a message. We are family, after all. Mother would want us to be united." Mrs. Fox had died the year before; Leah, who had spent as little time as possible with her while she lived, referred to her often now that she was dead.

At the door, Maggie put a gentle hand on Leah's shoulder. "I hope God sends you a son," she said. "For your sake. And mine. A baby would make you happy and fulfill you."

"And then I would leave you alone? Yes, I would. So pray very hard, Maggie. Let's see if your Roman prayers are effective."

Just a moment after the door closed behind Leah, Maggie, clearing the table, heard a knock. Now, what had Leah forgotten? There was no glove, no umbrella, no brown-wrapped parcel left on the floor.

But it wasn't Leah. A man, tough, burly, unsmiling, and with bruised knuckles, stood on the threshold. Maggie knew him.

"I've already paid my landlady," Maggie said, trying to close the door on him. His huge, thick-shoed foot wouldn't let her.

"Ain't paid me," he said.

His eyes scanned the room. He swaggered to the table, helped himself to the thin wad of bills he found at the bottom of her shabby tapestry bag, tipped his hat, and was gone. The greedy, all-powerful Tweed Ring of Tammany Hall had found her and from now on a percentage of her earnings would buy their 'protection'; otherwise her clients might be blackmailed or séances would be disrupted by hooligans.

When he had left, Maggie sighed and knelt down to say her rosary. She was starting to feel nostalgia for the farm in Hydesville, for Mrs. Turner's Academy for Young Women, places where in her youth she had believed herself to be miserable. One can attend mass and say the rosary just so many times during the day. A promise of heaven helps, but there is also the threat of hell, and when prayers fall dead on the lips a different type of assistance is called for. The ruby-colored bottles of laudanum tincture were emptied faster and faster. Maggie, sighing, found the vial in her nightstand drawer and poured most of it into her cold cup of tea.

On April 15, 1861, war was declared. The city exploded in a ferment of flag-waving, parades, and victory predictions for the Union; the war would be over in a couple of weeks, was the popular consensus. President Lincoln called for seventy-five thousand volunteers to march against the Confederacy, promising they would be home again soon.

Maggie leaned out her window and watched the handsome, beardless boys parade in their new uniforms. She cheered because everyone else was cheering; she threw confetti. War is entertaining at first, when the fighting is done with brass bands, embroidered mottos, speeches, and farewell parties. Mothers dream of the medals to be displayed on the mantels, lovers take liberties undreamed-of in peace, brothers look forward to souvenir sabers that will be brought home.

Lines formed outside Maggie's door at the beginning of the

war, when people were so optimistic they wanted to know the future—the future at this time consisting of one question: How soon will he come back?

Then came the battles, the lists of dead and wounded, telegrams to nearest of kin, hospitals, sheets torn into bandages. The marching bands disintegrated, as one by one the musicians joined call-up regiments; the cobblers disappeared, and the bakers and the farriers and the delivery boys. New York became a city of women, children, and old men.

Maggie was left with just a handful of customers after the Confederate victory at Bull Run, when four thousand men were lost in a four-hour battle that left New York shaken and gloomy. People forgot it was supposed to be over in a matter of weeks, and fell into the rhythm of war: parades, speechmaking, victory, defeat, more parades, more victories, more defeat.

The lines outside the recruitment stands in Union Square, like the lines outside Maggie's door, shriveled and dried up like an earthworm on a hot sidewalk. Funeral processions took their place, and there was talk of conscription, though the women of the city complained that few-enough sons and fathers were left to protect the city.

Others celebrated—in private. A new breed of millionaires arrived, the war contractors who sold uniforms, weapons, and cheap coffins, who now drove in gilded carriages to the Band Concert in new, unfinished Central Park each Sunday even as growing armies of war widows, freed slaves, orphans, and one-armed or one-legged war veterans begged on every corner. Inflation pushed bread up to a dollar a pound, and eggs, when they were available, were two dollars for six.

New York's well-heeled Four Hundred, some of Maggie's best customers in better times, retreated to their comfortable country houses in green, rustic Harlem; those left in the roiling city had no cash for fripperies like talking with dead Aunt Mathilde who died of apoplexy, or Handsome Johnny who went to war and didn't come back. Masses of unemployed house servants joined the ranks of the newly poor. Maggie took in an Irish girl to help with the housework (the last one had left to work for a wealthier household); the girl agreed to work for room and board, no pay. She was a red-faced, bitter, silent creature who filled the small apartment with street pamphlets calling for money and clothing to send to Ireland, which was in the grips of the Great Hunger.

Maggie, her bank account almost empty, prayed for those starving in Ireland as well as the soldiers of both armies, read the pamphlets, then used them as kindling.

Flame seemed an appropriate metaphor. Burn. Down to the fingertips. Scorching, singing. Elisha had told her how, in the frozen North, he had dreamed of huge, crackling bonfires, and how frostbite started out as a burning sensation, then grew numb, then the toes and nose tip turned black, as if they had burned.

Maggie, during the difficult war years, wrote and published her memoirs, calling them *The Love Life of Dr. Kane*. She no longer had to fear reprisal from his family, as they had long since ceased sending her the small pittance they had allotted for her maintenance. They gave nothing, so there was nothing they could take away, no way they could hurt her.

The memoirs, despite the racy title, did not sell well. Perhaps if educated Elisha had been there to help her write . . . But he wasn't. Perhaps, in the midst of the war, Maggie's little scandal with Elisha seemed insignificant and old. Her time was passing by, she felt it racing, heard the whir of mortality's wings at her ears.

She changed addresses frequently, trying to find cheaper rooms, and to stay one step ahead of Boss Tweed's rent collectors, but they always found her. Maggie joined the demimonde, the whores and bookies, magicians and runaway servants of New York City who bought their liberty from the all-powerful Tweed, on the installment plan.

She took up traveling, north and south, east and west, anywhere people would pay a dollar a head to talk with the dead—anywhere Leah wasn't. Maggie always ended up back in New York, not because she loved it, but because she needed it.

> Oh! just, subtle, and mighty opium! that to the hearts of poor and rich alike, for the wounds that will never heal . . . bringest an assuaging balm . . . that . . . for one night givest back the hopes of his youth, and hands washed pure from blood; and to the proud man, a brief oblivion . . . thou hast the keys of Paradise, oh, just, subtle, and mighty opium!
>
> —THOMAS DE QUINCEY

Opium dens were no longer found just in Chinatown; the Tenderloin district had a long line of them, dark, sweetish-smelling places where the doorman didn't ask for names, just took the offered money and showed clients to a cot and a pipe. New words entered the American vocabulary, never to leave it: *dope* and *joint* and other verbal remnants of the opium craze.

Maggie used her share of the 105,000 pounds of opium imported annually from Turkey and China. She knew where the houses were; she knew which pharmacists sold the stuff; she had her own layout—the long pipe, the lamp, the brick of dope, the scissors used to cut out little pills, the scraper used to clean the pipe. She knew to save the ashes because the dregs could be smoked again on those nights when there wasn't money for good stuff.

On the evening of April 14, 1865, just as newly reelected President Abraham Lincoln was entering his private box at Ford's Theater in Washington, and wishing that instead he could be out walking in the warm spring air, Maggie was leaning out her window enjoying the same spring night.

She had just emptied a long pipe of opium, and the visions were already starting. Paradise surrounded her. Colors heightened.

Cat yowls turned to music. Street shadows danced a friendly country jig and the moon smiled at her.

She loosened her hair, letting the heavy black coils cascade over shoulders and face, and felt Elisha's hands combing through it, brushing it, loving it, in death as he had in life. She was at peace.

The room was thick with spirits. They jostled and pushed and poked and she had to soothe them with a song, since Elisha was shy of them. He did not approve of this crowd. She had a question for Elisha, a question he always evaded by disappearing just as she gathered the courage to ask: If she had reached Havana before his death, would there have been the wedding he promised?

Maggie sat in the dark, waiting for Elisha to speak. He seemed worried. He sat, stiff and slightly transparent, his white collar gleaming in the darkness, and the afternoon paper was under his foot. President Lincoln was the cover-page photograph once again. Maggie picked up the paper and shivered.

"Why, dear? What is it?" Maggie crooned. The silence, if anything, had grown even more silent; the darkness, darker. Suddenly she was alone. The spirits had been called elsewhere; something bigger was afoot than a lonely woman's questions. This silence had happened before—usually on the eve of the great battles and massacres; once before a stock-market crash; and again when her neighbor had been robbed and left to bleed to death on her way home from the butcher's.

What was happening tonight? Suddenly she missed Washington—how jealous dear Elisha had been of those senators and congressmen who sat in the dark with her! She was overcome by a strange longing to visit that popular theater she had never had time to visit. Ford's.

Maggie closed her eyes and imagined President Lincoln, the Great Emancipator, sitting in his theater box, proud and very, very alone. His eyes were closed. There was blood on his frilled evening shirt.

Maggie screamed.

CHAPTER
TWENTY-TWO

$\mathcal{N}$ot a total fraud," had been Jude's summation of Maggie. "Wouldn't you like to have a cup of tea and a chat with her? Today, she'd be a subject in paranormal experiments. She saw Lincoln's death, you know. Tried to warn him. Sent a letter to Washington. No response. Do you think anyone tied to warn Kennedy?"

Jude, do you remember what you were doing on the day JFK took his last ride through Dealy Plaza? Senior Latin honors class; working on a translation of Virgil's *Georgics,* you told me once: "'Above our heads the zenith always towers, beneath our feet is dark Styx where the lower ghosts behold the nadir...'" You remembered it all those years later when, before my cozy hearth, we talked of the assassination of dreams. I had been skipping my chem class, sitting in an ice-cream parlor and wondering why the deejay had interrupted "Smoke Gets in Your Eyes," when the report began. I cried.

I am thinking of JFK because he taught us much about mortality and the ending of millennia. Perhaps time is infinite and events occur over and over; soon Lincoln will be shot. Then, a hundred years later, JFK will be shot, and a few decades after that, I'll meet Jude and we'll talk about what we were doing that day. We'll make love for the first time, again.

I've worked through another night and day, and every muscle in my body is stiff with cramp and cold. But there's a different quality to the air. Its sharp edges are gone; it doesn't tingle the nostrils to breathe in. Instead, a wet, raw smell, the perfume of spring, is seeping into my workroom. I can hear water dripping. It's a miracle day. There's a thaw. Winter, finally, is in retreat.

With the curtains pulled back, the view out my window, past the bars of melting icicles, is encouraging. The sky is a clear, faultless blue with clouds fluffy and white as a child's drawing of them, and the snow in the field is almost visibly receding. When I stand, my head swims a little and I clutch carefully at the handrail as I make my way down the staircase, through the dining room and kitchen, to the mudroom.

With eyes half closed from sleepiness, I reach for Jude's coat but instead of soft cloth my fingertips feel empty space, then the hard wood of the closet. The coat isn't here. I must have worn it and left it draped over a chair somewhere.

I'll worry about it later. First I want to get out of the workroom, out of the house, out of winter, into the first afternoon of spring. I have lived in a world of gray-and-white for too long. My eyes are hungry for color, for the green of pine and the red of cardinals and the ochers and golds of last fall's leaves.

Outside, though, reality has betrayed me once again. The garden and forest are still a dreary sepia print of death and loss. It will be weeks before the yellow daffodils and forsythia bloom, before the ferns unroll their green, feathery stalks, or the purple crocus sticks its head out of the muddy beginnings. The snow is melting, but spring exists only as a green fragrance.

I walk toward the shadowed forest, inhaling the air in great gulps and moving heavily through the thawed field, now spongy and dangerous with mole holes and fallen branches. My legs feel unpracticed at this art of moving through space. Suddenly I have an overwhelming feeling that Jude is with me, staring at my back, pulling at my sleeve. I turn to him, smiling, joyous. But no one is there. Stillness reigns. I am alone.

Breathing a little more shallowly, I stride deeper into the forest, stepping over fallen, half-rotted pines, avoiding moss-slippery rock piles where snakes hibernate. When I miss my footing and stumble on a rock, I fall to my knees and rest like that, trying to calm myself in this great pagan cathedral of a forest. Hidden eyes watch me.

This article must be finished soon. I must finish, and return the library books and the archive manuscripts, store the disks, file the notes, get Maggie Fox out of my life. I am weary to the bone, and with more than the stress of a deadline. I am tired of questions, of longing, of life itself. I am too tired to continue this walk. With the damp cold seeping through my clothes, I rise and turn back the way I came, through forest and field. When I reach the place where I have seen the stag, I stop and look up at the house, as he does. The setting sun glares against the windowpanes, making the glass almost opaque, yet I see someone in my room, sitting at my desk. It's a man, wearing Jude's coat.

It's Jude.

He's looking at me. He lifts his hand in the same halfhearted, sad wave he gave me at the airport when he was about to board the plane to Rome. I lift my arm to wave back, I mouth the words *Wait for me!* then run toward the house. I look down at the ground, unsure of my footing as I run, and when I look up again he is gone.

Wind sighs and stirs the pine branches. The biggest trees groan in protest and where they grow too close together there is a kind of wail as they rub against each other. The window is empty, a frame with the painting cut out of it. Clouds shift overhead, changing the light, and setting sun again turns the window orange and opaque.

Defeated, I trudge back to the house.

Maybe I didn't want to see him badly enough? This is the game disappointed children play by the Christmas tree after the packages are all open and that one most desired gift is not there.

In the kitchen, sipping a cup of tea laced with scotch, a new panic overwhelms me. I can hear water beneath my feet, beneath the floor, swirling and gurgling and pouring. " 'We are as water spilt on the ground,' " Jude said. Oh Christ. The thaw is flooding the basement and the sump pump isn't working.

The cellar has a fieldstone foundation, and I can tell from the gurgling and rushing sounds beneath my feet that the water is high enough, strong enough, to cave in a wall unless I do something now. In the mudroom again I pull on tall rubber boots, grab a flashlight, and with all my strength yank up the heavy trapdoor that leads to the cellar. I put my foot on the first step, which is still dry, and hesitate.

When I first moved into this house, this cellar terrified me. The fusebox is down here, and much wiring and plumbing, but whenever I had to come here I would sweat in fear. Even during the day it is pitch-black down here. At night, which it is now, it is blacker than black. There are snakes down there in the summer, and probably rats in the winter. And the door could come loose from its chain and slam down, locking me in . . . like Maggie in the cellar . . . Don't think like that.

Flashlight in hand, I clomp down the eight concrete steps, into the darkness. And where the round circle of the flashlight lands, I see a torrent of muddy water that is two feet deep and swirling in a small, dangerous whirlpool around the furnace. A fountain of water pours down one of the walls: thawed snow seeping through the stones. It's a nice effect for a hotel lobby but dangerous for an old house; some of the stones in the foundation are already bulging out.

The water is over the top of my boots and they fill with wet and slime, becoming heavier with every step as I make my way to where the sump pump is, or should be. It's completely underwater. Little bastard. I plunge my hand into the dark, icy water, fumbled, find the switch, and with a diseased, death-rattlelike gurgling the pump starts up.

The cellar is small, only ten by ten, and in just a couple of minutes, the flood starts to recede, inches down the walls and then the sloping floor, as the pump chugs and sputters. When the water is down to my ankles I take off the rubber boots, turn them upside down to empty them, and stand there in my sodden socks, shaking with exhaustion.

Back upstairs, where my sodden socks leave wet footprints on the kitchen floor, I pour a hefty glass of whiskey. This has not been a good day.

I'm standing there in my sodden socks and jeans, shivering, pondering, when I feel a hand lightly touch my shoulder. I jump a foot into the air.

It's Douglas, standing there and beaming in a blazer and creased trousers. Thursday.

"Sorry," he says. "I knocked, but you didn't answer the door. I let myself in the kitchen door, to make sure you were all right."

"Christ, you scared me."

"Didn't mean to. Hey, this gives 'casual' new meaning," he grins, taking in my wet clothes and mud-smeared face.

"Problem with the sump pump in the cellar. It's been that kind of day." I pour a second glass for Douglas and wipe a strand of hair out of my eyes.

"The thaw has flooded the streets downtown," he says, taking the glass and eyeing it warily. "That's a generous pour. You been drinking like this for long?"

"Don't lecture me," I snap.

"Sorry. Didn't mean to. It's just . . ." His voice dies away.

"I know." And suddenly, I do know. He cares for me. Beyond the initial lust and despair of our first meeting. Something else is growing, forming in the darkness of solitude and reaching for the light. I take his hand and kiss it. His thick, callused fingers seem strangely vulnerable.

Douglas blushes and sneezes, and I stare at the muddy footprints I've made on the kitchen floor.

"You've got a cold."

"Just a little one. No problem. But you should get into some dry clothes, I think."

"Yeah. Look, instead of going out, I'll cook. I've got some pasta, chicken in the freezer, stuff for salad, I think."

"I'll help."

Another silence. This time I catch Douglas staring at my eye, the scar. My hand goes up to it, to hide it.

"No," he says, taking my hand and moving it away from my face. He touches the scar gently, as if to smooth it out. "It wasn't that. It's the mud. Maybe you should have a shower, and I'll start dinner."

Later, Douglas paces back and forth in front of the empty fireplace.

"Damp is coming up from the cellar," he complains. "Be sure and check the sump pump again tomorrow."

"Right. You sound like a homeowner. Are you? I know nothing about you, Douglas Howard." He comes and sits next to me on the sofa.

"Right. I am a homeowner. Renovated Arts and Crafts style bungalow on Willow Drive."

"Sounds classy. And expensive."

"It was a bargain. A fixer-upper, which, you may have noticed, I am pretty good at."

"And you live alone, Mr. Howard?"

"No, I have four wives and twelve children."

"Just asking. Tell me more."

"I'm working on my PhD in architectural history. Have been for about six years."

"Aha. A laggard graduate student. A specialist in architecture and fixer-upper projects could come in handy. Why architecture? Why not political science, say, or physical therapy?"

"I think I like houses better than people. Better than most people, at least. Houses are predictable. Build a wall, it stays a wall. People . . . that's another story."

"This house isn't so very predictable."

"Still hearing the noises?"

"Almost every night."

"Maybe you need less time alone. By the way, it's freezing in here. Shouldn't we have a fire?"

"No. No fire." The empty hearth is an act of fidelity.

CHAPTER
TWENTY-THREE

$\mathcal{S}$trange fevers arise from battlefields—the most dangerous part of any slaughter occurs after the fact, when the dead are left strewn among the living and the miasma of hate mixes with the needs of life.

After the Civil War, the battlefield fever that shook the United States was Spiritualism, and Maggie's star was again ascendant. Half a million had died, leaving behind widows, mothers, sisters, fathers, brothers—all mourning, all desperate to communicate with the beloved. And in the cold winter of 1872, Maggie, almost respectable in new clothes and better-quality rooms than she had been able to afford during the war, opened the door to one of her most famous visitors.

She came attended by a single maid who would not enter

Maggie's parlor but stood in the doorway, patient and wary as a watchdog.

"Good child. Wait there," the visitor instructed her maid, and without waiting for an invitation, sat heavily in a chair. "I have been told you can bring me messages from my dead husband," she said. Her voice was weak; her plump fingers in their black kid gloves trembled.

Maggie sat opposite her. "I can. But I usually receive several people at one time."

"I insist on complete privacy."

Maggie considered. The visitor's clothes were neither new nor stylish, yet there was an air of wealth, of privilege, about this widow. In response to Maggie's inspection, the woman lifted her veil. Maggie instantly recognized the long, narrow eyes, puffy face and full double chin of Mary Todd Lincoln.

"Yes," Maggie said. "We will have privacy."

Maggie poured a cup of tea for Mrs. Lincoln and waited while the guest finished it with breathless, noisy sips. Then, she stood and dimmed the gaslights. The curtains were already tightly drawn. Comforting semidarkness descended on the parlor. Maggie walked around the room several times on tip-toe, thinking, considering, waiting. Before each session she felt an uncomfortable tightness in her chest, and could not begin until that knot had loosened and words were already beginning to form in her head. In this way, she believed, God worked through her, sending His spirit to guide her so that she might help others. Her own conversion and the brutal war had convinced Maggie that despite her tricks, she was a conduit to divine energy, to God. She believed.

When she finally sat down, she took Mrs. Lincoln's hands in her own. She closed her eyes in concentration, and held the hands tightly, alternately stroking and grasping the fingers.

"Oh, my. I feel such a strange sensation. It almost makes me dizzy. What are you doing?"

"Close your eyes," said Maggie. "Your nerves must be calmed, if you are to speak with one on the other side. I think the forces are strong enough that we will dispense with the spirit alphabet and ask the spirit to speak directly through me."

"Yes," agreed Mrs. Lincoln. "Yes."

And so Maggie held the widow's hands and comforted her with loving messages from her dear departed husband, Abraham. The messages were not difficult to focus; Mrs. Lincoln's beloved son, Tad, had died just months before. She needed comfort and reassurance that Tad was happy in heaven with his father. She was still wounded by charges made years before that she had stolen the White House silver, depressed by her lack of friends, anxious about money. She needed advice about her health.

"Your heart is not strong, my dear," Maggie said slowly and in a deep voice, as a husband would. "You must take care of yourself. Excessive grief will harm you. I recommend a resort."

"I have been having palpitations. Would you name a place?" asked the widow, eyes still tightly shutly, hands still clenched in Maggie's.

"Waukesha. Wisconsin," said Maggie after considering. Leah had gone several years before, still seeking the elusive victory of pregnancy. It hadn't worked, and now Leah was too old for babies but she still remembered the resort with some fondness. She had enjoyed herself there, away from Underhill's demands and annoying habits.

"Wisconsin, then," said Mrs. Lincoln who, like other war widows, had grown fond of traveling. Enemy lines and privation had held them as captive as surely as the prisoners of war and the freedom to travel was a prize of peace.

"What else do you have to say to me, Abraham?" the widow asked two hours later. Maggie had been silent for some moments. She was tired and emptied. Yet somehow this session had not finished itself.

"I . . . I," Maggie stuttered. "Wait." She rose, fetched a piece of paper and pen, and sat back down. "Put your hand over mine.

Help me write," she said in her own voice. "There is another message, but I am having trouble. It needs to be written."

Together, the two woman's hands and the one pen rested on the paper. Slowly, of its own will, it started to move. Maggie held her breathe.

"L.A.M.O.N." the moving pen wrote. "Beware. Lies. Mother truly wed. Defend."

The pen fell and rolled across the table. Maggie slumped in her chair. Mrs. Lincoln rose unsteadily to her fate.

"Oh, it is as I feared! Have no fear, Mr. Lincoln, I will defend your reputation!"

Maggie stared at her, bewildered. Who was Lamon? How could he harm Abraham Lincoln's reputation?

"Thank you, thank you so much for warning me," said the widow, much relieved. "May I come back? May I see you again?"

"Of course," said Maggie. "Send a message and I will see there are no other visitors that afternoon. Any time I can give comfort, come."

She watched Mrs. Lincoln join the watchdog-maid and totter gingerly down the snowy sidewalk to her waiting carriage. The veil had been lowered; the famous face had been hidden once again. Maggie waved though no one in the carriage waved back.

Who was Lamon?

She discovered the answer two months later, when Ward Hill Lamon published a biography of Abraham Lincoln, asserting, among other faults and shortcomings, that the assassinated president had been born out of wedlock, that his religious values were deficient, that his own marriage had been forced and unhappy.

The name had just come to her, she recalled with satisfaction. Sometimes, it happened. (Not a total fraud, Jude whispers to me. Remember what William James wrote in *Varieties of Religious Experience*: "Many persons possess the objects of their belief not in the form of mere conceptions but in the form of quasisensible realities directly apprehended.")

Her success with Mrs. Lincoln led to other opportunities. A very wealthy, very eccentric Philadelphian named Henry Seybert invited Maggie to reside in his Spiritual Mansion, a fine city home appointed specifically to house mediums and their ghostly guests.

Maggie didn't like Seybert. His collar was so high and stiff it hurt her to look at it, and he wore a bow tie, an affectation which Elisha scorned. But his offer meant a salary, three squares a day, a feather bed, an upstairs maid, lace curtains, Turkish rugs, a rose garden for noontime meditations—all those little luxuries that her bitter, worn mother had yearned for thirty years before, in Hydesville.

"You will be the high-priestess of this new temple of unseen entities," Seybert promised. Maggie winked at her new maid and made faces behind her patron's back.

The arrangement was not a success. Like those who have lived hand-to-mouth for too long, Maggie could no longer enjoy luxury without qualms ("These pork chops must have cost a dollar each!" she commented at dinner. "I'll just save half of mine for later.") and the rich clientele irritated her. They were the very kind of people who had tried to turn Elisha against her. Maggie put her nose in the air and imitated them, even when they could see her mince and lift her little finger to mock. She gave her required sittings in the Spiritual Mansion with ill grace, and often she arrived in the séance room drunk and cantankerous.

Mr. Seybert gave out that Maggie was frequently pursued by mischievous spirits, hence her dark humors. She still drew a crowd, but more and more, the crowd was made of curiosity-seekers and one-timers who never came back for a second sitting.

Seybert correctly thought Maggie was a drunkard, and even a little loose in the head. She, just as correctly, thought he was gullible, foolish, and too wealthy for his own good. Matters between them came to a head when Seybert asked her to convey messages from the saints. Oh, sweet Jesus, Maggie said, crossing herself. Blasphemy! Socrates and Herodotus were pagans, after all, but she would not carry messages back and forth to Saint Anne or Saint Paul or the archangel Gabriel.

"Do not the saints have voices? Do they not deserve to be heard?" Seybert stormed.

"I will not," Maggie insisted. She also refused to manifest ectoplasm, the latest trend in Spiritualism, thanks largely to little sister Katie, who had spent the war years as the exclusive medium for a rich New York banker whose wife had died in 1860. Katie, after almost five years and five hundred sittings, had materialized the dead wife, brought her back, not just as a voice, or presence, or signature, but "in the flesh," as a full-figured phantom who held her husband's hand and stood framed in the large parlor window, an unearthly light illuminating her diaphanous robes.

Why wouldn't Maggie do the same for her clients? Seybert wanted to know. Gentle knocks patiently answering questions, ribbon-adorned trumpets descending from trick ceilings, magic slates that spirits left their brief messages upon—those were yesterday's manifestations. Sitters now wanted more concrete evidence that the spirits did indeed come back. In the more adventurous séances held elsewhere, entire parades of phantoms marched about the room and posed in otherwordly tableaus. Voices and messages were not enough; believers wanted flesh and blood as well, or at least the spirit equivalent of flesh and blood: ectoplasm.

Maggie eyed Seybert, wondering if he was mad or merely ingenuous. So-called ectoplasm was, in fact, no more than very fine, white netting hidden in books or hollowed bootheels. At the appropriate time, the medium's assistant would shed her clothes, drape herself in the netting, and appear from a closed closet or cabinet.

Or, the "spirit" would dress in black tights and leave visible only a single arm whose eerie paleness would be enhanced with luminous paint: a popular handbook for mediums listed eight recipes that would make mundane flesh glow in an unearthly manner.

Maggie would have nothing to do with it. In this, at least, Maggie still had a conscience. Words of comfort, of hope from the other side or a few timely insults when appropriate, were one thing. Tricks involving naked men and women draped in nets were another. Maggie refused to materialize phantoms, so Seybert helped her pack.

New York felt old and stale. And after too many years of wandering from rented room to rented room, of nights spent alone with gin dreams, strange things started to happen to Maggie. She would enter a room and see Elisha leaving through the other door; she would look up from the street and see Elisha sitting in the window, waiting for her. She could never catch up to him. She had grown stout and her heart wasn't strong. Her lungs were heavy with fluid and opium residue. Sometimes she heard his voice whispering in her ear. She set two places at table, put a second pillow on her bed.

"Is the soup hot enough?" she would ask, spoon in midair. "Isn't it a nice day? Shall we take a walk?" Sometimes he answered.

"She's soft in the head," the street children yelled back and forth. "Look, here comes Crazy Maggie! Maggie, talked to any ghosts today?"

Maggie Fox, founder of American Spiritualism, was more famous than ever; but Maggie Fox, who, like the rest of us, pays bills and feels gnawing hunger when meals grow sparse, became an oddity, an unkempt woman with messy hair and untied laces whom people crossed the street to avoid.

Leah, however, continued to pursue her with both threats and promises, trying to force Maggie's appearance at her Wednesday-evening Spiritualist receptions, whence gathered Horace Greeley, James Fenimore Cooper, John Greenleaf Whittier, Washington Irving, and other celebrities.

But Maggie refused to join those gatherings, adhering to Elisha's request that she avoid the company of her scheming older sister.

She's a tigress, Elisha whispered in her ear. Watch out for her.

Maggie was lonely. She had lost the bravado of youth and had learned to number the things there are to fear; she missed her little sister, who had started on this strange journey with her that night so many years ago in Hydesville, when they had dropped apples out of bed. Katie had gone off to England, married an English barrister and bore him two sons.

"Come," she wrote to Maggie. "I miss you." And Maggie, ever restless, began to dream of sea voyages, of seagulls overhead and whitecapped waves and the chimes of Big Ben.

In the winter of 1876 Maggie arrived in England, sponsored by a wealthy London physician, Dr. H. Wadsworth, who was eager to talk with inhabitants of the spirit world and believed two Fox sisters would be better than one.

Little sister Katie met her at the wharf.

"Oh, I'm so glad you're here," Katie said in her little-girl voice, running into Maggie's arms as soon as she had tottered down the gangplank. "I've been so lonely! No one to talk to, not really. The English scare me, use the wrong fork at dinner, and they'll talk about you for weeks! And they want so much from the spirits, so very, very much. You must help me, Maggie. You must. Boys, say hello to your auntie!"

Maggie, hat askew and breathless, hugged Katie, then stepped back and looked at the boys—tall for their ages, a little sullen-looking, but handsome enough in their serge sailor suits and caps. "Ain't they fine-looking?" Katie cooed. They rolled their eyes.

Maggie looked closely at the little sister she hadn't seen in many years. It was like looking into a mirror. They shared the same long, broad noses, thick, straight eyebrows, and turned-down mouths. The black hair was shot with gray, deep furrows lined the pale foreheads. They were even dressed alike, both in black crepe, seams strained at the waist, the little bit of brightening white lace at the neck limp from lack of starching.

"Katie," sighed Maggie. "Oh, Katie. How we both have changed." They giggled.

"They don't look at my ankles anymore," Maggie whispered behind her hand so that the boys wouldn't hear. "Remember when they used to tie our ankles with their handerchiefs, and the men in the audience would almost break their necks, trying to see more?"

"Oh, you look fine," Katie cooed, fingering Maggie's new black picture hat and the little false ringlets of horsehair that hung down the sides of Maggie's face.

"And you, too," said Maggie, wondering if she looked as awful as her sister. Little slender Katie had grown fat and red-faced. Her fingers were plump as overfilled sausages.

"Let's get to our digs," Maggie said, looking for a porter. "I could use a glass. And then we'll discuss the sittings." Arm in arm, the two boys following behind, the sisters walked to a cab stand to find porters for Maggie's trunks.

"The sittings," Katie echoed. "We'll have to talk about that."

Spiritualism was as popular in England as in the United States, and Katie gave séances—at first because her husband, a firm believer in Other Worlds, had wished her to, and because her celebrity had assured her coveted invitations to country-houses (where Gilded Age youths and Regency dowagers discussed Oscar Wilde's latest witticism and Lily Langtry's scandalous doings), and to midnight suppers in London where the guest of honor was always titled and clattering with metals.

But Katie's husband, Mr. H. D. Jencken, although a barrister, had no knack for earning and much for spending, and soon Katie was giving seances for the old reason: to earn money. She had an expensive rented townhouse near the Crystal Palace, an upstairs and a downstairs maid, and her sons' educations to plan. And she had legal expenses.

Katie had been arrested several times for drunk-and-disorderly behavior. Like Pa Fox, like Maggie, Katie had found comfort in strong spirits.

"It is expected that a little bit of ectoplasm be produced during a sitting—a hand rising from a box, a shadowy figure seen dancing behind a gauzy curtain, a shimmering unworldly face reflected in the Pier Glass Mirror," Katie explained as soon as they were home, and the gin poured.

"Nice parlor," Maggie said, trying to change the subject. She unbuttoned the top of her blouse to breathe easier and put her feet on a velvet ottoman.

"Maggie, anybody can crack their toes and bounce the table around," Katie said. "More is expected." Her voice ended on a high, peevish note.

Maggie looked at her and tried to see the sweet little sister who had cowered under the coverlet in their shared bed in Hydesville, frightened by the scarecrow flapping in the cornfield. She saw only a thick-waisted, middle-aged matron with a peevish face.

"It's sinful," Maggie insisted. "Elisha wouldn't like it."

"Then let Elisha pay the bills," Katie snorted. That ended the quarrel. That evening a spirit (a pretty actress down on her luck and willing to appear dressed only in her underthings with a little gauze over them) paid a visit to Katie's London townhouse, and permitted three of the gentlemen clients to kiss the pale, iridescent hand she poked through the heavy black curtains hiding her.

The evening was a success, but Maggie's conscience pricked her. Do spirits have to be young, pretty, and half-naked girls? How will trickery of this sort bring believers closer to God?

The next séance cast Maggie into a worse funk of black mood and prickly conscience, for Katie insisted on making a spirit picture for one of the sitters. Glumly Maggie watched all that morning as an artist (down on his luck, like the actress) painted a nicely executed portrait of Mrs. Wendell Rishelm, who was to call that evening. He used special paints—tannin for black, sulphocyanide of potassium for red, sulphate of iron for blue, all chemicals which became invisible as they dried on the canvas. The artist was paid and ushered out, no questions asked or answers provided, and by late afternoon the framed canvas looked dusty, a little muddy, but the portrait had disappeared completely.

"Spray this over it," Katie said, showing Maggie a little copper fern-mister. "When the portrait is wet again, the picture will show up. Put this up your sleeve. I'll make a diversion, and you spray the painting when they're not looking at it."

"You're a fraud," Maggie said. Katie slapped her.

They were both tipsy, as Katie liked to say. Rip-roaring smashed, her sons said. Between the two, Katie and Maggie had emptied a large bottle of gin. They slumped deep into the red cushions of the settee, their legs sprawled on fringed ottomans, their black skirts twisted up to their knees and revealing runs and holes in their knitted stockings. The already dark, heavy atmosphere of the room was blue with smoke from the little cigars they enjoyed in private. ("Strange. Herbert never smoked in this life. Why did he take it up in the Other Place? I know I smelled cigar smoke in the sitting room," Lady Bushnell had said just the other day.)

The sisterly reunion was not successful. Katie resented Maggie's holier-than-thou attitude, and Maggie despised Katie's cheap trickery. Silences grew thick and long.

And for Maggie, there was neither safety nor salvation in London, with actresses coating themselves with iridescence, portrait painters moonlighting as envoys of other worlds, and the local constabulary waiting in line for their bribes. There was deceit and gin and cynicism.

Worse for Maggie, London was crowded with phantom Elishas, thin, pale men with dark beards, top hats, and canes, who strode confidently down Bond Street and St. James and through Trafalgar Square, their chins high, their shoes polished, the silver heads of their canes gleaming. They never stopped when she called, "Elisha!" They never slowed down and let her catch up. Maggie chased these phantoms down streets and lanes thick with yellow fog, through the pews of incense-smoky churches, through the bawdy entertainments of Piccadilly. All of this exercise and stimulation left her breathless. Maggie's heart began to skip and leave her dizzy.

Unhappy, irritated by Katie's antics at the séances, her conscience and Elisha's voice constantly pricking her, Maggie left London and returned to New York.

She spent another another decade on her own, wandering from rented room to rented room, growing older, more disillusioned, lonelier. And then, in 1888, a letter came from Katie. Leah was trying to take custody of her boys. Mrs. Fox-Jencken, the letter stated, was a harmful influence on her children, which meant her children were to be taken from her to be raised by Leah Underhill.

Did Leah really want the boys? Perhaps she merely wished vengeance on Katie and Maggie, who had deserted her and, worse, were more famous in stylish London than she was in old-hat New York.

Whatever Leah's reason, Maggie, more than anything in this world, hated bullies. Elisha's family were bullies. Tweed's rent collectors were bullies. And now Leah was bullying Katie who, despite what the years had made of her, was still the youngest, the most vulnerable of the three sisters.

Whatever intent, whatever emotion Leah had surrendered to when she instructed her lawyer to send that letter, she would have ample cause to regret. Maggie would see to that. No more little battles. This would be war.

CHAPTER
TWENTY-FOUR

I get up from my desk and turn off the worklight. I sit in the dark, very quietly. I imagine Jude downstairs in the kitchen, moving around. I'm sorry, I tell him in my thoughts. You were right, Rome wasn't a good decision. I shouldn't have badgered you to go, shouldn't have been so proud.

"I knew Jude," Douglas says the next day, sitting at my kitchen table. We're eating cheese sandwiches and drinking strong coffee. On the floor, next to him, is a new bucket of yellow paint. He's going to paint the upstairs room, he says. A freebie. Well, not quite a freebie. I have to go with him to the senior prom. A joke, he says. Laugh.

And then: "I knew Jude," Douglas repeats.

"Pardon?"

"I knew Jude," he repeats. He looks at the expression on my face and speaks a little slower, more clearly, as if I'm hard of hearing. "It's a small town. Your relationship wasn't exactly a secret. And I know Madelyn. She's on the historic-preservation board."

We are still sitting at the table, coffee cups in hand, birds chirping outside the window, but the room seems to have shifted. I feel off balance. I should have tried to get some sleep last night.

"I didn't mean to upset you," Douglas says. "But . . . I thought you should know. I don't want blank spots and silences. I would like to get to know you very, very well, but it has to go both ways."

"Yes," I agree. "I should know. You were Madelyn's lover?" *My friend,* Jude had said. *My ex-friend.* Douglas?

"It was all a mistake. Okay, not all a mistake. I enjoyed it. I cared for her. I knew she was married. I was friends with Jude. But she came over to my apartment one night, I was still just an undergrad. She and Jude had quarreled about something. Summer camp or a private tutor for the kids or something like that. I was part of her revenge. She stayed the night. Came again. I got kind of attached. And by then, Jude had met you."

"She was pretty," I said.

"Very. And fun, too. I know how you must feel about her . . ."

"Stop saying you know how I must feel."

"I can imagine how you feel about her, but she was a human being, and a kind of nice one at that."

"Jude thought she was a bitch." He called her that, once: Bitch. She had phoned and screamed at him about . . . what? I can't remember the details of that scene, only that it was months before Jude was to go to Rome and he had grown quiet and pale with worry.

"Jude only said that," Douglas says. "What did you expect the husband to say about the wife in front of his mistress?"

Ah. This young man knows how to wound. At that moment

I realize that he cares for me, he hasn't come over just to discuss paint. But Jude . . .

"That was unnecessary. Jude was going to divorce Madelyn when he returned from Rome. We were going to get married. More coffee?"

Douglas clears his throat a second time. "Better bring out the whiskey," he says. "Jude wasn't going to divorce Madelyn. He was going to stay with Madelyn. She wanted to get back together. End the separation, work harder at the marriage. She'd try if he would try. He said he'd think about it. Then, after he left, he sent her a letter from Rome. He wanted her to give up her lover. And he would give up his. There would be no divorce."

"How could you know that?" I am numb.

"She showed me the letter. It was the last time I saw her . . . except for meetings of the historical-preservation committee, of course."

I tilt my head to look out a window, where fussy white curtains frame an aquamarine sky. Such a pretty day. All winter, for months now, I've been waiting for a beautiful day like this, a day that promises spring and sweetness and some future better than the past few years have been. And now it's spoiled. I lost the future three years ago, and now I've lost the past. It never really existed, not as I knew it, because as soon as Douglas has said it, I realize I knew it all along. And so did Jude. He wouldn't divorce Madelyn. Christ, I'm stupid.

"That thaw was a surprise, yesterday," I say.

"Not really. It was forecast on the Weather Channel." Douglas is still speaking very carefully, watching me too intently.

"I don't watch TV. I think I'll get the bottle of scotch."

"Two glasses. Please," he says.

I come back, and pour. We sit at opposite ends of the table, as far from each other as possible, nursing tall glasses of scotch, staring at the glasses so we won't have to meet each other's eyes.

"You should have told me before," I finally say.

247

"When? When I first picked up the phone and didn't even know who was calling? When I came with Sheetrock? 'Hi, I'm here to fix your wall and to tell you your lover wasn't going to marry you.' Right. I couldn't find the time. Not till today. And I guess this was the wrong time, too."

"No, it wasn't. You were right to tell me. But . . ."

"I guess you want to be alone. I should leave."

He sits there, staring at glass of scotch, his eyebrows knitting back and forth.

"Are you sure you want me to leave?" he says.

"No. But leave anyway."

When Douglas is gone, I pace from room to room. "Come out!" I yell. "Show yourself. Explain yourself! Jude!"

Silence. My own footsteps echoing. Make-believe is over.

An hour later, I sit alone watching out the window, until the afternoon turns to twilight and twilight turns to night. Things move in the darkness. Shadows a shade darker than the night itself flicker and disappear like black flame. Raccoons, maybe, or deer. Maybe the stag is back.

I've been drinking steadily, but my head feels clearer than ever. My thoughts are clear water, I can see through them to the bottom, where it is murky and thick with pity.

Jude was, essentially, a kind person. It was not his nature to hurt, to harm. He was gentle. And the last decision he ever had to make was deciding which woman to betray: his wife, who had legal and moral claim, or his scarred and frightened mistress who had come to depend completely upon him.

No wonder his conversations were filled with musings about loyalty and duty. But perhaps that wasn't it at all. Perhaps he simply did not love me. Or was tired of me, disgusted by me. Perhaps he simply preferred Madelyn. I wrap my arms tightly around myself, shivering, lips clamped together to maintain the absolute silence that surrounds me.

~

At two in the morning, I'm still wide-awake. How shall I mark the anniversary of Jude's death? Before, I felt sorrow, guilt. Now there is also anger. I want to face him, accuse him, throw myself at him. We had promised honesty to each other. We had promised truth. I did not know it was possible to begin a new quarrel with someone who has been dead for three years. But Jude and I have a new quarrel.

You should have told me, I say aloud.

I sit, silent and still, willing him to speak, to show himself. The room grows colder and darker, but the emptiness, if anything, grows more complete. I am alone. But the answer comes to me. He knew how painful it would be and he was afraid of pain. Broken bones and bruises he could nurse, but not a broken heart.

You were a coward, I tell the empty room. Just like Maggie. Couldn't face reality. Instead you filled it with phantoms and lies.

I slept for four hours and woke to a silvered, slow dawn and a world filled with a new, even more painful reality than the old— the reality that Jude had left me and was never coming back.

Work. Finish Maggie's story. Don't think about love and lies. Jude chose loyalty and old vows; he fled back to safety, to known ways, and could not stay with me.

Some mornings, writing is like a gift, but this morning the words creep and hesitate, arthritic and unwilling. It takes an hour to produce six sentences based on stray thoughts, subjects and verbs and modifiers sulking in corners, refusing to come together, to mingle. When the phone rings I welcome the excuse to put my computer into sleep mode.

As I pick up the phone, I stand and push back the curtain over the window behind my desk. It's about ten in the morning and the sun is a promising gold ball hovering in the middle of the eastern horizon. The spring thaw has lasted.

"Hello?"

"Hi, Helen. It's me. Madelyn."

I sit back down.

"Madelyn." My voice is wooden, unfriendly.

"Yes, Madelyn. Don't say how pleased you are to hear from me, or anything ridiculous like that."

"I wasn't going to."

"I talked with Douglas. He called."

"I don't want to have this conversation," I say.

"I'm not exactly pleased about it either. But Douglas was rather insistent. At any rate, I wanted to explain about Jude. Douglas wants me to explain about Jude."

Silence. I can't think of anything to say.

"You're not making this any easier," she complains, in a voice I suddenly remember all too well. *Rise and shine, little adulterers. This is the wife calling.*

"Madelyn, I don't know how to make this easier. Not for either of us. Believe me."

"Okay, I'll just cut to the chase. He converted, you know. To Roman Catholicism."

"No," I say. "That was Maggie. Maggie converted to Roman Catholicism." My heart is pounding as if I've run up Piety Hill.

"Who? What are you talking about?"

"Nothing."

"He converted. He'd been thinking about it for a while, but when he went to Rome he made it official."

"He was the ultimate souvenir-shopper, wasn't he? First he brings you home from England, then in Rome he converts to Catholicism."

I hear Madelyn's ragged intake of breath. I've offended the widow of my dead lover. Must life be this complicated? I yearn for simplicity sometimes.

"It was always in him, you know, that religious part. I used to joke that he should have been a monk," she finally responds.

"Funny, that was never my impression of him."

"My dear, don't confuse sex with sexuality. Or with worldli-

250

ness. He converted. And when he was in Rome he decided he'd follow the rules. No divorce. I'll show you the letter, if you want."

"Was I suppose to be his Katharine Hepburn?"

For the first time, Madelyn laughs. "Something like that, probably. And I would play the patient, dutiful wife. Look, if it's any consolation, I think he just got temporarily unhinged by all that incense and architecture and masses in Italian. Midlife hits some men harder than others."

"You wanted him to stay with you."

Her turn to pause. "Yes. I did. He was my husband, after all."

Silence again.

"Will you come to the memorial?" she asks. "I think he would have wanted you to."

"I can't."

"Well, have a nice day." A click, a dial tone.

He betrayed me. For a little incense. For a bad church choir singing "Stabat Mater" on Good Friday. For ashes and palms and the sacraments. Forgiveness.

Forgive me. The words arrive in my head like flowers left on a doorstep. Jude's melodious voice. I shake my head.

No, I don't forgive you. You left me. Not once. Not twice. Three times. Elisha went to the Arctic, but he came back to do his dirty work, his betrayals, in person. You went to Rome and didn't come back.

The phone rings again. I glare at it, but it continues ringing.

The worst part of working at home is that people always know where to reach you. This time, when I bark a wary "Hello?" into the receiver, Alicia's high, fluting voice returns the greeting.

"You're avoiding me, Helen. I miss you."

I have forgotten how hard it is, this speaking to the living, to people who still believe in futures.

"I'm avoiding everybody," I say. "I have a major article to finish."

"Now I know you're avoiding me. You never used work as an excuse before. Is it because of Tom? Do you feel left out? You could join us, you know, I'm more than happy to share with my best friend."

I laugh, as she intended. "It's not because of Tom. Yes, it is. In a way. It's like you've gone through the looking glass, Alice. I can't follow. I can only watch and feel shut out. It's dismal. It's true that misery loves company, two people speaking the same emotional language. You have a language now I don't have. I have forgotten it."

"Good. I think, my friend, you have finally moved on to the next stage of mourning. I think soon you will join life again. You are beginning to want. Come back, Helen, you've been living with the dead for so long."

"When we bury the dead, we go into the grave with them, for a while."

"The Orpheus myth. But the living come back to the living."

I can't tell Alicia that Jude chose Madelyn. That he left me in every way that a man can leave a woman.

"See you soon," I say.

If I had to define reality now, I could not. Truth is a guess we make based on faulty perceptions. Death is irrelevant since the dead come back to wound us; they are more effective at that dead than when still alive.

The phone rings a third time. Enough. I really do have work to do. I let it ring till the answering machine takes over with a click and whir of tape winding itself, and Douglas's voice fills the room.

"Helen? Are you there? Helen, call me, will you? We have to talk. I'm worried about you. Call me, please."

Later. Maybe. I pull the phone cord out of the jack.

Love creates its own hierarchy of happiness. There are those at the summit who meet, fall, win each other, quarrel just often enough and bitterly enough to enjoy ending the quarrel, and have many years together to learn the dance of intimacy. They are worlds unto each other. Those in the middle of the hierarchy meet, fall, and win each other, but either they love unequally, or they are unable to pull out completely the poisoned darts left after each quarrel. They stay together, but they grow bitter and love looks more like habit.

At the bottom, you'll find Maggie and me. Women like us meet men and learn to love and then something goes very, very wrong. There is a death, or a scandal, a betrayal, an illness. Something steps between us and love, and puts up a plate-glass window so that we can look, but not touch. And we never really get over it. We are the ones who make others feel lucky.

CHAPTER
TWENTY-FIVE

*O*nce Maggie decided to confront and destroy Leah, she went to no little effort to make that decision incarnate.

Maggie was going to put a stop to it. She would give the death blow, as her memoir termed it, to Spiritualism. Another era was about to end. The millennium was coming, and truth would be its prow, its masthead, just as Elisha had always said.

And Maggie was so very tired. She had tried to bring comfort to others and to keep herself out of the poorhouse, but her deceit had been costly. She had lost Elisha and herself. Now she would save Katie's children, regain her soul, destroy Leah . . . and in the process, earn a sizable fee for the performance: Promoters were once again backing her.

What a coup! Margaret Fox-Kane, founder of American Spiritualism, was going to prove, in public, that it was all a hoax! It would be like the old days in the lecture halls of Rochester, with the smell and sizzle of gaslights and sweat and expectation rising from the audience, except now she was going to show that the dead do not speak. It would be, for the audience, the revelation of a lifetime.

And for Maggie, what a revelation to learn that you can be paid for truth as well as a lie, and at the same time destroy an enemy! Leah, who had established a chapel in her parlor for the spirits, who had built a large and reverent following based solely on her reputation as one of the Fox sisters, who was received in many upper-crust homes and ballrooms because of this reputation, would be destroyed.

It had been spring when Maggie Fox arrived in New York City for the first time. It was a bone-chilling autumn when she arrived for the last time.

On the windy, blustering evening of October 21, 1888, a crowd of fifteen hundred people sardined themselves into the Academy of Music, the largest entertainment hall in New York City, to see a very well advertised demonstration by Margaret Fox-Kane, founder of American Spiritualism.

America's love affair with the spirits was about to be sorely tested.

The crowd would not be friendly. Because of Maggie, they had been happily speaking with the dead, tilting tables, rapping at walls, and displaying spirit portraits on the parlor mantelpiece. They would not be eager to hear they had been deceived by an ignorant farmgirl.

However, they had come not for proof of truth, not for an end to deception, but to witness yet another spectacle. It would be the best entertainment in town that night. Maggie's new promoters had placed ads in all the papers for weeks beforehand, and other performers had taken the night off, knowing audiences would be sparse or nonexistent this evening, except for the crush down at the Academy.

As on earlier occasions, police were called in to restrain the crowd; when Maggie descended from the hired cab, one of them opened the door for her and helped her down. He was young, with cruel eyes. He pushed a program under her nose.

"Sign it. For the kids," he said. "Wait'll they hear I met Maggie of the Spirits." But the crowd pushed so thickly against them she dropped the pen he provided, and it was trampled underfoot. A wave of humanity pressed her into the theater. She felt as though she were drowning. River Jordan, wash my sins away! she prayed.

Maggie—as always, dressed in her dismal widow's weeds, her only reminder that she had once been loved by Elisha Kent Kane—was not cheered and applauded when she walked onstage, as she had been on earlier occasions. She was greeted with a silence as vast and hostile and cold as the air of Baffin Bay. (*Take courage, dearest,* she heard Elisha whisper in her ear.) A few rotten tomatoes flew with admirable aim from balcony to stage, landing close enough to Maggie's bare feet to make her wish she'd had another glass of gin before leaving her dressing room.

She peered out over the flickering gaslights into the darkness from whence arose a miasma of sweat and hatred. She was sober enough to feel fear and inebriated enough to see a few Elishas sitting out there, nodding sternly, prompting her.

She waved at him and smiled coyly.

The audience did not wave back. They saw a middle-aged woman with bloated features and slovenly attire flapping a soiled handkerchief at them. The first rows could see the calluses, bunions, split toenails, and chafed skin of her bare feet. The swollen ankles, snakelike varicose veins, were visible all the way up to the first cross-aisle. Did anyone in the audience remember, and still see, the young Maggie Fox, fresh from Hydesville, shining in her pretty youth and high spirits, with her pretty little bare feet?

Maggie, tottering a little, stood her ground and glared past the too-bright sunrise of the gaslights. All this, from dropping apples over the side of the bed and fooling Papa! She looked to the side, where Katie sat, teary-eyed and hopeful—Katie, fresh from England, alone, her sons taken from her as soon as she docked in New York and locked up somewhere in the bowels of the Society for the Prevention of Cruelty to Children, a branch of the animal-protection league, which now extended jurisdiction over children as well. Maggie smiled at Katie, who nodded back and dabbed at her eyes with her handkerchief. Katie looked frightened.

Maggie stood still and waited till the auditorium grew silent except for the occasional cough and jeer. Then, carefully, she took her skirt in her hands and lifted the hem up to her knees, just to make sure everyone could see.

"This is how it's done," she called to the audience. Lips pulled back a little from the effort, she made a small, barely-perceptible movement with her right foot, then her left, then the right again. She seemed almost motionless. Yet raps sounded . . . from all over the hall—from stage right, stage left, even the balcony.

The audience watched and listened and was stunned.

Maggie, looking as if she was enjoying herself, repeated the raps for several minutes. Then, a committee of physicians was ushered onstage and invited to hold the erstwhile medium's feet and ankles. They did so with less enthusiasm than such an invitation had invoked years before: her ankles were swollen and a rank order of stale gin wafted from her dark clothes. Maggie sat stiffly upright in a chair thumped in place by a stagehand and the physicians knelt before her, their formal black evening coats trailing onto the stage like splashes of ink, merging with the ink of her dress.

Dr. Devarry, a pince-nez clamped onto his nose and white muttonchop whiskers framing his face, was closest to the audience, and it was his face many in the audience watched as Maggie began the rappings again. The noises were softer this time, because of the imprisonment of her feet. Dr. Devarry's expression changed from pompous self-importance to curiosity, to alarm, to anger. Finally, in the complete and outraged indignation possible only from men of high status wearing dark suits, he dropped his pince-nez and rose to his feet.

"I felt it. Her foot moved. She is producing the rappings," he roared to the audience.

A silence—the silence parents would hear if children came down the stairs on Christmas morning and found there were no gifts under the tree—filled the hall.

The physicians returned to their seats. Maggie rose, dropped her skirts, and stepped closer to the footlights—so close the gas flames cast black shadows around her eyes and flickered on her brow. Her face was heavy with remorse.

"That I have been chiefly instrumental in perpetrating the fraud of Spiritualism upon a too-confiding public, most of you doubtless know," she recited, looking frequently at a cue card in her palm.

"What's that? What's that?" muttered an elderly gentleman sitting too far back. "Elroy, where's my ear trumpet?" The audience tittered nervously. *Speak from the diaphragm,* Elisha told her. *Stand straight, enunciate.* Maggie took a deep breath to steady herself and continued in a louder voice:

"The greatest sorrow of my life has been that this is true, and though it has come late in my day, I am now prepared to tell the truth, the whole truth . . ." She spread open her hands, palms up, being careful to keep her thumb pressed over her cue card so that it wouldn't fall. ". . . and nothing but the truth, so help me God. There are probably many here who will scorn me for the deception I have practiced, yet did they know the true history of my unhappy past, the living agony and shame it has been to me, they would pity me, not reproach . . ."

Good, said Elisha. *Let them know you were used too. The blame is not entirely yours. Remember the tigress, remember Leah.*

"The imposition which I have so long maintained began in my early childhood, when, with character and mind still unformed . . ."

(*Tar the rats again today, there's some good fat ones in the trap, or you can go to bed hungry,* her father hissed.)

". . . I was unable to distinguish between right and wrong." Maggie remembered the child she had been. She was visibly weeping. "Those who were older, who should have known better, who already knew right from wrong, encouraged me in this deceit, and taught me to be yet more deceitful." That was for Leah. *They'll know who you mean,* Elisha whispered.

"I repented it in my maturity. . . ." (Oh, Elisha, how I repented it. I cast my pearls before swine, when I might have had you.) "I have lived through years of silence, through intimidation, scorn, and bitter adversity, concealing as best I might, the consciousness of my guilt. Now, thanks to God and my awakened conscience, I am at last able to reveal the fatal truth, the exact truth of this hideous fraud which has withered so many hearts and has blighted so many hopeful lives."

The crowd held a collective breath, uncertain yet if it should applaud her honesty or jeer at her history of deceit.

"I am here tonight as one of the founders of Spiritualism, to denounce it as an absolute falsehood from beginning to end, as the flimsiest of superstitions, the most wicked blasphemy known to the world." Maggie finished with a flourish and a clumsy curtsy, bowed her head, and waited.

Silence. Fitful rustlings. A baby cried, and a nurse shushed it.

But once Maggie's words seeped into the thoughts and consciousness of the audience, into the darkest corners of their minds where despair and hopelessness lurk, the audience made up its collective mind. They shrieked their disapproval. They cursed and stamped their feet in anger.

"Tar and feather her!" someone shouted, and there was a mad

scramble as people jumped into the aisles, toward the stage where Maggie still stood, Maggie Fox, who had promised an afterlife of happiness, a new life of hope where the door between life and death would be unlocked, and who now claimed that it had all been a bad joke, a hoax.

The auditorium manager, watching from the balcony, signaled to the waiting security guards. The audience was turning into the kind of crowd that slashes seats, breaks lamp chimneys, and throws boots through expensive windows. Police moved down the aisles, nightsticks dangling from from their fists.

Maggie stood onstage, trembling, confused. Someone threw a black cloak over her and hustled her offstage, through the wing, out a side door into the dark street.

It was raining. Water soaked the black cloak, soaked her black widow's dress, plastered her untidy hair to her neck and ran in rivulets down her back. Oh, what a beautiful rain was falling! Washed in the River Jordan, freed of deceit, happy again for the first time in years, Maggie sloshed through the streets, mindless of the six-inch-deep puddles pooled in the potholes, the sudden sprays of muddy water when a carriage rushed by, the jeers of the men hanging out of the tavern doors. *Don't fret, dear,* said Elisha, tenderly taking her arm. *Soon we'll be together.*

"Oh, Elisha, you were right all along. Truth is the way. Oh, how naughty I've been!" She twirled, almost fell, leaned against a wall to regain her balance.

She headed home, to Elisha, to her gin dreams. She had earned them. She had scotched Leah and her followers so well they'd probably never have the opportunity to tip another table or rap another message. They wouldn't get Katie's boys. They wouldn't get Katie or Maggie. They'd never bother her again. It was over.

She felt young again—oh, ever so young. Still barefoot because she had left the theater so quickly there hadn't been time to put on her shoes, she squished mud between her toes and kicked at a pebble in the street, the way children do. She tugged at her sodden skirt and skipped merrily.

"Look at that old whore," muttered a drunk leaning against a fence.

Don't worry, my dear. You did the right thing, Elisha whispered in her ear.

"I know, Elisha. And did you see the looks on their faces? Serves them right. Oh, I wish I could see Leah's face tomorrow!"

Dance in the rain, Maggie. Joy is fleeting. But you learned that all too well. Even truth becomes a kind of lie, and now that you've confessed your sin there will be penance to do. "It's not that simple," Jude had tried to explain, when I encouraged him to go to Rome. I didn't believe him.

Many of Maggie's former clients and followers did not believe her.

Maggie's jubilation, like hope, was a false spring, she saw the next morning, when she sat at her little breakfast table with a cup of tea and the morning editions. Every paper in the country, and eventually most papers in Europe, too, covered the story of Maggie's confession; it was news. With trembling hands and a torturous hangover she scanned the headlines of the New York papers. The reporter from the *Herald* had been impressed:

By throwing life and enthusiasm into her big toe Mrs. Margaret Fox-Kane produced loud spirit rappings in the Academy of Music last night and dealt a death blow to Spiritualism, that marvelous world-wide fraud which she and her sisters founded in 1848 from their cabin in Hydesville. The wildest excitement prevailed at times during the evening. It was a most remarkable and dramatic spectacle. There she stood in her widow's dress, working her big toe and solemnly declaring that it was in this way she created the excitement. . . .

The audience, he wrote, hissed and booed.

" 'Hissed,' " she laughed, sweeping her teacup from the table. "That they did. And more." She unfolded the next paper, the *New York World*. Standing barefoot, sometimes sitting on a plain wooden stool, "Miss Fox produced those mysterious sounds which for forty years frightened and bewildered hundreds of thousands of people in this country and Europe," the paper reported.

Only the most prejudiced and bigoted fanatics of Spiritualism could withstand the irresistible force of this commonplace explanation and exhibition of how spirit rappings are produced. The demonstration was perfect and complete, and if spirit rappings find any credence in this community hereafter, it would seem a wise precaution on the part of the authorities to begin the enlargement of the States' insane asylums without any delay.

It was over. How could anyone continue a belief in Spiritualism after reading sentences like those? Maggie's joy, the glowing radiance produced by testifying the truth, dimmed a little with the first tug of regret. Spiritualism had made her famous and paid her bills. It had brought Elisha to her . . . and separated her from him. She had spent most of her life talking with spirits. Now gone. Over.

But not completely, she saw when she refilled her teacup and opened *The Spirit,* a Spiritualist newspaper. Its reporter, Mrs. Jemimah Wilson, reported that Maggie had been used by spirits who did not wish to be believed in, that she was a deluded alcoholic bent on revenge and making a quick dollar. Mrs. Wilson simply didn't believe her confession or her demonstration. "The poor Fox girls have become hopeless alcoholics," Mrs. Wilson wrote. "They are to be pitied. But not to be believed. Bad, mischievous spirits made her do it. There are certain spirits who do not want

262

us to know they exist, for reasons of their own, who enjoy playing tricks, and they played their tricks on Maggie, by forcing this false confession."

Maggie, sitting at her breakfast table, sighed. Once a liar, always a liar, her mother had said once, when, as a schoolgirl, Maggie had told a falsehood.

Disheartened, she saw that Spiritualism had outgrown her; it no longer needed her. It had a life of its own, a life she could no longer stop.

"Oh, Elisha," she said.

She was successful in stopping Leah, however. Ruined by the publicity, shunned by her fancy friends, her own Spiritualism business in a shambles, Leah had decided to avoid further negative publicity and not press the lawsuit for custody. Leah hid behind her thick oak front door. She stopped receiving guests; few came, after Maggie's confession. Soon other matters, more serious matters, distracted her from the feud and troubles with Maggie and Katie. The pain in her chest grew increasingly persistent. She had trouble breathing.

With the money that Maggie had earned from her October performance at the Academy of Music, denouncing Spiritualism, Maggie and Katie were able to live quietly in retirement. Occasionally Maggie gave lectures describing the tricks of Spiritualism, but she no longer liked appearing in public and limited her engagements and would not travel far. Travel was tiring. Maggie and Katie grew fond of simple pleasures, of uneventful days, and long evenings no longer spent at round tables, cracking their toes and manipulating trumpets with wires.

Age and ill health, those uninvited guests, those penances for lives too ardently lived, arrived quickly. One afternoon, in the humid July of 1892, after Katie and Maggie had taken a long walk in the park, reminisced about Hydesville, and then gone home to finish the usual afternoon bottle of gin, Maggie was seized with a choking sensation. Her vision went red. When she looked at Katie, sitting opposite her, glass still in hand, she had a vision of Katie, flat on a bed draped with sheets, her hands folded over her breast, her eyes closed and weighted with coins.

She blinked hard. Katie was as she should be, wide-eyed and concerned. But Maggie knew, and was not surprised when, a week later, Katie fell from her chair. The fall took forever. Maggie watched, her mouth open in a shriek, her hands extended to her little sister, who did not take them.

The funeral was small. Katie's boys, now almost grown, looking solemn in long pants and dark coats, looking sad and perhaps a little relieved, came back from school to see their mother laid to rest. They threw a handful of dirt into the grave and remembered toasting bread in English hearths, puppies, Katie singing lullabies, Katie calling on the spirits, Katie weeping as Leah tried unsuccessfully to steal them from her, Katie drunk. They had been returned to their mother's keeping and now that her guardianship was over forever they reflected and agreed that perhaps it was just as well that childhood ended.

Leah was not there; she herself had crossed over two years ago, not long after Maggie's confession of fraud.

Maggie, last of the three sisters, read Katie's favorite Bible passage, from Corinthians:

" 'The trumpet shall shound and the dead will be raised, incorruptible, and we shall be changed. . . . When the corruptible frame takes on incorruptibility and the mortal immortality, then will the saying of Scripture be fulfilled: "Death is swallowed up in victory. O grave, where is your victory? O death, where is your sting?" ' "

But death did sting, Maggie thought as she cast a handful of dirt over Katie's coffin. Where was that bright, cheerful little girl who liked to listen to ghost stories during long winter nights? Gone—leaving her, Maggie, behind.

Alone, Maggie drank even more heavily than before. Soon her bank account was empty again. Poverty was a loathsome acquaintance she couldn't hide from. He kept turning up, kept finding her. Poverty and his friends Hunger, Shabbiness, Defeat. Elisha had grown silent and offered no advice.

So, not knowing what else to do, she went back to her old profession, speaking with the dead. Maggie wrote a retraction of her confession—believers had never accepted that confession of fraud anyway—and began giving performances again, a dollar a head, rapping out messages from Aunt Claudia, unnamed lovers, and children who had passed over.

"This unfortunate woman had sunk so low that for five dollars she would have denied her own mother and sworn to anything," a Dr. Funk told a young trapeze artist, soon to turn magician, Harry Houdini.

CHAPTER
TWENTY-SIX
New York City~1893

$\mathcal{M}$aggie had the last laugh.

When death came nipping and worrying at her heels, hungry for the last of the famous Fox sisters, Maggie had a surprise for it.

March. A cold winter night, six months after Katie's death. Spring is a memory, not a promise. The wind blows through the window frame, shaking the curtains and moaning like one of the heavy-fingered tawdry Broadway mediums who just can't get the act right. The wind blows and chills Maggie—right to the bone, as Mother Fox would have said.

Maggie lies in state in a wide, high bed piled with comforters and wool blankets, but she still can't get warm. Her fingers are like ice. *Let me warm them for you, dear heart,* says Elisha, and he takes them tenderly and chafes them. *Oh, Maggie, how cold it was, in that little tent on the ice. How I dreamed of you, missed you.*

Her heart beats as erratically as the faulty metronome Leah used to have, in the old days, before the money came in. How Leah hated giving those piano lessons for the neighborhood children, the hundreds and thousands of "Für Elize"s she sat through, the scales and études hammered out by sticky little fingers, the smells of boiled cabbage and puppy shit that followed the students in and out of the rooms like odiferous ghosts. Maggie, half asleep, half awake, chuckles as she remembers Leah's discomfort and impatience and misery in that old rented room in Rochester.

"Is she asleep?" Maggie's hostess, Mrs. Emily Ruggles, whispers to the maid. "Give her another hot-water bottle."

"Not a boat of water bottles going to warm that woman," the servant mutters. "She's cold enough for the grave."

Mrs. Ruggles lets out a sob and wipes at her streaming eyes.

Maggie was lucky in this: She always found a friend of sorts, someone willing to stand by her. Katie, Elisha, the Washington senators, Mrs. Lincoln . . . even old whiskered Seybert had tried to be of use, but had been, ultimately, just too silly. Now there was dear Emily.

"Oh, my dear friend," Mrs. Ruggles wails. "Must you leave me?"

Maggie opens one eye and winks.

"Not dead yet," she says. "Bring me some whiskey, dear Emily."

"Do you think you should?"

"Absolutely. And let that young man who has been waiting in the hall come in now. I'm ready."

The young man is a journalist, fresh to his trade and eager for a story. He'd heard through his sister, who had a friend who had a maid who was friends with Mrs. Ruggles' cook, that the famous Maggie Fox lay dying in Mrs. Ruggles' guest room in her Brooklyn townhouse.

He tiptoes respectfully into the room and sits in the straight-backed chair put next to the bed.

"Mrs. Fox—Mrs. Kane . . ." He isn't certain how to address the personage shivering in this great bed. He's never had a death-bed interview before. He's a little frightened.

"Call me Maggie, dear," she croaks at him; then winks, so upsetting him he drops his pen and notepad.

"Maggie. Are the spirits with us now, in this room?"

"You bet," she says, winking again.

"How can I know so?"

"You just wait."

And so he waits.

Maggie's breath, despite the comfort of the whiskey, grows increasingly ragged and uneven. The sun begins to set, casting long shadows through the lace curtains. The day dies in sympathy with Maggie. She seems to sleep; twitches occasionally, smacks her dry lips and flutters her eyes. A clock ticks. In the street, a dog barks.

He waits. Mrs. Ruggles peers into the room at regular intervals, then totters back down the hall, wailing.

Just as twilight turns to night, Maggie Fox heaves a great sigh that shakes the bed, gurgles, and then relaxes deeper into the feather mattress, as though she has just been emptied of a great weight.

The young journalist leans away from the bed in fear, then closer to it. This is it? The great interview she has promised him? She's dead!

Suddenly he hears a noise. A tapping. Slow, solitary, almost like a second clock. It gets faster and louder and erratic. The noise fills the room.

Spirits! Maggie has kept her promise!

Hallelujah! Maggie Fox has brought the spirits!

He has learned the spirit alphabet. He counts the taps, jots down the letters, twists in his stiff chair, eager for the message, which is jumbled, incoherent, senseless, a volley of words: *heart-strings, icebergs, son, father, Elisha, come, go, yes, yes, yes*. He writes it all down and when the room finally grows quiet again, dashes into the hall, down the stairs, out the door, jubilant, victorious, carrying the words not from Maggie Fox, but from the spirit of Maggie Fox.

Upstairs, Maggie sits up and rubs her aching toes.

Now she is truly alone. The performance has taken a toll. Her heart, no longer even a faulty metronome, flutters and stalls like a faltering Ford motor in one of the new horseless carriages.

Alone. The thing in life she most hated. No, not alone.

Papa is angry; as usual, the room is filled with hostility. But little Katie snuggles closer.

"Look," she whispers. "The scarecrow is waving at us."

"Dragon's breath," Maggie whispers. Her voice sounds like the hissing of a kettle. "Things don't have to be seen to be real."

Maggie's eyes flutter open.

She is no fool. She knows what is to come. She will be with Elisha again, physically, after the resurrection of the body. He undoubtedly will have stern words for her, he usually did, but eventually he will take her hand and call her his own dear little girl, as he used to do in his gentler moods. And she and Katie could have tea together again. Could they lace it with whiskey and giggle and gossip together, as in the old days?

That would be nice.

But she might meet up with Leah. That reunion was bound to be unpleasant. Would Leah's pinches and slaps and tongue-lashings be worth the sweetness of being with Elisha again?

Were there rats waiting to be tarred in the Summerland?

And do the dead ever really speak to the living? Finally Maggie will know what really happens after the big crossover.

Her heart skipped and fluttered one more time and a giant invisible hand clamped down and pressed the air out of her chest. Her hand shot out from under the bed linen, knocking over the glass on her night table, her eyes opened wide in surprise. And then Maggie was still. She had passed over to the sweet by-and-by; she had joined the spirits.

CHAPTER
TWENTY-SEVEN

I had believed, when I began, that the dead were immutable. Now I find that the dead are as changeable as the living; at least, our opinion of them can change. I catch myself liking this woman I started out hating. Maggie and I know many things in common, but especially this: A long solitude followed by a brief passion, followed by an even longer solitude, as if love is no more than a flicker of time surrounded by infinity. When a proton does die, it happens so quickly the event can be recorded only in milliseconds, like a love lost too soon.

Maggie was a farmgirl who played tricks to outwit the too-long winter nights; a young girl who was thrust too soon into a larger world of greedy adults; a young woman who loved truly and not at all wisely; an aging woman who mourned the passing of too many things, including her own innocence.

In many ways she was a fraud, but she comforted those who mourn, and comfort is not an easy thing to come by. A dollar a head for words of comfort and release is a bargain. What is fiction? What is fact? Who draws the line between what is real and what is not? In the long run, does a lie really matter? There are so many betrayals.

I have finished Jude's task for me. I have told Maggie's story and I, who trusted only in the perceivable, the knowable—I, who hated fraud and mystery and doubt—have forgiven her.

My workroom is quiet and filled with a gentle, late-afternoon light that shimmers over the wood floor and white walls and the rows of books in the bookcases. There's an underwater quality to the light—this is the thick, mottled light that whales swim by; the light of the green water where glaciers calf; the cold light of the story of Maggie and Elisha, the spirits and the Eskimos and the unknown that confronts us all at some time. It is a good light for completion, for endings.

Jude and I never said good-bye. Even when I saw him off to Rome I had said, "See you in six months." Never *good-bye*.

A voice in my head, Jude's voice, repeats a passage from Seneca: " 'The most shameful cure for sorrow, in the case of a sensible man, is to grow weary of sorrowing. I should prefer you to abandon grief, rather than have grief abandon you.' "

It is a time for farewells.

I switch off the computer, pack up my computer disks, notebooks, and loose papers into a folder, put the folder beside other dog-eared, bulging ones, in an olive-green manuscript box so they can be shelved for three years, then discarded. I empty the waste bin, return books to shelves, tidy up pencils. Photocopies of old photographs—Elisha Kent Kane in evening clothes; Maggie and Katie next to a Christmas tree; Maggie and Elisha posed in summer whites and wicker chairs; Maggie by herself, staring forlornly into the camera, puzzled and bitter—are unpinned from the wall over my desk and put into a folder.

An hour later, when I finish, the room is exorcised of Maggie Fox.

And now, there is one other who must be exorcised.

I know why Jude wanted me to write this piece, to explore Maggie and what she stood for. He knew—not perhaps of his own death, though that is a possibility, but that I would grieve for him, eventually, and I did not know how. Death, for me, had always been near misses. Someday it was bound to become real. Death of the body, or of love? Which did he most fear for me? Through Maggie I have learned that a time comes when we must close doors behind us.

I put away the last file, shut the supply closet, and go downstairs, playing an old game with myself, trying to step on each stair in that one secret place where it doesn't squeak or groan; an impossible game in this house, where the old wood is warped so that it moans like a Greek chorus marking my passage.

Why did I ever buy such a big house? So many unused rooms, so many corners and alcoves, I feel separated even from my own shadow. This house was built for a family, for relatives and summer visitors, not for a solitary woman. I have been playing tag with memories for too long. Time to confront the thoughts I have been running away from. Jude was going to go back to Madelyn. For three years the question has been, Does he forgive me? New question: Do I forgive him?

"You were a good listener when you were here," I say out loud "You weren't a good talker, as it turns out. There was so much unsaid. The nature of your love, for instance. Your passion for loyalty. Your need for a God who would not let you change your mind. Vows, Jude. You should have told me."

There is one good thing discovered in all this debris of regret and doubt and deceit. I am not a murderer. I did not force Jude to go to Rome, to his death. He wanted to go. To think about what really matters.

And what does matter, exactly, Helen? *Something* must have importance. Truth is important, but often misunderstood; love is not to be counted on. Ultimately, the only thing that matters is moving forward, living and changing, and accepting change with goodwill and courage, not getting stuck in time like a coward, because time is merely the cosmos breathing, and we are part of that breath. That is what death is. The inability to change. And I have died. I can't move forward.

I go into the parlor where Jude and I used to sit, and I wait. I close my eyes. His voice in my head grows stronger.

Did you love me? I ask him. Do you love me?

The voice comes.

Yes. Yes.

But love is not the only important thing, is it? It is time to leave.

Yes, he says. *Almost.*

I wait for the touch of his hand on my head, on the scar. It comes, light as a draft of air.

We forgive each other, I tell him. We must, for the alternative to forgiveness is hatred, and I can't hate you.

Forgive, the voice says.

Good-bye, Jude. Good-bye. Rest in peace.

Deep, dark night, darker than I remember it being for a long time, prowls outside my workroom window. There are no more white fields to reflect the moonlight. The black, slumbering meadow absorbs the light, holds it greedily, will not give any back. I fall asleep, dreaming of sea changes and green light and new growth on the tips of branches.

Spring is not a gentle season. It is bloody and muddy and filled with the rutting, gasping turmoil of life trying to resurrect itself, preserve itself, push itself into an unknown future.

But ultimately spring is betrayal, because spring always lunges forward into the hope-breaking oven of a summer heat wave, or retreats into a false, upside-down, shaken-snowglobe scene of winter, with big white flakes landing on Santa's shoulders. Spring is inconstant.

When I wake up, cramped from my fetal position on the sofa, the parlor is startlingly silent. No mysterious knocking. No rumbling of the furnace. No whooshing of the sump pump in the basement. As silent as the grave.

The room is like an icebox. A chilly, damp spring day has turned tail and retreated back into a frozen, winter night. Time has moved backward, not forward. And there's no heat in the house, not even the usual lukewarm currents that spill out of the registers.

Turning on lights as I move down the hall into my bedroom, into the dressing room I use as a walk-in closet, I rub my hands up and down my arms, shivering. I put on three sweaters, one over the over, and two more pairs of socks, and a beret. It must be as cold inside as out; the pipes are going to freeze and burst. Damn. I have to go back into the basement and see why there is no heat.

In the basement, with only the thin, tired beam of a flashlight to guide me, I press the red restart button on the furnace. Nothing. Press again. Nothing. Not even a hiss or pop. The flood in the basement must have damaged it.

Back upstairs, I plug in the phone and put it to my ear, steadying my nerves for whatever rate the repairman will charge for such a late night call. Should I call Douglas? No. Yes. No.

Call Harvey, he's been pampering the furnace for years.

I pick up the phone and stab at the dial, then listen.

There's no dial tone. I can't call anyone.

It's happened before. Wires come loose. Poles fall. Circuits short out somewhere up the line.

There's nothing to do but sit tight and wait for morning. In the kitchen I pour a tall glass of scotch. I hesitate, then pour it into the sink. Enough. Instead, I pour a cup of cold, leftover coffee and carry it back into the dark parlor where I curl up again on the sofa with Jude's old coat draped over me. As I sit there, resting but not sleeping, the light slowly changes. The room grows less dark, not with dawn but with spring's betrayal. It's snowing outside, so thickly that the snow reflects light back and makes a false day.

Flakes as soft and chubby as a baby's hand drift thickly through the night, reflecting moonlight, falling so densely that I can see nothing but them; the road, the trees, the stars, are obliterated. It is just a few hours since I last looked out the window, yet the landscape, the world, in that short time has been transformed.

This is the beginning of a major blizzard.

Disaster usually arrives slowly in this part of the world. It creeps on rickety legs like an old man, giving its victims time to worry, fret, decide. In Hawaii, a lava flow or mudslide rearranges your life and future in minutes. California has earthquakes. Florida has hurricanes. We have spring floods that take days to happen, and summer heat waves that come and go like lazy tourists, never moving too quickly, and blizzards that arrive slowly, stately, building to a fine crescendo like the piano background of a silent movie.

This blizzard is not slow. It is not stately. It is furious. Snow falls, lethargic yet ominous, past the window. I'm inside one of those glass globes, trapped.

There's still time to get into the car, fishtail down the hill, and be in safe walking distance of town before I get snowed in. I can hole up at the College Hotel where there's plenty of food and people to wait on me, a pool and sauna . . . or stay here, where the power lines may come down and leave me in cold darkness, completely isolated from the world. I can't remember the last time I went to the supermarket. Is there anything in the house besides peanut butter? Is there even peanut butter?

Sit tight. The road looks treacherous, undrivable. No more accidents, thank you. I've waited out blizzards before. I'll wait out this one. It's too close to the anniversary of Jude's death, his heavenly birthday, as the Victorians called it, to be wandering around Eleusis. I'd be like Maggie, imagining I saw him every time I went into a strange room or turned a corner. We have finally said good-bye, I think.

I sip the cold coffee and think of Elisha Kent Kane, feverish in his tent on the ice floes of the Arctic, seeing monsters moving through the darkness. No, not monsters. Merely strange beings, creatures of our own invention who wear the misshapen face of dreams poorly realized. We make the monsters out of our own thwarted needs and desires, and then we destroy them or let them destroy us.

But when the snow falls this thickly, even the monsters must be still. It is eerily beautiful, this white world outside the window where all seems pure and preserved, past corruption. A Victorian conceit, that: comparing the white snow to a concealing shroud. This same snow now covering Piety Hill is falling on the Holy Word Cemetery, where Madelyn placed a tombstone for Jude, though there was little to put beneath it. Jude and I went hiking once on a night like this, tramping through the night like runaway children, falling onto the softly shrouded ground and swinging arms and legs to leave behind the impressions of snow angels.

Should I go to the memorial ceremony? Of course, it will be tedious. All those silly speeches, the insincerity, the lies. The looks I'll have to endure, of shock—*What nerve, coming here!*—and pity—*Poor woman, all alone, unlike Madelyn who got on with her life.* A public stoning might be easier.

I sit in the kitchen alcove, wondering what to wear for a public stoning, watching the snow fall and fall and fall. I call up Jude's image as a test. Does "farewell" empty the memory? No, I can remember every detail of his face, down to the fine, graying hairs in his straight eyebrows and the small scar on his left temple, left by a fishhook when he was eight, when he was the child I never knew.

Snow comes down even heavier, faster. I hear mini-avalanches sliding off the roof.

Restlessly I pace through my old house, back and forth, up and down. I'm looking for something, but I don't know what. I open drawers, kick through the debris in closet bottoms, paw through the medicine chest in the bathroom. I did this after my mother died, too, searching through her things, her house, neither knowing nor finding what I sought, until Dad finally took my hands to still them.

"Let her go," he said. He was crying. It was the only time I ever saw him cry.

Now, on a blizzardy night in April, twenty years after my mother's death, three years after Jude's, I continue to rifle through drawers and boxes, jacket pockets and cupboards, looking for what can't be found. The memory doesn't exist in objects; love can't be found in drawers and storage boxes. Yet we look, we search the dark corners, and hope.

The snow falls and falls, and I abandon the search for what is missing and can't be found, and go back into the parlor. I slide into a restless sleep again on the sofa, shivering under a blanket. Consciousness runs ahead of me, a laughing child carrying balloons, racing down a street thronged with the faces of old hopes and older fears. I can't catch up with her, but the effort of the pleasant chase brings me to alertness. Wide-awake again, I sit up, surrounded by a twilight grayness made up of night and moonlight reflected by snow. I fell asleep with every light in the house still switched on, and now the house is lit only by spring's betrayal. Power's out.

And the house is throbbing with noise. A strong, steady beat shakes the walls and moves the still air into tidal waves of anticipation.

Someone is pounding on the front door.

It's one o'clock in the morning and still snowing, and someone is pounding at the door. Car accident, I think, jamming my feet into shoes, combing back my hair with my fingers and running down the hall. Teens, even their parents, get blasé about winter and forget how quickly even a four-wheel-drive can go into a spin coming down steep, curving Piety Hill when it's covered with ice and snow; I learned the hard way. I run to the front door, prepared for the worst.

I take a deep breath, trying to remember where the nearest first-aid kit is, and swing open the door onto the black-and-white night.

Douglas stands there, smiling feebly, his arms full of water-streaked, sagging grocery bags.

"Hadn't intended to arrive so late. Had some trouble getting here. Car went into the ditch about three miles back."

Speechless, I open the door wider and pull him by the sleeve out of the snow, into the house. His wool overcoat is dripping wet, his black beret is frosted with ice. His face is white and pinched from the cold, his gloveless hands red.

His appearance here, now, has the feel of inevitability, of rocking chairs on the front porch and toothbrushes side by side. Weeks ago, when he first appeared to mend the wall upstairs, our hands had touched and the tectonic plate of reality shifted.

"Kitchen?" he asks, nodding at the bags, and without waiting for an answer, heads down the hall. He already knows his way around.

I follow, and as he unpacks cheese and fruit, white-wrapped bundles of meat, cans of tomato sauce and tuna, plastic bags of lettuce and broccoli, I fill the kettle and put it on the gas stove.

Douglas takes off his coat, hangs it over a chair back, and sits at the table, watching me finish putting away things. I am conscious of his eyes following me, and it feels like the sun warming my back.

"Bet you were working so hard you never watched the news today," he says finally, gulping down hot coffee.

"You win the bet." I scrutinize the label on a jar of tomato sauce to avoid looking into his eyes.

"Blizzard. Big one."

"That much I have managed to figure out for myself."

"Very big," he continues. "It's going to snow for three days, nonstop. They say upstate New York will come to a standstill for another two days. While you were typing away upstairs, the rest of Eleusis has been emptying out the supermarkets and preparing to be snowbound for a week."

"You thought I was going to starve?"

"Maybe not actually starve. But I thought a few basics might come in handy."

" 'Basics'?" I hold up a five-pound box of chocolate-covered cherries.

"Helen, don't give me a hard time. I needed an excuse to drop by. We have some unfinished business."

"Do you always visit so late at night?" I am giving him a hard time and enjoying it, because it intensifies the look in his dark, beautiful eyes.

"I told you, I went off the road and had to shovel out. Not once. Not twice. Three times. It took me hours to get here and I spent a couple of hours in line at the supermarket before that. More coffee, and this time with a shot of whiskey, if you don't mind. I'm freezing." He claps his hands together and rubs them.

I put the cherries on top of the refrigerator, next to the walnut-colored pottery bowl Jude bought for me one day at a farmers' market.

"They'll have to cancel Jude's memorial," I say. "No one will be able to make it."

"Postpone. Madelyn has her outfit all picked out—she won't cancel."

"You still keep in touch with her?"

"I do. She's a friend."

"I see."

"No, I don't think you do see. She's a friend, Helen. It wasn't like this."

Douglas takes my hand and pulls me onto his lap. He smiles up at me. Can things really be this simple?

"I've finished the Maggie Fox piece."

"Congratulations. Maybe you'll have time for other things. How did Maggie fare? You were no fan of hers, as I recall."

"She was a fraud in some things. Not all things. But now . . . well, there's always pity, isn't there?"

"Pity for Maggie, or her customers?"

"Both. It was all about need. And grief. And fear. Who would judge them for that? Maybe death isn't as final as I once believed. Hey," I say, pulling away. "You're soaking wet. You're shivering." I put my hand to his forehead. It's hot.

"Just a cold," he says. "It's cold in here, by the way. Trying to save on the fuel bill? You writers are a miserly lot." As he speaks, gusts of frost billow from his mouth, as if in evidence.

"No heat. Furnace went out."

"I can think of one great way to get warm," he says, grinning. But then he sneezes and coughs and his eyes pinken and water.

"Later. First I'll get some dry clothes for you, and towels. You don't look so good."

I fetch some of Jude's old things and help Douglas out of his sodden clothes. He stands naked in the kitchen, white and shivering as I towel him down, rubbing briskly till his skin turns pink. His face is hot and flushed; his limbs are clammy and chill.

"My Romeo. Comes to rescue me and I have to nurse him instead," I tease.

"I'm freezing," he complains, no longer smiling. Even after he is dressed in fresh, warm sweatpants, sweater, coat jacket, and scarf, he stands there shivering.

I pause, hands on hips, deciding.

"Come," I tell him. In the parlor, I pile four dusty logs on top of each other in the fireplace and wad a piece of newspaper under them for kindling. I struck a match and let the hearth, cold since Jude's death, warm again with flame. It takes awhile for the logs to catch, but when they do I kneel there, matches in hand, fascinated. The paper catches easily; the wood takes more time, but in a few minutes I have a roaring blaze going. Good-bye, good-bye.

"Closer, it's warm here," I tell Douglas, who is slumped on the sofa. He comes and kneels next to me and holds his hands to the fire. "Get warm. I'm going to go upstairs and pile every blanket I can find on the bed and get out the hot-water bottles."

Later, when the wood has burned to ashes and we've taken shelter in bed, we burrow together under a dozen blankets, his knees pressing into the backs of mine, my rump resting against his belly. He has finally stopped shivering and his hands explore the hills and valleys of my body. We are still new terrain to each other, borders to be crossed, maps to be completed. Love is discovery and we are eager explorers.

Sometime during our lovemaking the lamp on the nighttable flickers on and then goes dark again. "Ghosts," I say, laughing. "You said the house was haunted."

And then we return to our beginning, our private prehistory where words have not yet been invented and language is formed in the fingertips, the quickened breath, the oceanic slap of flesh against flesh like waves breaking over the shore of a new world.

When I awake for the second time that night, Douglas is asleep beside me, breathing in a long, slow rhythm. I close my eyes and listen to this new rhythm and enjoy his closeness, the warmth, as the minutiae of genesis seeps back into my own pulse, quickening it. I open my eyes again upon his sleeping face and drink in the sight, the feel, the scent of him. So alive. Outside, the night is still light with snow and its moonlight reflections. Snow veils the world in soft white mounds, obliterating color, obliterating sharp angles and straight lines. Everything has gone soft and pure and I am new again, returned from the dead.

But just as I am making peace with this, the room fills with the scent of bay rum, Jude's aftershave.

The odor is slightly off. It has turned bitter, and has undertones of smoke, of scorching.

Douglas is still asleep. He senses nothing. But for me the house and the night have come alive; things move in the corner of my eyes; stairs creak; somewhere, something taps against a wall. In the time it takes to blink, I move from the peace I felt a moment before, to a sense of heightened awareness and danger. Moving slowly so I won't wake up Douglas, I slide out of bed.

The scent of aftershave is even stronger in the hall, stronger yet at the top of the stairs. There's a blue mist in the air. Already knowing what I will see, I look down.

Jude stands at the bottom of the staircase. He is looking up at me, smiling. I see the hair curling at the nape of the neck, the scar over the eyebrow.

He has appeared. Words weren't enough; he wants to be seen by me. Why? Fear prickles the hair on the back of my neck, on my arms. We had said good-bye, it was finished. My own powerlessness overwhelms me. We do not command the dead. This has not been a game. He has an existence outside of my own need and my reality.

Jude, transparent but complete in form, turns away, walks down the hall. I run down the stairs, stand where he stood, inhale his scent. The house is freezing, I expect to see ice hanging from the ceilings, it is so cold, yet sweat drips down my forehead. My heart feels like a caged tiger ramming against the bars of the cage.

He's ahead of me, looking over his shoulder, beckoning from the other end of the hall.

His features aren't as clear as they were when I was farther away, they have blurred, so that as he passes the Currier-and-Ives print hanging on the wall I can see the skating figures, the horse sleigh, through the cloud of Jude's face. I follow.

He stops outside the parlor where, hours before, Douglas took me by the hand. Jude steps through the doorway and looks at me over his shoulder. *Come, Helen. This way.*

I step through the doorway after him.

The parlor is filled with smoke. It strikes me in the face, the chest, leaves me breathless and choking. I flail my arms at it uselessly. Smoke closes over and around me, hotly suffocating.

Chimney fire. The chimney hasn't been cleaned in years. Sparks from the blaze must have caught hold in creosote and debris. My house is on fire. I run back upstairs to the bedroom and shake Douglas, but he has fallen into a deep sleep, enhanced by the cold medication I gave him earlier. His breathing does not even change rhythm as I hold him and shake him like a huge, limp rag doll.

Suddenly the thought comes that we could die like this. Smoke is already inching up the stairs. The coroner reported of Jude's death that he died from smoke inhalation, not flames.

I can't carry Douglas down the stairs; he's half again my own weight, and unconscious. If I drag him . . . No, there's no carpeting on the stairs—his head would hit each tread.

Okay. It's up to me. I race back downstairs to the kitchen where I keep the all-purpose fire extinguisher, and then sprint back to the parlor, my skin and nerves jumping with adrenaline.

I fumble with the safety seal and lever, the task made more difficult by the smoke that blinds my eyes and leaves me gasping for breath, but finally the extinguisher is ready for use. I wade through the thick smoke to the chimney, point the extinguisher up, and press. Sizzles and pops and hissing fill the parlor and the smoke worsens. Coughing and gasping, I drop the extinguisher and when I pick it up, fumbling in the smoke the way I had fumbled in the dirty water of the basement flood days earlier, I see Jude standing by the window, expressionless, like a cardboard cutout.

Damn, the fire extinguisher is empty. No, I've just loosened my grip on it. Pay attention, Helen! I look back at the hearth, aim the red canister back up the chimney and press harder on the level. A last spray of chemicals shoots up and then, slowly, the hissing and snapping dies away. The fire is out.

I drop to my knees, gasping. The windows in this room have been painted shut. My lungs are on fire and can't get enough air; I grab the lamp and shatter the window. Jude had been standing here. Where is he? Cold air washes over me, the sooty curtains flap in my face like angry bird wings. Over by the sofa. Thinner. Fainter. But still there. I see him out of the corner of my eye, through the dispersing smoke.

His eyes meet mine. Just before everything goes black, the last thing I see is Jude smiling at me.

CHAPTER
TWENTY-EIGHT

The days following the fire are strung together with little islands of bright if confused consciousness, surrounded by a gentle ocean of nothingness.

A nurse, taking my pulse, adjusting knobs on a gleaming machine next to my narrow hospital bed. The pressure of her fingers at my wrist is warm and firm . . .

"Any pain?" she asks. I am too tired to open my eyes. I wonder what she looks like, to have such a pleasant voice.

"No, no pain."

"Sleep," she says.

I do.

~

"Nice work," says a stranger, bending over my bed. He has a name tag on his jacket: Ted Newton of the Eleusis Volunteer Fire Department. His jacket is bright orange against the white curtain behind him.

"Thanks. My house . . . ?"

"Just fine. A little damage to some interior walls, but you got it out in time. Nice work," he says again.

"Helen? Are you awake?" Douglas bends over me.

"Hey," I say, smiling at him. "We started a fire."

"We sure did. You probably saved my life, you know," he says. "Thank you."

"No problem."

And so I have been redeemed. I did for Douglas what I could not do for Jude. With Jude's help. He warned me. Together, we righted the wrongs we had done each other.

Night again, but night as it happens in the hospital: filled with metallic sounds, whispers, footsteps in the hall, and made artificially bright with streaks of overhead fluorescent tubing. Douglas is there again, or still there, I don't know which it is. I try to sit up but my arm is strapped down where an IV drips into it.

"Sedative," Douglas says.

"How did you get an ambulance? The phone was dead."

He frowns. "The phone was working, Helen."

"Not when I tried it."

"Don't worry," he says. "Everything will be fine.

A dream. Sitting at a round table, large enough to hold eight in a circle, but it's only Maggie and me. She pours. She has grown young again; she is not the shady hag I described in the last pages of my article, but a young woman with steady eyes and black hair and a rounded chin held quite high in the air. She pours tea for me, sweetens it with sugar and milk.

I ask her, "Was it all a lie?"

"Not all of it," Maggie says. "Though Elisha said it was. Jude, though . . ." She winks at me. "Jude had his suspicions. I could have convinced that one. More tea?"

She begins to cry. Her face screws up, her eyes close, her mouth trembles.

"He tried to take care of you," I tell her. "He cared. His family . . ."

"My dear. Do you always talk to yourself?"

They kept me in the hospital for several days, not so much for smoke inhalation as for what the doctor, being somewhat elderly and quaint in his terminology, called "nervous exhaustion." I was anemic and underweight and, when unconscious, prone to delirium. I insisted, Alicia told me later, that I had seen Jude.

My mother's generation would have said I was suffering from a nervous breakdown. The Victorians would have said I was suffering from neurasthenia; medievalists would have called it "accidie." We've always had a word for it, because that kind of break from reality, from what passes as reality, has always been with us.

But when the restless delirium passed and the sedative was discontinued, I felt only an overwhelming sense of peace, for myself and for Jude. I know, now, why there are still those who push aside credulity and lessen the pain with the impossible. What is rationalism compared to consolation?

Douglas insists that the vision of Jude was a dream or a hallucination. We're both right. Of death, Samuel Butler wrote in his notebook, "To die completely, a person must not only forget but be forgotten, and who is not forgotten is not dead." Memory is the alternative universe of the physicists, the place where miracles happen, where the dead talk.

When they let me return home, I entered that old house happily but somewhat cautiously, I admit. I sniffed at the aftersmell of smoke and still found, at the bottom of it, the scent of Jude's aftershave.

The parlor was in ruins. I sat on the soot-covered sofa, staring at the gaping black mouth of the fireplace, planning new paint colors for the walls and stain removers I could try on the marble-topped tables. Perhaps I should get some new furniture, I mused, modern, not ever owned by anyone else. This house had been too much like a museum.

"Too much like living in someone else's past?" Douglas said, which was exactly what Jude had said years before. The odds on that happening are too difficult to figure, they are somewhere, floating down that riverbed between skepticism and faith.

Jude's memorial was delayed a full week because of the blizzard, but when the group invited to celebrate Jude's life and work was gathered in Sage Memorial, I was part of it. I sat between Tom and Alicia, in the pew right behind Madelyn. When she saw me, Madelyn rose and gave me a hug. I hugged her back. Jude had loved her. There was that connection between us. And I saw in her eyes that she was thinking exactly the same thing about me.

The service was as bad as I had anticipated, full of easy sentiment and old clichés and the kind of indiscreet gloating that the living feel in the presence of the dead. Jude would have enjoyed it. He would have taken notes to work into an essay, something paralleling modern mourning methods with Greek blood sacrifice.

I was nervous. I half expected to hear voices again—Jude or that female voice that passed as Maggie's. I was still a little unsteady on my feet, still prone to hearing buzzings and waves and little statics of conversation. But . . . nothing. Emptiness. Quiet. It was even quiet at the cemetery, where I drove out with Madelyn, part of the smaller group that had been closer to Jude than the colleagues now having lunch in the rathskeller back at the college. I threw a rose onto the little alcove where Jude's urn and ashes were placed and bowed my head in prayer, did all the motions of grieving and parting that I had avoided three years before.

The rituals of parting felt like playacting, but they helped. When I went home, I left Jude there, in the cemetery, with the other dead.

The past had no more to say to me.

In the spring I began repairs on the house. Douglas helped. We tore out false ceilings, stripped layers of paint, took down makeshift walls, and in general began a restoration project that should make my house—our house, now—a Victorian beauty authentic enough to appear in the local guidebooks. I estimate we'll be finished when I'm approximately one hundred and ten years old. "But who's counting?" Douglas says.

To help pay for the restoration, I accepted another major assignment form *Savant,* this time on the lives of traveling salesmen during the Great Depression. Douglas is worried about that.

"Weird things will happen," he says. "Traveling salesmen will start showing up or something."

The tapping has not come back. Whatever it was, it has ceased. The night of the fire resolved it somehow. I don't think about it too much. Why frown over questions that have no answers?

All my dead are buried.

And this is the end of Maggie's story, culled from a continuing trail of newspaper clippings down through the 1930s and 1940s, when her cult was stronger than ever. When the cabin in Hydesville where her story began was torn down, a skeleton was found in it, behind a wall in the cellar. The lie that had founded Spiritualism had had some truth to it. Maggie had known the unknowable.

Had the victim talked to two small, mischievous girls? Had the dead spoken with the living?

I would have said it was impossible, of course, before I began my story on Maggie. Now, I am not as certain. There are mysteries here, questions that cannot be answered with numbers and the scientific methods of observing, measuring, repeating results. Hauntings, if hauntings they were (in both Maggie's story and mine), are often the result of a poorly-laid spirit, or one not laid to rest at all, according to experts I would not have taken seriously a year ago. Maggie's cabin had a restless spirit, a murdered man over whom no prayers of farewell had been said. As for me, I had Jude.

Hauntings, or "visitations," a far kinder word, often seem to be marked by fire. After the skeleton was found, the Hydesville cabin caught on fire and was badly damaged. It was rebuilt and moved to a new location, a camp where Spiritualists could gather around it and call on Maggie. It burned again. It was rebuilt again. It burned a third time. It was not rebuilt a third time.

There have been no more fires in my house, though the hearth is regularly used.

What is left to say? I close the notebook on Maggie—for the second time—with a verse by Robert Browning, written by him after attending a series of séances with his wife, Elizabeth:

> I tell you sir, in one sense, I believe
> Nothing at all,—that everybody can,
> Will, and does cheat; but in another sense
> I'm ready to believe my very self—
> That every cheat's inspired, and every lie
> Quick with a germ of truth.

AUTHOR'S NOTE

As I worked on this novel, I asked various people if they believed in ghosts. The most common answer was "No. But . . . ," and then I would hear another ghost story about the strange odor in the stairwell, the glowing lights at midnight, the voices in the next room when no one was there. Even non-believers are not immune to the otherworldly.

Was Maggie a fraud? Perhaps. But there had to have been some truth, some provision of the spiritual for Maggie Fox to have earned her historical title. The Founder of American Spiritualism. This novel is based on what we know of her childhood home, her public life, her informal marriage to the explorer, Elisha Kent Kane, her confession of fraud, and her later rescinding of that confession. I have occasionally manipulated fact, as novelists do, since while we know a good deal of Maggie's whens and wheres and hows, we can only imagine the why. The stranger details of her life are real, not inventions: the spirit house in Philadelphia, her meeting with Abraham Lincoln's widow, and, of course, the simple fact of the beginning of her tale on the eve of April first—April Fools' Day.